INSIDIOUS INSURRECTION

OVERWORLD CHRONICLES
BOOK FOURTEEN

JOHN CORWIN

ISBN- 978-1-942453-09-3

Printed in the U.S.A.

To my wonderful readers, my amazing editors:

Thanks so much for all your help and input!

Books by John Corwin:

The Overworld Chronicles:
Sweet Blood of Mine
Dark Light of Mine
Fallen Angel of Mine
Dread Nemesis of Mine
Twisted Sister of Mine
Dearest Mother of Mine
Infernal Father of Mine
Sinister Seraphim of Mine
Wicked War of Mine
Dire Destiny of Ours
Aetherial Annihilation
Baleful Betrayal
Ominous Odyssey

Overworld Underground:
Possessed By You
Demonicus

Overworld Arcanum:
Conrad Edison and the Living Curse
Conrad Edison and the Anchored World
Conrad Edison and the Broken Relic

Stand Alone Novels:
No Darker Fate
The Next Thing I Knew
Outsourced
Seventh
Mars Rising

Join my VIP Club at
www.johncorwin.net

HEAVEN IS HELL

Civil war tears apart the Darkling nation. The Eden army is too small, too battered to overcome the warring Darkling factions. Even more insidious, Justin discovers that Victus built a small army of demon golems created from parts of Nightliss's soul—and these dolems may soon control the Darkling legions.

The only army large enough to overcome the threat is controlled by Kaelissa, but she has her own designs on ruling Seraphina. But Justin has an idea that might just win the war and give him control over the Brightling Empire. It's time for one last desperate gambit.

It's time for an insurrection.

Chapter 1

The ambush struck in the middle of the Northern Pass.

We thought we were ready for it. We were wrong.

Elite Daskar in their shiny black armor launched from concealment on the cliffs and swarmed the *Falcheen*. Illaena shouted commands, and her first mate, Tahlee, roared them to the rest of the crew. The weaponized gems on the sides of the flying ship pulsed as magic surged through them. Light beams speared toward the attackers, blasting too few from the sky before they reached the ship.

Only weeks ago, we'd battled Kaelissa in Atlantis. Since leaving there, we'd fought two dragons that had come through rifts between Seraphina and Draxadis. I'd hoped that we could reunite with Thomas Borathen and the rest of the Eden forces without another engagement, but the renegade leader of the northern legion apparently had other plans.

"Holy mother of assburgers, Justin!" Shelton shouted. "I thought you said Kohval's entire legion went south to Tarissa!"

I channeled an orb of Brilliance around my right fist and blasted a Daskar from the sky before he could land on the deck. "Well, at least Kohval didn't completely abandon the borders."

1

He whirled his staff and unleashed a fireball toward another attacker, but it glanced off the enemy armor. "Is that your way of looking at the bright side?"

I didn't have a chance to answer.

A squadron of Daskar hovered off the port bow, their full-faced helmets staring at us with dead, black eyes. Aether gems in the palms of their armored gloves glowed ultraviolet an instant before beams of malevolent energy lanced toward us.

I threw up a flat shield and willed the surface to become reflective. The magic bounced back, narrowly missing the attackers. I altered the angle up a touch and grinned with satisfaction when the ultraviolet beams smacked right back into the Daskar before they ceased fire.

They dropped out of the sky like burning flies, vanishing beneath the *Falcheen.*

"That's so wrong." Shelton held his staff in front of him. "It's like grabbing someone's wrist and making them punch themselves."

I spotted Elyssa aft, leaping back and forth, firing the magical bow given to her by the people of Atlantis. Jagged lightning bolts cut through enemy armor and sent Daskar spinning out of control. The few who made it past her light show were greeted by her short sai swords.

Adam Nosti stood behind her, casting oil spells on the feet of enemies, causing them to stumble and fall, making them easy prey for Elyssa and the Mzodi.

The Daskar gave up trying to get past me and made a concerted effort to land on the bridge next to Illaena and Tahlee. I sprinted aft, firing beams of ultraviolet from my left hand and brilliant white from my right, knocking Daskar over the side of the ship on my way.

During my time in Atlantis, the humans there had allowed me to feed my Seraphim side on their essence. For reasons unknown, it amped my angel magic exponentially. It was the reason Daelissa had been so powerful, and it was the reason these Daskar didn't stand a chance against me.

If only Illaena allowed her crew to do it too. So far, the Mzodi crew held their own, but if they'd fed on human soul essence, this battle would have been a rout.

A Daskar swooped in at Elyssa's back as she fought off two other attackers. I blurred in and smacked one out of the air with a Murk-enhanced fist. Someone screamed. I glanced port as Daskar pulled two navigators from their posts and threw them overboard. Six navigators powered and guided the levitation foils on the ship—three on each side.

If we'd lost one navigator from each side, the *Falcheen* might have limped along. Losing two on one side was like having a front tire blow out on a car. The sky ship lurched hard to the left. The hull slammed into the cliff wall. The impact threw around everyone on deck like rag dolls. Only the other navigators, buckled into position, managed to stay in place.

I tethered myself in place with strands of Murk and grabbed Elyssa. "I got you, babe!"

She gritted her teeth and plunged her sword through the narrow seams in an attacker's black armor. The Daskar stiffened and let out a feminine shriek. Elyssa reared back her foot and booted her over the railing. The *Falcheen* smashed into the cliff again, hurling Daskar and Mzodi crew alike across the deck.

"Can you take one of the navigation spots?" Elyssa shouted over the roar of grating rock and the cry of battle.

I nodded. "You got my back?"

3

She slapped my ass. "Always."

Another impact hurled a Mzodi soldier toward the railing. I caught her with a strand of Murk and pulled her back to safety. She waved gratefully and channeled her own ultraviolet tether.

Tahlee shouted something at me, but I couldn't make it out. There were too many bodies fighting between me and her. I strapped myself into the stool in front of the crystal control rod at the first station on the port side. I gripped the rod and channeled into it. Pulled right on the rod to steer the ship away from the cliff face. Nothing happened. I poured more magic into the rod. It should have fed the levitation foil on the lower hull and given me more control. I felt no resistance, no connection.

Elyssa finished off another attacker and turned to me. "What's wrong?"

"I think the levitation foil is toast!" I released the strap and got up. The ship's railing ground against the cliff face in a shower of sparks, dislodging rocks and stone that crashed down where I'd been sitting. Ignoring the danger, I ran to the next control rod and tested it with the same result. The collision with the cliff had damaged the levitation foils.

This was worse than a flat tire. If the *Falcheen* was a jumbo jet, we'd just lost two engines.

I was about to relay the dire news to Elyssa when the front end of the ship sank about fifteen degrees. Rocks, gravel, and dead bodies slid down the decline. Elyssa and I leapt over obstacles and worked our way aft toward the savage melee between crew and Daskar.

I reached Illaena. "Are we going to crash?"

Eyes tight with apprehension, the captain of the *Falcheen* nodded. "Our only hope is to control the descent."

"Son of a bitch!" Shelton roared as a gout of ultraviolet light nearly took off his wide-brimmed hat. He retaliated with a shackles spell. A flaming bolo wrapped around the offending Daskar, immobilizing the soldier and smashing him into the cliff.

"Finally got one!" he shouted. "These assholes can take everything I dish out." Another enemy dove toward him. He flicked the screen on his arcphone and a honeycombed shield sprang up around him. The Daskar fired. One hexagonal section of the shield blinked out. The shield rotated to absorb another hit and another.

"Damn, you got your geodesic shield working?" Adam called out as he dodged another attacker.

Shelton gave the thumbs-up just as his shield sparked, flickered and died. "What the hell?"

Adam spun his staff like a propeller and thrust it toward another group of Daskar. Dark clouds enveloped their heads. They veered crazily through the air, some smacking into the cliff and others crashing into the ship.

"Dammit, I thought this spell would work!" Shelton fiddled with his arcphone, but couldn't get the barrier back into place.

"I don't know if you'll need it," Adam said grimly and pointed up.

The remaining Daskar leapt into the air and hovered far above us, their black visors watching the doomed ship drift toward the ground far below.

"Bastards." Shelton opened a slot on his staff and checked a chunk of black rock inside. "At least this new aetherite amplifier works. Almost makes me feel useful."

"Is that the stuff we found in Voltis?" Elyssa asked.

5

"Yeah, it's super-concentrated aether." Adam checked a similar rock inside his staff. "I was able to modify our staffs by connecting the aetherite to the magic generators. You might say this is the first field test."

The *Falcheen* creaked and groaned as it listed side-to-side.

Shelton's face paled. "Man, I think I'm gonna be sick."

My stomach flip-flopped as the ship bounced on a pocket of turbulence. I swallowed uneasily and steadied myself. "Two of the levitation foils are out on the port side. I don't think there's anything we can do to keep the ship in the air."

"Crash landing?" Adam said.

I nodded. "Crash landing."

Shelton pressed his wide-brimmed hat against his head as a gust of wind threatened to dislodge it. "How in the hell are we supposed to walk the rest of the way to Tarissa?"

"What makes you think the Daskar will give us a chance to walk?" Elyssa looked up at the enemy soldiers where they paced the crippled sky ship. "Depending on how hard we land, they're going to swoop in and kill us before we can defend ourselves."

Shelton sighed and pinched the bridge of his nose. "Dammit, woman! You're really putting a damper on my day."

"You mean a dhampyr?" Adam said with a grin.

We groaned.

The *Falcheen* fell in slow motion, but even an impact of twenty miles per hour would be enough to break bones and send people flying. Most of the Mzodi could channel wings and glide safely to the ground, but they weren't nearly as maneuverable as the Daskar in the air and would be easy targets.

My heart thudded against my ribs like it wanted to sprout wings of its own and fly away. "We're gonna be fish in a barrel if we don't do something."

"If you channel wings, I will ride on your back like a baby," Shelton said.

Adam grinned. "Man, you're desperate, aren't you?"

Shelton stuck out his chin defiantly. "I ain't too proud to admit I can't fly."

I thought back to our harrowing journey through the Voltis Maelstrom to Atlantis. We'd faced situations worse than this. There was one thing that could save us. I interrupted a heated discussion between Illaena and Tahlee. "Can we use the emergency wings?"

Tahlee pointed to the cliff face about twenty feet from the side of the ship. "How are we supposed to engage the wings without ripping them off?"

I tried to remember how long the wings were, but only remembered they were huge. "How much space do you need?"

"Too much." Illaena shook her head. "Forty yards at minimum."

"Christ," Shelton muttered. "Can't we steer the ship away?"

"The navigators are barely holding it off the cliff face as it is," Tahlee said. "If we try to pull any harder to starboard, we risk losing control."

I ran through half a dozen options in my head. Could I fire a Murk web to the other side and pull us over? The opposite canyon wall looked a little over a hundred yards away. Fully charged, I'd be hard pressed to channel enough power to fire a shot that far. Even with everyone on board helping, we'd lose a battle of tug of war with the ship, especially since it was still moving forward and downward at the same time.

"We need a kinetic blast." Adam pushed nonexistent glasses up on the bridge of his nose and made the universal gesture of throwing a fireball with his hands. "The levitation foils allow us to glide on the air like a ship on water, but with considerably less friction. That means if we could slam a solid blast of Murk against the cliff wall, it might propel us out and away."

"Sort of like using a pole to push us off shore," Shelton said.

Adam nodded. "Exactly. The problem is, we need a really big pole."

"I don't think I can channel that much raw power," I told him. "We're talking about moving a big-ass ship forty yards to starboard."

Adam steadied himself as the ship lurched and pointed toward the huge gem mounted on the front of the ship. "We might be able to use the portal gem."

The portal gem was something we'd stolen from Kaelissa after driving her out of Atlantis. It allowed a Seraphim to focus a beam of magic on the aether storm surrounding Voltis and create a portal through it.

"It won't work," Shelton said. "The gem is attenuated for specific magic."

"Not if I remove the Chalon." Adam staggered across the shuddering deck to the large brass frame holding the gem. He lifted a lever to unlock the cogs and rotated it ninety degrees to port, directly at the cliff wall. Another rod held a small obsidian orb just in front of the gem. The orb was a Chalon, a master key used to open portals between realms.

"You sure it isn't going to blow up in my face?" I said.

Adam looked up and tapped a finger on his chin. He nodded and focused on me. "About ninety percent sure."

"Wonderful," Elyssa said. "Just remember, if Justin blows up, we're all gonna blow up."

I stepped around corpses, trying not to look at the sightless eyes of the dead. There were more Daskar than Mzodi, but I'd gotten to know the crew of the *Falcheen* during our odyssey into the unknown. Seeing familiar faces made an already heavy burden even heavier. I shoved aside a Daskar corpse so I could line myself up with the focusing gem.

Adam stood next to me, aiming his hands toward the gem as if lining up the shot. "Yeah, that looks about right."

Elyssa looked over the railing. "Better do it fast. We're running out of air."

I planted my feet, balled my fists, and reached for the invisible aether flowing all around me. My senses closed around Murk, the cold, ultraviolet power of creation and channeled it into my body. My left arm and fist felt as if I'd plunged it into a snowbank, energy surging along the limb and gathering in a sphere.

I held my arm above my head and shouted, "By the power of Greyskull!"

Adam pumped his fist. "Feel the power, baby!"

The power massed until I could hold it no longer. I aimed at the gem and focused all my willpower on one giant blast. "I have the power!"

Elyssa face-palmed.

Murk lanced into the focusing gem. The facets sparkled, chiming like shattering ice crystals. A gout of Murk exploded from the other side of the gem. It crashed against the cliff wall. The ship shuddered and bounced away. Rubble exploded from the rock wall and tumbled out of sight only feet away.

I fell back on my ass, gasping for breath, sweat freezing on my forehead from the chill of Murk. Face grim, raven hair whipping around her face, Elyssa gripped my hand and pulled me to my feet. When I looked at the cliff wall, I knew why.

We'd gained maybe fifteen yards of distance. Nowhere near enough room to open the emergency wings.

Chapter 2

Adam's forehead pinched with worry. "Can you do it again?"

My knees wobbled, and my insides felt like a frozen microwave dinner, but I nodded. "Yeah, I need a moment."

"We don't have a moment," Elyssa said, looking up at the Daskar circling like vultures overhead as they waited for us to slam to earth.

Illaena rushed over to us, eyes wide. "What are you doing?"

"Making space," Shelton said.

Adam snapped his fingers. "Of course! We could use the ship's weapon gems at the same time!"

"Same time as what?" Illaena asked.

Adam held out hand, lining it up with the gem. "Justin's going to ram Murk against the cliff to push us away from it. Can you give us all you've got from the port side cannons?"

The captain nodded and shouted commands to Tahlee. "Power port side cannons. Fire on my mark!"

Tahlee relayed the orders and the tactical soldiers manned the stations. I took a deep breath and steadied myself. Elyssa put her hands on my shoulders and braced me. "I've got you, babe."

I can do this. My best friends were on this ship. My true love was right behind me. I had to do what it took to save them.

I summoned all my strength and channeled Murk. I was too tired to make jokes this time. Too tired to hold my arm up. Elyssa gripped my forearm and steadied my aim. I felt her warm breath against my neck. Felt her soft curves pressing against me.

"Justin, I think you're redirecting your power somewhere else." Elyssa said.

I blinked my eyes and tried not to think about Elyssa for once. "Sorry, got distracted."

"I'll distract you all you want later," she murmured.

My core temperature shot up and suddenly the Murk didn't seem so cold after all. I gathered my willpower and nodded. "Ready. Aim. Fire!" I unleashed everything I had. The ultraviolet energy gathered on the gem and exploded from the other side.

Illaena threw forward her arm and the ship cannons fired.

The crystalline tinkle of Murk filled the air and the ship lurched starboard. The massive explosion ripped gouts of rock from the cliff. Dust filled the air and was just as quickly blown away by the wind. Elyssa kept me from falling this time, but my vision went blurry and I nearly blacked out.

I heard Shelton whooping. Felt Adam clap me on the back. I shook my head and the world swam back into focus. We'd gained over twenty yards—more than enough room for the wings. Illaena's shouts filled the air. Crew ran to long levers set flush in the deck and pulled on them with all their might.

Elyssa and the others went to help. I sat down on the deck to gather my strength. The lifeless gaze of a dead Daskar peered at me through a broken mask—a single green eye glazing over in death. I reached toward the helmet, determined to pull it off and see one of the bastards who'd attacked us when my stomach sank like a rock and gravity toppled me over.

The wings locked into place with thuds and the ship leveled out its descent. With the assistance of the remaining levitation foils, the *Falcheen* rose ever so slightly and the violent turbulence stopped vibrating the deck.

Cheers rose from the crew. Shelton raised his staff overhead and shook it at the Daskar pacing us. "Who's got the power now, bitches?"

"Lock foils, prepare for assault!" Tahlee shouted as she relayed another order.

The dozen remaining Daskar joined a tight arrow formation and dove. The levitation and weapon gems on their armor glowed brighter and brighter, as if they were charging everything all at once.

"What in the blazes are they doing?" Shelton said.

Adam's mouth dropped open. "They're overloading their gems. When they hit the ship with that much magic, they'll explode!"

I raised a trembling hand and then dropped it. "I'm too tired to stop them."

Elyssa reached for her light bow, but it wasn't on her back anymore, probably lost in one of the earlier scuffles. "We're screwed."

Shelton slammed the butt of his staff onto the deck. "Not if I have anything to say about it." He ran to the focusing gem and rotated the housing. "Adam, aim this damned thing for me."

Adam rotated the brass housing up, eyeballing the distance. "I won't be able to touch the gem while you're firing."

13

"Lead them a little," Shelton barked.

I stumbled over and pushed Adam out of the way. "Let me aim it. I can survive a little magic damage."

"Don't count on it," Shelton said. "You touch the wrong side of the gem and you'll lose a hand."

I summoned a trickle of Murk—just enough to tether the top and bottom of the housing. "I can aim up or down. Adam, you rotate."

Adam knelt and gripped the rotation lever on the base. "Ready!"

Shelton spun his staff in a pattern. The lines of the pattern glowed brilliant orange, hovering in place before the Arcane. The magic sizzled with heat. Sweat broke out on Shelton's forehead and his face reddened. He thrust forward his staff and shouted, "Ra!"

The lines of glowing energy poured into the gem until it lit up like the sun. Orange flames gouted from the other side, miniature solar flares. Fire licked at the sky, missing the Daskar by a wide margin.

"We're too high!" I yanked on the bottom tether and lined up the shot.

Elyssa motioned at Adam. "Ten degrees starboard!"

He pushed on the lever and the solar flare spell raked across the Daskar. A chorus of screams went silent in an instant as the aether gems on their armor overloaded. Ultraviolet energy cascaded across the sky, thunder rumbling the final death cry of the attackers. The edges of the explosion washed across the deck, pushing the *Falcheen* forward on a tidal wave.

"Nice work, Shelton!" Adam clapped him on the back.

Shelton didn't look happy. "It took a damned magnification gem to make me halfway useful in a fight."

We grabbed hold of the gem housing and held on for dear life as the sky ship rocked and swayed in the turbulence. We careened hard starboard. The emergency wing on that side grazed the cliff, sending another shudder through the vessel.

The navigators wrestled back control before the wing could tear loose.

Massive columns appeared through the haze several hundred yards ahead. Adam swallowed hard. "We're almost to the shield wall."

"Why didn't Kohval's people wait to attack us at the wall?" Shelton said. "They could've pinned us in."

"Possibly," Elyssa said. "Kohval probably knew we'd anticipate an attack at the shield, so he tried something different."

"Kohval anticipated our anticipation," I added helpfully.

"I'm sure he had eyes on the coast just waiting for us to make an appearance," Elyssa said. "He knows Justin is the biggest threat to his plans."

Adam rotated the gem toward the shield and latched the Chalon back into place. "Let's just hope my brilliant plan for piercing the shield works."

Shelton looked at me doubtfully. "We didn't plan on Justin being out of juice at this point."

Adam's plan had been pretty brilliant. If Kohval had waited until we'd reached the shield to attack us, we would have punched a hole through it using the portal gem and been on our merry way while his forces were trapped on the wrong side. Adam had tested his theory on

15

my shields, and while it had worked fine, the shield wall used to keep Brightling invaders at bay was far more powerful than anything I could muster.

A curtain of sparkling violet light shimmered between the giant columns braced against the canyon walls. A handful of Daskar hovered in the air before it, but they were far fewer than what had attacked us earlier.

Shelton laughed and slapped his leg. "They blew their load on us already! All we gotta do is punch a hole and we're home free."

"Don't count your chickens yet, Shelton." Elyssa folded her arms and focused on the objective. "Kohval might have another surprise waiting."

"Justin can't power the gem," Adam said. "We need the crew to help."

Illaena was already on it, shouting at a group of people near the aft section. A bald seraph pushed through the others and made his way forward. "I am more than prepared to save the ship," Eor bellowed. "You may place your faith in me." He took the Chalon and set it back in its holder on the magnifying gem.

Illaena didn't look exactly pleased to see the head gem sorter, but at this point, we couldn't afford to be picky. The soldiers and deck crew looked exhausted, leaving our fates in the hands of the last people on the ship to see action—the gem sorters.

Eor and five of his people gathered before the focusing gem.

"Do you know what you're doing?" I asked.

"Of course." He waved away my concerns. "I watched you test this many times." He gestured toward the Mzodi paired off to either side of him. "They will chain with me and allow me to focus energy on the Chalon."

"One hundred yards and closing to shield wall," Tahlee shouted. "Two minutes to impact!"

Adam flinched at the interruption then turned back to Eor. "Channel Brilliance into the Chalon and then will it through the gem. The gem will do the rest."

Eor sighed dramatically. "I know, boy. Now, let me save the ship."

Adam's jaw tightened and he muttered something.

Eor's eyes widened. "Why would you say such things about my mother?"

Adam bared his teeth. "Just pierce the damned shield, okay?"

Tahlee's voice rang out again. "Seventy-five yards, one minute, thirty seconds to impact!"

"Stop scaring me!" Shelton hollered at the first mate.

The other gem sorters made a chain, touching the shoulder of their neighbor with Eor at the center. The head gem sorter cracked his knuckles, cleared his throat, and then held out his right hand. A beam of white Brilliance speared into the Chalon. The orb levitated from the brass frame and spun in the air. Intricate patterns etched in its surface glowed softly at first, growing brighter and more intense with every second.

"One minute to impact!" Tahlee shouted.

Eor flicked his fingers and energy poured from the Chalon and into the gem. A large, diffuse beam shot from the other side and hit the shield wall. Nothing seemed to happen.

"Oh, crap," Shelton said.

Adam tried to push up his nonexistent glasses again, eyes growing round as dinner plates. "It's got to work!"

Tahlee piled on with another reminder. "Forty yards, Thirty seconds!"

The shield wall flickered and misted away, leaving a space large enough for the *Falcheen* to fly through.

The gem sorters cheered.

"We ain't out of the woods yet," Shelton said. "What about the damned emergency wings? They'll never fit through that hole."

Elyssa leaned forward against the bow railing. "We'll lose altitude too fast without the wings."

She was right. Adam had aimed the gem just a bit lower than the ship, giving us a dozen yards of clearance all around, but without the wings, we'd drop well below the threshold and the lower hull would smack into the shield. I didn't want to imagine the wreck after an impact like that.

Illaena held up a fist and the crew manning the wing levers tensed.

"Twenty seconds," Tahlee cried. "Ten seconds!"

Illaena dropped her fist.

The crew pulled on the levers, muscles bulging, arms tensing with the strain. The massive wings groaned, folding back but not fast enough. The edges skimmed the hole in the shield, snapping the wings shut with a loud clap. The impact threw bodies across the deck, both living and dead, but with the wings out of the way, the *Falcheen* plowed onward through the hole and into Darkling airspace.

The hole in the shield shimmered and solidified behind us, just as Adam had expected. When we used to gem to make a gateway through the Voltis Maelstrom, it might remain in place for an hour or more, but its effects didn't last long against shields.

Without the wings open, the sky ship rapidly lost altitude. The crew struggled with the wing levers and opened them in time to keep us from smashing into Kohval's military headquarters, a tall black building. The last time I'd been here, the facility had been crawling with soldiers. Now the entire town looked deserted. Aside from the welcome wagon left behind in the Northern Pass, it seemed Kohval had taken everyone with him to invade Tarissa, the capitol city of Pjurna.

The crippled ship flew just past the town before Illaena spotted a grassy field that offered the best place for us to crash land. Without all the levitation foils functioning, there was little chance of making a nice, soft vertical landing.

We dropped lower and lower, strain showing on the faces of the navigators as they struggled to slow the ship. The tops of trees brushed against the bottom of the crystal hull, wood creaking and screeching. By the time we reached the field, we were less than a hundred feet in the air.

Ever the bearer of good news, Tahlee shouted, "Brace for impact!"

The crew who weren't helping the navigators channeled wings and glided away into the air. Illaena and Tahlee gripped their stations on the bridge, committed to going down with the ship.

I turned and watched the ground with growing horror. It was like rushing headlong toward death and I felt completely powerless to stop it. I was too tired to channel wings or even Murk to tether myself. "This is going to hurt."

Tahlee shouted another command. "Wings full tilt."

The crew on the emergency wings pulled sideways on the levers. The wings rotated nearly ninety degrees, braking the ship hard enough to send more bodies and rubble skidding across the deck.

Elyssa held onto the portal gem base with both hands, and wrapped her legs around my waist to hold me in place. I couldn't help but grin. "I could die a happy man like this."

She laughed. "I can make you even happier alive."

"Will you two shut up?" Shelton said between gritted teeth. "I don't want to die if the last thing I hear is your lovey-dovey cooing."

Elyssa gave him a sharp look. "As if you wouldn't say the same thing to Bella right about now."

Shelton didn't have a chance to answer. The ship thudded onto land with a loud boom. Rubble, corpses, and the living bounced and slammed back down. The ship ground through the earth, grating, rumbling, and vibrating for what seemed ages though it was probably more like a minute before coming to a stop.

Tahlee looked at Illaena and nodded in satisfaction before belting out new orders.

The Mzodi captain strode over to us, her tall strong frame bending with exhaustion. "We are not far from Kohvalla, and the repairs will take a day at least. I suggest you rest while you can because it will not be long before the Daskar reach us and attack."

Chapter 3

I pushed myself up off the deck and felt the hope drain right out of me at the sight of so much carnage and destruction. "There must be a ton of rubble from the cliff on the deck."

"So many bodies," Adam said. "I don't see how we're going to get this ship airworthy before Kohval's soldiers catch up."

I bent down to lift a fallen Mzodi, but Elyssa stopped me. "Justin, this is no time for you to pitch in. You need to rest and feed or you won't be able to fight the next battle."

"Or the next one, or the next one after that." I threw up my hands in disgust. "When we get back to Tarissa, I'm going to cram a Daskar down Kohval's throat!"

"That would be a sight to behold." Shelton sighed happily and looked up at the sunny sky. "I'll make sure to record it for posterity."

Adam snorted. "There's no reason we can't use a little magic to clean up this mess while the Mzodi replace the levitation foils."

Shelton flexed a hand and winced. "Man, after the light show I put on, I gotta rest too. That black aetherite definitely takes a load off my spell casting, but I need a break."

Elyssa looked up at the crow's nest where a Mzodi scanned the horizon behind us. "We should have a decent warning with the

22

lookout up there." She gripped my bicep and pulled me toward one of the rampways leading below decks. "You need some sleep, pronto." I was too tired to resist and let her lead me back to our quarters, a small room with a cloud bed.

The bed was powered by its own aether gems, so it responded right away when I lay down on it. I meant to say something to Elyssa, but drifted off to sleep before I could get it out.

I'd expected alarms to wake me—a call to arms as enemy soldiers swarmed the ship. Instead, I woke up after a strange dream about me eating ice cream with my sister Ivy. I lay in the darkness for a moment, pondering the afterimages of her smiling face. *I hope she's okay.* Ivy was stranded in Eden, tricked by Yuuki Wakahisa into staying behind while Victus sabotaged the Alabaster Arch—the only way to traverse the realms.

Let me rephrase that—the only *known* way to traverse the realms.

We'd determined that the Voltis Maelstrom was actually a giant malfunctioning portal that might offer a way to reach the other realms. We'd left a flying ship and equipment with the Atlanteans so they could research the possibilities in our absence.

I stood up and stretched, feeling invigorated. I drew upon the aether and summoned a glowing white sphere. It felt like I still benefited from the effects of feeding on human soul essence. The effect wore off after time, but it was also cumulative, and I'd fed on humans a lot during the Second Seraphim War.

Our great enemy at the time, Daelissa, had completely consumed the light essence from the souls of humans, killing them in the process. It had made her incredibly powerful, and just as incredibly insane.

23

I left the room and jogged up the ramp at the end of the corridor to the top deck. The sun was low on the horizon, meaning I'd probably slept through most of the day. The deck was completely clear of debris and bodies, and only a lone sentry stood atop the crow's nest. I walked to the railing and looked over the side, but the angle of the ship made it hard to see if the levitation gems were repaired or not.

I spotted a lone figure in the field dancing through martial arts poses I'd seen a hundred times before. I ran down the gangway and joined Elyssa in her daily routine. She smiled but said nothing, continuing the poses, the stretches, her silent dance she used to greet the day.

When we finished, I wiped the sweat from my forehead and kissed her on both cheeks. "Why did you move your routine to the evening?"

She laughed. "Better check the sun again, hon."

It took me a moment to realize what she meant. The sun hung higher than it had earlier. I took out my arcphone, Nookli, and checked the compass. The sun was in the east. *That means...* "Wait a minute, I slept the rest of the day and through the night?"

Elyssa punched me on the shoulder. "Bingo!"

I was stunned—and not by the length of my slumber. "No attacks, from Kohvalla? Nothing?"

"Nada." She shrugged. "Illaena sent some scouts to keep an eye on our surroundings, but it's been all clear so far."

"What about the remaining Daskar at the shield wall?"

"No sign of them." She bit her lower lip. "There's something else you need to see."

My stomach tightened. "It makes me nervous when you say that."

"Yeah, well, maybe you should be." Elyssa's forehead pinched. "I hardly believe it myself."

I gulped. "Great."

As we walked toward the ship, I noticed the new levitation foils affixed to the hull, one blue and polished to a nearly mirror sheen, the one behind it sparkling like a giant topaz. The crushed remains of the old ones lay on the ground nearby. In fact, it looked like most of the weapon gems on this side had been replaced as well. It still amazed me how the gem sorters could enchant aetherite for so many different uses.

Corpses bundled in white cloth were arrayed neatly next to the old levitation foils. Beyond that lay piles of Daskar armor, some of it sorted into complete sets. I picked up a chest plate and leggings, holding them up to my body, but they looked too short to fit.

"Doubt you find any in your size or mine," Elyssa said. She waved me on. "I'll show you why." She led me around piles of rubble to an unsettling sight—dozens of unwrapped bodies stacked like so much meat in a slaughterhouse.

"The Mzodi don't plan to bury the Daskar?" I said.

"They aren't sure what to do with them." Elyssa pulled me over where four soldiers lay next to each other, still clothed in tight black underwear that resembled gym clothes.

I gasped so hard, the air nearly shot out of my ass. "You've got to be kidding me."

"I wish."

I sank to my knees and tentatively touched the hand of a female soldier. She looked like a mix between Nightliss and her fake daughter, Issana. The female next to her looked virtually identical, save for a few tiny differences like a freckle on her nose, slightly thinner lips, and larger hands.

Her eyes were green, skin olive toned, hair dark as midnight. The other two seras—female Seraphim—bore the same characteristics.

"What in the hell is going on, Elyssa?" I looked at the other bodies and realized every last one of them could pass for relatives of my dead friend. I choked back tears and heard my knuckles crack as hands formed fists.

"You remember how my father said Issana is some kind of golem?" Elyssa said.

I nodded. "Was he right?"

She took me to the back of the pile. I shuddered at the sight of a dissected Daskar, but I'd seen too much death for it to make me turn away.

"Dried blood, white bone, entrails—everything looks normal," I said.

"For the most part it is." Elyssa knelt down and picked up a crystalline sphere then held it up to me. It was about the size of a baseball and transparent.

I recognized it. "It's a spark vessel like what they use in golems."

"It was located right next to the heart." Elyssa pointed to a socket next to the vital organ. "To deactivate most golems, you have to break its spark vessel."

I frowned. "The Daskar seemed to die like anyone else when you stabbed them in the right place."

"Exactly. When their vital organs stopped working, the sparks died along with them." Elyssa blew out a long slow breath. "Justin, I used to think Fjoeruss was the only Seraphim who played god like this. It's obvious that Cephus took it to a whole new level."

"My first time in Seraphina, he kidnapped Nightliss." I bounced the vessel in my hand. "He somehow used her to make these clone golems."

"You know what makes the least sense?" Elyssa stood, eyes still locked on the bodies. "How did these golems use magic?"

Fjoeruss had created an army of gray-skinned golems, the gray men. Most of them were completely controlled by their creator—all but one. Cinder had achieved sentience through a magical accident. Though he looked and felt convincingly human, he was a golem. As such, he couldn't do even the simplest of magic tricks like forming a circular containment field. In other words, he couldn't draw a line in chalk and trap aether inside it.

These clone golems had channeled Seraphim magic through their armor. "Hang on—did you make sure their armor isn't enchanted to make it look like they're channeling magic?"

"Eor looked at it, but said the gems in the armor require the user to channel through them." Elyssa shrugged. "We saw Issana use similar armor to fly."

I touched one of the bodies in the pile. The skin felt cold and waxy, just as it did on a real dead body. A foul odor emanated the bodies, not unlike rotting flesh. "Did Adam look at the bodies?"

"He took a tissue sample, but said it would take his arcphone a while to analyze it." Elyssa took my hand and briskly walked away from the bodies. "I think I know what he's going to find though." She looked over her shoulder. "I think those bodies are made of real flesh and bone just like ours. I think your term clone golem is right on the nose."

"Even if the bodies are made of flesh, you need a soul to use magic." I shook my head. "At least that's how it was explained to me."

"Maybe it's different with Seraphim magic?" The rise of her tone at the end made it more of a question than a statement. "There's got to be some logic behind it."

"Regardless of the hows or whys, we have an even bigger problem on our hands." I stopped and looked back at the dead Daskar. "Kohval may have a way to mass produce elite soldiers. These guys—gals—make Cephus's brainwashed flying soldiers look like pigeons." Cephus had captured Tarissan citizens and surgically altered them to make them mindless flying soldiers. I'd thought Daelissa was a heartless bitch, but Cephus had done his best to match her on the evil scale.

"That bastard." Elyssa's hand tightened around mine. "I wonder why Cephus didn't use Daskar instead."

"Maybe he wasn't ready yet." I winced and freed my hand from her painful grip. "Maybe there are answers in his old digs at the Ministry of Research."

"Kohval controls that section of Tarissa now," Elyssa said. "It'll be a miracle if we even get inside the city at this point."

The Mzodi had helped relocate the Eden army to the east of Tarissa out of harm's way while Kohval and Meera battled for the capitol city of Pjurna. It seemed likely that, after the Darkling legions destroyed each other, Kaelissa would swoop in and extend the Brightling Empire.

We continued walking. A cool breeze rustled through the tall red grass and the blue-leaved trees bordering the field. We found a boulder and perched on it in silence for a while. I tried not to think about what lay ahead. I tried to enjoy the moment alone with the woman I loved. All the trying in the world couldn't keep the troubling thoughts from finally boiling over.

"I'm so sick of this shit." I tossed a stone into the trees. "My god, remember when I complained about how hard it was to unite the lycans and felycans? When I bitched and moaned about how stubborn the Daemos were?" I threw up my hands a barked a sarcastic laugh. "Uniting all those different supernaturals was cake compared to getting the Seraphim to cooperate."

Elyssa gave me a sad look, but said nothing.

"I can't even trust the Darklings to cooperate." I held out my fingers and started listing my grievances. "Cephus betrayed me, then Victus stabbed us in the back. We finally beat Cephus and expected Kohval to jump at the chance to rebuild the Darkling legions, but *no*, he bends us over and rams us up our backside by marching on Tarissa so he can have it for himself!"

"Well, if you're naming names, Kaelissa betrayed us too."

I snorted. "Kaelissa was never with us to begin with. She's as crazy as her daughter, Daelissa, and just as hell-bent on ruling the world."

Elyssa bent her legs and rested her chin on her knees, violet eyes lost on the horizon. "There are plenty of good people out there too, like Flava."

"Most of the good people are dead." I squeezed shut my eyes and saw Nightliss's battered body in my arms. Saw the light fade from her eyes. "Cephus killed Ketiss and most of the Tarissan Legion when they came back to confront him. It looks like Kohval wants to finish the job."

Elyssa turned her gaze to me. "What are you saying?"

"I'm saying I won't trust another damned Seraphim I don't already know." I tossed another stone into the forest. "I'm going to kick Kohval's ass, then I'm going to kick Meera's ass, and then I'm going to take control of the government and tell these idiots how things are."

"Dictator Justin." Elyssa made a thoughtful grunt. "Doesn't sound quite right. Maybe Overlord Slade would strike fear into the hearts of the citizens."

"I think you're right." I was only half kidding. "The Darklings and Brightlings have hated each other for millennia and for what? Nothing!" I looked for another stone to throw but I was all out. "They're like a bunch of bigoted kids who will never get over their differences unless the adults come in and make them behave."

Elyssa chuckled. "Well, if we're the adults here, then the Seraphim are in big trouble."

"That's for sure." I lay back on the boulder and stared at the cloudy sky. "Well, I guess saving the world is better than sitting at home being bored all day."

"Never a dull moment for us." Elyssa traced a finger down my chest. "And it leaves no time for my favorite way to enjoy those moments."

All the troubles faded like mist, and my heart beat a little faster. "This moment is really dull."

She laughed. "Yeah? Is it?"

I nodded fervently. "It's the dullest of all moments."

Elyssa leaned over and gently nipped my neck, my ear. "Maybe I can fix that."

Her breath felt so hot against my ear it made my tender bits tingle. I was a fish caught on her alluring hook. "Please, fix it."

"That was not a damned fox!" Shelton's voice echoed from the trees an instant before he and Adam appeared at the edge of the field.

Adam saw us and waved energetically.

I whined like an angry kid. "Please, god, why now?"

Elyssa deflated and groaned. "Never a dull moment when you really need one."

Shelton took out his arcphone and showed us the picture of a furry blue creature with long ears and a tail. "That's a fox, right?"

I sighed. "Well, *Harry*, that depends on if it said what a fox says."

Shelton's eyes widened, primarily because I almost never used his first name. He looked back and forth between me and Elyssa and cleared his throat uneasily. "Uh, maybe this can wait."

Adam didn't seem to notice the tension, instead digging into his jeans pocket for his beeping arcphone. He took it out and grinned. "Hey, the analysis is complete."

"What analysis?" I asked.

He raised an eyebrow. "Now we can finally get to the bottom of the golem mystery."

Chapter 4

I was all ears. "Well, what does your phone say?" I asked.

Adam's eyes went round. "Dude, you're not going to believe this."

"Believe what?" Shelton crowded next to his shoulder. "Whoa!"

I got up off the boulder and leaned over Adam's other shoulder. Cyrinthian symbols scrolled down the screen next to a picture of olive-toned skin. Red text flashed at the bottom. *Epidermis Daemi.*

"Demon flesh," Shelton said.

"Now I'm really confused." Elyssa pushed herself off the boulder and crossed her arms the way she did when she was expecting a damned good explanation for something. "Demons don't have flesh."

"Well, yeah, technically." Adam pocketed his phone and held his hands apart as if about to launch into an exposition, but paused with his mouth open for a moment before actually saying anything else. "When summoned with a ritual pattern, demons must enter the physical world in physical form."

I scrunched my forehead. "Yeah, but it's only temporary. The bodies melt when the person who summoned them ends the spell.

Besides, the summoned demons are chained to the ritual pattern the entire time so it's not like they can wander away."

"Well, they can wander away if they break free," Shelton said. "But they lose cohesion after a while and return to Haedaemos, leaving a decaying body behind."

Adam snapped his fingers. "Exactly. Under normal circumstances, that shell disintegrates without a life force to maintain it."

"That's where the golem spark comes in," Shelton said. "Give the demon body life, and it'll remain, looking just as real as you or me."

I jabbed a finger over my shoulder, more or less in the direction of the dead Daskar. "In other words, all those dead bodies will be dust soon?"

"Probably in a day or so," Adam said. "They look and smell like regular rotting bodies, but they're not."

"Sounds a lot like when I summon a hellhound," I said. "That primordial goo creates the body for the spirit to inhabit."

"Exactly," Adam said.

"No, this still doesn't add up." Elyssa quirked her lips, a sign she was really thinking this through. "A golem spark isn't the same as a soul. It shouldn't be able to animate or maintain a demon body."

"That's where it gets tricky," Adam said. "A golem spark is essentially a collection of enchantments infused into a ball of aether and trapped inside a specialized vessel. Without the spark, a golem becomes inanimate."

"The Daskar died without us damaging the spark," Elyssa said. "That means instead of just the bodies being reliant on the spark, the connection goes both ways for them."

"Yeah, it certainly breaks the basic principles of golem crafting," Adam agreed. "Then again, I've never heard of golems created with demon flesh. Wood, stone, clay—you name it, I've heard of it, but this is new ground for me."

I scowled. "It's obvious that your favorite person and mine is responsible for these monstrosities, and I'm not talking about Cephus."

Adam nodded. "Definitely stinks of Victus."

"Why don't the bodies smell like brimstone?" Elyssa said.

"That's a damned good question." Shelton took off his wide-brimmed hat and scratched his head. "Maybe it's because there's no demon inside them."

"That would be my guess." Adam nodded his head back toward the *Falcheen*. "On the other hand, we have a live specimen to study back on the ship."

"We captured a Daskar?" I said.

"Just found out about it this morning," Adam said. "Apparently, she—it—was trapped beneath a boulder lodged in one of the aft rampways."

"Well what are we waiting for?" I said. "Let's go question it."

We started walking back toward the ship, tossing ideas back and forth, but unable to nail down exactly how Victus had managed such an incredible feat.

34

"You ever feel like the bad guys are just way too damned smart?" Shelton said. "I mean, Adam's a friggin genius"—he turned to his friend—"Don't let it go to your head."

Adam waved away the compliment. "Wouldn't dream of gloating about my intellectual superiority over you, Shelton."

Shelton continued speaking as if he hadn't heard a word. "But Victus is up there with Fjoeruss when it comes to next-level sorcery."

"He's found a way to create life," Elyssa said. "It's appalling and amazing all at the same time."

My stomach tensed at the thought. "My god. What if he's back in Eden making an army of these things?"

Adam clapped my back. "Best not to think about it, man. We've got enough issues to deal with here."

"You're darned tootin'," Shelton said. "We can worry about Victus when and if we ever get back to Eden. Right now, we've got Kohval and his group of merry demon golems to worry about."

"We can only hope that Kohval doesn't have the means to make more," Elyssa said.

"Speaking of which," I said, "why would Kohval have them under his control in the first place? Unless I'm missing something, he wasn't allied with Cephus."

Adam stared at the horizon beyond the *Falcheen*. "I have a feeling there's a huge can of worms hidden in Kohvalla that might just give us the answers we need."

Elyssa flicked her gaze his way. "Are you saying we should take the time to root around in Kohvalla while Kohval and Meera tear apart Tarissa?"

"At this point, I don't think it would hurt," Adam said. "There's literally nothing we can change by rushing into Tarissa. Your father led our army to safety, so it's not like there's a pressing concern to get there."

Elyssa didn't look convinced.

"Maybe Victus dealt with Kohval without telling Cephus," Shelton said. "Victus might have used him as a backup plan in case Cephus failed."

"That makes sense," Elyssa said. "That could also be why Kohval didn't attack Cephus, but then turned around and betrayed us once Cephus was out of the way."

"Can you imagine how long Victus must have planned for all this?" Adam's mouth dropped open and his eyes widened like someone who'd just glimpsed the Matrix. "All of this would have taken years, maybe even more."

"Considering we didn't even repair the Grand Nexus until recently, I sincerely doubt Seraphina played into his plans." Elyssa plucked a strand of red grass and wound it through her fingers as we walked. "I'd bet Daelissa shook up Victus's original plans to conquer the Overworld."

Shelton snorted. "Yeah, nobody saw that crazy bitch coming until she was breathing fire up our asses."

"I wonder how long he's had the ability to make these demon-skinned golems." A shiver ran down my spine. "What if he has the capability to produce ones that look like leaders in the Overworld community?"

"He wouldn't even have to fire a spell from his wand," Adam said. "He could take over from the inside."

"I'm beginning to lean toward Adam's idea about searching Kohvalla," Elyssa said. "If we can find any records of interaction between Victus and Kohval, that might clear up a lot."

"Yeah, but Seraphim don't use paper files or computers." Shelton rolled a small communications gem in his fingers. "They use these tiny things. It'd be like searching for a needle in a haystack *if* anything actually exists."

"Back before Tarissa was nearly wiped out, every Darkling wore one of those gems," I said. "They called them life gems because they essentially recorded everything about daily life."

"Nice way of keeping crime rates low." Adam pursed his lips. "You think Kohval and his minions wore similar gems?"

I shrugged. "Kohval wore about a dozen gems on his uniform. Any one of them could have been recording video."

"Yeah, but said gem would be on Kohval way the hell over in Tarissa," Shelton said.

Elyssa turned to me. "Didn't you say all those transmissions were sent to a central location for analysis?"

"They had a hub, but I have no idea if people actually reviewed the video, or if it was done magically." An idea nudged my brain and made my right eye twitch. "When Cephus explained their system to me, he said each city had a repository for important records. If that's true, it's probable that Kohvalla has such a repository."

"If we find Kohval's records, does that mean we have to fast forward through this dude's daily life?" Shelton said. "I don't want to suffer through weeks of watching Kohval sit on the toilet with a newspaper."

Adam snorted. "The gems are worn on the uniforms, so you'd be seeing everything from Kohval's perspective, not a third-person perspective."

We reached the ship and climbed the gangway to the top deck then walked down the rampway to the lower levels where we found Illaena and Tahlee talking in the corridor. Illaena raised an expectant eyebrow when she saw me. "Feeling rested?"

I danced a little jig and ended with a show of jazz hands. "Does that answer your question?"

Elyssa covered her face and groaned.

Tahlee shook her head disapprovingly. "It appears his mind was severely damaged in the attack."

"Oh, his mind was damaged a long time ago," Shelton assured her.

Adam barked a laugh.

I looked at Adam and motioned toward Illaena. "Tell her what you told us about the Daskar."

He pushed up his non-existent glasses and cleared his throat. "The Daskar are created by summoning a demon with a ritual pattern and forming a body."

Illaena's forehead pinched with concern. "A demon?"

"Yep." Adam pushed on the bridge of his nose again. "My theory is that somehow a golem spark is inserted into the body so when the demon vacates it, the body doesn't disintegrate."

"We do not have much experience with demons in this realm." Illaena glanced at me as if to indicate I was the exception. "Can the demon control what its form will look like?"

"Now that's a tricky question," Adam said. "Usually, the summoner is the one who forms the demon."

"Here's another thought," Shelton said. "Hellhounds can morph into human and other forms. Could the Daskar be some kind of hellhounds?"

I shook my head. "Hellhounds can morph, but their forms are crude copies and they have limited range."

"Could you summon a hellhound in the shape of a human?" Adam asked.

I waggled a hand. "Yes, but the forms are limited. Most spirits are tethered to their ethereal forms. That's why all scorps look the same. It's why crawlers all have the same number legs, and it's why hellhounds look like dogs most of the time."

Elyssa nodded. "The only variance is size."

"That's right." I'd fought scorps the size of dogs, and a couple the size of school buses. "I don't have a lot of experience summoning higher demons, but even they are bound to their ethereal forms."

Shelton grunted. "In other words, the summoner can't just will a demon to look like a rodent of unusual size?"

"I don't think so." I tapped my left temple as if that might jog loose a memory. "I'm wracking my brain here, but out of all the demons I've fought, none of them looked all that human."

"There are humanoid demons," Elyssa said. "Emily Glass's boyfriend."

39

I snapped my fingers. "Yeah, I completely forgot about him."

"The Great Banisher," Adam said, awe in his voice. "Man, I wish she was here to answer some questions."

"That boyfriend has a name, you know," Shelton said. "Tyler Rock."

"Aww, did we objectify a man?" Elyssa said as if speaking with a baby. "I'm so sorry."

Shelton threw up his hands. "It hurts okay? Did you know that most of the Arcanes call me Bella's man, or Bella's husband? It's like she gets all the credit whenever I do something really cool."

Adam started giggling like a kid. "Oh man, that's great."

I clapped my hands loud enough to startle the others. "Hey, let's stop talking about Shelton's man card issues and get back to demon facts." I looked at Elyssa. "Did Emily Glass come to Seraphina?"

She shook her head. "No, the Custodians were too busy fighting some major battles of their own when we came through to Seraphina. In retrospect, I think Victus wanted to keep Emily busy because she's probably one of the few people who could have wrecked his plans."

"Victus might be a super powerful demonologist, but Emily could kick his ass three ways from Sunday," Adam said.

"Maybe you ought to marry her," Shelton said. "Sounds like you worship her or something."

Adam looked hurt. "Dude, that's just mean."

"Do you children always speak in circles?" Tahlee said. "I do not see how you get anything done."

"Hey, we ain't kids!" Shelton stuck out his tongue to drive home the point, drawing another groan from Elyssa.

I dragged the conversation back to demons. "I had a conversation with Emily about demons once. She said that you could sometimes tell the kind of demon by its color. Yellow demons are caustic and destructive. They're the ones that like to possess humans, but their presence slowly kills the body. Blue spirits are compatible with humans."

"Your dad was a blue spirit before he merged with a human and became Daemos," Shelton said.

I nodded. "That's why my eyes light up blue when I get angry."

"Or excited," Elyssa said with a smirk.

My face heated up. "Uh, yeah." I cleared my throat. "Tyler Rock is a green spirit. I think Emily said he's extremely rare."

"There are red demons too," Adam said. "I think they're compatible with human bodies to a certain extent, but they're also physically strong."

"What does all of this have to do with the Daskar?" Illaena asked. "Are they possessed by these humanoid demons?"

I shook my head. "No, but I'd be willing to bet a humanoid type demon helped make their bodies. We just don't know exactly how."

"Looks like Heaven is full of demons," Shelton said with a grin.

Illaena and Tahlee exchanged confused glances.

"Can we talk with the prisoner?" I asked Illaena.

She nodded and walked to the wall next to me where a small gem protruded. Illaena shot a spark of aether into the gem. Part of the wall dissolved into a door, revealing a small room with no furnishings. A woman in Daskar undergarments sat in the middle of the room, legs crossed, green eyes staring angrily at the door. Her resemblance to Nightliss stabbed me in the heart.

I realized that the pain in my heart wasn't sadness. It was anger. Burning hatred for Victus. That rat bastard had been behind the crystoid attack on Eden. Everything he'd orchestrated led to Nightliss's death when she'd saved us from a nuclear explosion. It was as if he'd made an army of Nightliss look-alikes just so I'd have to kill her over and over again until one of these monsters finally killed me.

I took a deep breath and cleared my thoughts. Becoming irrationally angry wouldn't help at all. Once again, I looked at her, but instead of noting the familiarities, I noted the differences between her and Nightliss.

Her hair hung short just below the chin and ran at an angle to match her jawline. Light green eyes glared at me, not the familiar dark jade of my dear friend. This creature's nose was too long, her chin too square, her eyes too small. She was a pale imitation of a beautiful person—gross mimicry instead of true art.

I felt Elyssa's hand on my shoulder. Felt her concern. I squeezed her hand and smiled. "I'm okay."

The Daskar tried to rise, but dark ultraviolet shackles and chains held her in place.

I tried to form the first question, but the question lodged in a dry throat. Elyssa stepped in and started with something easy.

"What's your name?"

The Daskar bared her teeth and snapped them together like an angry dog.

Elyssa knelt in front of the golem. "Look, I want to help you get out of here. I want to get you safely back to Legiaros Kohval, but first, I need to know your name."

The Daskar's eyes narrowed suspiciously. "You lie. You mean to kill me no matter what I say."

"What harm is there in knowing your name?" Elyssa said.

"There is no harm," the golem said. "I simply do not care to answer."

Elyssa nodded. "I know you're angry and you don't trust us, but we want to help you."

The Daskar yanked on her bonds again. "I do not want your help, invaders. I will gladly die for the glory of the Overlord's will. I will kill you or die trying."

Elyssa frowned and raised an eyebrow. "Who is the Overlord?"

"My one true master."

"Is Kohval the Overlord?"

The Daskar shook her head. "No, he is the Overlord's proxy. He is the one assigned to lead us to glory here in this world."

A thought punched me in the gut. "Is Victus the Overlord?"

The Daskar's brilliant green eyes lit on me. "Who are you to claim familiarity with the Overlord? You will not speak his name in my presence, or I will surely kill you the first chance I have."

"Promises, promises," Shelton said. "Listen here, sweetheart. You wouldn't stand a chance against any of us, so you'd better calm down and answer questions or we'll make it really unpleasant for you."

The Daskar snarled and leapt. The Murk bonds clanked and jerked her back to the floor. She strained at them, like a dog at the end of its leash, screaming and snapping her teeth until her lips were flecked with spittle.

Illaena took out a gem and channeled through it. A hazy blue beam enveloped the Daskar and the golem dropped to the floor like a sack of flour. "She's asleep."

Elyssa sighed and stood. "This is really, really bad."

"Yeah, we're never getting answers from her," Adam said.

"Worse than that." Elyssa shook her head sadly. "Kohval has an elite army of complete fanatics at his disposal. Unless we find a way to disable them, there's no way our army will ever have a chance of retaking Tarissa."

Chapter 5

Elyssa's words wrapped around me with all the comfort of wet sheets in a freezer. "That thing can still answer questions for us." I turned to Adam. "Experiment on it. Do whatever it takes to find out what makes that thing tick so we can shut down the rest of Kohval's puppet army."

"I cannot permit experimentation on a living being," Illaena said.

"It's not alive," I said. "It's not a being. It's a creation, a thing."

"Does it feel pain?" Illaena asked.

I bit back an angry denial, but I'd heard the Daskar cry out in pain during our battle. "Yes," I said.

"Does it feel emotions?"

"It's only programmed to simulate emotions and pain," Adam said. "It's just a robot."

"Like those metal creatures from your world?" Tahlee said.

"Exactly," Adam replied. "The Daskar are enchanted to behave like people, but everything about them is fake."

"Simulacrum," Shelton said.

Illaena pursed her lips, her expression skeptical. "We cannot be sure. Until you prove to me this soldier is not a living being, you cannot harm it."

"But you killed them during the fight!" I said. "You've killed other soldiers and even thrown them overboard."

"During battles," Illaena said. "This prisoner is completely at our mercy. She is our responsibility and I will not allow torture or cruel punishment while she is in our custody."

Elyssa nodded. "I agree."

I flinched back. "Hang on—you agree with protecting that thing?" I walked over to the unconscious Daskar and jerked its head up by the hair. "Look at it!" I shouted. "It's nothing more than an animated demon shell made to look like Nightliss!" My eyes burned. "That bastard did it just to hurt us—to remind us that he's really the one who killed her!"

"Justin, you're not making sense." Elyssa touched my hand. "Calm down, babe. We'll figure this out."

"It's not real!" I pounded a fist on the floor in disgust and glared at Elyssa. "I can't believe you're protecting this thing." I released the Daskar's hair and let its head thump on the floor. "Adam needs to find out what makes these things tick, and you're throwing up roadblocks."

"What would Cinder think if he heard you talking like this?" Elyssa said in a calm, cold voice.

Shelton's eyes widened, and he swallowed hard. He shook his head at me, obviously wanting me to keep my mouth shut.

He didn't have to tell me because I didn't have an answer for Elyssa's question. Cinder was a golem, but he was also our friend. If I considered him sentient, what made him any different from this Daskar?

"Look, I've got plenty of harmless tests to run," Adam said. "It's not like I need to cut her up or anything."

"Cut *it* up," Shelton said. "Best we don't humanize this thing."

Elyssa turned her glare on him, and his face went pale.

I swallowed my anger and nodded. "Do what you can, Adam." With that, I turned and stalked out of the room.

I couldn't hear her, but I knew Elyssa was right behind me. I walked a ways down the corridor and turned to face her. She crossed her arms, raised an eyebrow, and stared at me. I didn't see anger in her eyes. Instead, I saw something a lot worse—disappointment.

So what? You know you're right! I wasn't sure if that was my inner demon or just ego talking. I swallowed it like a bitter pill and sighed. "I'm sorry. I let my emotions control me."

"I understand," she said in a neutral voice. "You were closer to Nightliss than anyone else. You loved her like a sister and then Victus took her away from you. Finding out he modeled an army of super soldiers on her is like rubbing salt in the wound."

"A knife in the guts," I clarified. "Yeah, it is, but it doesn't excuse me losing my mind in there."

Elyssa's expression finally softened. "You haven't been through years of Templar training like me, and half your soul is made up of an angry demon who just wants to watch the world burn."

"Yeah, but—"

She put a finger on my lips. "Justin, let me finish." Elyssa moved her hand to my cheek. "I don't blame you for what you feel. Just try your best not to let someone like Victus turn you into the monster he'd love for you to become."

It felt like a vice clamped around my heart had loosened. I pulled her into a hug and rested my chin on her shoulder. "I'd be lost without you."

She chuckled. "That's for sure."

I pulled back and rolled my neck to relieve some of the tension in my muscles. Images of Nightliss's burnt and battered body kept flashing through my mind. She wouldn't want me to lose my humanity over this. Maybe the Daskar really were just *things* enchanted to act like real people, or maybe Victus had figured out how to make them into living beings. Just because he'd played god didn't give me the right to do the same with our prisoner. I was just kidding myself if I thought that torturing or killing a prisoner wasn't taking on the role of god.

It seemed like just yesterday I was talking to Nightliss and consoling her on the eve of the arctic battle that claimed her life. I shook it off and squeezed Elyssa's hand. "I think we need to get to Kohvalla and recon the area in case there are still soldiers stationed there before we start snooping around."

"Spoken like a Templar," Elyssa said with a wink. "Just the two of us?"

I shook my head. "Let's see if Shelton wants to go."

She groaned. "I was kind of hoping we might find a secluded spot."

"We can call in Shelton after we finish the recon," I said a bit too quickly.

48

Elyssa leaned over and whispered in my ear. "You're smarter than you look."

I was about to jokingly ask what she meant by that, but her tongue on my earlobe made me forget how to talk.

We stepped back into the room where the Daskar still lay on the floor. Tahlee and Illaena spoke to Adam. Shelton shifted worried looks back and forth between me and Elyssa. The stupid grin across my face seemed to reassure him.

"What's the plan?" he said.

"Elyssa and I are going to scout Kohvalla to make sure the coast is clear," I said. "Then we'll poke around a little."

Shelton nodded. "I'll come with you."

I shook my head and a look of realization swept across his face. Shelton snorted. "I know what kind of poking around you want to do."

Elyssa burst into laughter while I turned fifty shades of embarrassed.

Illaena and Tahlee finished outlining the rules of interrogation for Adam then turned toward me.

"What do you hope to find in Kohvalla?" Illaena asked.

"Answers about the Daskar," I said. "Maybe discover any links Victus had with Kohval."

She nodded. "Very well. We have another day of repairs ahead of us, and we must bury our dead. The ritual will be this evening."

I nodded. "I'll be back in time."

49

Elyssa and I went to our room to grab some equipment first. She reached into a black duffel bag. "I'm glad they found my bow after the fighting was over." She withdrew and unfolded the compact black bow given to her by the human citizens of Atlantis. A tug on the bowstring produced an arrow of shimmering silver light, crackling and humming with energy.

"Where was it?" I asked

Elyssa blew out a breath. "Under one of the bodies."

"It came in handy during the fight." I slid a katana into a sheath on my back. The Nightingale armor we'd worn to Atlantis had been shredded during previous battles, so we were stuck with the Atlantean approximations of jeans and T-shirts that they'd made for us before departure.

Elyssa's brow furrowed in concentration and the shining silver arrow turned black and then golden. The sharp arrow tip morphed into a square block and back into a point. She eased off the bowstring and the arrow vanished. Her fingers stroked the dark wood gently.

I grunted. "If I didn't know any better, I'd think you're in love."

"It's not the first time I've fallen in love with something dangerous." She compacted it by folding the ends and slid it into a holster on her back, a grin spreading her lips. She slid sai swords into the sheaths on her thighs. "You ready?"

I stared enviously at her light bow and sighed. "Guess so."

Elyssa rolled her eyes. "Look, you can shoot lasers out of your hands and eyes, so don't give me any guff about my bow." She shrugged. "Besides, the Atlanteans only had a handful left after all these centuries."

"Maybe it would be redundant for me," I said with a shrug, "but think of all the stylish action moves I could pull off."

"Ha!" She punched me in the shoulder. "Guess you'll just have to watch me."

There was one last thing we needed to do before leaving the ship. We went to Illaena's cabin where she let us use the ship's communications gem since ours weren't powerful enough to reach Elyssa's father, Thomas Borathen.

Illaena's quarters were fancier than most: a wide crystal table stood in the center and a cloud bed hugged the curve of the hull in the back. Large crystal windows offered a view that was magnificent while the ship was airborne. Like most women, Illaena had a shelf with an assortment of knick-knacks purely for ornamental value.

A nasal male voice answered. "This is the *Uorion*, how can I help you?"

"This is Elyssa Borathen," Elyssa said. "I need to speak with Thomas Borathen."

"I cannot connect to him directly right now," the operator said. "We will have a ship in the area in one hour."

"Why aren't there any ships near our army?" Elyssa said.

"I cannot answer that question," the operator replied. "I can relay a message for him to contact you."

Elyssa scowled. "Just tell him we're investigating Kohvalla and I'll contact him when we return."

"Very well," the operator said.

Illaena deactivated the connection. "I believe Xalara ordered Mzodi ships to carry as many refugees from the warzone as possible. That is why there are no ships in his immediate vicinity."

Elyssa nodded, mollified. "That's a good thing. We need to get as many civilians out of Tarissa as possible."

I squeezed her shoulder. "Ready to go?"

"Yeah." She walked out of the door and headed down the gangway. Within a few minutes, we entered the forest.

Blue and yellow leaves whispered in the wind atop the creaking boughs of trees. A chittering red squirrel dashed from cover between mushrooms that reached as high as my waist. One of Shelton's blue foxes watched us curiously from atop a rotting log. I made some barking noises, but it simply tilted its head curiously and watched us go by.

"Next thing you know you'll be swinging from vines and yodeling at all the forest creatures," Elyssa said. She leaned her head against my shoulder. "We can lead a jungle rebellion against Kohval."

I snorted. The rustle and crackle of boots on twigs and fallen leaves jerked my attention to our surroundings. Elyssa pulled me down and put a finger to her lips. I made a *Duh* face. *As if I didn't already know to keep my mouth shut.*

She motioned me to stay in place and slipped into the trees in full ninja mode. I went down on my belly and peered around the stalk of the mushroom I'd ducked behind, its pungent, earthy aroma filling my nostrils. The underbrush wasn't thick due to all the giant mushrooms, but the undulating landscape made it difficult to see very far.

I crept forward for a better view and spotted movement just up the hill. Two figures clad in Daskar armor edged around the trees, knees bent, steps slow and cautious. One of them pressed something at the neck of their armor. The faceplate on the helmet split in half and the helmet retracted into the back. The other did the same.

Two variations of Nightliss looked at each other, mouthing something to each other. One of them pointed in two different directions, apparently wanting to split up. The second shook her head. She cupped an ear and pointed in my direction.

They must have heard me earlier.

I didn't know why I'd been so careless. These woods might be crawling with enemies. Then again, the *Falcheen* had been sitting in one place for more than a day and we hadn't seen any sign of enemies. Since the Daskar didn't seem to know exactly where I was, I decided to put my critical thinking skills to the test.

Why are they walking instead of flying?

That was puzzling. Their flight armor gave them a major advantage. Even the Brightling archangels would be hard pressed to match their speed and agility. On the other hand, we'd decimated the force that attacked us in the Northern Pass. Maybe they'd attacked us with nearly everything they had and were down to only a few soldiers.

If that was the case, then it made sense they'd want to keep a low profile until they assessed the enemy. They may not have even discovered that we'd landed just a couple of clicks from the city.

I couldn't help but stare at the pair of soldiers trying to sneak through the forest. Backs hunched, knees bent, eyes darting toward every noise, they did their best to remain as quiet as possible. They also failed miserably. Daskar were made for balls-to-the-wall combat and flying, not ninja operations.

More movement up the hill and to the east caught my eye. I spotted Elyssa waving at me from cover behind a tree. She pointed two fingers at her eyes and then toward the soldiers.

Duh, I already see them. I would have rolled my eyes, but she probably wouldn't have noticed. I gave her a thumbs up.

Elyssa slid the light bow from its holster, drew back the string, and aimed a black arrow at the targets. She seemed to be aiming way too high, and even if she hit one of the soldiers, she couldn't take out both of them at once. She released the arrow. It sailed in an arc that carried it way over the soldiers and into a tree.

The arrow sliced through a branch. It fell and knocked loose a large, waxy sphere that splatted on the ground right in front of the Daskar. An explosion of angry golden bees swarmed the soldiers. The pair shouted in surprise and ran in circles, arms flailing comically. One of them came to her senses and fired beams of Murk at the insects to drive them off.

When that failed, she summoned a shield that did little to protect against the bees that had already invaded her armor. The first Daskar punched the top of her breastplate. It snapped open on a hinge and she pushed it off, then did the same with the leg armor. Her comrade followed suit while doing the ants-in-your-pants dance.

Red welts covered their exposed skin, but the bees weren't done with them yet. The Daskar ran through the trees, the swarm trailing after them. When the sounds of their frenzied escape faded in the distance, I stood up and looked at Elyssa's last position.

"Looking for me?" said a voice at my shoulder.

I bit back a cry of panic, but still jumped about four feet off the ground. I growled and glared at Elyssa. "Aren't you the same person who didn't want me torturing those golems?"

She smiled innocently. "What I did wasn't torture. I simply got rid of them in a non-lethal manner."

"Unless they're allergic to bees." I *tsk*ed and shook my head sadly. "I'll bet they didn't even bring any epinephrine with them."

Elyssa patted the bow in the holster on her back and sighed. "Yeah, I'm definitely in love." She pulled back her arm as if aiming a bow. "That thing is so quiet and accurate!"

"Next thing you know, you'll be naming it."

Her eyes flashed with excitement. "That's a great idea!"

"How about Bowie?" I suggested.

Elyssa groaned. "You've literally come up with one good name in all the time I've known you, and that wasn't it."

"I think Captain Tibbs and Cutsauce are just a small sample of the awesome names I've come up with."

"You literally named a dog Mr. Licks." She crossed her arms and raised an eyebrow in challenge.

"He liked to lick things," I protested.

"You call your phone Nookli."

I waved off whatever she was about to throw in my face next. "Fine. You come up with a name for your bow. *I'm* going to Kohvalla."

We continued at a stealthy pace until we reached the outskirts of the residential part of the city. I scanned the sky, but didn't spot any lurking Daskar.

Elyssa took a deep breath. "You ready?"

I nodded. "Let's do this."

We crept forward into enemy territory.

Chapter 6

Kohvalla was a ghost town.

Crystalline paths wended through a landscape of empty houses in the residential sector. It seemed the soldiers' families had packed up and moved when Kohval took the legion on the southern skyway to Tarissa.

Elyssa peered through an open doorway on a cube house. She shook her head. "They didn't even bother closing the doors on most of the houses."

I poked my head inside a dome house across the way. It was completely bare from floor to ceiling. I walked across the path to her. "Probably in a big hurry to march south."

She peered around the corner of the next house and down the path. "Clear so far, but let's not take any chances."

I didn't argue. If there was anything I'd learned from past experiences, it was that anything could happen. The early ambush in the Northern Pass had proven that. We crept through the residential sector and reached the buildings where the residents ate.

I hesitated to call them restaurants or even eateries since no one actually served the food or prepared it there. If anything, they were more like cafeterias, sans surly people with hairnets dishing out food behind a sneeze guard.

The cafeterias had also been stripped bare of food. Even the heating box—a magical microwave—was gone. I stepped around a squashed glurk on the floor and leaned against a table. Something about this situation bugged the hell out of me, but I couldn't put my finger on it.

"You look like you just ate that glurk off the floor," Elyssa said. "You must be thinking the same thing I am."

"Why would Kohval strip the last defenses of the northern border and march south to Tarissa?" I ran a hand down my face. "It doesn't make sense to attempt a coup while leaving your back open to attack."

"Agreed," Elyssa said. "It's almost as if he doesn't care."

"It goes beyond that." I pushed off the table and walked to the doorway. "Let's say he wanted a quick offensive on Tarissa in the hopes that he could secure the city and then send enough troops back to guard the northern border."

"Not a bad strategy," Elyssa said. "But Meera invaded with her legion and bogged him down."

"Exactly." I motioned back the way we'd come from. "If he wanted a lightning offensive and quick victory, why did he take all the civilians too? It's as if he decided that nothing in Pjurna is worth holding except for the capitol city."

Elyssa's forehead scrunched with worry. "I wonder if Meera did the same with the western borders."

"There's no quick way to tell without traveling all the way there, and we don't have time for more detours." I stepped back to the doorway and made sure the coast was clear. "If Kaelissa gets wind of this, she's going to ram the Brightling army right up our collective asses, and there won't be anything we can do to stop it."

"The only thing standing between Pjurna and a massive invasion force are its impassible natural barriers and the narrow routes that would funnel enemies into a death trap." Elyssa looked toward the dark towers of the military base in the distance. "Once they get this far, they've practically stormed the castle."

My stomach knotted as I realized just how urgent it was that we put a cork in the bottle. "We need to move the Eden army up here so they can guard the pass in the meantime."

Elyssa's worried face seemed to reflect my own. "You're right. We'll need to send scouts to the west to see if Meera left that border as open and unguarded as this one."

"Good god. What in the hell is wrong with those people?" I looked toward the mountains and the Northern Pass where we'd run the gauntlet only hours ago. I half expected to see an army of Brightlings flying through, but it remained mercifully empty of invaders.

"I think we've got a little time before Kaelissa realizes what's happened," Elyssa said. "Hopefully, all her forces are still in Cabala, half a world away."

Kaelissa had apparently relocated most of her troops to the western coast of Azoris—the Seraphina equivalent of North America—in a failed attempt to assault Atlantis. "I hope you're right." I punched my left fist into my right palm. "In the meantime, I think we should clean up the rest of the Daskar in this city so we don't have to worry about them later."

"Agreed." Elyssa stepped outside and onto the path. "Let's head straight to the military towers and see if we can get a headcount. Once we know what we're dealing with, we'll return to the *Falcheen* and contact my father to let him know the situation."

"Then we bring Shelton and the others and knock some Daskar heads together?" I said.

A grin spread across her face. "Sounds like a date."

We didn't come across any other patrols until we crossed into the military sector. The training grounds, normally a beehive of activity, were wide open and empty except for a pair of Daskar several hundred yards in the distance.

Elyssa pointed to the command center, a black square squatting against the cliffs of the Vjartik Mountains behind it. Dark towers rose around it, each one usually manned with sentries. In this case, only the one facing the Northern Pass held a lone occupant. Elyssa held up a finger and made a circle.

I mimicked her. "You could've just told me that we're going to circle around the back way instead of using one of your fancy hand signals."

She held up her middle finger and circled it in the air instead, staring at me with a quirked eyebrow for emphasis. "How's that for fancy?"

I made a sad face. "I don't want to go on secret missions with you anymore, meanie!"

Elyssa snorted. "You're such a goof."

I pecked a kiss on her nose. "Someone has to counterbalance your dark, brooding personality."

"I think you're confusing me with my brother."

"Eww." I wrinkled my nose. "You're a lot cuter than Michael."

She made a show of tossing back her hair. "Because I moisturize." Elyssa grabbed my arm. "Let's get a move-on, lover boy."

We clung to the edges of the residential sector, making our way toward the mountains towering over the military headquarters. We circled around the back of long rectangular barracks, running from cover to cover until we closed to the final fifty yards of open ground between us and the target building.

Elyssa looked up at the nearby sentry towers, but nothing had changed there. The lone Daskar paced around the edges of the circular platform at the top, dead eyes of the facemask surveying the land. We waited for the sentry to turn north and then dashed across the open ground to the command center.

From there we had to be quick, sliding our backs along the black crystalline surface until we reached the east side of the building—the front entrance. From there we had an unimpeded view across the training grounds, which meant we'd see any oncoming patrols, but that also meant there was nowhere to take cover if anyone looked our way.

We skirted the front and peeked through the front entrance. The lobby was unguarded, so we slipped inside and pressed our backs against the wall. My pounding heart slowed, and my nerves unwound with relief.

Elyssa made a hand signal, and I didn't argue with her this time. Now was the time for absolute stealth. The building had a simple layout—administrative offices on the first floor, training and briefing rooms on the second and third floors, and Kohval's top-level war room on the fourth.

We took our time clearing the first floor. Two levitator shafts offered access to the second floor, but we took the auxiliary stairwells in the back to avoid any surprise encounters. The second and third floors were just as abandoned as the first. As we left the stairwell on the fourth floor, Elyssa held up a fist.

I stopped in my tracks.

She cocked an ear and closed her eyes, then pointed forward down a familiar corridor leading to the main war room. That was where Thomas Borathen had spoken with Kohval and where the Darkling Legiaros had threatened to have us arrested. When we'd left, Daskar had ambushed us outside and chased us through the Northwest Pass where we'd narrowly escaped with our lives.

As we crept down the corridor, faint voices reached my ears. The war room wasn't quite soundproof, but it muffled the voices so I couldn't understand what the occupants were saying.

Elyssa bit her lower lip and stared at the room a moment before shaking her head and pointing back the other way. She was the one with ninja instincts, so I nodded and went along with her suggestion.

We made a circuit of the rest of the floor, clearing each room except the main war room, and took cover back in the stairwell. Elyssa leaned against the wall and bit her lip again, eyes narrowed in concentration.

"What now?" I mouthed to Elyssa.

She pointed to the floor and then made some other hand gestures I didn't recognize. I frowned and tried to make sense of them, but failed miserably. I gave her the universal squad signal for *What in the hell are you trying to tell me?*

Elyssa rolled her eyes and held up finger to her lips. She pointed to me, to her, and then to the floor. Jabbed a thumb over her shoulder toward the war room. Held out the palm of her hand flat and mimicked a person walking with her fingers across it. Elyssa pointed to her and me again and then did the little person walking thing again.

I almost snapped my fingers when I got it. *We're going to follow whoever is in the room.* I gave her a big thumbs up and a grin.

She pressed the palm of her hand firmly against her face and shook her head.

I sidled up next to her and whispered in my quietest voice. "It's not my fault you didn't teach me advanced hand gestures."

Elyssa put a finger to her lips and shook her head.

I didn't know why she was so worried about being heard. Anyone in that room would be hard pressed to hear someone whispering outside it.

A good twenty minutes passed before we saw movement. A section of wall misted into a doorway at the end of the corridor. I caught a glimpse of a seraph in silver Daskar armor and two seras, one in metallic blue armor and the other in red before I ducked back into cover.

Boots stomped down the corridor and voices became clearer. "I will go below and check their progress," a male voice said. "We must be ready before more invaders try to breach the pass."

"Wait, Zero," a female said. "What of the foundry? We are dangerously low on personnel. I do not believe we have enough soldiers to carry out the task."

"Why did you not bring this up with Kohval during the meeting, Two?" the male, presumably Zero, said.

"I do not want to disappoint our leader," Two replied. "I want him to think us capable of carrying out his wishes."

"They took all foundry personnel with them to Tarissa," another female said. "There is no one here with the knowledge to work its Arcane secrets."

"It is as Thirteen says," Zero replied. "We might as well try to bake soldiers from clay as attempt to work the foundry. Without help from our true master, we can do nothing." The boots walked past and in the direction of the levitators. "Kohval will contact us in twenty-four hours. We must be done with the task by then."

I peeked around the corner for a glance. The female in red spoke. I identified her as Two by her voice. "As you say," she said. "I will gather the others."

"I still think we should have looked for that Mzodi ship," said Thirteen, the other female. "They could have been the precursor to a larger force."

"If we complete the task, there will be no need to worry," Zero said.

Their voices faded as the levitator carried them down.

Elyssa and I exchanged worried looks.

What task are they carrying out?

While Two and Thirteen bore resemblances to Nightliss, Zero looked quite different. He reminded me of someone but I couldn't put my finger on it.

Elyssa's gaze locked onto the war room at the end of the hall. She looked up and down the intersecting corridor and then walked purposefully toward the room where the Daskar had met.

Several dark red gems lay in neat rows on the table. I charged the first one. It rewarded me with a holographic image of Kohval's floating face staring intently at me. His square jaw, hooked nose, and lean face made him look like a hawk, but his rich voice made him sound like he should have gone into voice acting.

"I have moved up the timeline for your mission, Zero," Kohval said.

Zero was not in the image, but his voice spoke. "As you command, Legiaros. We are ahead of schedule and nearing completion."

I freaked out and deactivated the gem before someone heard it.

"They must have recorded their briefings with Kohval," Elyssa said. She noticed my concerned expression and smiled. "I don't think anyone is left in the building, so we can talk freely for now." She nodded at the gem. "Keep playing it."

I resumed the recording.

"It is vital that you complete it soon," Kohval said. "Our borders must be secure."

"Of course," Zero said.

Kohval offered a curt nod and the holographic image faded. I charged the next gem. Kohval appeared alongside three people I didn't recognize. I realized they were standing around this very table when the recording took place.

"I've called you here today to discuss the invasion of Tarissa," Kohval said. "Reports from the west indicate Meera has plans of her own, and we can't allow her to control the capitol."

The gray-haired seraph to his right spoke first. "Sir, I thought you were coordinating a meeting with Meera to discuss peaceful transfer of power."

"That was indeed true, Horus, but plans have changed to match the circumstances." Kohval looked grimly at each of them. "Meera no longer desires peace, but conquest."

A stout female with short-cropped hair frowned. "That information is not congruent with what I've heard. My spies tell me Meera is still intent on a peaceful transition."

Kohval glowered at her. "Perhaps you forget who is in charge here, Voda." He turned his glare on a tall, thin male. "What is on your mind, Uthor?"

Uthor didn't look the least bit cowed by Kohval's demeanor. "As you well know, in the case of a power vacuum, the remaining legion commanders are to elect a temporary leader until such time as the population can elect a new Trivectus." Uthor raised an eyebrow and drew nods from Horus and Voda, then continued. "As subvectus for this province, I have the authority to replace you if I deem you unfit for duty."

Kohval's jaw tightened. "You wouldn't dare."

"Something about you changed the day Cephus attacked Tarissa," Voda said. "You have always placed Pjurna first."

"You once told me that war was a last option," Horus said. "Kohval, my old friend, what has changed?"

"We know about this secret army you've been building," Voda said. "We know about the foundry."

"The world has changed," Kohval growled. "It is time we take control of the shattered remains of our nation and mold it into the war

66

machine it could be. We will raise armies and cast our might across Seraphina." He held up a fist. "The Brightlings will one day know what it is to be conquered!"

Uthor's eyes widened with disbelief. "No, I will not allow it." He pounded his fist on the table. "In the presence of your other top advisors, I do hereby declare you unfit for duty and assign Voda the position of Legiaros."

Kohval bared his teeth in a feral grin. "You no longer hold authority over me." He touched a red gem at his collar. Daskar flooded into the room. "You said you know of my secret army?" He flourished an arm toward the armor-clad soldiers. "Here they are, the elite Daskar."

"What are you doing?" Horus said. "I have known you since you were a child, Kohval!"

"No, old seraph, you have never known me." Kohval reached toward the table and the recording went dark.

Chapter 7

"Holy crap," I hissed. "Looks like Kohval suddenly went off his meds or something."

Elyssa frowned. "This must have been just before we came here."

"Sounds like it." I charged another gem, but it was a long, boring border report. Another gem carried news about Cephus's attack on Tarissa, and yet another dated all the way back to the day I'd been framed for murdering the Darkling Trivectus. I shivered at the memories of that terrible day.

The next gem showed Kohval in a meeting with the three advisors from the earlier recording, but in this one, everyone looked a lot happier.

"My spies report no border activity," Voda said. "Well, they did catch Legiaros Pagos toying with another of his mistresses in the ocean."

Uthor grinned. "That old Brightling couldn't turn down a female's advances if he tried."

Kohval chuckled. "What else is he supposed to do? His career was over the moment they assigned him to our shores."

Uthor barked a laugh. "I think the only reason the Brightlings hold onto the Vjartik beachhead is so they'll have someplace they can send useless commanders."

Elyssa gripped my arm. "Pause and zoom on Kohval's face."

I didn't really want to look any closer at the madman's face, but I froze the holographic image and pinch-zoomed until I could see the pores on Kohval's hooked nose.

Elyssa huffed. "Not that close." She pinched her fingers on the image until Kohval's face filled the view. She bit the inside of her lip. "Can you put the first video we watched next to this one?"

"Sure." I picked up the first gem and charged it. When Kohval's grim face filled the view, I paused it and put the images next to each other.

Elyssa looked back and forth a couple of times then pointed to a small mole on the upper right of Kohval's forehead. "Now look at the other image."

I examined the two foreheads. The mole wasn't present in the newer recording.

Elyssa gripped the image of the smiling Kohval and twisted it to show his profile then did the same for the grim Kohval. "Look at his chin and his nose." She traced her finger along each profile.

The differences were minute, but discernible. Kohval's nose in the older video had a small bump right where it began to hook downward. Grim Kohval had no bump, but a smooth transition. His chin was slightly rounder in the older recording.

I peered closer. "I don't suppose Kohval had plastic surgery since the first recording was made?"

Elyssa shook her head slowly. "What if Victus made a demon golem that looked nearly identical to Kohval and replaced him?"

"That's terrifying," I said. "Do you really think Victus could waltz in here and pull that off without anyone figuring it out?"

"I think it would explain why Kohval went from this guy"—she pointed to the smiling visage in the older recording—"to this guy." Elyssa's finger traced the profile of the grim-faced Kohval. "We need to examine all these gems and the foundry they mentioned."

"I don't think we have the time to look at all the gems," I said. "It'd be better if we waited until we took over the city first."

Elyssa frowned but nodded. "You're right. Let's poke around a little more and then we'll rendezvous with Shelton."

We went back to the stairs and took them down to the bottom floor. I leaned my head around the corner and looked into the central corridor. Just then Zero shot up the levitator shaft in the corridor and vanished to one of the higher floors. Luckily, he was studying something in his hand and didn't look up or he would've seen my surprised face peering around the doorway.

I jerked back into cover. "That was strange."

Elyssa hadn't seen him. "What is it?"

"There must be another floor beneath this one." I told her what I'd seen.

"Zero mentioned going below." She touched the walls in the stairwell. "Do you see any gems that might open another stairway?"

"No." I edged back to the doorway and looked at the levitator alcoves. "Something tells me that's the only way to get down there."

70

"What if you need a password?" Elyssa whispered.

"Then we're screwed." I tiptoed down the hall and stepped into the shaft. An invisible platform held me in place. Light glowed in the alcoves on the floors above me, but below was only darkness. Levitators were the magical equivalent of elevators, except they didn't use buttons. Instead, you willed them to take you to a specific floor.

Take me down.

Nothing happened. *Take me below. Go down. Sublevel One.* I sent it a stream of commands, but the levitator didn't know what to do with me.

"You look constipated," Elyssa said in a quiet voice. "What are you doing?"

"Trying different commands." I sighed. "Nothing's working."

She stepped on next to me and the platform seemed to drop out from beneath us. In the space of time it took me to stifle a shout of surprise, we stopped at in a black-walled corridor.

"Hmm." Elyssa grunted in satisfaction. "Level Zero did the trick."

I groaned. "Why didn't I think of that?"

Noises echoed from ahead. Elyssa put a finger to her lips, activated stealth mode, and stalked down the hallway like a panther in search of prey. I shadowed her and hung back while she checked the corner at the end of the hallway. She motioned me forward and we emerged in a large room lined with shelves. Sets of black crystal armor filled the shelves, and on the other side of the room were tables fitted with the sort of gems I'd seen the Mzodi use to rebuild damaged sections of the *Falcheen*.

71

Three people with shaved heads stood near the tables, their backs to us. Before them were three silver frames, each one holding a gem the size of their bald heads. The gems were mottled and ugly as a Hawaiian shirt with dog barf on it. Shelton had come across a smaller but similarly splotched gem in the hold of the *Falcheen* and asked Eor what it was good for.

Eor had promptly thrown it out, saying those sorts of discolored gems were good for nothing. The baldies down the way from us had apparently found some use for the ugly things.

I ducked around the shelves and crept down to the end near the tables for a better angle, Elyssa close behind. From here, the people stood in profile to us, though I could only see the one on our end since he blocked the view of the others.

Brow furrowed in concentration, sweat dripping down his face, the seraph channeled ultraviolet energy into the mottled gem. Crackling static beamed from the other side and into a large transparent gem clamped onto the table in front of him. The energy emerging from the mottled gems arced and undulated like a wild snake, sometimes missing the target gem and splashing against the back wall where it left black furrows.

The target gem sparkled with malevolent energy like a diamond spinning in the rays of the sun. I'd seen this sort of energy before. I'd seen it lay waste to an army and had nearly been killed by it.

I pulled back into cover and looked with alarm at Elyssa. "They're channeling malaether."

Her eyes flashed, forehead pinching into a V. "Are you sure?" she whispered.

I nodded and looked back at the channeling seraph. Two more crystal clear gems sat on the floor next to the table bearing the target gem. Another table farther down held two more gems. Beyond that was a doorway leading into a tunnel.

One of the channelers gasped and buckled. The other two stopped and went to his aid.

"I can't continue this pace," he said. "It's too much."

"We're almost there," the second said. "Just two more and then we can join the army in Tarissa."

"We should already have more than enough to complete the task," said the third.

"Let us take a brief break before continuing," the first said. "We will have to channel all night if this is to be ready by the deadline."

"Agreed," said the third.

The first seraph sat with his back to a shelf and closed his eyes while his comrades did the same.

A figure in Daskar armor but no helmet appeared in the tunnel followed by five more.

As with the others, they looked like variations of Nightliss, all slightly taller and stouter, but undeniably made in her image. The first one scowled at the dozing seraphs. "Sleeping again?" She booted the one closest to her and he jumped up with a shout of alarm. "Get back to work. We need to finish so we can leave."

"We're exhausted!" the first baldy protested. "We'll never finish if we burn ourselves out."

The Daskar bared her teeth. "Fifteen minutes, then back to work. I'm eager to join the conquest of Tarissa." She turned to her comrades and barked orders. The other four Daskar each hefted a gem sparkling with malaether and then vanished back down the tunnel, leaving the bald seraphs in peace.

"I'm taking thirty minutes," the first one said once the Daskar were gone. "I haven't properly rested in days."

Elyssa and I waited until the trio were snoozing again and sneaked back to the levitator. We took it up to the first level and then made our way back outside. We timed our run so the lone sentry in the tower wouldn't see us and took cover behind the barracks.

"I want to check out the foundry," Elyssa said.

"I want to know what they plan on doing with those malaether gems," I said.

She grunted. "Looks like they're making bombs to take on Meera."

"Just a couple of those gems would probably level half the city." I stared at the command center and shook my head. "I don't think Kohval wants to destroy Tarissa."

"What if it's not Kohval?" Elyssa said. "What if the seraph in charge of the legion is one of those demon golems?"

I shuddered. "Then there's no telling what it'll do."

"Cephus is dead and Victus is out of reach in Eden." Elyssa tapped a finger on her chin. "If Kohval is a clone, that means he's got no one to give him orders."

"A demon golem ordering around more demon golems." I blew out a breath. "This is crazy."

"So far, I've counted thirteen enemy combatants," Elyssa said. "The two Daskar in the forest, Zero, Two, and Thirteen, the three bald seraphs, and the five Daskar."

"Don't forget the one up in the sentry tower."

She flashed a smile. "Sometimes you're more observant than I give you credit for being."

I snorted. "You were testing me, weren't you?"

She shrugged. "Maybe."

"Why don't we take out the sentry so it's easier to move around?" I suggested.

Elyssa shook her head. "No. If the sentry is checking in with someone else, they'll know something is wrong when she goes dark."

I pursed my lips, nodded. "You're right." I nodded my head toward the far end of the building. "Let's see if we can find the foundry."

We tiptoed around the military sector, keeping an eye out for more enemies and adding them to our count as we went along. It was hard to be certain if any of them were part of our original number since the Daskar all looked so similar whether they wore their helmets or not. Zero seemed to be the only male golem.

After an hour of methodically creeping through most of the sector, we found an octagonal building tucked away in the northern section of the military zone behind rows of barracks. The obsidian octagon measured about twenty feet tall and maybe thirty yards in length and width.

There were no trees or other places to hide between us and the open doorway, so we'd have to run for it. Elyssa surveyed the area and shook her head. "We shouldn't risk trying to make it inside."

"What if it's the foundry?" I said.

Elyssa grabbed me and pulled me behind the corner of the barracks as Zero, Two, and Thirteen walked around the corner of the neighboring barracks, no more than forty feet away. Just the three of them wouldn't have worried me, but close behind them marched over a dozen fully-armored Daskar.

I pressed my back to the wall and held my breath, afraid they might hear my panicked breathing. Elyssa gripped my hand and squeezed. She peered back around the corner, ducked back, eyes filled with alarm. I risked a peek and was happy to see the formation heading away from us and toward the Northern Pass.

Then I saw what worried Elyssa.

A cloudlet laden with malaether gems floated not far behind their formation, and behind it, another and another. If each one of those gems could level a city, what havoc could three dozen wreak?

Why are they going north? There's nothing up there except—

I pulled back and let my gut instinct guide me. I knew why Kohval had abandoned this city and why he wasn't worried about Kaelissa attacking his rear. That many malaether gems were for one thing.

Before I jumped to conclusions I told Elyssa what I was thinking. "Am I crazy or is Zero going to collapse the Northern Pass?"

Elyssa nodded. "I don't see what else he could be planning."

Kohval's insane solution to a Brightling invasion was to seal the northern border.

Chapter 8

Kohval's plan was a crazy one, and not the sort that just might work. It was the fantasy of a madman to think he could seal the Northern Pass with a few explosions. "That fissure is a couple hundred yards wide and nearly a mile deep. Even if he blows up half the mountain, will he have enough rubble to fill it?"

"I don't see how." Elyssa stared up at the crack in the Vjartik Mountains. "All he'd do is create another gap."

The mountains were impassibly high—an entire range rivaling Mount Everest. Even if someone flew to the top and didn't suffer from severe oxygen deprivation, aether storms pummeled the peaks.

Pjurna had remained safe from the Brightlings for so long because of the dangerous natural barriers all along the coasts. Not only was the landmass the geographical equivalent of Australia in Eden, but like Australia, everything here could kill you. It even had giant spiders that spun aether webs and small but vicious drop bears.

I still had nightmares about my first encounter with what I'd thought was a sweet little koala bear.

The convoy of cloudlets stopped in front of a boulder that looked as if someone had chiseled a V-shaped crack down the center.

Zero stopped and held up something pinched between his bare thumb and forefinger. I magnified my vision and discerned a small clear gem.

"Looks like he's going to demonstrate the process," Elyssa said.

Unfortunately, Zero's troops positioned themselves between us and him, so we couldn't see what he was doing.

"This way." Elyssa headed around the opposite side of the building and crept to the far end. Before we got there, a loud boom echoed through the valley. An instant later, it sounded as if a bull had charged through the biggest china shop in the world, like a thousand plates crashing onto a marble floor all at once.

Echoes and the ringing in my ears gave way to silence.

Elyssa and I froze, staring at each other with unease.

"What in the hell was that?" I hissed.

She shook her head and poked her head around the corner. I knelt down and took a peek. The crack in the rock was completely filled with what looked like shattered crystal. *No, that's not crystal.*

"Those gems don't explode like malaether crucibles," I said. "They seem to solidify airborne aether into crystal."

"Suddenly their plan doesn't seem so crazy after all." Elyssa bit her lower lip. "We need to get back to the ship."

Before we could leave, more soldiers drifted into view, some on cloudlets, others marching with comrades. Before long, a cheering crowd had gathered in front of the boulder with Zero, Two, and Thirteen raising their fists in the air in victory.

"In a few hours, we leave for Tarissa," Zero shouted. "Soon, all of Pjurna will be justly governed by its rightful ruler, Kohval!"

"Looks like we way underestimated the force here," Elyssa said. "I count thirty Daskar."

"Thirty flying menaces," I muttered. "This is going to be harder than we thought and we only have a few hours to stop them from sealing the pass."

Elyssa nodded. "We'd better get back to the ship fast."

The need for stealth slowed our progress. It took us nearly an hour to clear the military sector, and another thirty minutes to get through the village. We saw only a couple of guards patrolling, but any one of them could have put the entire base on high alert. Our chances of stopping the Daskar were a lot better if they didn't know we were coming.

Shelton gave me a disgruntled look when he saw us emerge from the forest. "Man, I thought you were going to meet up with me. I must've waited for an hour near the edge of town."

"I'm sorry, man." I clapped him on the shoulder and pointed toward the ship. "Let's get onboard. We've got problems to discuss."

Adam met us at the top. "You guys were gone for a while."

"We've got a good reason for it." Elyssa told him and Shelton what we'd witnessed.

"Fascinating." Adam put a hand on his chin. "These mottled gems must create a slightly different kind of malaether than what we've dealt with in the past. It sounds like they act as a catalyst to solidify airborne aether, causing a crystallizing effect."

Shelton blew out a sigh. "Imagine if those were some sort of malaether gem bombs."

"I don't want to imagine it," Elyssa said. "They'd make the ones Daelissa used look like firecrackers."

"We have an important decision to make," Adam said. "Do we stop the Daskar, or let them seal the pass?"

"Why in the blazes would we let them seal the pass?" Shelton said. "We'd have to go all the way to the west just to get out of the damned country and it would take forever to go back to Atlantis."

"There are other ways in and out of Pjurna," Adam said. "It's just that the Northern and Western Passes are the only ones big enough to march an army through."

"Exactly," Elyssa said. "It means Kaelissa could bottle us up here as long as they want. We'd never be able to launch an offensive against her."

"Not like that's gonna happen anytime soon," Shelton muttered.

I held up a hand. "Look, we're not making any decision without consulting Thomas, okay?"

"Amen," Shelton said. "Atlantis might be the key to us getting out of this hellhole and I don't want to make it any harder to get there than it is already."

Adam snorted. "Let's not call Pjurna a hellhole in front of the Darklings, okay, Shelton?"

"I ain't talking about Pjurna," Shelton shot back. "I'm talking about Seraphina!" He made a disgusted grunt. "We had to go all the way to Atlantis just to get a decent hamburger!"

"Otherwise it'd be just fine?" I said.

Shelton pursed his lips and considered it. "Toss in pizza and it'd be bearable."

"Well, thank god Atlantis gave us enough Eden-style food to last a while," Adam said.

Shelton shuddered. "I can't even look at glurk without gagging."

"Enough food talk," Elyssa said. "Let's contact my father."

Illaena had seen us coming up the gangway and had gone into the captain's quarters ahead of us. Thomas's holographic image appeared above the table, the dark fabric of a tent behind him. Illaena moved as if to leave, but I stopped her.

"You'll want to hear this too," I said.

Her eyes narrowed. "As the Muhala Kajeen has made clear, we are not a part of this war. Though we will help refugees, we will not fight with you."

I waved off her concern. "This isn't about just us anymore."

"Kaelissa hijacked your ships and kidnapped Mzodi crew," Shelton said incredulously. "Why in the hell won't you people fight?"

"The civil war in Tarissa is a completely different matter than the fight with Kaelissa," Illaena said. "The Mzodi cannot embroil themselves in such internal matters."

"I still think you'll want to hear this," I told her. "Believe me, Xalara will agree."

Illaena frowned. She didn't nod, but she didn't leave the cabin either, so that was at least something positive.

"Commander, what's your location?" Elyssa asked her father.

Thomas looked around at each of us. "I take it you made it through the Northern Pass and are enroute to meet us?"

"Not exactly." Elyssa folded her arms across her chest. "I need to know where the army is now."

"Ooskai—Kaelissa's former village." Though he didn't even flash a smile, he seemed amused. "The villagers have been very accommodating, and are helping us create more domiciles for the refugees the Mzodi are bringing with them daily."

"I'm not sure if that's irony or not," Shelton said.

Elyssa held up a hand to keep Shelton from going off on a tangent. "I'll keep this short. Kohval may be a golem. His elite Daskar are all golems created in a likeness to Nightliss, and the remaining Daskar in Kohvalla are about to close the Northern Pass with malaether gems."

Illaena gasped at the last part. "Close the pass? Impossible."

"Totally possible," I said. "Those gems solidify aether right out of the air and he's got enough of them to pack the Northern Pass a mile wide and deep."

"That is a major trade route," Illaena said. "I must speak with Xalara at once."

I gave her a satisfied *I told you so* look, but she seemed too preoccupied with the grim news to give me a proper scowl.

"What's the soldier complement in Kohvalla?" Thomas asked.

"Thirty to thirty-five," Elyssa said. "We can't stop them unless the Mzodi help."

83

Thomas already had a handle on the bigger picture. "Kohval wants to seal off the pass so he can concentrate on Tarissa without fear of the Brightlings invading behind him. That means if we stop them from damming up the pass, we'll need to station our own forces there to protect the border."

"That's why I wanted to know your location," Elyssa said. "We need you to get here as soon as possible."

Thomas turned to Illaena. "Will you help them stop the Daskar?"

The Mzodi captain stiffened but offered a curt nod. "If Xalara approves, yes."

"There's more," I said. "If Kohval really is a golem, it means other important people could have been replaced."

"Cinder has been spending a great deal of time with Issana," Thomas said. "He's been unable to determine how she can use magic."

Adam pushed up on the bridge of his nose. "I can summarize."

"Proceed."

"The Daskar are made flesh and blood by summoning a demon in their likeness and then replacing the demon spirit with a golem spark." Adam frowned. "I still don't understand how that maintains the demon flesh or enables them to channel magic, but it does. As you know, golem sparks are not the same as spirits."

"Don't tell Cinder that," Shelton said. "It'd break his heart."

"We think they're making the golems in a place called the foundry," I said. "Elyssa and I weren't able to infiltrate it."

Adam's eyes widened. "You didn't mention that earlier."

84

"We found recorded communications between Kohval and his top lieutenants," Elyssa said. "He's apparently moved foundry operations to Tarissa. I don't know if there's anything useful left at the one in Kohvalla."

"It doesn't matter," Adam said. "I'm dying to know how they did it."

"Victus is how," Shelton said grimly. "We think he may have dealt directly with Kohval at some point."

"No collusion between him and Cephus?" Thomas said.

"We won't know until we've searched the command center from top to bottom," I said. "We need to capture the city and hold it." I looked at Illaena. "As I said earlier, we can't do it without Mzodi help."

Thomas pinched his chin between thumb and forefinger. "Illaena, can we coordinate with the Mzodi to relocate our forces to Kohvalla?"

"I will speak to Xalara and let you know," she replied.

"Very well." Thomas nodded at Elyssa and me. "Good work. Inform me once Xalara has made a decision." The holographic image faded to black.

Illaena didn't waste a moment and contacted the Mzodi flagship, *Uorion*. The same nasally male voice greeted her. "How may I help you?"

"This is Captain Illaena of the *Falcheen*. I must speak with Xalara on a matter of great urgency."

"At once, Captain." A moment later, a tall woman, her long brown hair hanging in tight braids about her face, appeared. Xalara, the Muhala Kajeen of the Mzodi, looked like a mix between an Italian and an Amazonian warrior.

Xalara didn't beat around the bush. "What is of such urgency, Illaena?"

"Kohval's forces seek to close the Northern Pass." Illaena held up a hand as Xalara's eyebrows rose in disbelief. "I know it sounds impossible, but he has devised a weapon that crystalizes aether."

Adam raised a hand. "Um, maybe I can explain a little better."

Illaena and Xalara deferred to him with nods.

"It would appear that these malaether gems are charged using those splotchy gems that Eor told us are useless—"

Xalara's brow arched. "Kohval's people are using slag gems?"

It took a moment for me to translate that from Cyrinthian into English and back again since I hadn't heard that term before. It was probably a term native to the Mzodi dialect. "The gems were mottled with all sorts of colors."

"Slags," Xalara said. "Sometimes an aether vortex will fuse many gems into one, rendering them useless for our purposes. Not even our gem can separate slags. We discovered that any attempts to enchant these gems only destroys the aether channeled into them."

"We call it malaether," Adam said. "It was used during the war to create weapons of mass destruction."

Xalara's dark eyes flashed. "Is this what Kohval means to do?"

Adam waggled his hand. "Not exactly. It seems that these large, clear gems magnify the discharge of malaether and coagulate the magical energy in the air like rancid milk."

86

"Milk?" Xalara frowned. "Is this a human food?"

"Like coagulating blood." Adam took out his phone and projected a drawing of the Northern Pass that looked like something a kindergartener had drawn in a hurry. "Sorry about this rough sketch, but if a malaether gem discharges, this is what we can expect to happen." He played a brief video of a stick-figure gem breaking and filling part of the pass with scribbles.

"Man, that is the worst illustration I have ever seen," Shelton said. "Did you make that on an Etch-a-Sketch?"

Adam gave him a dirty look then turned back to Xalara. "Based on my calculation, one gem can pack a hundred square yards with up to ten feet of crystalized aether." He flicked to a series of numbers. "That would mean Kohval's people have just enough of these gems to fill the pass all the way to the top."

The Muhala Kajeen's gaze went distant. She turned to Illaena. "I authorize you to assist them in any way necessary to stop this from happening. If the Northern Pass is closed, that will severely limit our trade routes."

Shelton raised a hand. "Speaking of which, how is trade these days? I mean, Kaelissa hijacked your ships and all. Are you still doing business with her?"

"There is more to the Brightling Empire than their leader," Xalara said. "We do not judge an entire nation based on the actions of a few."

Elyssa's mouth dropped open. "After all they've done to you, you don't plan to retaliate?"

Xalara shook her head. "I will not lead the Mzodi to war."

Once again, it seemed we were on our own against the Brightling Empire.

Chapter 9

"Maybe you should reconsider that," Shelton said. "At the very least, maybe you should help us get rid of Kaelissa."

"I have discussed the matter in depth with my advisors and the fleet captains," Xalara said in a cold voice. "This is not the first time we have had conflict and it will not be the last. We made the decision to enact trade sanctions on the capitol city of Zbura and the Brightling military." She stared at Shelton a moment. "Do you find that acceptable, Edenite?"

Shelton's fists tightened and instead of backing off, he doubled down. "Maybe you think because I'm not Seraphim that I'm intellectually challenged or something." He squared his wide-brimmed hat. "Frankly, I don't give a damn. Kaelissa ain't no better than her maniac daughter. If anything, she's worse, because she's got the whole damned Brightling Empire at her back now. That means these limp-wristed trade sanctions ain't even a smack on the ass. If anything, she'll see that she can get away with hijacking Mzodi ships and just do it again. If she can't trade gems, she'll steal them right along with your ships." He folded his arms across his chest. "Before long, you won't have a fleet left and the Brightling military will be hunting you down with your own sky ships."

I didn't like Shelton's tone, but damn if he wasn't right on the money about Kaelissa. At the risk of getting booted off the ship or worse, I tossed my own two cents into the conversation. "Shelton's right. Kaelissa is licking her wounds, but the moment she finds out about these trade sanctions, she'll devote everything she has to stealing more Mzodi ships."

Illaena glared at me. "The Edenites express themselves poorly, Muhala Kajeen, but in this case, I must agree with their reasoning. I fought Kaelissa. I saw her madness firsthand. She is ruthless and will not allow any slight to go unchallenged."

Xalara reeled back, apparently just as surprised as the rest of us at Illaena's outspoken agreement. "You did not voice such an opinion during our deliberations."

"Of course I did not," Illaena said. "I was not invited."

"Not invited?" Xalara's dark eyes glowed ever so faintly. "I sent the invitation to all ships' captains."

"Perhaps I did not receive it because I was in Atlantis," Illaena said. "Communications there were difficult."

"I told my second to ensure all ships received the communique." Xalara shook her head. "I will speak with Naja on the matter."

Illaena nodded. "That is good."

The Mzodi leader tilted her head slightly. "So you believe open war with the Brightlings is the answer?"

Illaena shook her head. "Absolutely not. I believe we should ensure none of our ships venture alone into Brightling territory. We should be wary and prepared for attacks. If the Brightlings attempt another hijacking, then we should retaliate."

"What about the Mzodi crew Kaelissa kidnapped?" Shelton said. "Are you doing anything to get them back?"

"The Brightling prisoners we took said that the crew are imprisoned on Guinesea," Xalara said. "So far, our attempts to communicate with them have been ignored."

I grimaced. "That's the island just north of Pjurna, right?"

Illaena nodded.

"Maybe if we stop Kohval's people, we can try to mount a rescue for the crew on Guinesea." I turned to Xalara. "I think with us you'll have a better chance of getting them back."

The Mzodi leader looked from me to Illaena. "Would you be willing to undertake such a rescue?"

Illaena bared her teeth in a fierce smile. "Gladly. It has been over a month since our people were taken captive. The time for talk is past."

"Very good, captain." Xalara turned to me. "I take it there's more you wish to discuss?"

"We want to relocate our army to Kohvalla so we can defend the pass," I said. "We need your help to make that happens as quickly as possible."

Xalara nodded. "I will coordinate with Commander Borathen. I believe we can have most of them transferred within a few days."

"In the meantime, there's not much we can do to secure the Northern Pass," Elyssa said. "Once we clear out the rest of Kohval's forces, there won't be anything between the Brightlings and Pjurna but us."

"You will have to do your best," Xalara said. She held her gaze on Illaena a moment. "If there is nothing else..."

"We are done," Illaena said. "Next, we mount an attack on Kohvalla and stop the Daskar from destroying the pass."

Xalara held out her hands as if to grasp Illaena's. "May the winds blow with you, captain."

"And also with you." Illaena touched a gem and the hologram vanished. She turned to Elyssa. "You have proven yourself an apt strategist. We do not have much time to plan an attack, so I would like to hear your suggestions."

Elyssa smiled and blushed. "Wow, I didn't realize you thought of me that way, Illaena."

"I can hear her head swelling already," Shelton muttered.

Elyssa elbowed him lightly in the stomach without even looking his way. "Illaena, do you have a holographic map of the area?"

"Of course." The Mzodi captain set a gem on the table and zapped it with white energy. A three-dimensional landscape of our surroundings floated over the table.

"This is gonna take a while," Shelton said, "and it's getting stuffy in this cabin."

"I'm going above decks with Shelton." I pecked my girlfriend on the cheek, but she was too busy studying the terrain to notice.

"I'm going to stick around here for a little while." Adam tapped notes on his arcphone. "I may have an idea in case the Brightlings decide to invade before the rest of the army arrives."

"You do that," Shelton said. "We're all depending on you."

Adam pretended to pick up something off the floor. "Hey, Shelton, looks like you dropped a pile of steaming sarcasm on the floor here."

"Yeah, just don't sniff it," Shelton said as we walked out of the door.

We walked up the ramps to the top deck and enjoyed the sweet-smelling breeze drifting in from the forest.

"How are you feeling?" I said. "A little more confident?"

Shelton's hand went to the compact staff holstered at his side. "A little. The aetherite power enhancement helps, but I can't help but feel like a third wheel sometimes. I mean, every native in this world is ten times more powerful than me."

I leaned over the railing and looked out across the field. "I don't think that's true."

"Dude, your Arcane Potential score was forty-one. I'm half that." Shelton sighed. "The only reason I was able to hold my own in the fight against the Daskar is because they weren't paying attention to me."

"What about your sunray spell?" I said. "What about when you shackled that Daskar before she could attack?"

"In a one-on-one fight with a Seraphim, I'd lose," Shelton said. "I've just been lucky that hasn't happened yet. If I could get that geodesic shield to work, that would be something."

"Most of the Seraphim here haven't fed on humans," I reminded him. "They don't have the kind of firepower Daelissa had."

Shelton took off his hat and ran a hand through his short hair. "I hope you're right. It just sucks that the only reason I could contribute was due to the aetherite power modification Adam made to my staff."

"I don't think that's it at all." I plucked his hat from his hand and plopped it on his head. "You're one of the most powerful Arcanes there is, man, and spell casting is a lot different from channeling." I mimicked waving a wand. "You can program entire spells into your arcphone that I could never perform just by channeling."

"Yeah, but I don't know how much good that does me."

"Get creative." I clapped his back. "And stop feeling sorry for yourself."

He chuckled. "Yeah. Guess I'm starting my own pity party." Shelton's face brightened. "How about I cook up some burgers while we wait on your chief strategist to come up with our battle plan?"

"Sounds good to me." I went below with him to the pantry where the food the Atlanteans had given us was perfectly preserved by Seraphim magic. It didn't take us long to cook some hamburgers and gussy them up with all the fixings. By the time we finished eating, Elyssa and Illaena were ready to lay out their master plan for taking Kohvalla.

The entire crew of the *Falcheen* gathered on deck and Elyssa addressed them. "Xalara has authorized us to take Kohvalla by force."

Eor raised a hand and spoke without waiting for acknowledgement. "I find it hard to believe that Xalara would authorize such a thing! We are sky fishers, not barbarians."

Illaena flashed a sharp glare at the gem sorter. "Perhaps you would like to wait here while we go prevent the Northern Pass from being destroyed."

That comment drew a chorus of gasps and surprised shouts from the crew.

"But without the Northern Pass, our trade routes will be untenable," Eor whined. "This is an outrage!"

Elyssa let him finish his tirade before continuing. She explained the situation and then laid out the battle plan. It was divided into two parts and sounded simple in theory. I had a feeling the execution might be trickier than it sounded.

After she finished speaking, Illaena took over. "While I do not condone starting a fight, the Daskar have left us no choice. If the Northern Pass is blocked, it will add weeks to our northern trade routes. If you do not wish to fight, you may disembark and wait here until we return." She gazed out at the crew, but nobody took her up on the offer. "Very well. Report to your teams."

Elyssa gathered a group of short Mzodi around her and led them down the gangway to prepare for their part in the assault while the rest prepared the ship for takeoff.

Adam rubbed his belly. "Man, I'm hungry."

"I got some leftover burgers down in the galley," Shelton said.

"I'll take them to go." Adam's eyes brightened. "I have something I want to show you."

We swung by the galley and grabbed some food for Adam, then followed the excited nerd down to a cabin he'd used as a work room. A disassembled set of Daskar armor sat on a workbench, dozens of empty spark globes piled in a shimmering net hanging from the ceiling.

Adam moved aside the armor and picked up one of the crystalline spheres. Unlike the others, this one wasn't empty. Aetherial vapors drifted inside, a multicolored cloud of magical energy, sparkling like diamonds in a sandstorm. Smoky strands of gray coiled about the aether like a ghostly snake.

"Watch carefully," Adam said.

Shelton and I leaned in closer, watching the undulating gray coils that seemed to hold the aether into one cohesive form. A sphere bulged in the smoky substance. Small protrusions morphed into a nose, lips, and ears.

Shelton's mouth dropped open. "Is that a face?"

"Watch it," Adam said.

I did and felt nausea clumping like rancid milk in my stomach. The mimicked face was smoky and amorphous, but in brief instances solidified into a countenance I recognized. "It looks like Nightliss."

"I solved how the golems can do magic," Adam said in a hushed voice. "Every one of them is infused with a little piece of Nightliss's soul essence. Cephus must have extracted it from her when he took her prisoner."

"That soulless bastard," Shelton growled through clenched teeth. "I hope to hell he's rotting for all eternity in the Void."

I backed away, the nausea clawing up my throat. "Her soul is trapped inside these monsters?"

"It's not precisely like that," Adam said. "When you feed on humans whether it's for your demon or angel side, you take some of the energy that makes up their souls. In essence, you take a little bit of them with you."

"But it's energy, not soul essence," I argued.

Adam waggled a hand. "It's a little bit of both. That's why Daelissa killed those poor people she sucked dry. It's how Daemos can literally devour souls." He put a hand on my shoulder. "Justin, Cephus wasn't working alone."

"No joke," Shelton said. "He and Victus were besties."

"Actually, neither Cephus nor Victus could extract soul essence in such pure form." Adam looked at the ghost inside the globe and shook his head. "There are very few entities capable of it."

"Then who the hell could pluck a soul and slice it up like that?" Shelton said.

"Only a Daemos." Adam turned to me. "Cephus and Victus are behind the demon golems, but now I'm certain they had a Daemos helping them."

I should have been surprised, but I wasn't. "Probably Yuuki Wakahisa or someone from her house." Thinking of them only made my spirits sink lower. "She's the one who tricked Ivy into staying behind while Victus sabotaged the Alabaster Arches."

Shelton shuddered and looked away from the spirit sphere. "Dude, put that thing away. It's giving me the creeps."

Adam set it on the workbench and clamped an opaque dome around it to keep it from rolling around while the ship was in flight.

Shelton took off his hat and set it on the bench then pinched the bridge of his nose. "I need something explained to me. How does one take so much soul essence from someone without adversely affecting them?"

Adam held up a finger. "Ah, now that's where it gets interesting."

"And hopefully less sickening." I took a deep breath and swallowed the ill feeling.

"So far, I've located three of these spirit globes," Adam said. "In one of them, the soul is very small, barely even a wisp. In this one, it's nearly four times larger."

"Maybe they used more essence for this one," Shelton said.

Adam shook his head. "No, it's not that at all." He placed a hand over his heart. "Our souls usually mimic our physical shell's size and shape."

"But they're not solid," Shelton said, gesturing toward the covered globe. "They're pure energy."

"More than just energy," Adam said, "but you're right—they're not solid so they can fit inside different vessels." He took out his arcphone and projected the outline of a person with a ghostly gray substance inside. "A Daemos can pluck bits of a soul from a person and store it in their psythus."

I touched my chest and nodded. "Yeah, it's like my demon stomach."

"Precisely," Adam said. A man with demon horns appeared in the hologram. He reached into the outline of the body and pulled on the soul. A part of it tore off like cotton candy and the demon swallowed it. His outline became transparent to show the soul fragment in a circle labeled *Psythus*.

"Hey, isn't this from our elementary social studies class about different supernatural types?" Shelton said.

Adam chuckled. "Yeah. I remember the teachers terrifying us with this lesson."

I shuddered. "They show elementary school kids how a Daemos eats souls?"

"Yeah." Shelton blew out a breath. "Arcane elementary schools like to scare the hell out of children."

"It's horrifying!" I shook my head in disbelief. "Talk about scarring your kids for life."

"I'm about to get to the scary part," Adam said. "You're definitely not going to like this."

My heart clenched. "Spit it out."

Adam looked at the opaque dome covering the soul globe. "In Daemos, the psythus digests the soul fragments, causing them to slowly dwindle to nothing. When they're kept in a container like those globes, something else happens."

Shelton's eyes went wide. "You mean—"

Adam nodded. "Yeah."

I was a second behind Shelton in realizing what it meant, and the prospect terrified me.

Chapter 10

"The soul fragments regenerate," I said.

Adam nodded. "Yeah, which means whoever made these golems has an endless supply of Nightliss's soul essence." He pressed his lips together. "Meaning, they could make as many as they want."

I reeled back, and not because I feared an army of demon golems. It was because somewhere, someone was using the soul of a beautiful person to create monstrous warriors. I swallowed the knot in my throat. "Is it possible that if the soul grows enough, the golem will have Nightliss's memories and personality?"

Adam's forehead scrunched. "I've given that a lot of thought, Justin, but I think these soul wisps are entirely reliant on the spark to remain in the vessel."

"If the soul globe is broken, the wisp escapes?" Shelton said.

"That's right," Adam said. "There's nothing binding the soul wisp to the physical body."

"What makes it any different than demon possession?" I asked.

"Demon flesh has no soul." Adam touched his chest again. "A demon possesses people by latching onto its soul. Demon flesh cannot bind a soul since it's a magical vessel and not a real one."

"Look, it's just one of those things you're gonna have to accept and move on," Shelton said.

Adam offered a wistful smile. "I wish one of these soul wisps could grow back into the real Nightliss, but judging from the personalities of the demon golems, it would seem that Cephus took a dark part of our friend's soul."

I couldn't disagree with him there. "I'll bet the soul source was in the foundry. Kohval probably took it with him to Tarissa."

"They must have used Kohval's soul to make his demon golem," Shelton said.

"Are we certain Kohval is a dolem?" Adam said.

"A what?" Shelton's brow pinched and almost immediately relaxed. "Ah, I get it. Demon golem—dolem."

"I was thinking the same exact name," I said. "Either that, or gemon."

Shelton groaned. "Let's stick with dolem, okay?"

I tried to remember what we'd been talking about and snapped my fingers when I did. "Elyssa was convinced Kohval is a dolem. We even saw a side-by-side before and after comparison. Unless he had cosmetic surgery, I think she's right."

Shelton scratched the back of his neck. "Assuming that this ain't just wild theorizing, that means the real Kohval might be dead. It means the fake Kohval is in charge of a legion that's hell-bent on starting civil war. It also stands to reason the Daemos who helped pull this off is probably with him right now."

"Maybe the Daemos is calling the shots," Adam said. "Then again, maybe the Daemos went back to Eden with Victus and the fake Kohval can't produce anymore golems without help."

I snapped my fingers. "Yeah, he needs someone who can summon demons, because pure Seraphim can't do that."

"Let's hope that's the case," Shelton said. "It's gonna get real awkward if we get to Tarissa and find another thousand Daskar waiting for us."

"Kohval had about four-hundred Daskar," I said. "That's already more than I want to fight."

I turned to the other odds and ends on the workbench. "What's the deal with all the armor?"

Adam pushed a finger up the bridge of his nose. "I was trying to see if I could replicate the armor and adapt it to Arcane purposes."

Shelton snorted. "How in blazes is an Arcane supposed to use Seraphim armor? We're casters, not channelers."

Adam didn't seem put off by Shelton's tone. "That's what I'm trying to figure out. It'd be really cool to have flight armor."

"You're forgetting something real important." Shelton jabbed a thumb at his back. "We can't channel wings."

"Yes, but what if I could adapt the black aetherite into a power source that would allow us to cast wings?" Adam grinned. "We'd have to do it differently, but the end results would be the same."

"Might as well flap your arms," Shelton grumbled. "I'll stick with flying brooms."

"Except our brooms are in rough shape from all the action they've seen." Adam shook his head. "I wouldn't trust them in battle until they've been repaired by an experienced broom technician."

"Adam's right," I said. "Besides, I wouldn't mind a set of Daskar armor." I ran a hand down my bare arm. "My Nightingale armor is toast."

"Hmm." Adam held up part of a chest plate to me. "You're a bit tall and wide, but I'll see if Eor knows how to manufacture this stuff."

We headed back to the main deck to get ready for the upcoming battle.

Elyssa joined us moments later. "You guys ready?"

I nodded. "Everything work out with the soldiers?"

Elyssa tilted her head side to side. "More or less. I think we have enough to do the trick."

"We'll find out real quick if we don't." Shelton pushed back the flap of his leather duster and holstered his backup staff on the opposite hip of his primary.

Adam grinned. "How many of those things do you have, Shelton?"

"Never enough." Shelton narrowed his eyes at me. "I still can't believe you broke my all-time favorite staff over your knee."

I snorted. "That was ages ago! Besides," I reminded him, "you were trying to kidnap my dad."

"My favorite staff." Shelton shook his head sadly and turned to Adam. "Always keep a spare around. You never know when Justin is gonna flip out and break yours."

Adam barked a laugh. "Maybe if you kept your staff out of other people's business, it wouldn't get broken."

Elyssa winced. "Eww. I don't even want to think about that." She looked Shelton up and down. "I don't know why you wear that leather trench coat all the time. Doesn't it restrict movement?"

"Nah." Shelton pivoted and waved his arms. "See? Plenty of room for movement." He slapped the sleeve. "Plus it's enchanted with all sorts of spells."

Elyssa pursed her lips and gave a doubtful shrug, but she knew how futile it was to try to argue Shelton out of something. We headed down the gangway and joined two more groups of Mzodi. Tahlee led one while Illaena headed up the other.

Elyssa scouted ahead in the forest and the rest of us followed at a discreet distance. We reached the outskirts of the village without incident and the groups went their own ways, sweeping the civilian sector for lone targets.

We crept around one of the eateries near the center of the village and nearly ran into a pair of patrolling Daskar. Elyssa held up a fist and I pressed myself against the building. Shelton and Adam mimicked me.

Elyssa pointed to Shelton and Adam and made a circling motion then gripped my arm and motioned me to come with her. She and I crouched and padded quickly after the targets. We caught up to them before they turned the next corner. Knocking out fully armored soldiers wasn't easy. Elyssa would have brought her wrist-mounted lancer, but she'd run out of the knockout darts.

That meant we'd have to do this the old-fashioned way.

Elyssa sneaked up behind the one on the right and in one fluid motion gripped the helmet and jerked it up while I mirrored her actions on the other Daskar. The pair shouted in surprise and spun toward us before we could deliver the knockout blow.

When they faced us, Shelton and Adam burst from cover behind them. Green energy lanced from their staffs and clubbed the soldiers on the backs of their heads. The seras slumped to the ground, black hair spilling across their faces. Even though I'd known their faces would resemble Nightliss, I still had to repress a shudder.

It's like looking at ghosts.

I didn't know if I'd ever get comfortable with it, but I couldn't let their appearance sway me from beating their asses when the situation called for it.

Adam and Shelton grabbed the helmets and Elyssa and I carried the limp bodies back toward the forest. Illaena and Tahlee's groups waited for us with four more unconscious forms. Eor and his gem sorters gathered the Daskar and carted them off toward the ship where they'd be stripped of armor and secured.

"The civilian village is cleared," Illaena said. "If they were checking in with someone, we do not have much time before they notice."

"I'm counting on it," Elyssa said. "You should return to the ship. Be ready when you see my signal."

Illaena nodded. "It will be as you say." She turned and led the other Mzodi back toward the *Falcheen.*

Elyssa ran a hand over her equipment—sai swords, her light bow—and confirmed everything was still in place. Then she reached into the fanny pack she wore on her side and pulled out a tube of lip balm which she smoothed over her lips.

"Got a tissue in there?" Shelton said. "My nose is runny."

Elyssa didn't bat an eyelash as she whipped out a fresh sheet.

"Wow." Shelton took it and noisily blew his nose into it. He wadded it up and chucked it into the underbrush.

Adam shook his head slowly. "Litterbug."

"Better I litter than sneeze while we're being sneaky," Shelton said. He flipped a compacted staff in his hand and holstered it. "I'm ready for phase two."

Elyssa zipped up her pack and nodded. "I suspect the other Daskar will have noticed their patrols aren't checking in by now."

We jogged back into the village and made our way toward the military sector. I spotted a squadron of Daskar lift off from the command center and head in our general direction, their ultraviolet wings blazing against the blue sky. Elyssa led us to the closest practice field and stopped.

She pulled the magic bow from her back. "Give them a light show." With that, she launched a bright red arrow toward the Daskar. It zipped far to their right, but it got their attention lickety-split.

Adam and Shelton fired spells and I channeled a bright white beam at the enemy. Everything fizzled about a hundred yards out except for Elyssa's light arrows which lost altitude and fell back to earth where they vanished in a flash of light against the ground.

Another group of Daskar launched from the command center. I recognized the silver armor of Zero alongside Two's red and Thirteen's blue. Instead of helmets, they wore visors that covered their eyes. Somewhere in the distance, an alarm wailed. Another squadron appeared from the north.

"Holy unionized unicorns," Shelton breathed. "That looks like more than thirty Daskar."

105

I counted out loud, pointing my finger at each one like a teacher taking a headcount. Elyssa beat me to it. "Fifty-one," she said grimly. "There must have been more working on the malaether gems in the Northern Pass."

"Well, your plan worked." I backed up a couple of steps. "It looks like they're all coming for us." I really wished our brooms had been in working order for this part. I felt like a field mouse beneath diving hawks. While I could channel wings, I wouldn't be able to fly nearly as well as the Daskar in their fancy flight armor.

Zero made a series of hand gestures. The other squadrons angled toward our north and south flanks, then stopped and hovered in position about a hundred feet off the ground and maybe as many yards away. Zero kept on coming. He landed lightly on his feet, a shimmering shield of Murk emanating from the gem on the palm of his left armored glove.

He flipped the visor up on his forehead and stared at us. "You will surrender or we will be forced to kill you."

I held out my hands helplessly. "Actually, I was going to say the same thing to you." I jabbed a finger toward the north. "We've got a big problem with you blowing up the pass."

Zero looked comically confused. "Why should we surrender? Four of you cannot prevail against us."

"You might be surprised." I did my best not to look worried even though my heart pounded like I was a teenage virgin in a porn store. "How about we settle this with a good old-fashioned duel? If I win, your forces surrender. If you win, we'll surrender."

Zero didn't crack a smile. Instead, he looked at Shelton and Adam. "I am only offering you surrender because you have two of the Eden Arcanes with you. We have need of their services."

"Hey, my work ain't cheap," Shelton said. "I hope you're paying better than minimum wage."

The Daskar leader's forehead pinched, but he plowed forward anyway. "I will be a kind master to you if you surrender. Otherwise, we will have to resort to unpleasant methods." His voice didn't hold an ounce of bluster or threat in it. Instead, it sounded as if he was reading off a grocery list.

He looked so familiar, but I still couldn't place the face. *Whose soul fragment does he have?* "It's for the foundry, isn't it?" I hoped my words threw him off balance and nearly grinned when I saw his shield waver along with his concentration before he shook it off.

"How do you know of the foundry?"

"I know that you were made by a man from my world." I was bluffing, of course. It might have been Cephus, but this seemed like a good chance to wring some information from the seraph. "A man named Victus and a demon spawn who worked with him."

Zero's eyes widened. "Can your Arcanes replicate his work?"

Elyssa stepped into the conversation. "I thought Kohval took the foundry personnel with him to Tarissa. Why do you want to make more of your kind?"

He glanced back at the hovering squadrons. "That is none of your concern."

There was something subtle in his voice, a tremble my demon super-hearing picked up. "Wait a minute—this is personal isn't it?"

Zero backed up a step. "I have given you every chance to surrender. Will you take it, or must I do this by force?"

I sensed an opportunity, a chink in Zero's armor that I tried once more to exploit. "Zero, if you and your people surrender and join us, we will help you with your foundry." I held out a hand imploringly. "We can do this without violence."

"I cannot betray my oath." Zero squared his shoulders and wings blazed to light on his back as he rose into the air. "We will try not to kill you, Arcanes."

"Sounds totally reasonable," Shelton shouted. "We'll try not to cut off your nuts with a stray spell, how's that?"

Zero rejoined Thirteen and Two. He held his hand, palm flat, then closed it into a fist and pulled it down. The Daskar swarmed into arrow formations to the south, the north, and the west. Zero flung out his fist.

The Daskar attacked.

Chapter 11

"We gotta work on your peace talking skills." Shelton whirled his staff. "I thought we might get out of this one without a throw-down."

"I want Zero alive," I said. "He's different from the others, and I want to know why."

"Is he the only male you've seen?" Adam asked.

Elyssa shook her head. "No, I've seen other male golems, though not many. None of them looked like Nightliss."

"It's not his gender that makes him different," I said. "It's just a feeling."

The Daskar closed in. A hundred yards. Malevolent energy gathered in their palms. Seventy yards. Fists aimed toward us. Fifty yards. The Daskar opened fire.

Elyssa launched a blazing red arrow straight up into the air. I threw up a dome shield and deflected the first salvo of fire. The squadron from the north closed into firing range and hit the shield from that angle. Every blow felt like a sledgehammer to my brain.

"Damn these guys hit hard!" I winced as another volley rained down.

Elyssa's arrow exploded into fireworks.

The Daskar pummeled my shield, driving me to my knees. "I can't hold on much longer." My head ached and my brain felt like a hippo was using it as an easy chair. The Murk shield cracked. Zero and his squadron hovered twenty feet away and hammered it. More cracks ran through the shield and the vice around my brain ratcheted tighter and tighter.

I clenched my teeth and roared with effort, but it was simply too much. The shield shattered.

Shelton flung a volley of sizzling blue discs at Zero while Adam whirled his staff overhead. White bubbles coalesced at the end of his staff and floated up into the air. He looked like a kid with an oversized bubble blower. The Daskar were too busy dodging Shelton's attacks to see the bubbles at first.

Elyssa gripped my arm and helped me up. "Run!"

We took off to the east, the only clear way out of there.

Zero shouted. I turned back and saw his squadrons falling back into formation after avoiding Shelton's attacks. Just then, the bubbles burst into a kaleidoscope of colors. Blinding light strobed in all directions, as if someone had tossed a truckload of disco balls into the air. I turned away to preserve my retinas and heard the Daskar crying out.

"Where the hell is our backup?" Shelton shouted. "I could really—" He stopped in his tracks as another squadron of Daskar streaked in from the east and came right for us. "Are you kidding me?"

Elyssa grinned. "Right on time."

The new squadron flew over our heads and engaged the enemy group from the north. A loud hum filled the air and the *Falcheen* burst into view, its hull only a few feet above the tops of the trees. The weapon gems burst into light, webs of energy flying out and snaring Daskar. The immobilized soldiers fell to the ground, unable to fight free.

Yellow paint streaked the arms of the Mzodi in Daskar armor, allowing the crew of the *Falcheen* to avoid their own people.

Adam pumped a fist. "My weapons enhancements are working perfectly!"

Shelton raised his staff overhead and whooped. "Get wrecked, bitches!"

Elyssa took me to the side of a domed building and made me sit down as the battle raged behind us. I eased onto the ground, panting, my head pounding.

"I should have fired the arrow sooner," Elyssa said. "I just needed them to feel overconfident."

I waved off her concern. "It's fine. You fired almost right away." I spotted Shelton and Adam watching the fireworks overhead, occasionally adding their own to the battle. "I hope Shelton feels a little more confident after this fight."

Elyssa frowned. "What's the problem?"

I sighed. "Performance anxiety. He feels useless against the Seraphim."

"I know how he feels," Elyssa said. She stroked the light bow. "When the Atlanteans gave me this, it felt like I suddenly had some power in this world."

I touched her cheek. "Babe, you have power everywhere." I took a deep breath. "I feel better now. Let's go help the others."

The element of surprise had already proven decisive. Nearly half the Daskar forces were down, rendered immobile by the energy webs fired from the *Falcheen*. Zero, Two, Thirteen, and a handful of others were the only ones left flying. Zero raised a fist and circled it. The tattered Daskar forces formed up around him then turned tail and fled toward the Northern Pass.

"That's right!" Shelton shouted. "Run away, you wimps!"

A massive ball of blazing energy coalesced atop the sentinel towers near the command center. I magnified my vision and saw a Daskar aiming the spherical gem Elyssa and I had seen earlier toward the *Falcheen*. Illaena must have seen it too, because the *Falcheen* banked hard to port. The sizzling energy beam struck a tall building to the south, shattering it into crystalline rubble.

Another of the tower weapons lit up and fired, followed by two more. Buildings exploded. The *Falcheen* strafed side to side, but it wasn't fast enough to avoid so many weapons. A blast slammed into the aft section. The hull cracked. The ship spun wildly.

The Mzodi in Daskar armor stopped pursuit of Zero and streaked toward the sentry towers. Though they hadn't had a lot of practice with the armor, they proved too nimble for the sentry tower weapons. Malevolent energy flashed and the first tower weapon went silent.

"I hate not having a broom," I growled as we raced on foot toward the towers. Zero and the others streaked unhindered into the Northern Pass and an uneasy feeling coagulated in my stomach. The super-soldiers seemed too duty-bound to make an escape. Since they couldn't kill us, that meant only one thing.

"The sentinel towers are only buying time," I said. "Zero is going to blow the pass."

Shelton huffed and puffed. Adam had already fallen behind, holding his side. Neither were able to match Elyssa's and my supernaturally enhanced physiques.

"Go as fast as you can," Shelton gasped. "I'm done." He stopped and bent over, hands on knees.

I looked at Elyssa. "Ready for warp speed?"

"Three, two, one." Her legs blurred and Elyssa leapt forward.

I gave it everything I had, caught up, and passed her. My long stride ate up the ground. I was fast, but not as fast as the flying targets. Zero and pals already had a generous lead, but I refused to let it dampen my efforts.

The *Falcheen* swooped up from behind another building and blasted a sentinel tower with a full-on broadside from its light cannons. The charged weapon gem in the tower exploded. Light cascaded in a ring around it, slicing through nearby structures. Crystal towers shattered and fell in on themselves.

The ship veered out of the path of another blast from the last tower. The Mzodi in Daskar armor silenced the enemy there before they could fire another shot.

I touched the pendant on my shirt. "Justin to *Falcheen*. Come in, *Falcheen*."

"This is Tahlee. Go ahead."

"I need pickup. Zero is headed to the Northern Pass." I gulped a breath. "They're going to blow it."

"On the way." The ship dipped lower. A long shimmering rope dropped from the side, dragging the ground behind me. Elyssa caught the rope as it passed by her, and scrambled up a few feet. I grabbed it when it reached me.

The *Falcheen* climbed upward, matching the altitude of Zero and gang. Two Daskar reversed course and flew straight at me, fists out like they were superheroes. They zipped beneath weapons fire from the ship. Ultraviolet blazed from their fists, splashing against the hull just above Elyssa's head.

"They're trying to cut the rope!" I shouted.

"Catch me if I fall!" Elyssa said, and wrapped her leg around the rope. She let go with her hands and pivoted upside down. In one smooth motion, she unfolded her light bow, nocked a blazing arrow and loosed it at the nearest Daskar.

It punched into the narrow seam between the chest plate and arm protection. The Daskar screamed and spun out of control, blood trailing behind. Elyssa hadn't paused to see if her arrow hit and had already launched another at the second target.

The other Daskar dove to catch her comrade and the arrow missed. The pair fell together until the injured one regained control of her flight armor. I took advantage of the moment and fired a watermelon-sized fist of Murk into the back of the injured soldier. It did the trick and knocked the breath out of her, causing her and her comrade to spin out of control.

They plummeted toward the ground, slowed at the last minute and bounced across the grass practice fields, coming to rest in a heap. I spotted Shelton and Adam going toward them and hoped my friends could handle the grounded Daskar.

Elyssa holstered her bow and gripped the rope to right herself.

"That was mighty fancy," I said.

She grinned. "It was kind of badass, wasn't it?"

"Totally gnarly, dudette." I looked ahead and saw Zero and gang a hundred yards in front of us. We were gaining quickly, but they'd already reached the malaether gems.

A flash and a boom rumbled from far below. Aether crystallized and crackled at the bottom of the gorge. A shockwave rocked the *Falcheen* as another gem erupted. The Mzodi in Daskar armor opened fire on Two and Thirteen. The two Daskar zipped around our fire and closed in on the Mzodi with expert precision.

"Our people can't take them," Elyssa said.

It was obvious our newbies were outmatched by the Daskar Wonder Twins, but the *Falcheen* couldn't open fire without risk of hitting our people. Zero was already at the next gem. He hit it with a beam of Murk and zipped upward before the malaether explosion rocked the boat again.

"Climb!" I shouted to Elyssa. "I've got an idea." *She is not going to like this.*

Elyssa nodded and shimmied up the rope fast as a greased snake on a waterslide. I brute-forced my way up, hand-over-hand, and leapt over the railing. The moment my feet hit the deck I raced for the front of the ship, channeling aether and concentrating on my back until I felt an itch in my shoulder blades.

I motioned toward Tahlee as I raced past the bridge toward two giant crossbows bolted to the deck near the bow. "I need you to shoot me off the ship!"

The first mate's eyes flared. She looked at Illaena for guidance. The captain scrunched her face like she thought I was crazy but was apparently used to my shenanigans and nodded.

"What in the hell are you doing?" Elyssa said.

I flashed a grin. "Trust me."

Tahlee ran with me to the prow. "Where am I launching you?" she asked.

I zeroed in on Zero and pointed my finger toward the next malaether gem affixed to the cliff wall. "Right there."

She gripped the ballista, swung it left and up. Murk channeled from her fingers and into the weapon. A thick ultraviolet bow string formed between the prongs. "I am ready."

Elyssa pecked me on the lips. "Please don't die."

"I'll do my best." I climbed onto the ballista, hands held out in superhero position, and braced my feet on the bow string. I slid backwards as the energy stretched taut.

Tahlee almost seemed to be smiling as she cried, "Launch!" and jerked back her hand.

The g-force slammed my stomach against my liver. Wind whipped against my face. I soared out from the ship and into open air, zipping straight for Zero at incredible speed. He turned and saw me at the last instant, eyes and mouth opening wide with surprise.

My shoulder met his armored midriff with a loud crack. I shouted in pain and Zero grunted. The pain ripped through my concentration. I forced myself to focus on the itch in my shoulder blades and channeled my wings. Hot and cold blades knifed through my flesh and my wings unfurled an instant before Zero's back slammed into the cliff wall.

We dropped twenty feet and crashed onto a narrow ledge. Dust and rubble rained down on us. Zero broke free and leapt into the air. I caught his leg and slammed him onto the ledge. The flight gems on his armor sparked and cracked. He twisted away from me, a sphere of Murk flickering on the end of his fist.

"Surrender," I growled. "Don't make me do something nasty."

Zero wiped a trickle of blood from his forehead, his eyes never leaving mine. Without warning, he thrust his hand out. I slammed a shield in place, but the angle of Zero's arm was all wrong. I realized he wasn't aiming for me, but for something above and behind me. I looked back and saw an aether gem planted on the cliff face about twenty yards up.

"No!" I redirected my shield to block the shot, but it was too late.

Time seemed to slow down as my demonic survival instinct ramped into "Oh, shit!" mode.

Zero tried to fly, but his suit was too damaged. My wings were still extended, but I didn't think I could outrun the shockwave. The malaether gem sparkled and the air began to crackle. In a few seconds, tons of crystallized aether would bury us.

I turned toward the *Falcheen*. The ship was fifty yards out and thirty below me, besieged by Two and Thirteen while the Mzodi in Daskar armor futilely tried to keep them at bay. While the pair weren't doing much damage, they were doing precisely what Zero wanted— keeping the *Falcheen* in the perfect spot to get buried by an avalanche of crystallized aether.

There was only one thing to do.

Time seemed to return to normal as the decision hit me. I feinted toward Zero. He threw up his hands in a defensive stance as I delivered my real attack—a beam of Brilliance at an outcropping of rock above him. Large chunks of rock pelted him and I blurred in with the distraction.

He tried to block me, but a rock the size of a glurk smacked him on the noggin. Zero lost his balance and toppled over the ledge. I helped him stay upright with a hard left hook to the jaw. A grunt exploded from his mouth. Crimson splashed my fist.

The malaether gem hummed as the energy built toward detonation. I grabbed Zero by an arm and a leg and hit my comm pendant. "Justin to *Falcheen*! A malaether gem is about to explode right above us. Come get me!"

No one replied, but the ship lurched toward me, beams of light spearing from the cannons, Two and Thirteen deftly dodging the attacks. I couldn't glide down to the ship with Zero's hefty form in my arms, so I guesstimated the distance and flung him out into the void. He spun like a rag doll, glanced off the ship railing, and skidded across the deck.

I leapt, spread my wings, and aimed for the ship. A crackling roar filled the air, like two icebergs smashing together. My breath frosted into ice and the shadow of crystal aether eclipsed the sun.

There was no way in hell I could survive this.

Chapter 12

Adam swiveled the ballista. Tahlee pulled back with her arm and the giant crossbow launched a chunk of unrefined aetherite straight up into the air. I twisted sideways to avoid colliding with it and at the same instant, saw Shelton frantically waving his arms at me.

He cupped his hands to his mouth. "Dive, Justin! Dive!"

I didn't need further encouragement and folded my wings. I dropped like a rock, straight toward the deck. At the last second, I spread my pinions and tried to brake. I was partially successful and slowed down a little. The partially unsuccessful part started when I tripped over my own feet and rolled a few dozen feet across the deck.

I came to a stop on my back just as the red gem met the onrush of crystals forming in the air above the ship. The freezing aether blotted out the sun and for an instant, there was no light, just frigid air and the sound and fury of a porcelain store during an earthquake.

A blaze of red light erupted, like a dying star going supernova. Orange light licked at the mass of aetherite falling toward the ship.

"All stop!" Illaena shouted.

I tried to scramble to my feet. Tried to scream, "Are you crazy?" at her, but all the speed in the world couldn't save us, caught here

119

beneath an aether hail storm that was going to bury this ship and smash it into the ground like a toy.

As the crystals passed through the light of the red gem, they lost cohesion and evaporated like steam. The avalanche roared past us on all sides. Razor shards passed so close to the railing I probably could have reached over and lost a hand to them. A huge crystal crashed onto the aft section, rocking the boat like a weeble-wobble.

The navigators wrestled the *Falcheen* back under control and nudged it into the safe zone provided by the umbrella of red light overhead. The next few seconds felt like eternity. The rush of crashing crystal subsided to a tinkle as the remaining shards covered the bottom of the pass. The red gem spent its charge and slammed onto the deck with a dense thud.

I worked my jaw back and forth to dislodge the tinnitus whining in my agitated eardrums. Elyssa appeared at my foot and held out a hand. I took it and she yanked me to my feet.

"What was that?" I asked.

"That was a super-concentrated gem carving enchantment." Adam jogged over to us, Shelton shuffling along behind. "It was totally a shot in the dark."

Shelton snorted. "Literally and figuratively." He booted aside a chunk of crystal. "Turns out Eor was working on a way to clear the pass in case we didn't stop Zero in time."

Eor strode up behind the pair, lips pursed in satisfaction. "It worked precisely as planned."

I looked around the ship. Crystal shards jutted from the deck where the enchantment had been unable to stop them. The toughened Murk shell of the *Falcheen* had more pits and scars than a prizefighter's face. The Mzodi crew rushed to uncover comrades buried by rubble and the rest of us went to help.

Amazingly, no one had been impaled or crushed by the crystals that had reached the ship, and we got some bonus prizes as well. In addition to capturing Zero, we found Two and Thirteen trapped beneath separate piles of crystal.

The Mzodi stripped them of their armor and secured them in the hold with the other Daskar prisoners.

"What of the other bombs?" Illaena asked Adam and Eor, after we'd secured the deck. "Can they be removed without setting them off?"

"They're dangerous, but I don't see why we couldn't remove them," Adam replied. "I'd rather leave them here, though, until I have a chance to study them."

Eor tutted. "Considering how adeptly I rescued the ship, disarming these bombs should be elementary."

Illaena and Tahlee looked at each other and seemed to come to an unspoken agreement. "We will leave them in place until such time as we can safely disarm them," Illaena said.

Eor's mouth dropped open. "But—"

"Reverse course," Illaena said. "Land us in Kohvalla."

Tahlee dug down deep in her diaphragm and roared the instructions to the crew and the *Falcheen* headed back into the village.

There was no time to rest once we set down. We combed the military installation and searched for the dead and wounded. A complement of Mzodi had remained behind to secure prisoners and we found them standing guard around nearly thirty Nightliss look-alikes who'd been stripped to their underwear and bound with the same shimmering ropelike material the Mzodi used for the gem nets.

I couldn't bear to look at them for long and did my best to put the dolems out of my mind.

By the time we finished securing the military zone, the sky had grown dark and we'd counted our losses.

Jayla and Raja, two Mzodi soldiers were dead. Another three were wounded, but expected to survive. Even though I wasn't truly a part of the crew, I'd been through so much with these people that it felt like losing family.

I'd talked to Raja only days ago and even convinced her to eat one of Shelton's French fries. She'd been insatiably curious about Eden, and in particular stand-up comedians. Adam had made the mistake of showing her a stand-up show he'd saved on his arcphone and Raja had been entranced ever since. A sad smile crept over my lips as I remembered her trying to tell us one of Shelton's recycled jokes.

Jayla, on the other hand, wanted nothing to do with us Edenites. She thought we were a corrupting influence on the crew and despised us for eating meat. Only Elyssa had escaped her derision. Jayla, like many other crew, admired Elyssa and requested training sessions.

For supper, I stuffed a cold hamburger in my mouth and forced it down. My body desperately wanted sleep, but my mind wanted answers and there was one place we hadn't searched yet.

Shelton chowed on a plateful of cheese-covered French fries across the table from me in the galley of the *Falcheen*. "Where to next?"

Elyssa already knew what I was thinking. "The octagonal building." She glanced at me. "Right?"

I nodded. "I think that's the foundry."

"The place where they make the golems?" Adam dropped a half-eaten hamburger on his plate. "Dude, I'm dying to see that place."

I clenched my hands to stop them from trembling. It was hard enough seeing Nightliss look-alikes dead or imprisoned by us. I dreaded what might be inside that building, but really had no choice.

Elyssa put her hand on my back. "Are you okay?"

I nodded. "Just trying not to let this get to me."

Shelton let out a loud burp. "I'm right there with you, man. These Daskar are creepy as hell. I feel like I'm fighting Nightliss's extended family or something."

Adam didn't seem all that bothered. "They're just physical shells." He shrugged. "I mean, just think of them as Halloween masks or something."

Shelton shuddered. "Hell no! Halloween makes me think of the most terrifying things in the universe."

I met his gaze and said the dreaded word in unison with him. "Clowns."

Elyssa groaned. "You're saying we'd lose if the Daskar dressed up in oversized shoes and big red noses?"

"Damn straight," Shelton said. He pursed his lips. "Or maybe it'd just make me fight even harder."

I raised both eyebrows at my girlfriend. "I seem to recall you nearly nuking a house because you found a spider in it."

She shivered. "Spiders are different, Justin."

"You fought demon crawlers!" Adam said. "Those things have a lot more legs than spiders."

"Yes, but they're big and I can see them coming." Elyssa grimaced. "Spiders like to crawl all over you while you're asleep."

Shelton snorted. "Yeah, and into your mouth."

"Gah!" She slapped him on the shoulder. "Why'd you have to give me that visual?"

I got up. My joints popped like an old-timer's. I stretched to work at the stiffness while the others debated the pros and cons of spiders versus low-level demon spawn. When Shelton started to agree with Elyssa, I decided it was time to break up the conversation. "Let's get a move on. I want to look inside before my body gives out."

We headed above deck and then walked down the gangway to the military training fields. The Mzodi had moved the prisoners from the field and the ship into the prison facility located near the command center. I was thankful I didn't have to look at the dolems again today.

Grow a spine, man! Nightliss had been one of my dearest friends, but I couldn't afford to let the revulsion I felt toward her demonic copies drag me down or slow me in a fight.

When we reached the entrance to the octagonal building, I stopped at the threshold and took a deep breath.

Shelton clapped me on the back. "We can take a look around, let you know what's in there if that'll help."

124

I shook my head. "No, I need to just plow through."

"Spoken like a true man," Elyssa said dryly.

I ignored her jibe and stepped inside. A corridor ran to the right and left around the inside perimeter of the building. I followed it since there was no other way to go until it ended at a wall with a gem. I charged the gem, but nothing happened. Two more attempts yielded no more success than the first.

"Must be locked." Adam took out his arcphone and scrolled through a long list of spells. He selected the one titled, *Gem hack*, and ran it. It took about twenty minutes to work its magic, allowing our imaginations to run wild about what waited on the other side.

"God, I hope it's not filled with bodies," Shelton said. "Or body parts, like Cinder's workshop."

Adam wrinkled his nose. "Yeah, I wish he wouldn't leave his experiments lying around."

"I think he just tosses extra parts onto the floor and forgets about them." Shelton snorted. "Maybe he ought to build himself a helper to keep the place clean."

"Cinder will probably want to set up shop right here," I said. "I hope he doesn't try to make dolems."

"Naw, he can't even make golem sparks on his own," Shelton said. "Poor guy can't do a lick of magic, much less summon a demon."

Adam's arcphone chimed and displayed a series of Cyrinthian symbols—the password for the door. They weren't just any old random symbols. In fact, they formed a name.

Naelissa.

Shelton sucked in a breath between his teeth. "That's Nightliss's given name, ain't it?"

"So Kaelissa said," Elyssa answered.

Adam shrugged. "Not all that strange given this entire project is built on Nightliss's soul and DNA."

"It's not strange," I said. "It's twisted as hell."

"Horrific," Elyssa added.

I sent a charge of Murk into the gem on the wall and mentally sent the password. *Naelissa.*

The wall dissolved to reveal a wide-open space. I located a gem on the inside wall and charged it. The ceiling emitted a bright white glow, illuminating the huge chamber from end to end.

A long table ran against one wall. Pairs of short, rectangular pedestals with curved cradles jutted up every few feet. All of them were empty save one at the far end, which held a smooth, clear gem in the cradle nearest the edge of the table.

The rest of the chamber looked empty, but it wasn't.

The floor was light gray, crystalline and hard. Only a few feet from us, black lines formed an intricate pattern within a perfect circle that measured about five feet in diameter. A row of similar patterns formed another circle that curved around the entire room. Thick black lines connected the circles while others braided yet another pattern inside the big circle.

Shelton walked to the edge of a smaller circle and knelt next to it. "What in the hell is this? Some kind of off-the-wall demon pattern?"

Adam took out his phone and snapped a picture. "This reminds me of something I read about the Demon War."

The patterns on the floor drew my eyes along their twisting, curving lines. I felt my inner demon jerk awake, a sharp tug on the nether half of my soul. A presence, something dark, watched me. The hairs on the back of my neck prickled and my heart constricted with dread. A thousand voices seemed to shout in my head all at once.

KHO VA JUSLAD.

I shouted and nearly fell over backwards in my haste to get away.

JUSLAD KHO VA MI?

It felt like a question, but one that terrified and confused me all at the same time. For once, my inner demon didn't want anything to do with this. Instead of trying to break out, it seemed to be cowering in its cage.

"Justin, what's wrong?" Elyssa gripped my hands and looked at the others. "He's not responding."

I squeezed shut my eyes and retreated inside to my mind's eye. I saw the huddled form of my demon soul. It looked like me, but glowing blue and with horns and a tail. Just beyond it hovered the window in my soul, the spiritual link to the demon world of Haedaemos. My inner demon usually resided there, but had retreated as far as it could go.

I sensed something huge and ominous just on the other side of the window. The voices echoed like thunder again and again, crashing against my mind like powerful waves. I moved toward the window, fighting an invisible tide with every step.

JUSLAD!

I gritted my teeth, reached forward, and slammed shut the window.

I slumped to my knees, panting and looked at my demon spirit. It glared back at me and bared its teeth.

"You know if you weren't such an asshole, I'd let you out a lot more." I flashed my teeth at this odd part of myself.

"You are weak," it said in a deeper version of my own voice. "It should all be yours. All!"

"And this is why we don't talk." I cut the spiritual connection and blinked back awake in the real world.

"Justin?" Elyssa smoothed hair back from my forehead. "Can you hear me?"

I pinched the bridge of my nose to ward off an impending headache and nodded. "I just had a close encounter of the demonic kind."

"Really?" Adam was suddenly all up in my face. "What happened?"

"Lots of loud voices and shouting." I accepted a hand up from Elyssa and rose to my feet. "I had to close my connection with Haedaemos just to shut them up." I gave them the details.

"Well, they sure weren't talking Cyrinthian," Shelton said. "Or if it is, it's a dialect I've never heard."

Adam looked up from his phone. "I ran it through my translators, but zero hits." He pursed his lips and looked out at the pattern. "I wonder if that had something to do with it."

128

"Probably. I felt another presence the moment I looked at it." I squeezed shut my eyes and tried to recall what we'd been talking about before the riot broke out in my head. "Adam, didn't you say something about a demon war?"

"Yeah, it blew up around the same time as the war against Daelissa." He tapped a finger on his chin. "I think that was a few months after the Demonicus Incident."

I strained my brain for a clue, but came back with nothing but a dull ache in my forehead.

Elyssa rubbed the back of my neck. "It's okay. I didn't even know about the Demon War until I read the after-action reports."

I threw up my hands. "There was another war and nobody bothered to tell me?"

Adam didn't look up from his phone when he answered. "It wasn't widely talked about because the Second Seraphim War kind of stole the headlines."

Elyssa hooked a finger on my chin and turned my head toward her. "Obviously, Emily and the Custodians won the war or we wouldn't be having this conversation."

Shelton shrugged. "I don't remember hearing anything about it either."

"Aha!" Adam held up a finger. "This is a variation on a demonicus."

"It sure as hell ain't no finger painting." Shelton walked around the edges. "Man, this is some work."

I held up a hand. "Wait, a demonicus?"

Adam pushed up on his non-existent glasses and adopted a lecturing tone. "Each of the smaller patterns you see"—he pointed out the smaller circles—"is the representation of a lesser demon name, many of which are listed in the demonomicon—a directory of known demon names. These demons tend to be more humanoid and range from the caustic to the symbiotic."

Shelton toed the edge of a pattern. "For example, this entire circle contains the name of one demon."

"Exactly." Adam tapped his phone. "I'm searching the demonomicon for names corresponding to the patterns."

"What about that?" I nodded toward the big pattern in the middle.

"Well, that's where it gets tricky." Adam pressed his lips together as if thinking of what to say next. "A demonicus tends to consist of lesser demon patterns surrounding those of greater demons, with the pattern for a demon lord in the center."

"This one only has two circles," I said.

"Yes, but…" Adam's eyes darted around the outer circle as if something had just occurred to him. Using a finger, he pointed at each circle and counted them. "This building isn't an octagon—it's a nonagon."

"Huh?" Shelton counted them out loud. "Well what do you know? This place does have nine sides."

"Nine sides, nine circles surrounding a huge complex pattern at the center." Adam's forehead pinched. "Dude, this isn't the pattern for a demon lord—it's for an overlord." His eyes filled with wonder. "If Victus made this, I think he intended to conquer Seraphina with a demon army."

Chapter 13

I wasn't convinced. "I don't think Victus had any plans to conquer Seraphina."

Shelton snorted. "Far as Victus is concerned, this place is just one big prison for his worst enemies."

Elyssa frowned. "If that's the case, why make a demonicus? Maybe he intends to return later."

"Good question." Adam's phone beeped and he groaned. "The scan program I used to identify the diagrams crashed. It can't handle the big picture, meaning I'll have to take pictures of all the diagrams individually."

"While you're doing that, I'm going to look at that gem on the pedestal." I pointed to the one on the last table. "I'd bet it has something to do with this puzzle."

"I'll help Adam," Shelton said.

Elyssa and I went to the gem on the pedestal and looked it over.

"It looks like they took the other gems but left this one," I said. "I wonder why."

Elyssa ran a finger along the bottom of the gem. "Probably because of this." The bottom of the stone looked as if it had fused with the cradle.

"Well, well. Looks like a malfunction." I motioned her away from the pedestal. "Step back. I'm gonna channel into the gem."

Her eyebrows shot up. "Are you sure? What if it malfunctions again?"

"That's why I want you to back up." I waited for her to do as I requested and then sent a gentle trickle of Murk into the gem. The ultraviolet energy flowed through the gem. Transparent webs sparkled out of the other side, twisting around each other and forming the outline of a sphere in the cradle of the other pedestal. Well, it would have been a sphere, but the bottom began to sag and warp, probably due to the defective gem.

"It's a soul sphere," Elyssa said. She looked down the tables. "They must have mass produced them here."

I amped up the energy output and finished a lopsided sphere within a few minutes. I pulled it off the cradle and inspected my handiwork. "I wonder how they put the spark and soul essence inside."

"No wonder!" Adam said in an excited voice. He jogged over to us, eyes lit up with excitement. "I identified the demons associated with the diagrams." He set the arcphone on the table and projected the image of an amorphous red shape with train wreck of letters and a circular diagram beneath it.

"Is that supposed to be a name?" I said.

"Yeah." Adam scratched his head. "Gxlilitharth? Gixilthruth?"

Shelton groaned. "Will you just get to the point?"

132

Adam smiled apologetically. "Sorry." He flicked through several images, some of ghostly humanoid shapes, and others of fully summoned demons in human form. "What we have here is a collection of ruby, topaz, and an amethyst spirit or two." He stopped at a green one. "Even the rarest of the rare—a jade spirit."

"These are demon types?" I asked.

He nodded. "Yeah. Emily Glass is the one who started listing them like gemstone colors. The only ones she doesn't list like that are the yellow spirits—the caustics."

I stared at the dark green form. "Colors aside, I assume these spirit types are humanlike when summoned?"

"Exactly." He pointed to the diagram beneath the name. "That symbol represents the demonic name, which is what forces spirits to appear when summoned." Adam flicked to the last image, this of the largest diagram. "Apparently, Victus wasn't using just any old demons for his cloning process."

Shelton sighed impatiently. "You never get to the point, do you?"

Adam held up a hand. "Fine, fine, I'll skip past all the tantalizing setup and ruin the surprise, okay?"

"What surprise?" I said.

"The humanoid demons I showed you aren't random." Adam milked the suspense a moment longer, turning his gaze on each of us in turn. "These demons are the children of a far more powerful entity." Adam switched to another image, this one of a shapeless mass of blacks, grays, reds, whites, and all the spectrums of the rainbow.

The name beneath was so long I couldn't even begin to pronounce it. "Is that a demon overlord?" I asked.

Adam shook his head. "No. This is the big cheese. The grand poobah of all demons." He grinned. "This, my friend, is the pattern for your dear, sweet grandfather, Baal."

I didn't have anything in my mouth, but I still managed to choke on my breath. "Baal, as in the ruler of Haedaemos?"

"The very same." Shelton let out a long, low whistle. "I wonder if Victus actually summoned him."

Adam shrugged. "The only person to successfully do it in recent memory was Emily Glass. From what I understand, Baal is powerful enough to resist a summons even if the summoner has his name perfect."

"Holy hellhounds in a fruit basket." Shelton blew out a breath. "You think Victus wanted to make a mega-Nightliss clone? A giant Daskar?"

"I think he wanted to make something beyond super-soldiers," Elyssa said. "He wanted to raise an army that could lay waste to anything."

"Christ," Shelton growled. "Do you think he's doing that in Eden right now?"

"Man, I hope not." Adam reached for his eyes as if to adjust eyeglasses and then stopped himself. "There's something else to consider. If Kohval moved the foundry to Tarissa, that means he must have someone on hand who can create the patterns and summon the demons."

"In other words, bad news all around." I tossed my misshapen soul sphere on the table. It clunked around and came to rest on its warped bottom. "Maybe that's why I heard all those voices in my head."

"Man, I wonder if Baal was able to reach through the pattern to you somehow." Adam rubbed his hands together nervously. "He must be insanely powerful."

"No doubt." I could almost feel the tidal wave of power pounding against the closed window in my soul. *Could that possibly be Baal?* "We need to find out who did this and stop them from helping Kohval."

Elyssa's upper lip curled with distaste. "Who'd be crazy enough to summon Baal?"

"Crazy ain't a strong enough word," Shelton said. "More like bat-shit insane."

"What happens if Baal breaks free of the pattern?" Elyssa said.

"That's something we don't want to find out," Adam said. "Baal's pattern is the work of a master." He knelt and put his cheek to the ground. "My god, it's even three-dimensional and hardened. We'd have a heck of a time destroying this."

I followed his example and put my eye level with the floor. From that angle, the lines seemed to hover off the floor, even if only by a millimeter. "Incredible." I stood up and brushed off my hands. "You think Victus designed this?"

Adam sat up on his knees and nodded. "That's the highest probability. I can only hope that whoever is helping Kohval can't recreate this pattern."

"That makes all of us," Shelton said grimly. "The last thing we need is a loose nut unleashing Big Daddy Baal on Seraphina."

"I think we're looking at this backwards," Elyssa said. "I doubt anyone makes Baal do something he doesn't want to do."

Shelton's eyes fluttered. "Wait, you think Baal is large and in charge?"

"That's a distinct possibility," Adam said. "An entity that powerful uses people, not the other way around."

My insides went cold at the thought of Baal's possible involvement. Somehow, we had to shut down this place and ensure it couldn't be used again.

Elyssa squinted, eyes locked on something at the other end of the room. "Is that a gem on the wall back there?"

I followed her gaze and saw a small imperfection. "I can't tell what it is from here." I jogged around the perimeter of the black line encircling the other patterns, unwilling to risk physically touching it, especially after my cranial invasion.

"Just go on without me," Shelton shouted. "I've had enough of running today."

Elyssa and I reached the opposite wall. It wasn't a gem we'd seen, but a hole in the wall about the size of my fist. I peeked through. Dim light glinted off shiny surfaces, but I couldn't see what was inside.

Elyssa shouldered me out of the way for a look. "It's too dark." She backed away and examined the wall. "Does this open?"

I touched the smooth hole. "It must open somehow." I gripped the edges of the hole and tugged. The wall didn't budge. I traced a finger along the corner where this wall met the next, but it looked seamless.

Elyssa walked past me, running her hand on the wall and stopped. "I found something." She lifted her hand to reveal a small bump in the crystal.

It was a dark gem that almost perfectly matched the wall in color and texture. I channeled Murk into it and was rewarded when the wall misted away into an opening. I stepped into a corridor like the one leading inside the foundry, but this one ended in the dim room I'd seen through the hole. I channeled a globe of light and sent it hovering overhead.

Elyssa hissed a breath through her teeth at what we saw.

I recoiled in horror at the sight of nearly a dozen transparent crystal caskets, each one occupied by a withered humanoid form. I swallowed hard and stepped closer. A female clothed in a purple gown stared blindly back at me. All skin and bones, her withered flesh looked as if someone had vacuumed out her insides and left her to die.

That comparison wasn't far from the truth. I'd seen this before. Seen the effect of draining someone of too much soul essence all at once. It was exactly how Daelissa had killed humans when she fed on them.

Are these humans?

Seraphim didn't feed on one another. They exchanged greetings by splaying their fingers toward one another, sometimes exchanging aether, but not soul essence. Besides, feeding on another Seraphim wouldn't amplify their magic.

"Justin, come here." Elyssa hovered over a casket near the back of the small room. She backed away so I could stand next to it.

At first, I didn't know what I was supposed to see. It looked like the withered husk of a man, also wearing a robe like the others. As I stared at the gaunt face, I realized it was familiar. The sunken eyes and hollow cheeks made it harder to see, but once I saw the resemblance, I knew who this was.

"It's Kohval." I flicked my gaze to her. "The real one."

She shivered. "He's completely drained." Elyssa waved a hand around the room. "Just like the others."

I stared long and hard at each of the occupants to see if I recognized any others, but none bore a resemblance to anyone I'd met before. I walked back over to Kohval's still form and studied the tortured lines in his face.

Adam and Shelton entered the room.

Shelton looked inside the first crystal case and shouted in surprise. "What the hell kind of freak show is this?"

"Fascinating," Adam breathed. He gripped the sides of the casket and swiveled it from side to side. A tug on the bottom inclined the case vertically. The body remained in place instead of sliding around inside.

Shelton huffed. "What kind of sicko likes to play with bodies in coffins?"

"I'm not playing with them," Adam said. He walked over to the hole in the wall. "I'm figuring out something."

Elyssa stood next to the hole and looked at the crystal coffin. "If you swivel the cases upright, the tops line up with the hole in the wall."

"I think a gem fit into this hole," Adam said. "They probably siphoned the soul essence straight from the bodies during the ritual."

"Why do that when they could grow a whole new soul in a soul globe?" Shelton said.

"I don't know," Adam said. "Maybe they wanted to mass produce some demon golems in a hurry."

"They might have been using the souls of these poor bastards to fuel the demons too," Shelton said.

Elyssa motioned Adam and Shelton to the back of the room and showed them Kohval's case.

"Well, I guess we know for sure that ain't the real Kohval leading the legion," Shelton said. "Did you find Meera in any of the other coffins?"

"I don't even know what she looks like," I said.

Adam turned his phone to us and displayed the stern face of a woman with a shaved head. A small nose hung above a wide mouth and dark amber eyes seemed to bore into whoever took the picture. Next to her stood a male and female with equally grim faces. "This is Legiaros Meera and her top lieutenants, Talus and Ganja."

"Aw, don't they look sweet," Shelton said. "I'll bet if I asked Meera to make me a sandwich she'd cut my arms off."

Adam tutted. "They don't eat sandwiches in Seraphina, Shelton, but she'd definitely cut off your arms just because you're a grade-A jackass."

Elyssa snorted. "She'd make you her bitch."

He waved off the comments. "Yeah, you're probably right. Hell, even Bella won't make me sandwiches. She's always making me eat those damned Colombian *arepas*."

Adam barked a laugh. "No wonder you cook for yourself."

I walked around the room, looking at the females in the crystal cases, but none of them remotely resembled Meera. "If Meera's body isn't in here, does that mean the one in Tarissa might be the real deal?"

"It means she might be defending Tarissa instead of conquering it," Shelton said as he fiddled with the case containing Kohval. "Maybe we can talk alliance with her and take on Kohval." He pounded on the side of the case and grunted.

"Maybe not." Elyssa took Adam's phone and held it next to one of the male bodies. "This is Talus." She walked over to another coffin. "And this is Ganja."

"Damn." I shook my head. "Even if Meera is still in command, her top people are dolems."

Shelton pressed down on a bulge in the side of Kohval's case. "Hey, I think I got it!" With a loud hiss, the top misted away. Kohval's eyes flicked open and a hoarse scream tore from his throat.

Chapter 14

I screamed right along with Kohval. Shelton scrambled backwards, shouting curses, and Adam fell on his ass with a yelp. Elyssa pressed a hand to her heart and steadied herself on a nearby coffin.

Elyssa came to her senses first and rushed to Kohval's side. "Kohval, we're here to help."

The seraph reached a feeble hand for her, but couldn't hold it up.

Adam tapped on his communication pendant and reached Tahlee. "We need a healer in the foundry stat." He stepped outside the room. "That means pronto—I mean, right away!"

Elyssa patted the withered arm and leaned closer as Kohval tried to speak. "What are you saying?"

"Victus," Kohval wheezed. "From Eden."

I stood on the other side of Kohval. "Yes, we know who Victus is. Was he here with Cephus?"

"Air." A ragged breath sent a shudder through Kohval's body. "Air is."

"You're not making any sense," I said. "What are you saying?"

141

"Air on is." It was as if he was saying a word he didn't know how to pronounce.

"Is that English?" Elyssa said. "What are you saying about air?"

Kohval's chest sunk and rose as he gasped for breath. "Demon…woman."

"He needs to rest," Adam said. "I think this coffin is like a preservation chamber. We need to close it back up and keep him alive until help arrives."

"No." A hint of command crept into Kohval's voice. "Dead already. Too much."

"That's not true," Elyssa said, eyes running up and down what had once been the stout muscled frame of a Legiaros. "A healer can restore you."

"Air on is," he said again. "Demon woman. Both legions subverted. Daskar army." Kohval tried to say more, but his eyelids fluttered and his head lolled to the side.

"Oh, crap." Shelton inched closer and peered in. "Is he dead?"

Elyssa felt the seraph's neck. "He's alive, but barely."

Elsa, one of the Mzodi healers rushed into the room. "I am here. What is—" her dark eyes went huge. "What is this place?"

"This seraph needs your help." I motioned her over to Kohval. "They were being drained of their souls."

Elsa bit her lower lip and nodded. "I will do what I can." She placed her hands on the dying seraph's chest and closed her eyes. A soft ultraviolet halo glowed around her hands and her brow furrowed in concentration.

142

The rest of us backed out of the room to give her space.

"What in the blazes did he mean by air on is?" Shelton said. "It's nonsense."

Adam tapped a finger to his chin. "Air on is. Demon woman."

Shelton grunted. "Like I said, zero sense."

"Demon woman?" I leaned back against a wall. "Could he mean the dolem versions of Nightliss?"

Adam kept repeating the phrase over and over again.

"Saying it a million times won't magically transform it from gibberish," Shelton said.

Elyssa snapped her fingers. "Aerianas, demon woman—a Daemas."

"Whoa." I pushed myself off the wall. "That's impossible. I kicked her ass at my dad's wedding and the Daemos locked her up."

Shelton's face went white as a sheet. "No. You're wrong."

"Didn't she crash that shindig and try to send Kassallandra to Hell?" Adam said.

"Even worse," I said. "The Abyss." Technically, it was a special holding place where the Apocryphan were imprisoned after their war splintered Earth into separate realms.

Elyssa grimaced. "The Daemos transferred Aerianas to Templar control just before the war. Both she and Vadaemos were imprisoned by Templar factions loyal to the Synod."

"You gotta be kidding me." Shelton spit on the floor. "I thought that bitch was permanently out of the picture."

143

Adam's worried gaze met mine.

Shelton had a bad history with Aerianas. She'd seduced him with her Daemas wiles and made him do some really bad things when he was a bounty hunter. He'd sent innocent people to prison.

Adam put a hand on Shelton's shoulder. "Dude, are you okay?"

Shelton shook it off and scowled. "I'm trapped in a realm where all the natives can kick my ass with magic and just found out a woman who used and abused me might be here raising an army of demon golems." He glared at us. "To answer your question, I'm just peachy."

"I thought you were over the whole Aerianas thing," I said. "You're married to Bella now. You've got your happily ever after."

"Aerianas is a succubus, Justin." Shelton's hands clenched. "You know better than anyone what kind of control Daemos can exert over people. She practically controlled my mind. She made me do whatever she wanted me to do. I was her stupid, helpless puppet." He pounded a fist on the wall and winced. "Let's just say I ain't the least bit happy to hear that a criminal I thought was locked up for life might be roaming free."

Elyssa took Shelton's fist and pressed it into the palm of her hand, her violet eyes full of sympathy. "Harry, I understand. If Aerianas really is free, we'll do everything we can to put her away again."

Shelton blinked, obviously taken aback by Elyssa's demeanor. "Uh, thanks."

"Daemos like Aerianas and her father, Vadaemos, are the kind who gave all Daemos a bad name," Elyssa said.

"Don't forget about Yuuki," I said through clenched teeth. I put my hand on top of Shelton's where it still rested in Elyssa's palm. "Don't worry, brother. I'm right here with you."

"Me too." Adam put his hand on mine. "We're gonna send that demonic whore right back to Hell!"

Shelton snorted. "Demonic whore?" He burst into laughter. "I don't know why, but that's the funniest thing I've heard all day."

"Should we count to three and do a cheer?" I asked.

Shelton took back his hand and grunted. "Nah. I feel better already."

Elsa pulled her hands from Kohval and let out a deep sigh. She turned and came into the corridor. "I cannot keep him alive. His soul is too damaged and his body too frail."

"Is he dead?" Elyssa asked.

She looked back at the room and shook her head. "No, but he will be soon."

I had more questions for her, but those could wait. I rushed back to Kohval's side. He looked up at me with bleary eyes. "Who are you?"

I didn't have time to tell him everything—he'd probably be dead before I finished—so I kept it short. "Someone who wants to keep Victus from destroying Pjurna."

Kohval nodded. "Victus came around the time news of a war in Eden reached us. He told us he would help us build an army to defeat Daelissa and the Brightlings. He brought with him a woman, Aerianas, who would help us. I gave her all the resources she needed."

"Your people built the foundry?" I said.

"Yes." His eyelids fluttered. "She guided the builders into drawing the patterns on the floor. We did not realize what they were."

"Demon summoning patterns," I said.

Kohval tried to nod, but seemed too weak. "She tricked me. Took part of my soul and summoned a demon. It took my form and that was the last thing I remember."

"That's awful," Elyssa said from behind me.

I was confused. "How did Aerianas take a part of your soul?"

"Demon magic," he whispered. Kohval's eyelids fluttered shut. "Soulstones." A final breath rattled from his throat and the real Legiaros Kohval went still.

I looked at Shelton. He looked at Adam. Adam looked at Elyssa. She looked at me. I stuck out my tongue and crossed my eyes to break the tension. It didn't work.

Shelton gave me a sour look. "Soulstones are no laughing matter."

"Correct me if I'm wrong," Adam said, "but soulstones can only capture soul essence at the moment of death, right?"

"As far as I know," Shelton said. "That was why we used them against the Nazdal."

Elyssa grimaced. "The Nazdal absorb the life force of the dead and dying, but the soulstones sucked it up before they could."

Adam waved a hand toward the room of crystal coffins. "If a soulstone did that, then it's a different kind than what I've heard of."

146

"His soul was torn," Elsa said. "Badly damaged."

That still didn't answer something. "Daemos can consume soul essence, but they can't just transfer it into a soulstone, can they?"

"No," Adam said. "I suspect Aerianas has a modified soul stone, or maybe even a gem."

I walked toward the other coffins. "Can you check out the others? See if anyone else is alive?"

The healer nodded. "I will do what I can."

Shelton showed her the bulge on the side of the coffin. "Push in on that if you need to open one, but it'll also break the preservation spell."

Elsa ran a finger along the surface. "Can they be closed again?"

Shelton pressed the bulge on Kohval's coffin and the top misted back into place with a hiss. "Looks like it."

Adam touched the hole in the wall. "Maybe this is where they placed the soulstone."

"I need to understand the process from start to end." I looked through the hole at the pattern. "How did they get the soul fragments into the soul globes? How did they get the globes into the demon bodies?"

"I don't know much about golem creation," Adam said, "but the globes are made first and the sparks are created inside of them."

"Yeah, but how do you get the soul fragment inside?" Shelton said. "The globes are three-dimensional containment circles, so the aether for the spark is already trapped inside. I imagine you'd also have to charm the globe to keep the soul fragment locked inside too."

"Cinder might know," Adam said. "I suggest we give him something to research when he gets here."

"Oh, he'll eat that up like candy," Shelton said.

"Can we get out of here?" Elyssa shivered. "This place gives me the creeps."

"Amen to that." Shelton gave one last look of disgust around him and left, the rest of us close behind.

We circumnavigated the foreboding demon patterns on the floor and took a collective deep breath when we got outside again. This place had been home to dark magic that might plunge Seraphina into chaos. We needed to destroy everything inside once we studied and understood it better.

The first Mzodi ships with our people began arriving early the next morning, sleek majestic curves glinting in the sunlight. The flagship, *Uorion*, floated serenely overhead, its levitation foils glowing brilliantly. The massive ship set down in the practice fields and the three relatively smaller ships landed side-by-side in the neighboring field. Moments later, Templars began streaming off the *Uorion*.

"The cavalry has arrived!" Shelton shouted.

The huge felycan leader, Saber, strode down the gangway of the *Rekt*, McCloud, the lycan pack leader, by his side. The elite vampire soldiers of Red Cell marched from the *Kestra*, and beyond them, Arcanes and Blue Cloaks emerged from the *Ogan*.

Two massive ships resembling blue whales, the *Krstuk* and *Volante*, sailed low over the trees and landed well away from the others. Their gangways disgorged a mass of people dressed in the ultraviolet and dark hues of civilian attire commonly worn in Tarissa. They favored tight-fitting cloaks, pants, and shirts more like uniforms than standard clothes.

"Cinder is probably on the *Uorion*," Adam said. "I'll go fill him in."

"My baby is on that ship too," Shelton said, a little skip in his step. "Man, I can't wait to see Bella." He set off at a quick walk and the rest of us hurried to catch up.

Adam chuckled. "At least I know one thing that'll make Shelton run."

The *Uorion* had six gangways, each one filled with Templars marching in orderly fashion off the ship. Though they still wore black uniforms, most were not in Nightingale armor. Despite the strict demeanor, the soldiers looked tired, eyes longing for a realm they might never see again—Eden.

"They look bad," Elyssa whispered to me. "Looks like someone drained the spirit right out of them."

"I know how they feel." I looked up the ramp at the line of grim faces. "We came here to unify Seraphina, but instead this realm is even more fractured than before."

A wide command platform lifted off from the deck of the *Uorion* and drifted down to land nearby. Commander Thomas Borathen's ice-blue eyes met ours as he stepped off, leaving the Templar crew behind to guide the platform where the rest of their equipment was being gathered.

Elyssa pressed a hand to her chest in salute. "Commander."

"At ease," Thomas said. He looked toward the command center in the distance. "Follow me."

149

I wasn't used to such a curt welcome from Thomas, but then again, he probably didn't want to show too much emotion in front of the troops. He tended to have a stick up his butt about such things.

"Baby!" Shelton shouted, and ran toward one of the other gangways where a short Colombian woman waved wildly back.

"See, I told you he'd run," Adam said. His eye caught on a blonde walking down the gangway behind Bella, and a grin split his face from ear to ear. "Uh, I'll be back later." He set off at a dead run after Shelton.

"I guess Meghan and Bella are in for some intimate reunions," Elyssa said with a chuckle.

I snorted. "It's been a while."

Elyssa tugged on my sleeve and we followed Thomas toward the command center. When we got inside the deserted building, Thomas faced us, fresh urgency in his eyes. "What's the situation here?"

Elyssa gave him a quick rundown of everything we'd done and the mysteries we were working on solving now.

"The real Kohval is dead." Thomas's lips formed a grim line. "I was hoping we could use him to convince his troops that they're following an impostor."

"He's virtually unrecognizable," Elyssa said. "Besides, they might think it's a trick."

Thomas pounded a fist into his palm. "We need solutions and we need them fast."

"Hopefully, Cinder can figure out how the Daskar are made," I said. "In the meantime, there's no telling if Aerianas is making more."

"That's a name I'd hoped never to hear again," Thomas said. "Unfortunately, many top-priority prisoners escaped during the war. Some were released by the Synod to fight for them, and others escaped damaged facilities."

Elyssa's forehead furrowed. "Dad, what's going on? Why are you so antsy?"

Antsy was not a term I'd ever use to describe Thomas, but in this case, he really did look unsettled. "Yeah, you do look a little anxious."

Thomas went absolutely still, face as hard as a rock. "The civil war in Tarissa was short-lived. Shortly after we finished evacuating, our scouts reported that Kohval and Meera joined forces and now control the entire city." He folded his arms across his chest. "It's only a matter of time before they attack us."

Chapter 15

I gulped. "You think they'll come up here and attack us?"

Thomas paused a moment then nodded. "Reports indicate that they are turning their eyes north, perhaps because you prevented Zero from finishing the task of blocking the Northern Pass and reporting to Tarissa." He pursed his lips. "I suspect closing the pass was a last resort. It's possible Aerianas has her eyes set on Guinesea and beyond."

"Is Meera still in charge of her legion?" I asked.

"I don't know, but it would appear that the golems who took the place of her top lieutenants may have done something to her." Thomas's gaze went distant. "She may have been replaced or killed."

"I'd guess killed," Elyssa said. "I don't think it's that easy to make identical copies of people or we'd have an epidemic on our hands."

"Agreed." Thomas turned to her. "In any case, we may soon have the combined legions marching north. I left sentries to watch for and capture enemy scouts, but it's only a matter of time before Kohval figures out we're up here."

"Kohvalla isn't defensible from the south," Elyssa said. "There's nothing stopping a force from marching in and wiping us out."

"Even with the Mzodi, we'd be hard pressed to defeat both Victrix and Gallix legions," Thomas said. "Our chances are even slimmer if they're producing more Daskar."

I raised a hand. "Uh, dumb question, but what should we do?"

"Retreat to Atlantis?" Elyssa said.

"It's an option." Thomas put a hand under his chin. "Think about it. I'm meeting with the other faction heads later so we can discuss options." He saw the worry on our faces. "We sabotaged the skyway leading from Tarissa to Kohvalla, so that will buy us some time."

"Days, maybe," Elyssa said. "Unfortunately, we need years."

A team of Templars arrived to help Thomas set up the command center, though I wondered what good it did to get comfortable if Kohval might send forces north at any time. Elyssa and I went back outside to locate Shelton and Adam, but they were nowhere to be found.

"Must be getting some afternoon delight," I said.

Elyssa offered a wan smile. "They deserve it. I feel like I haven't seen everyone for a year."

"That trip to Voltis wasn't just a walk down the street." I weaved my way between hundreds of people disembarking the sky ships, my gaze darting from face to face in hopes of finding familiarity.

A female on a flying carpet flew overhead shouting instructions. "All Tarissan civilians please report to the location of the yellow flares for your housing assignments!"

I spotted the flares she mentioned, bright yellow fireworks shooting high into the sky near the civilian sector. Templars filed into the barracks near the command center while the vampire army marched to ones on the other side of the training grounds.

As the crowd thinned, I spotted two familiar faces coming our way—my mother, Alysea, and father, David. David pointed at something and laughed, but Alysea's nose wrinkled as if she didn't think it was very funny.

My parents looked like a young couple in their early thirties. The kind of couple just starting out in life and looking to buy a house, adopt a dog, and start a family. In reality, they were each over two thousand years old and from opposite sides of the tracks. David started life as a demon—a blue spirit that successfully melded with a human to form the first demon spawn in the world. Alysea was from Seraphina, a Brightling who'd once been besties with Daelissa.

Even to this day, I found it mind-boggling that an angel had fallen for a demon and had kids. I also didn't understand how anyone could deal with all the lame jokes my father came up with, especially over eons.

David ruffled Alysea's blond hair and kissed her on the cheek. She responded by thoroughly mussing his black hair until it stood on end and then burst into musical laughter. David looked my way and waved when he saw me, completely unconcerned that he looked like he'd just woken from a long nap.

Elyssa and I jogged over to them. Alysea embraced Elyssa while I gave David a handshake and one-armed bro-hug. He ruined it by wrapping both his arms around me and squeezing.

"Great to see you, kiddo." He ruffled my hair like he'd done to Alysea and grinned. "It's good to see you still in one piece."

Alysea hugged me and kissed my cheeks. "As usual, David is completely understating how relieved we are to see you, son." She hugged me again and backed off. "It looks like we're already in the middle of another crisis."

David nodded seriously and motioned toward the civilian sector. "Yeah—do we choose the purple house, or the blue one?" He tapped a finger on his chin. "Then again, I've really got a thing for that canary yellow ranch style on the west side."

Alysea sighed. "I told you I don't like yellow houses." She smiled and turned back to me. "Can we please sit down and have dinner together? I just want some family time before we have to run from Kohval's army."

I squeezed her hand and smiled back. "That would be great. Shelton's got some Eden-styled food on the *Falcheen*. I could whip up pizza or something."

Alysea's eyes brightened. "You have pizza?"

David rubbed his belly. "Oh man, you'd better not be teasing me. I'm so sick of glurk and quintos I could puke."

Alysea took Elyssa's hands. "Will you join us?"

"I'd love to." Elyssa looked back at the command center. "Is it okay if I ask my father to join us?"

David wrapped an arm around her shoulder and gave her a hug. "Hey, there's always room for more family. Maybe Michael would like to come too."

"Yeah, if I can find him." Elyssa shrugged. "I think the next twenty-four hours are going to be very busy."

David squeezed my shoulder. "Hey, let's go make that pizza. Better make it four of them. I think I could eat an entire one myself."

I grinned. "You're got it!"

"I'll go tell my father," Elyssa said. "I think he'll be too busy to join us, but you never know."

"Meet us at the ship?" I said.

She pecked me on the lips. "See you soon, pizza boy."

I headed toward the *Falcheen* where it was parked near the entrance to the Northern Pass and undergoing more repairs after our last battle. Alysea hooked her arm in mine. "It's good to see you again son."

Her voice broke a little, and I knew why. "Thinking of Ivy again?"

"Always." She took a deep breath. "But this is a happy reunion, so let's not drag it down with talk of things we can't control."

"Tell me more about Atlantis," David said in the voice of an excited boy. "Do they have lasers and flying cars?"

I snorted. "They have a few futuristic weapons." I told them about Elyssa's light bow and the armor they'd worn for the fight against Kaelissa. "Otherwise, the best thing about Atlantis is that it's beyond Kohval's reach."

David clapped me on the shoulder. "And it has the ingredients for making pizza."

"And hamburgers."

"I'd just like a nice salad," Alysea said. "I used to love glurk when I was a child, but living in Eden corrupted me."

As we walked up a rise toward the ship, I stopped and looked back over the valley. People scurried about like ants. Flying carpets and brooms whizzed back and forth, and lights began flickering on in the civilian sector as Tarissan refugees settled into their temporary homes.

"I can't believe we're going to have to pick up and move again," I said. "Thomas said Kohval will probably march north to get rid of us once and for all."

"What's this I heard about Kohval being an impostor?" David asked.

I grunted. "Did you meet Issana?"

"Nightliss's fake daughter?" David nodded. "Yep, but only briefly." He grimaced. "She's a strange one."

I bit my lower lip and shook my head. "Dad, we think Aerianas is behind this."

The smile on his face died in a heartbeat. "You're kidding me, right?"

"No." I told them what the real Kohval had told us before he died, and explained more about the demon golems.

David's jaw hung open. "That's insidious!"

"It's awful," Alysea agreed. "How in the world are these demon bodies not disintegrating?"

"They have souls in them." David let out a low whistle. "Victus is a damned genius." He flinched as if just realizing what he'd said. "I mean, he's sick in the head, but still—I never would have thought up something like this."

157

"Aerianas can apparently only make near-identical golems in some cases," I said. "Otherwise, we'd really be in trouble."

"They don't even smell demonic." David's brow furrowed. "We need to come up with a way to detect them. Make sure we haven't been infiltrated."

"The odor of brimstone is usually the only giveaway," Alysea said. "If Daemos can't sniff them out, then no other person can."

David snapped his fingers. "You're right!" He pecked a kiss on her lips. "What would I ever do without you?"

Alysea frowned. "Did I miss something?"

David's grin returned with a vengeance. "Hellhounds." He looked back and forth between the two of us. "They can sniff a demon fart from a hundred yards."

"Wonderful analogy, David." Alysea gave me a hopeless look. "I'm glad you didn't inherit your father's scatological sense of humor."

I looked at David. "Demon farts." Then we both burst into laughter.

Alysea let out a sigh of the long suffering. "Over two thousand years old and still makes poop jokes."

"Hey, poop and fart jokes are eternally funny," David said. "If you can't laugh about bodily functions, you might as well hang it up."

"I'll keep that in mind." Alysea folded her arms over her chest. "So, we'll talk to Kassallandra and the others about sniffing out the army with hellhounds tomorrow?"

David stifled a laugh and nodded. "Yeah. We have a lot of people to go through."

"That's a lot of farts to sniff," I said with barely restrained mirth, and then the two of us burst into howls of laughter.

Alysea slapped David on the shoulder. "I'm going to fart on both of you if you don't take this situation seriously."

That only made us laugh harder. Alysea bit her lower lip, but couldn't hold back a laugh of her own.

I took a deep breath and tried to sober my attitude. "Mom's right. Demon farts are all fun and games until we have a demon golem army marching up our collective asses."

David followed my example and put a hand on my shoulder. "True."

"Provided we clean our forces of impostors, what then?" Alysea said. "We certainly don't have an army capable of withstanding two Darkling legions."

"Maybe we could replace Kohval with an impostor of our own," David said. "Take control from the top."

I shook my head. "We don't have any of his soul to make it with. Even if we did, making an identical clone seems difficult."

"We also have the impostors in Meera's army to deal with," Alysea said. "If we took control of one legion, that might cause the other one to attack it."

David frowned and put a hand under his chin. "In other words, we'd have to make two clones and take over both armies at once."

"Impossible," Alysea said. "Kohval and Meera are certainly on high alert and surrounded by their armies. You'd have a better chance of—oh, I don't know"—she gestured north—"going to Zbura and kidnapping Kaelissa."

David went still for an instant then turned toward me. I did the same exact thing as an insanely stupid plan flashed into my mind.

"Are you thinking what I'm thinking?" David asked me.

Alysea put herself between us. "No."

I nodded. "There's only one army in Seraphina big enough to take down Kohval."

"The Brightling army," David said.

"You'll never get her," Alysea said. "She's probably sitting in her crystal palace planning revenge on Justin."

I paced back and forth, letting my thought process mow through the weeds of doubt springing up in my mind. "What if we simply lured Kaelissa here and let her take on the legions?"

"Bad idea," David said. "She'd take over Pjurna and that's game over. We probably wouldn't live long enough to swap her out with a copy."

"In other words, we have to catch her while her guard is down." I stared at the Northern Pass where the crystallized aether from the malaether bombs filled the bottom. "If we're lucky, she's still in Zbura licking her wounds after the Battle of Atlantis."

An amused grin spread across David's face. "Is that what they're calling it now?"

"They will, once I tell everyone the cool official name I came up with."

Alysea grabbed David by the front of his shirt and gripped my arm with her other hand. "Let's get one thing straight," she said in a deadly serious voice, "you are not going to Zbura in some insane quest to replace Kaelissa with a clone so you can take over her armies."

"We'd need you too," David said. "You know how to help us blend into Brightling society."

She slashed a hand through the air. "None of us are going, David." Alysea looked at me. "Justin, forget this idea."

I pulled free of her grasp. "What are we supposed to do? Run off to Atlantis and hide until we luck out and find a way back to Eden?" I shook my head. "If we sit around with our thumbs up our asses, then Kohval will close off the pass and rule Pjurna, or Kaelissa will barge in and kill everyone."

"Not necessarily true," David said. "We overlooked the most important person in this equation."

"Kohval?" I said. "Meera?" I shrugged. "Who else could there be?"

"Victus is in Eden, so I assume his surrogates here control the demon golems." David motioned toward the foundry. "I'd be willing to bet that Victus replaced Kohval first then left Aerianas in charge and went back to Eden. It probably took her months to kidnap Meera's top lieutenants, but once she did, she marched on Tarissa and united her forces."

His reasoning hit me like a ton of bricks. "I never even thought of it that way."

Judging from the horrified expression spreading across Alysea's face, she was coming to the same realization. "Blocking the pass was just a delaying tactic," Alysea said. With her new legions united, Aerianas will probably set her sights on the Brightling Empire."

161

I filled in the final blank. "Unless we do something, Seraphina will have a demon spawn queen."

Chapter 16

"Queen Aerianas." David spit on the ground. "For all we know, Aerianas already has imposters in Kaelissa's court." He blew out a breath and rubbed his stomach. "Man, all this thinking makes me hungry." He jabbed a thumb over his shoulder toward the *Falcheen*. "Let's go make those pizzas."

By the time we reached the hold of the *Falcheen* and started looking through the ingredients, Elyssa showed up with her entire family in tow.

Her mother, Leia, greeted me with a hug. "I'm relieved to have you both back safe and sound."

Elyssa's sister, Phoebe, formerly long-lost and brainwashed by Daelissa, also gave me a warm hug. She resembled Elyssa so closely that the two might have been twins. "I hear Elyssa kept you mostly out of trouble."

I chuckled. "Just barely." I hadn't really gotten to know Phoebe all that much and wasn't sure where to take the conversation next. Michael stepped up next to her and saved the day, engulfing my hand with his and gripping it hard enough to remind me that he could kick my ass any time he wanted.

I pretended not to notice. "Hey, Michael, good to see you."

Michael and I had a complicated history, but it was long past being awkward. He'd made a deal with Underborn to protect me despite wanting to kill me for dating his little sister. Fighting side-by-side in the Seraphim war had changed that dislike to respect, though it hadn't turned him into a loveable fuzz-ball. He only seemed truly at ease around Elyssa.

"Alysea, David, I need some help grinding the wheat," Elyssa said. "Phoebe, can you help peel vegetables?"

"Well, duty calls," Phoebe said, and turned to go help her little sister, leaving Michael behind.

I nodded toward Thomas. "I'm surprised he actually came. He's not usually one to take time off when there's a war that needs planning."

Michael shrugged. "Everyone needs a break." He let go of my hand and looked at the array of ingredients on the table. "Even the Templar commander."

"Doesn't seem like that long ago we were celebrating the end of the Seraphim War with pizza." I sighed. "Never seems to end, does it?"

"Almost enough to make me think there's something driving this chaos, but we don't have enough information to see it." Michael ran a hand through his close-cropped hair. "Elyssa ended up undercover at your high school because of a new vampire drug. That drug led us to Maximus who was building a vampire army for Daelissa. That helped us uncover another conspiracy and another."

"You think this is a similar pattern?" I asked.

"On a larger scale, perhaps." Michael looked at his sister while she showed Thomas how to cut the tomatoes for the sauce. "For example, is Victus working alone, or with someone? How did Cephus

164

and Victus originally connect so they could stab us in the back, cripple our army, and strand us here?"

I'd made a few efforts to connect those dots, but hadn't exactly broken out the push pins and yarn. "Those are excellent questions. Any theories?"

"That Apocryphan who got loose during the war is one theory." Michael gave me a sideways look. "I have to wonder if any of them were able to somehow communicate with others in the outside world."

"Kind of like kingpins running their business empires from prison?" I said.

"Exactly." He shrugged. "Then again, Daelissa was probably acting on her own and everything that's happened since then has simply been a symptom of the war."

"I've seen enough conspiracy movies to know that it doesn't take an Apocryphan to pull the strings," I told him. "Victus wants to rule Eden. Cephus wanted to rule Seraphina. Someone who knew their true goals had to introduce them shortly after the Grand Nexus was repaired and travel between the realms was restored. That's the mystery."

"Agreed," he said in a grim tone.

"Yo, bro," Elyssa called. "I need you to knead the dough."

A faint smile curved the edges of his mouth. "Duty calls."

"Aye, yai, yai!" Bella stood in the doorway, eyes lit with excitement. She rushed over and kissed my cheeks before backing away to look me up and down with brilliant violet eyes. "Justin, did you grow another inch?"

"Maybe in the stomach," Shelton said with a grin.

"God, it feels like forever since I've seen you." I gave Bella a big hug and backed away. "I could swear you've gotten taller since the last time I saw you."

Bella giggled. "Oh, I wish." Her Spanish accent sounded even more exotic when paired with the Cyrinthian language. "I get such a neck ache looking up at all you tall people."

Elyssa jumped into our small circle and the two women cried out and cooed like two sorority sisters who hadn't seen each other in a decade. "Bella, I'm so happy to see you again!"

"I am just happy you're all safe and sound," Bella said. She kissed Elyssa on each cheek. "*Que linda.* You are looking beautiful as ever."

I preened my hair. "Yes, well that's because I moisturize daily."

Bella slapped my arm. "Oh, Justin, you're not looking too bad either."

Elyssa hooked her arm in Bella's. "Shelton brought back a lot of fruit and wine. Do you think you could make us your award-winning sangria?"

"You mean real fruit and wine?" Bella's violet eyes lit up with excitement. She turned on Shelton. "Harry, why didn't you tell me you had this?"

Shelton frowned at Elyssa. "I was gonna spring that surprise in a few minutes."

Elyssa smiled sheepishly. "I'm sorry, Shelton. You should have told me."

"Meh." He waved it off. "She looks plenty surprised to me."

166

"Aw, baby." Bella stood on tiptoes and kissed his nose. "You're so sweet, *papacito*."

Shelton's face turned bright red, but he kissed her back on the nose. "Anything for you, *mami*."

I felt my mouth dropping open in conjunction with a huge grin. "Shelton, I knew you had a sweet side buried in there somewhere."

Elyssa burst into laughter. "He's been suppressing it so long, I guess he can't help himself."

Shelton bared his teeth and growled. "Hey, I'm a sensitive guy, okay?" He took Bella's hand. "Come on, babe. Let's go make some sangria."

The next person through the door made my heart skip a beat. Tall, square-jawed, a silver mane of hair hanging to his shoulders, Cinder looked every bit like his creator, Fjoeruss, and maybe even a little bit more badass. Then he had to ruin it with one of those frightful leers he called a smile.

"Justin, it is a pleasure to see you again." Cinder crooked an arm around my shoulder and another around my back in a hug so awkward, I didn't even know what he was doing at first.

"Great to see you too," I said, backing away as quickly as possible without tripping.

"Cinder!" Shelton clapped the golem on the back. "How's the hammer hanging?"

Cinder stared at him unblinking. "I have not used a hammer recently, Harry." He turned to me. "I studied the foundry, Justin. Though it represents exciting potential for advances in golem making, I am not certain consorting with demons is safe."

"Did you learn anything?" I said.

"I determined how they infused the soul and spark, and found some gems with records of their early experiments," Cinder replied. "I have not had time to review them all." He chomped down on his lower lip and cradled his chin with a hand in a ridiculous attempt to look thoughtful. "Issana was disturbed to discover her origin as a demon construct."

I felt a pang of sympathy in my chest. "I can imagine. Why did you tell her?"

"It is only right that she knows." He dropped his hands to his sides. "She went into the foundry with me, but if she was created there, she remembers nothing about it."

"She told me she was working for Cephus, not Kohval." I sorted through the jumbled puzzle pieces in my head. "It's possible Cephus had his own foundry in Tarissa."

"Our theory is that Cephus was Victus's original partner," Cinder said. "Victus probably needed Aerianas's expertise with demons to make the foundry work. Without Cephus and Victus to guide her, she has, as they say, gone off script and is now doing her own thing."

"That'd be my guess," Shelton said. He looked around. "Where's Issana now?"

"She came onboard, but did not feel comfortable coming to see you all." Cinder looked genuinely downcast. "Issana feels like an imposter."

Shelton pressed his lips together. "Yeah, well, she can't help what she is."

Cinder nodded sadly. "It is not how we were created that matters, but what we do with our lives. I have not been successful imparting that wisdom to her."

"Dude, that's deep." I squeezed his shoulder and decided to change the subject. "By the way, how did your hair get so long?"

"Ah, yes." Cinder stroked his lustrous mane. "I experimented with artificial hair growth."

Shelton snorted. "Oh, brother. You growing pubes now, too?"

"I have not attempted hair growth on my nether regions," Cinder said. "Do you think pubic hair is a worthy endeavor?"

Everyone burst into laughter.

Adam and Meghan showed up when the pizzas were cooking in the magic-powered brick ovens he and Shelton had constructed during our time in Atlantis. Meghan wore her blond hair in a tight bun, indicative of her reserved demeanor. She gave Elyssa a quick hug and turned to me.

"Hello, Justin." Meghan held out her hand for a handshake. "I'm glad to see everyone is back safely."

"Meghan!" I gripped her in a hug and felt her reluctantly pat me on the back as I held on for an awkwardly long time. I winked over her shoulder at Adam, who barely repressed laughter. "It's so good to see you."

She sighed. "Okay, Justin, I'm uncomfortable now. Will you let me go?"

I released her and backed away. "You're no fun."

Meghan brushed at the hem of her gray skirt. "I suppose I'm too introverted to be your sort of fun."

"Believe it or not, I used to be an introverted little nerd," I said with a smile.

Alysea burst into laughter. "Honey, I'm sorry, but you were never introverted."

"That's for sure," David added. "You were an extroverted nerd if anything."

"But—but I used to be really shy!" I protested.

Alysea tutted. "You used to jump in front of girls with your toy sword raised and declare that you'd save them from evildoers."

"He used to terrify little Sally Kinklesberg," David said with a grin. "Always jumping around and fighting invisible monsters."

Elyssa giggled. "Sounds just like you, babe. Putting damsels in emotional distress and then saving them."

"Yeah, yeah." I held up my hands to ward off more stories. "But I was still shy at heart."

"Those monsters ain't so invisible anymore either," Shelton said from the table where he and Bella were slicing fruit and dunking it in the rich red wine the Atlanteans have given us.

Adam put an arm around Meghan and she seemed to melt with relief. "Some people don't do well at big gatherings."

"It's emotionally draining," Meghan added. "Then again, as a Templar, I have no choice but to do my duty."

"I hope you don't look at this as a duty," Shelton said. "It's supposed to be fun."

Meghan nodded warily. "It can be fun, just go easy on the hugs."

As the conversation continued, I thought back to my first encounter with Meghan. Stacey had been bitten by a hellhound and was dying. Meghan had used my blood to heal Stacey despite her hatred of demon spawn at the time. Meghan had certainly come a long way since then.

And that was when it hit me. Vadaemos had consumed the soul of her father. Vadaemos—the father of Aerianas. It had been a long time, but some wounds never healed. The joy drained right out of me as I thought about telling her the news. Then again, why did I have to tell her when I could delegate?

"Hey, Adam, I need to show you something." I motioned for him to follow me outside of the galley and into the hallway.

Adam looked at me curiously. "What is it?"

I lowered my voice. "Have you told her about Aerianas yet?"

"Ah." He leaned forward. "Yes. I told her all about it."

"Oh." I floundered for what to say next. "Was she upset?"

"Let's just say she wants Aerianas dead once and for all if she's the one behind this." Adam looked through the doorway where Elyssa had drafted Meghan into her army of food preparation minions. "She also asked me if we knew for sure that Vadaemos was still locked up back in Eden."

The question caught me off guard. "Underborn told me he'd killed Vadaemos, but who knows if that's the truth?"

"Yeah, nobody does." Adam shook his head slowly. "God only knows what criminals got loose during the war or what they're doing in our absence."

It certainly wasn't a pleasant thought. "I just wanted to make sure she knew so it didn't become a nasty surprise later."

Adam patted me on the shoulder. "It's all good, but thanks for the head's up. Meghan would have been pissed if she found out from someone other than me first."

David opened one of the ovens and sniffed. "Man, this pizza smells so good!"

"I'm starving," Shelton said. "Tell me those pies are good to go."

"I think they are." David slid a large wooden peel under one of the huge pizzas and pulled it out. Within a few minutes, he and Shelton had all the pizzas lined up on the central table in the galley.

Illaena poked her head inside the doorway. "I must admit this Eden food has a tantalizing scent."

Shelton pointed to a pizza on the end. "That's a vegetarian so you can eat it without lowering yourself to our carnivorous standards."

Illaena looked at him with narrowed eyes but stepped inside, Tahlee close on her heels. "I will try it."

Our simple dinner turned into a pizza party that went on for much of the afternoon. Illaena couldn't get enough of the veggie pizza or Bella's sangria, and when all was said and done, we polished off ten pizzas.

As we sat there recovering from our gluttony, Elyssa nudged Shelton in the ribs. "You were wrong. Michael ate two pizzas himself."

"Holy key-rist!" Shelton whistled. "Remind me not to invite him next time or I'm gonna run out of ingredients."

Adam leaned forward, elbows on the table. "I've been thinking a lot about that."

"About pizzas?" Shelton said.

"About Eden food." Adam traced his finger along the table. "We should make some gardens with leftover seeds. It'd be a real pain in the ass to make a run to Atlantis every time we needed tomatoes."

Shelton slapped a hand on the table. "That's a damned good idea."

I imagined fields of wheat, orchards bearing apples, and all the other agricultural needs of our army. "The thought of setting up farms makes Seraphina feel more and more like a permanent thing."

Elyssa took my hand. "Even if it's only temporary, we need a solution. I think everyone in the army is probably sick of the vegetarian diet."

"There are many in your army who have not abided by our traditions," Illaena said in a voice slightly slurred from all the sangria she'd downed. "I have heard that your wolf and feline shifters have hunted the native animals." She shuddered violently. "And eaten them."

Tahlee's lips curled with disgust. "There are many who want all of you gone even if you leave this world to Kohval and Kaelissa."

I raised an eyebrow. "Do you mean Mzodi or Darklings?"

"I can only say what others have overheard," Tahlee replied. "Many Seraphim do not like your customs or barbaric treatment of animals."

"But killing each other is okay?" Michael said.

Tahlee heard him, but didn't look his way. "Killing is not good, but sometimes necessary."

"Same with food," Michael replied calmly. "We need meat to survive, so we have to kill."

Tahlee finally looked at him. "Only because you are so huge! How many animals does it take to sate such a man?"

Michael didn't even blink under her harsh gaze. "A lot."

I clapped my hands together. "Alrighty, then! It was fun, but I think it's time to go."

Thomas stood first. "The meeting with the other faction leaders is in two hours. I need to—"

A klaxon sounded in the distance followed by another even closer. Without another word, everyone rushed above decks and gathered at the ship railing.

The tall crystal pylons that powered the north-south skyway glowed and a path of clouds ran into the distance.

"What in the hell is going on?" Shelton said. "I thought the skyway was offline."

"It was," Thomas said. "We disabled every pylon between here and Tarissa. Kohval would have had to send people in advance to repair each one."

A high-pitched whine rose to the north and an explosion rumbled through the air. Tons of crystallized aether tinkled down inside the Northern Pass and a horrible realization hit me.

"Aerianas's golems infiltrated the refugees and the army." I covered my ears as another explosion shook the ground. "They must have stayed behind and repaired each pylon after you left."

Thomas tapped the pendant on his uniform. "Sound general alert. All units board your respective Mzodi ships. This is a priority alpha evacuation order."

More explosions sounded in the Northern Pass, and tons more crystal packed the bottom of the pass. "They've got people setting off the malaether gems," I said. "If we don't leave soon, we'll be trapped!"

"Why the hell did we leave those in place?" Shelton said.

"We didn't know how to safely defuse them," Elyssa said. "I should have had them removed the minute the army arrived."

Hundreds of people flooded from the civilian sector, all of them running for the Mzodi sky ships parked in the fields.

Illaena raced to her cabin and the rest of us followed.

Xalara's holographic image floated above the table in her quarters in the middle of a sentence. "...an emergency evacuation order. All ships are to proceed through the Northern Pass and rendezvous at Mount Ulladon." She glanced to the side and worry spread on her face. "Kohval's forces are only minutes away."

Thomas clenched his fists. "I need to supervise the evacuation. I need to get to the command platform."

Leia grabbed his arm. "You've issued the order. There's nothing more you can do from the ground."

"Agreed," Michael said.

I turned to Illaena. "Are all the crew onboard?"

175

She nodded. "Yes, we can leave whenever necessary."

Another explosion shook the Northern Pass. I ran back up to the main deck and looked. The canyon was halfway full. I looked back down the rise toward the mass exodus taking place and realized with horror that they'd never board their ships in time.

Because, in minutes, the pass would be blocked and we'd be trapped between an army and a hard place.

Chapter 17

We are so screwed.

I wanted to fall to my knees and cry, but I'd been in tough situations before.

Thomas was already on top of things. "Illaena, we need to disable the skyway pylons permanently. Can your weapons take them down?"

The Mzodi captain looked at Tahlee. "What do you think?"

"Unlikely," Tahlee said. "They are designed to withstand attacks by the Brightlings. I do not think one ship can damage them."

"We removed the gems powering them," Thomas said. "But that takes time. If spies replaced the missing gems, then we'll never get them back out in time."

"We've got to try anyway," I said. "At the very least, we need to buy time for the refugees."

Illaena nodded. "We will try." She walked over to the bridge and gave her commands.

"Levitation foils full up," Tahlee roared. "Cannons at the ready."

The *Falcheen* lurched upward. Alysea and David stumbled around, clearly not used to emergency maneuvers while the four of us who'd been to Atlantis and back kept to our feet like the saltiest sea captains. I also did my best not to show how queasy it still made me feel.

The ship shot toward the pylons. The skyway, a literal road of clouds, trailed into the distance, bearing a dark mass of enemy soldiers. I couldn't tell how many were Daskar and how many were normal legionnaires. Even if we destroyed the pylons and shut off the skyway, most of the soldiers would be able to channel wings and glide or fly to safety.

The *Falcheen* strafed sideways, all port cannons facing the target.

Tahlee flung her arm forward. "Fire!"

Beams of magical destruction crashed against the crystalline Murk. Death rays that could melt stone to lava barely made a scratch in the dense material. It appeared the builders had used the same layering techniques here that they'd used on the buildings in Tarissa.

Unsurprisingly, the Templars were the first to finish boarding their ship, the *Uorion*, and the massive vessel lifted off and lumbered toward us. It presented its broad side to the skyway pylons and blasted it with a dozen azure beams.

Both ships continued to fire, chipping away slowly at the massive structure, but it was clear that it would take us an hour or more to topple even one. We had only minutes.

A voice boomed from the *Uorion*. "Protect the *Krstuk* and the *Volante* until they lift off, then make for the Northern Pass.

Illaena clenched her teeth. "Why are those civilians so slow?"

The *Rekt*, the ship with the felycans and lycans, lifted off next and guarded the final two ships as Tarissan civilians rushed onboard.

I turned my gaze toward the skyway even as we continued firing at it. A dark cloud of Daskar lifted off and zipped toward us. The Mzodi ships stopped firing on the pylons and focused their efforts on the incoming swarm of destruction.

Destructive beams lanced out from the ships. Smoking bodies spiraled to the ground. Six here, a dozen there, but the swarm adjusted course like a massive flock of birds, as if they were all of one mind, ducking and weaving all the weapons we brought to bear on them.

"How in the hell are they doing that?" Shelton said. "They should be crashing into each other."

I didn't know, and didn't have time to figure it out. The Daskar would be here in seconds.

The final two ships lifted into the air just as the first wave of enemies reached us.

A voice boomed out from the *Uorion*. "Full speed to the pass!"

The *Falcheen* rotated on a dime using a maneuver I'd taught them and dashed for safety. Daskar landed on the Uorion, firing aether beams from the weapon gems on their armor. Templars rushed forward to meet them, and a massive brawl consumed half the deck.

Another group of Daskar focused fire on the *Krstuk*'s levitation foils. The port aft foil exploded and the ship spun out of control. Illaena shouted commands and the *Falcheen* rushed to their aid. We butted up against the prow and managed to stabilize the ship, but it was badly damaged.

Howls and roars pierced the air as the Daskar engaged the shifters on the *Rekt*. Massive wolves and all manner of felines tore into the Daskar even as enemy aether beams sizzled through flesh and bone.

Another command blasted from the Uorion. "*Falcheen*, guide the civilian ships to the pass. We will cover your retreat."

"Cover our retreat?" Shelton yelled. "They're swamped with enemy soldiers!"

Illaena paused, seemingly unwilling to give the command. She stared helplessly at the crippled *Krstuk*. Fists clenched, she gave the command.

The Daskar focused everything they had on the *Uorion* and the *Rekt*, apparently realizing the bulk of our army was on the two ships. Blue Cloaks on flying carpets formed up around their ship, the *Ogan*, and launched a counterattack on the Daskar swarming the *Uorion*.

The *Kestra*, the ship with the vampire forces, hadn't even gotten off the ground. Ragged holes smoking where once there had been levitation gems meant it wasn't going anywhere. Vampires in red uniforms poured like army ants from a mound, retreating through the military sector in orderly fashion. The Daskar ignored them and turned on the remaining ships.

Crew from our ship tossed shimmering net ropes to the Mzodi on the damaged *Krstuk*, and tethered it to thick moors on the aft section. Illaena gave the order to retreat. The other civilian ship, *Volante*, glided by our side, smoke trailing from a damaged levitation foil. Healers attended the wounded Tarissans on the blood-stained deck.

Elyssa and I ran aft and watched the battle. The Uorion turned slowly north, but its decks crawled with enemy soldiers. I didn't see how our people would escape.

"Justin, that's our entire army back there," Elyssa said. "We can't just abandon them."

Spells flashed through the air. Daskar fired beams of ultraviolet at the attacking Blue Cloaks. Templars fought magic with silver and steel. But there were too many enemies to fight. If the ships broke free, they could outrun the Daskar, but how could that happen?

I realized the answer was straight ahead of us. "Get me a flying carpet."

Elyssa narrowed her eyes, but ran below and returned a moment later.

The *Falcheen* stopped outside the pass, leaving the refugee ships outside as explosions rocked the air. There was no way they could take care of the saboteurs while keeping the other ships aloft.

Crystallized aether rose more than halfway up the sides of the canyon. More explosions rocked the gorge and another ton of crystals rained down below. The ship faltered and slowed.

"What's wrong?" Elyssa said. "Why are we slowing?"

"The malaether gems suck the magical energy right out of the air," I said. "If the levitation foils don't have aether, they can't operate."

"Then why didn't we drop like a rock?"

"The levitation foils have a large reserve of emergency magic," I explained. "It's enough to hold up the ship for a few seconds before it drops."

"In other words, if our flying carpet is caught in an aether-free zone—"

"We drop like a lead brick," I answered. "Thankfully, Seraphina is so full of aether that it would replenish quickly."

"I hope you're right." Elyssa tossed the sleek black carpet on the deck. It was a military model that could keep up with even the high-performance brooms.

I stepped onto it and felt my feet stick to the material. I held out hand to Elyssa and said, "Come with me if you want to live."

She rolled her eyes and stepped onboard. "I think you meant to say die."

"Probably," I admitted, and lifted off.

"What the hell are you two doing?" Shelton shouted.

"Saving the day," Elyssa said. "Wish us luck!"

"You're idiots!" Shelton hollered back.

I scanned the area below and spotted the shadowy humanoid form of a saboteur far below. The moment I cleared the railing I took the carpet into a steep dive toward the target. The seraph wore civilian clothing and could have passed for a Tarissan citizen. He'd probably been planted with our forces when Kohval occupied the city.

He didn't look at all like Nightliss and rode a flying carpet, which meant he was probably a normal legionnaire and not a demon golem.

He didn't hear us coming until the last second, face filled with shock when he saw my fist inches from his face. I clocked him right in the jaw. He tumbled off the ledge and landed in the crystallized aether about twenty feet below. I heard a low hum emanating from somewhere on the other side of the canyon and realized someone else had primed a gem for explosion. Farther down the wall from us, another gem hummed.

Cold air mixed with the heat of the explosions, filling the pass with fog that made it difficult to see how many other enemy agents were activating the malaether gems. I didn't have time to deal with them, but maybe the *Falcheen* could.

More than anything, I wanted to get back on the ship and get the hell out of Dodge. My family and friends were on that ship, but I couldn't leave good people behind. I had to do what I could to help the rest of our army escape. I jerked the gem, but it wouldn't come loose from the rock face. Channeling a thin beam of Brilliance, I sliced into the rock. Molten stone dribbled down the cliff and the gem came free in my hands.

I spun the carpet south and headed for destiny.

"You're not going to throw that at the ships are you?" Elyssa said.

I shook my head. "No. We're going to take out the skyway." I tapped the pendant on my shirt. "Justin to *Falcheen*. There are at least three other enemy agents setting off the gems. You need to stop them or the other ships won't be able to get through."

Illaena answered. "Commander Borathen is already working on it."

Two more explosions rumbled behind us as we shot out of the foggy pass and back into clear air. Smoke trailed from two levitation foils on the *Rekt*. The crippled ship drifted steadily toward the ground even as a battle raged on its deck. The Templars on the *Uorion* seemed to have their fight under control, but ragged breaches dotted the hull, and gems spilled out of the main hold, glittering in the air, a storm of jewels.

The skyway teemed with legionnaires, now less than a quarter of a mile away. While they might not have the same flight capabilities as the Daskar, they would certainly have an easy time dispatching our grounded units. The *Rekt* thudded to earth, sending cracks through its crystal hull. The gangway dropped and the shifter factions abandoned ship.

The Daskar turned their attention on the *Ogan*, defended primarily by Blue Cloaks and Arcanes, while the *Uorion* shifted into position to defend the grounded units under fire from the sky.

I was so busy watching the battle I almost didn't see what was coming for us.

"Justin!" Elyssa grabbed my arm and pointed to two squadrons of Daskar coming for us.

"Why are they sending so many after us?" I said. "Two people on a carpet can't present much of a threat."

Elyssa slapped the huge gem sitting between us. "They saw this and they know what it is."

"Oh, do they now?" I grabbed the gem and held it over my head. "Hey, assholes! Look what I've got!"

They probably couldn't hear me over the sounds of battle, but the big gem sparkling in the sunlight certainly caught the attention of more enemy squadrons. Another three groups of twelve Daskar broke off their attacks on the ships and angled to intercept us.

It didn't take a mathematical genius to calculate our trajectories and come to the same conclusion I did. One squadron would reach us before we reached the skyway.

"I instantly regret my decision." I dropped the gem back on the carpet and turned to Elyssa. "I need you to drive."

"I still can't beat them to the skyway," Elyssa said.

"No, but I can fend them off until we get there." I channeled orbs of energy around my hands and prepared for battle.

184

Elyssa tapped her pendant. "All units prepare for loss of aether. We're going to detonate a malaether gem at the skyway."

The Blue Cloaks on flying carpets began to withdraw closer to their ship, doing what they could to fend off the Daskar swarms.

The closest enemy squadron cut us off. Daskar armor glowed with malevolent energy and unleashed an ultraviolet torrent. Wind whipped in my face as Elyssa took us into a steep dive and angled back up. I unleashed beams of Brilliance and punched a hole through the armor of the nearest Daskar.

A feminine shriek of pain drew regret and winces from me. *It's not Nightliss*, I reminded myself, and fired at the next enemy. The Daskar swarmed like bees, dodging my beams while I landed only an occasional hit. Only Elyssa's flying skills kept us from getting hammered.

"They're too damned fast," I said. "They're even harder to hit than the ones we fought before."

"Maybe you need a flyswatter," Elyssa said.

As we looped beneath another flurry of attacks, I observed how the squadron moved, how they split apart to dodge my attacks but quickly reformed. They were fast enough to dodge narrow energy beams, but what about something a little bigger? "You're a genius, babe."

"Obviously," she said.

I drew on Brilliance with my right hand and channeled Murk in my left. "Let's see how they handle this." I fired three short bursts of sizzling white energy. The Daskar swooped and funneled around the attacks with ease. At the last instant before they were upon us, I threw up a wide wall of Murk right in front of them and tied off the weave.

The Daskar didn't have time to react before they smashed into the barrier. The shield shattered and three Daskar plummeted for the ground. Their comrades dove to save them, and we darted past the remaining enemies toward the skyway.

I channeled into the malaether gem and threw it at the pylons. A hum filled the air. I sucked in all the aether I could and stored it in my well. The other squadrons of Daskar closed in and unleashed their attacks right when the bomb went off.

Chapter 18

I felt the magical energy drain from the air. To my magical senses, it was like trying to draw breath in an airless vacuum. Aether crystallized and rained down, leaving behind a magicless void.

Thankfully, I'd stored a reserve of aether. The Daskar, however, had not. As the shockwave rippled through the air, hundreds of Daskar found themselves without power. I channeled my reserves into the carpet to keep us aloft, but others weren't so prepared.

Bodies plummeted. The Mzodi ships faltered, levitation foils flickering, but reserve energy kept them aloft. The Blue Cloaks on their magic carpets had already landed on their ship. The skyway vanished and Kohval's legionnaires performed impressions of a cartoon characters who'd just run off a cliff.

Arms flailed and the screams and shouts of surprised legionnaires reached me even from hundreds of yards away. Luckily for them, they were distant enough to still have aether and most channeled wings so they could glide to the ground. The nearby Daskar weren't so lucky, bodies smashing into the grassy field below before more aether rushed in to fill the void.

Without power in their armor, the Daskar who'd boarded our ships were quickly dispatched or tossed overboard by Templars. As power flickered back on in the levitation foils of the two remaining Mzodi ships, they altered course to assist the grounded *Rekt*.

Thomas's voice came over Elyssa's pendant. "We stopped the saboteurs in the Northern Pass, but not before they mostly blocked the gorge," he said. "There's not enough space for the other ships to follow."

"Understood," Elyssa said. "We'll rejoin you shortly."

The Daskar who'd recovered before falling to the ground retreated south, presumably to rejoin Kohval's legion. The *Uorion* settled to the ground next to the *Rekt* and began taking on more passengers. The *Krstuk* and *Volante* drifted over from the impassible canyon and joined the other ships.

A voice boomed from the flagship. "Board quickly and prepare for departure."

"I think they're okay for now," Elyssa said. "Let's get back to the *Falcheen*."

I sat down on the carpet and watched the retreating swarm. "How are we supposed to defeat them, Elyssa?"

She cupped my hand in her chin. "I don't know, but we'll find a way." She managed a smile. "We always do."

Her brave front didn't alleviate the sinking feeling in my guts.

Elyssa spun the carpet around and flew back to the pass. The entire entrance brimmed with aether crystals. Only a small gap far above allowed us passage. Aether lightning crackled through the clouds thirty feet above. Powerful winds swirled and deadly energy crashed against the mountains.

The dangerous aether storms crowning the mountains would destroy or severely damage any Mzodi ships that tried to go over the blockage. Damaged as the sky ships were, it was likely they wouldn't make it far.

A shimmering bed of aether crystals filled the gorge for a hundred yards or more in front of us. Elyssa flew low as possible. Lighting struck the crystals at random intervals, narrowly missing us several times. I caught myself holding my breath in anticipation of the strike that would kill us in an instant. There was no way I could shield us from that sort of destructive power.

Elyssa gripped my hand and I held onto hers for what seemed like a tension-filled eternity. At last, we shot from the other side and immediately dove lower to put as much distance as possible between us and the aether vortex overhead.

The *Falcheen* waited for us not far ahead. As we came in for a landing, I saw Meghan and Bella on their knees before a still form. The wide-brimmed hat lying to the side sent a jolt of terror straight to my core.

I leapt off the carpet before we'd even landed and ran to Shelton's side. Blood caked his shirt and his leather duster. Eyes closed, face pale, he looked dead. A painful knot formed in my throat. I couldn't breathe. Couldn't think. "Shelton!"

Bella looked up at me with tears in her eyes. Meghan didn't move a muscle.

David grabbed me before I could rush to his side. "He's stable, son. Shelton is just sleeping."

Salt stung my eyes. "What happened?"

"He went on a flying carpet and fought off one of the saboteurs, but one of the gems went off before he could get out of the way." David grimaced. "A crystal shard stabbed him right in the gut."

Alysea stood next to David. "Bella brought him back, and Meghan managed to stabilize him before he lost too much blood."

The weight of everything seemed to drop on my shoulders all at once. Elyssa's arm around my waist supported me both emotionally and physically, otherwise I would have dropped to my knees and shouted at the top of my lungs.

"We lost almost everything today." I couldn't even begin to calculate how many lives had been snuffed out, how much damage had been done. "The vampires had to retreat on foot, and the *Uorion* had to pick up the shifters. The *Ogan* and refugee ships were the only other ones still in the air."

Thomas appeared by my side. Blood stained his uniform and speckled his face. "Kohval outsmarted us. I knew he had moles mixed with the civilians, but there was no way to root them out, no way to know they'd remain behind and repair the skyway."

"I don't understand how they repaired the skyway so quickly," Elyssa said. "It's almost like they anticipated it."

"I'll tell you how," Adam said. "When Kohval took his forces to Tarissa, they left repair gems hidden near each of the skyway pylons in case of sabotage."

Thomas frowned. "Is that a guess, or conjecture?"

"It's a guess, but an educated one," Adam said. "When we were looking through their gem warehouse, I couldn't find a single repair gem."

David blew out a breath. "It doesn't matter at this point. What matters is what we do next."

Shelton groaned and his eyes blinked open. Bella cried out with relief and peppered his face with kisses.

I knelt by his side. "How you doing, buddy?"

"I feel like I lost an ass-kicking contest with a unicorn." Shelton tried to fend off Bella's kisses but grimaced in pain. "Guess that means I'm still alive."

"Unfortunately for the rest of us," Adam said, relief spreading across his face.

"It's your second chance at life," I told him. "You have a chance to redeem your asshole ways."

"Screw that," Shelton groaned. "Take me now, lord."

Bella tutted. "Oh, baby, I'm so glad you're alive."

He smiled and looked up at her with adoration. "Ain't nothing as beautiful as you up in Heaven."

"Aww," Alysea said, brushing away tears.

"So cheesy," Adam muttered.

Bella kissed Shelton's forehead and started crying again, but this time with a smile through the tears.

Illaena emerged from below decks, face pale and tired. "The *Uorion* and *Ogan* recovered most of the shifters they could, but they are at full capacity. The rest will have to walk."

"What about the vampires?" Thomas said.

"They are headed southeast on foot." Illaena shook her head. "There is no easy way for them to rendezvous with us, and there are no other Mzodi ships in Pjurna to come to their aid. Xalara said the *Uorion* will unload passengers in a safe place and return for the others. Then they will find a way to meet us in the north."

"So much for retreating to Atlantis," Adam said. "We've got the only way in and out of that place."

"How long would it take to circle around and meet them?" Thomas said.

"We have to circle out to sea, navigate past the vortexes, and approach from the western pass," Illaena said. "We cannot take the shorter route to the east because that would take us right into Tarissa, a route Kohval likely has guarded. Because of the weather patterns this time of year, it could take weeks."

"Weeks?" I said. "What do we do when we get there? Just sit around and hope Kohval doesn't hunt us down?"

"We have to find a safe place where we can weather this storm," Thomas said. "I see no other alternatives."

David raised an eyebrow and looked at me. "There is that other idea we had."

"Anything is better than just sitting around," I said.

"No." Alysea gripped David's arm and shook her head. "It's an idiotic idea."

Thomas's cool gaze shifted back and forth between us. "What idea?"

I stood up and brushed off my hands. "Dad—David—and I don't think Kohval is the one in charge. We think Aerianas controls the dolems."

Meghan's lips peeled back into a snarl. "She needs to die."

"Yes, she does," David said. "But she's a hard target with the legions around her."

"Impossible to reach," I added. "We think Aerianas plans to grow her army by making more of those dolems. Then she'll attack the Brightling capital, Zbura, and take over the empire."

Michael grunted. "Then it's simple. We just sit back and let them destroy each other."

"That would be unwise," Cinder said. "If a Daemas is indeed involved in creating these dolems, then she could summon many demons at one time."

"True," David said. "Does that mean they can mass-produce those things?"

"Not precisely," Cinder said. "They are limited by how much soul essence they have. It is more likely they will try to clone Kaelissa or someone close to her and assassinate her from within rather than risk a direct assault. Then they need only one dolem instead of an army."

Thomas's lips pressed into a grim line. "I think he's right."

"Which is why we need to get to Kaelissa first," I said. "The Brightling army could easily crush the Darkling legions."

"Do we really want to crush them?" Alysea said. "There are thousands of innocent legionnaires who are only following Kohval's orders. They think they're driving invaders out of their homeland."

Shelton groaned. "Can someone get me to a bed before I die?"

"Yes, baby." Bella helped Shelton to his feet. With her dhampyric strength, she probably could have hefted him over a shoulder and carried him like a sack of potatoes, but with his wound, it probably wouldn't have felt too pleasant.

"Careful," Meghan warned. "I sealed the wounds, but they are still delicate right now."

"Understood," Bella said. "No rough sex."

The tension broke and most of us enjoyed a good laugh at Shelton's expense. Thomas, however, looked pensive as ever. After a time, he nodded. "I think Justin is right. It might be easier to get to Kaelissa before Aerianas does. Neither our army nor Aerianas's forces are a match for the Brightlings, but we could win this war with a clone of Kaelissa."

"Madness," Alysea said. "We'll never get to her."

I took her hand and squeezed it gently. "Mom, we have to try, and you're the expert who can help us succeed."

David put an arm around her shoulder. "He's right, honey."

Alysea looked at us as if we were madmen. A long sigh deflated her, and she nodded. "Fine. But don't blame me when we're all dead."

Illaena blinked and shook her head. "I cannot be party to this."

"Do we really have to go through this again?" I said. "Believe me, you do not want someone like Aerianas running the realm. She's probably crazy enough to engineer a total demonic takeover."

"They are right," Tahlee said. Her fiery red hair hung limp and dull and, for once, the indefatigable sera looked worn and tired. "We must put a stop to the madness. It is time to show the Brightlings and Darklings that unity is stronger than division."

Illaena's tired gaze shifted to her first mate. She nodded. "I will confirm with Xalara."

Thomas held up a hand. "Be sure Xalara is the only one who knows and that she keeps it to herself. We don't know if there are other spies in the Mzodi fleet."

"Today removed all doubt of that." Illaena headed for the bridge, Tahlee on her heels. The orders rang out and the crew of the *Falcheen* once again set a course that would take us into danger.

"Before we go too far, we need to confirm that Kaelissa is in Zbura," Thomas said. "It's too long a journey to make only to discover she's elsewhere."

Elyssa nodded. "I wonder if we could find out in Guinesea?"

"My idea exactly," Thomas said.

"How exactly are we supposed to find out where she is?" Alysea sounded exasperated. "Just waltz in and ask around?"

"That's precisely what we need to do." Thomas braced his chin with a hand. "The Mzodi are typically welcomed at all ports, so we could simply pass as them."

"I don't know about that," Adam said, pushing up on the bridge of his nose. "Kaelissa stole two Mzodi ships while they were docked in Guinesea. I don't think the Mzodi are any safer than we are in Brightling territories now."

"Especially since they helped us drive Kaelissa out of Atlantis," I added. "Might be best to keep this as covert as possible. Not to mention, there might be Mzodi prisoners still in Guinesea."

195

Thomas nodded his agreement. "Very well, then. We'll need to learn more about Guinesea and find out who to talk to."

I motioned toward Illaena. "I suggest we start by asking the captain."

An hour later, the *Falcheen* set down on in a cove on the northern shores of Pjurna. The crew needed a rest and the ship needed repairs. After dinner, Thomas, Elyssa, and I met with Illaena to discuss our next steps.

"Guinesea is a small island with a population divided almost equally between military and civilians," Illaena told us when asked. She displayed a holographic map over the table in her quarters and zoomed in on the island in question. In Eden, Guinesea coincided with Papua New Guinea, but a quick look at the map on my phone confirmed that this island was barely half the size of the one in my home realm.

The Mzodi map displayed few details other than markings for the military base and a single city named Novus. Illaena traced a finger in a space between the base and the city. "This is where we landed to trade gems for goods and services."

"Do you also believe that the Mzodi are no longer welcome in Brightling lands?" Thomas asked.

Illaena scowled and nodded. "They still hold the crews of the stolen Mzodi ships." She turned to me. "I would like to rescue them."

"I told you I would. We just need to know where they're being held." I looked at the map. "Where do you suggest we set down so we can enter the city?"

She pointed to a nondescript area just north of Novus. "The city is a ten-mile hike from this valley. You should have no problem walking that distance."

"I wish this map was more detailed," Elyssa said. "What's all this space in between the valley and the city?"

"Farms," Illaena said. "They grow glurk, quintos, and other foods to support the troops." Her nose wrinkled. "They also raise livestock. Some Brightlings consume meat."

"Doesn't sound too risky," I said. "We just need to dress like the locals and take a hike."

"We have suitable clothing in the hold," Illaena said. "You have another problem to overcome."

I raised an eyebrow. "Which is?"

"Your accents." Illaena cleared her throat and spoke with a slight lilt to her tone. "I should like to purchase a glurk." She stopped, repeated herself, but this time with what I imagined a redneck might sound like speaking Cyrinthian. "I wanna glurk."

"Are you saying we sound like the second example?" Elyssa said, looking as offended as I felt.

"Your accents are barely up to Pjurnan standards," Illaena replied coldly. "For you to pass as Brightlings, you will need to adjust how you speak, or they will immediately identify you as an outsider."

"Wonderful." I groaned. "We used a spell to implant Cyrinthian in our brains. Can we do the same with the accents?"

"Accents are learned over time," Thomas said. "I suggest you learn how to fake it."

"Maybe my mom can help out," I suggested.

Illaena shook her head. "Your mother speaks with a High Cyrinthian accent. That would stand out just as much."

I ran a hand down my face and looked at the captain. "Can you help us?"

She sighed. "Very well, but you must do exactly as I say."

It was going to be a long night.

Chapter 19

We spent hours practicing the pretentious accent used by urban Brightlings until I wanted to scream. Illaena finally let us go sometime after midnight so we could catch some shuteye.

"It sounds like an Irish accent," Elyssa said as we made our way to our room.

I grabbed my crotch. "I got their frosted lucky charms right here."

She giggled. "Maybe we should dress up like leprechauns."

I burst into laughter. "And bring a pot of gold."

Despite the humor of the situation, it took me a while to fall asleep that night. Tomorrow, phase one of Operation Kaelissa began whether we were ready or not.

The *Falcheen* glided low over the water to avoid detection while Alysea channeled a light-bending shield in front of the ship that made it harder for sentries to spot us.

Shelton leaned heavily on the railing, face pale, but eyes alert.

"Feeling better?" I asked him.

He grunted. "Feels like my ribs tried to make love with a grizzly bear, but otherwise, yeah. I feel peachy." He looked me up and down. "You look like someone who lost a bet."

I brushed my hands nervously on the silky white kilt Illaena assured me was all the rage in Brightling fashion. "It looks silly, but man, does it feel nice on my legs." I ran a hand along the billowing white shirt. "Besides, this makes me look like an Irish pirate captain."

Shelton snorted and turned back to the kilt. "You got panties on under there too?"

"Silk boxer-briefs." I flashed a grin. "Jealous?"

"Maybe a little." He looked back down at the water rushing beneath the sky ship.

Normally, Shelton would've mercilessly poked fun at me, but it was obvious he was pretty down on himself again. "Look, it was a hard battle. It's just bad luck a piece of that crystal got you."

"Yeah, right." Shelton spat over the side. "I'm just a level fourteen wizard against a world full of level ninety-nines."

"More like level thirties," I said, sticking with the nerdy reference. "If you can't overcome with brute strength, try being sneaky."

"That ain't my style." Shelton stood upright and winced. "That's like trying to turn a knight into a thief. You can't be sneaky when you're clanking around in armor."

"Now you're just coming up with excuses." I leaned my back against the railing. "If a bull is charging straight at you, are you going to try to overpower it?"

"I know what you're getting at," Shelton said. "Of course I'd jump out of the way. But a Seraphim ain't a bull. A bull can't spin on a dime and fire a damned death ray at your face."

"Would you shield against the death ray?" I asked.

He shook his head. "No, I wouldn't stand a chance. I still can't get that geodesic shield spell working right." Shelton's shoulders slumped. "But I can't exactly dodge a beam of light. I'm just not fast enough."

The *Falcheen* entered a shallow valley carpeted with pastel-blue grass. Short trees with brilliant orange leaves dotted the hillsides. The ship set down in a meadow and the gangway dropped.

It was time for me and Elyssa to go. I squeezed Shelton's shoulder. "Don't overthink it."

He *pshaw*ed. "I'm just gonna stay out of the way from now on."

Elyssa strolled over, looking rather delicious in a creamy white dress, her raven hair done up in small braids laced with white silk. The popular styles for Brightling seras were obviously less silly than what the seraphs wore, but Elyssa could make just about anything look good.

"Are you ready?" she said in an excellent imitation of a proper Brightling accent.

I held out my arm. "Yes, my good woman."

Elyssa wrinkled her nose. "You still sound stiff."

I groaned. "Maybe I should just keep my mouth shut."

Shelton snorted. "That's usually a good idea."

Thomas, my parents, and Illaena came over and wished us good luck, then Elyssa and I headed down the gangway and began the hike to Novus.

A patchwork of orchards and fields of grains painted the hilly terrain in brilliant colors. There were no skyways out here in farmland, no pylons or access points, just a white crystal road that looked as if it had been carved into the ground with Brilliance rather than constructed with a gem.

We didn't pass any farm houses, or if we did, they were concealed by the hills. A seraph tending to his glurk orchard waved at us as we walked past. We smiled and waved back, relieved that he didn't come over and try to talk to us. Once we passed him, we picked up the pace and broke into a run, keeping a careful eye out for anyone else.

It wasn't until the walls of Novus came into sight that the number of pedestrians increased. As Illaena promised, the males wore kilts while the females favored long, flowing dresses. Rich reds and royal blues dominated among females, but the males seemed to prefer pink.

"They must be a confident bunch," Elyssa quipped as we smiled and waved at another pink-loving seraph.

Children laughed and played, chasing each other in a meadow while their parents watched and conversed with their peers. Cottony cloudlets laden with foodstuffs glided down the road close behind the farmers bringing them to town. The gates of the city hung open in greeting, though Brightlings in crystal armor patrolled the walls.

"Doesn't look like they're too worried about a Darkling invasion," Elyssa noted.

"I doubt that's been much of a concern." I smiled and nodded at a couple walking a small blue fox like a dog. It sniffed me then promptly latched onto my leg and began furiously humping it.

"Sorry." The sera bent down and picked up the pet. "He's in heat right now."

I smiled stupidly, afraid to talk and betray my bad accent.

"Cute," Elyssa said.

"Yes they are," the sera's boyfriend said, his eyes lingering on Elyssa.

His girlfriend tugged his arm and the pair continued walking with their amorous pet.

The bored guards at the gate barely glanced at us when we stepped through and into the town. Whereas most of the buildings in Tarissa were ultraviolet, the Brightling town preferred white or transparent crystal.

A domed building with a sharp spire rising from the center sat in a grassy plaza at the end of the wide boulevard. The houses here rose three stories at a minimum, their exteriors adorned with latticework and statues, far more fanciful than their utilitarian counterparts in Kohvalla.

Shops displayed artwork, primarily lifelike statues and paintings that all bore a chilling resemblance to the last person I wanted to remember. One statue stood seven feet tall, a female figure holding her arms wide, each hand holding starry-white Brilliance as she prepared to destroy an unseen foe.

Elyssa read the Cyrinthian imprinted on the base of the statue. "Daelissa unleashes her fury."

A painting with a demure rendition of Daelissa drew my attention. "Forever our queen." Daelissa was the spitting image of Nightliss, but with creamy skin instead of olive tones and blond hair instead of black. But where Nightliss had been kind, Daelissa was cruel and uncaring.

"Forever," a nearby sera murmured. "Oh, how I long for her return."

"Keep still your tongue," her male companion hissed. "Kaelissa is the empress now."

"She is the mother of the greatest leader, but will forever live in her shadow." The sera turned an imperious glare on her companion. "I would like this for the house."

He sighed and began bargaining with a portly seraph who was probably the shop keeper.

We continued through the market, passing stands of food, a shop selling aether gems, and one displaying wares that brought me to a stop. Elyssa sucked in a breath. "Are those televisions?"

"You've got to be kidding me." We stared at the items on the shelves just outside the shop. Toasters, microwaves, smartphones, and more.

A pudgy Brightling with a shaved head smiled broadly and approached. "Hello my good people. These are authentic goods plundered from the evil Edenites."

Elyssa blinked couple of times and recovered her wits. "Do they work here?"

"Yes, of course!" The seraph produced a blocky red aether gem and pressed the plug of a nearby toaster to it. The prongs stuck to the gem. When he pressed down on the handle, the toaster hummed to life. "This device is for destroying a food they call bread." He ran a finger along a television. "And this is for dulling minds."

I nearly called him out on the toaster, but couldn't disagree with him about the TV.

"How interesting," Elyssa said. "Perhaps later."

"But you haven't seen everything." The shopkeeper took out a smartphone and flicked on the screen. "This strange device can turn thinking people into mindless automatons."

Elyssa backed away. "I already feel it numbing my brain."

I finally summoned the courage to speak. "Tell me, good man, did you procure these items yourself?"

The seraph clapped his hands together. "Ah, I can tell by your accent you are a native of our fair capitol, Zbura, are you not?"

"Yes, of course," I said, hamming up the accent as much as possible.

"Were you in the war?"

I cleared my throat. "Yes, but I do not wish to speak of it."

"Understood." The shopkeeper splayed his fingers and bowed. "High regards to you, veteran. I am Uro."

I splayed my fingers back in the standard Seraphim greeting, but didn't bow as deeply as the other man. "Thank you, Uro."

Two of the city guards paced by on the street, casting disparaging glances at the wares on display. One of them elbowed the television hard enough to knock it over and send it crashing to the street.

"Careful!" Uro shouted. "These are quite rare."

"How dare you sully our lands with this Eden trash," one guard said. "We told you to keep it off the street."

"But they are collectibles from the war!" Uro knelt next to the broken television and looked as if he wanted to cry.

The guard leaned over. "Get it off the streets. The empress doesn't like reminders of the failed war." He stomped a foot on the TV then marched away with his companion.

"Not very friendly," I said.

"Daelissa is still the queen in our hearts," Uro said. "She is still magnificent even in defeat, but her mother wants nothing more than to see that defeat forgotten."

Elyssa and I exchanged a glance. The first time we'd met Kaelissa she'd seemed pretty proud of Daelissa. Then again, she hadn't been empress back then. Maybe getting her ass kicked in Atlantis changed her outlook on the war.

"I have not been back to Zbura in some time," I said. "Is the empress there now?"

"Ah, rumors abound after nearly every legion was sent to Cabala for purposes unknown." Uro frowned. "After all, she took nearly every solider from our garrison and left us defenseless should the savage Darklings decide to attack."

Kaelissa had massed her troops on the western coast of Azoris, the Seraphina equivalent of North America, and used some of them to attack Atlantis. Why she'd needed so many troops for the effort was still a mystery.

"We wish to pay homage to her," Elyssa said. "Does anyone here know for sure if she is back in Zbura?"

Uro sighed and climbed to his feet, sad eyes looking at the broken TV. His brow furrowed as if something had suddenly troubled him and his gaze flicked to us. "You are a true supporter of Kaelissa?"

206

"Yes, of course." Elyssa quirked an eyebrow. "Why?"

He shook his head. "I am certain our empress is safely in Zbura or perhaps even Cabala, according to rumors, but who can say for certain?"

"I heard Kaelissa commandeered ships from the Mzodi," I said. "Is that true?"

"Oh, yes." Uro looked up as if a sky ship hovered overhead. "That was very bad for business. The crews were kept at the garrison for weeks and later taken elsewhere when the rest of the legionnaires left."

Well, no rescue just yet. Illaena wouldn't be happy to hear it.

Elyssa smiled at the shopkeeper. "Thank you for your time, Uro."

"It is my pleasure," he replied, turning back to the smashed TV.

We wandered around town for the better part of an hour questing for information about Kaelissa. Several citizens frowned and hurried away from us at the mere mention of the empress. One seraph displayed open hostility.

"Why should you wish to worship at her feet?" He pushed his chest against mine. "Kaelissa has stripped us of troops and left us at the mercy of the savage Darklings!"

Elyssa shoved the seraph away and we made a hasty retreat, dashing through twisting alleys until we lost him.

"I don't think Kaelissa is popular in these parts." I pounded a fist against the alley wall. "Guinesea is a bust."

"Tell me about it." Elyssa bit her lower lip. "I haven't seen a single statue or portrait of Kaelissa anywhere—just Daelissa."

I peered around a corner to make sure the street was clear. "Let's get back to the ship. I guess we're going to have to stop in Cabala to see if Kaelissa is there before going all the way to Zbura."

"Agreed." Elyssa took my hand, and we strolled back down the crystal streets toward the city gates.

As we passed through the market again, our friendly neighborhood television salesman saw us and waved.

"I wondered if you would come back," Uro said. "I know just who you can ask about the empress." He walked toward the shop doors. "Follow me."

Elyssa and I exchanged confused looks followed by shrugs.

"Couldn't hurt," I said.

Elyssa *pshaw*ed. "Provided nobody else tries to start a fight."

We followed the waddling seraph into the building. The inside of the shop looked like something that had been lifted straight out of a big-box retailer, complete with the shelving, marketing materials, and even industrial carpeting.

"Whoa." I stopped in front of a shelf filled with game consoles and turned in a circle. "It almost feels like we're home."

Elyssa touched a shelf almost reverently. "This is so weird."

"This way," Uro said. He channeled into a gem and part of the wall misted away into a downward-sloping corridor.

I hesitated. "Where are we going?"

"To the warehouse." Uro walked a few feet and stopped. "My comrade is a great admirer of Empress Kaelissa. He will certainly know where she is."

Elyssa's eyebrows arched. "You have a warehouse?"

"Yes, filled with the spoils of Eden." Uro puffed out his chest proudly. "You will never see another collection like it."

I decided there was no harm in asking this friend of his, considering the alternative was to give up and head to the ship, so I continued after Uro. "How did you get all this stuff?"

"It was not so hard once I found the right people," he said. "What you have seen above is only a taste of what I have to offer."

I knew the answer to my next question, but asked it anyway. "Do you know a way back to Eden?"

Uro shook his head sadly. "The Alabaster Arches no longer work, or I would import even more goods. If Daelissa had conquered the mortals, I would live in Eden now."

We reached the end of the corridor and stepped into a cavernous warehouse. A polished concrete floor, orange metal shelving, and rows upon rows of boxed goods made me feel as if I'd stepped through a portal and into a wholesale club.

Family-sized bags of Cheezy Poofs, complete sets of dinnerware, microwaves, clothing, jewelry, and all sorts of goodies were here for the taking.

I wonder if they have my favorite kind of underwear.

"Impressive," Elyssa said, letting her accent drop briefly.

Uro didn't seem to notice and spread his arms grandly. "Welcome to the Eden Emporium!"

"Wow." I touched an unopened bag of boxer-briefs reverently. "How much for these?"

"Aren't they exotic?" Uro grinned. "Edenites have such strange tastes in clothing."

I glanced down at his purple kilt, but kept the retort to myself.

"My comrade, Lando, is down here," he said. "Come."

Elyssa squeezed my hand and gave me a warning look. "I don't know if we should trust this guy," she whispered in my ear.

Her ninja senses rarely failed us so I nodded. "Be ready to fight, but act natural."

Elyssa pressed her lips together, but returned my nod.

We followed him through the warehouse and into an empty room at the back. Uro channeled into a gem and a doorway appeared. "Please wait here for a moment." He stepped inside and the wall misted back into place.

"Can you believe this place?" I said. "They have underwear!" I clapped my hands with delight.

Elyssa looked around warily. "It's the little things, isn't it?"

"Oh, definitely." I bit my lower lip. "I really want some Cheezy Poofs too."

A strange odor tickled my nose. I frowned and looked at Elyssa at the same time she looked back at me.

Her nose wrinkled. "Did you fart?"

That was the last thing I heard before everything went black.

Chapter 20

I snapped awake feeling like I'd just gotten eight hours of solid sleep. My senses were alert, my mind sharp, and for the first time in a while, I was ready to tackle the world.

Unfortunately, four blank walls and a ceiling severely limited my options. Elyssa jerked upright a few feet away and leapt to her feet. "Where are we?"

"That's a really damned good question." I traced a hand along the walls, inspecting each one for a gem, but this room had been designed to keep people in, not let them out. I thought about trying to brute-force my way out of this mess, but experience told me to save my strength. I had no idea what was on the other side of these walls, and I didn't want to exhaust myself trying to blow a hole through them.

"An even better question is why are we here?" I pressed my hand flat against the smooth surface of the wall and pushed. It didn't betray any structural weaknesses.

The minutes ticked past while we paced around the room testing every square inch for a way out. I pounded the bottom of my fist as hard as I could against one wall. If it had been concrete, it would have cracked. I didn't even make a dent.

The wall flickered and became black as pitch. I jumped back. "Did I do that?"

Elyssa pressed a hand to the darkness. "It's still solid."

A glowing sphere illuminated the darkness a few feet beyond the wall, and I realized what had happened. "It's turned from a wall to a window."

Three hooded figures stepped into the circle of light. One of them raised a finger and pointed at me. "You stand accused of being a true follower of Kaelissa, yet you followed Daelissa into Eden. What say you?"

Even though the voice was slightly deeper, I recognized it at once. "Uro, is that you?"

"Speak the truth!" he said.

"You look silly in those robes." I leaned against the wall adjacent to the window and tried to act nonchalant. "Is Lando one of your robed buddies?"

The figure to his right raised a fist and spoke in a feminine voice. "You will answer the question, or pay the price."

"Well, crap! I left my wallet at home. Will you take an IOU?"

Elyssa tugged on my sleeve and whispered, "Justin, maybe you should answer the question instead of antagonizing them."

Uro was really worked up now. He clenched his fists and roared something unintelligible, while the female tried to calm him down. The one who hadn't spoken stepped closer to the window, face still hidden by shadow.

"You speak with a strange dialect." His voice was low and gruff, but calm. "You speak like those reborn in Eden, millennia after the first great war."

Something about this guy made the hairs on the back of my neck rise. He was smarter than the other two, that much was certain. I held up my hands in a helpless gesture. "Yes, I was reborn and raised by Edenites. Even though my memories returned, I gained a different accent."

"That explains much." He folded his arms. "That is why you are such a proud, condescending creature."

"Hey, now, that's not nice."

The dark cowl turned to Elyssa. "Is she also reborn?"

Elyssa didn't have Seraphim powers and wouldn't be able to pass for one if they tested her, so I plucked another lie out of thin air and hoped it worked. "She is an Edenite. My faithful servant."

I nearly cringed at the ferocity that blazed briefly in Elyssa's eyes, but she covered nicely, managing a smile and a bow. "Yes, he is my master." She put a hand to her chest. "Verily, did he save me from the evil ones, and forever am I in his debt."

Talk about hamming it up.

The cowl bobbed in a nod and turned back to me. "Then I ask you this. Does your loyalty lie with Daelissa or her mother?"

Something in his tone made me think this was a trick question. What good did it do me to be loyal to a ghost? What would one of the real Brightling reborn say, especially those who'd been around when Daelissa ruled Eden?

While I hadn't gotten to know many who fit in that category, the brief encounters with a few gave me a pretty good idea. Qualan and Qualas, for example—pure sadists and all-around black-hearted brother and sister duo. If they'd survived, I guessed what their answers would be.

I stiffened my back and puffed out my chest. "Daelissa is dead. Kaelissa is a failure. While I would still gladly follow Daelissa if she lived, the only loyalty I have is to myself."

Uro and the female turned toward each other. I wondered what expressions hid beneath their cowls.

"That is not precisely what I wanted to hear," the seraph said, "but it sounds like truth to me."

"To hell with your truth," I shot back. "Why are we here?"

The seraph slid back the hood and I was shocked to see the guard from earlier who'd broken Uro's precious TV. *It was all a show—pun totally intended.* Without the armor and the helmet, I was taken aback by how regal he looked. He wore thick blond hair combed down in a Caesar, but with a sharp point instead of a flat line. His black beard was groomed into a point that ended several inches from his chin.

I hated to admit it, but he looked like a magnificent bastard.

"I am Ontidam, a Brightling reborn by our dear Daelissa."

I didn't recognize the name, but hundreds of Brightlings and Darklings had been husked by the explosion of the Grand Nexus during the First Seraphim War. The Seraphim called it the First Eden War, but Shelton referred to it as Supernatural Mega Crap Storm Uno.

That meant the odds were good Ontidam didn't recognize me either. "Did you fight in the first war?" I asked.

"Briefly," he replied.

That didn't help me much. I needed to place him so I could tailor my own story to fit. "Were you among the original rulers of Eden?"

"No, I was in the imperial army, called to serve when the Edenites rebelled." Ontidam shrugged. "I was there for the last battle and close to the initial blast when the Grand Nexus exploded. The next thing I knew I was a toddler in a nursery with other reborn, new children appearing every day. Within a month, I began to remember the horrors of the first war, only to find out I had been brought back to fight in the second great war."

"Talk about a short childhood," I said.

"Indeed."

The shortest of the three figures pulled back his hood to reveal he was indeed Uro. He raised a hand. "Master, what shall we do with them?"

Ontidam held up a hand without even turning to the other seraph and asked me a question. "What is your name?"

I'd been thinking about that very question for the last few minutes. I'd given some thought to saying I was Fjoeruss. After all, I bore a very slight resemblance to him, and Kaelissa hinted he might even be my many-greats grandfather. On the other hand, he was probably famous enough that Ontidam had seen him at some point and would quickly realize I was not him.

The other option was to make up a name, and as Elyssa and my friends often pointed out, I sucked at names.

Elyssa bowed in my direction and saved the day. "Why, he is Justias of course."

Ontidam frowned. "I do not recall that name." He tilted his head slightly and looked at me. "Then again, I served with many."

"I was in the second wave," I told him. "I was there for the start of the war, but being husked and reborn cost me many of my memories."

"As it did me," Ontidam said, a smile replacing his frown. "Tell me, brother, would you support the downfall of Kaelissa?"

I nearly blurted out a yes, but had to reframe the response from the perspective of a haughty Brightling reborn. "That depends on who is to take her place."

Ontidam laughed. "Of course, brother."

I prodded him for more information. "I assume you wish to rule?"

"No, not I." Ontidam pressed a hand to his chest and shook his head. "Nor do I support that dog, Arturo, who has forgotten his true queen and serves Kaelissa."

That wasn't the answer I'd expected. I couldn't hide the curious note in my voice. "Then who?"

"We are here to pave the way for the true savior of Seraphina, and the ruler of Eden." Ontidam spread his hands and looked up as if praying to a god. "We serve Daelissa's chosen successor, Victus."

I felt my jaw drop and my heart skip a beat. I opened my mouth to say, "Are you freaking kidding me?" but Elyssa grabbed my arm and bowed. "Victus is a worthy candidate."

Her quick thinking jerked me out of my shock and back to role-playing. "Ah, Victus." I faked a smile so hard it hurt. "You prepare Seraphina for him?"

"Yes," Ontidam said. "He has already destroyed the Darkling nation, but left the fate of the Brightling Empire in our capable hands."

I knew beyond a shadow of a doubt that this person wasn't the real Ontidam, but a dolem just like Issana and the others. Victus's devious planning had gone far deeper than I could have imagined. In fact, his minions might have already taken over the Brightling Empire had not Kaelissa suddenly taken an interest in picking up where her crazy daughter left off.

I pretended to think about it. It would be out of character to agree too quickly. "What makes you think Victus a worthy successor?"

"He is no Seraphim, but he has the powers of a god." Ontidam once again looked up in prayer. "Victus can create life. He is powerful in the magical arts and the sciences of mortal men. He has already set in motion plans to unite all the realms under one rule."

That plan sounded ambitious even by Victus's standards, but I pretended to be convinced. "Yes, I heard tales of his powers. I even saw him summon creatures from the nether realm, Haedaemos."

My inside knowledge of Victus's abilities lit a fire in Ontidam's eyes. "Truly, you have seen his works?"

I nodded. "Yes. Even though it pains me to admit it, Victus is more powerful than me."

That last statement seemed to seal the deal as far as Ontidam was concerned. He looked at Uro and the third hooded person. "I believe Justias would be a worthy addition to our effort."

Uro frowned thoughtfully then added a nod of his own. "Agreed."

The third figure lowered her hood to reveal a face so familiar, it didn't even surprise me. The third mystery person was yet another Nightliss look-alike, albeit taller and thicker than my dearly departed friend.

218

"I am not so certain," she said. "There is something he is not telling us."

I frowned and tried to deflect. "She does not look like a Brightling."

Ontidam smiled. "Ah, you are very perceptive, Justias." He put a hand on the sera's shoulder. "Bliss is a Darkling."

I hated that name, because this creature brought anything but bliss to my thoughts. "Why do you consort with Darklings?"

Bliss's eyes burned with anger, but Ontidam replied before she could. "Though Daelissa despised Darklings, Victus showed us that we must unite with our brethren if we are to overcome Kaelissa. Even now, we prepare a Darkling army to help us in our quest."

I wondered if he knew that said army had just sealed up the Northern Pass and wouldn't be joining them anytime soon. Then again, why would Kohval seal the pass if he had co-conspirators up here in Guinesea?

I played the role of haughty Brightling and grimaced. "A Darkling army?"

"Do you really trust this seraph?" Bliss asked Ontidam. "I think he is hiding something."

"Oh, I am certain of that," Ontidam replied. "But that does not mean he cannot serve our goals."

I glared at Bliss. "I would be foolish to trust you so quickly."

"And we would be fools to trust you," she shot back.

"You would be wise to accept my help." That kind of logic made me feel like a fourth-grader trading insults on the playground. I turned back to the other two as if I was done with Bliss. "How many support the cause?"

"Over a hundred," Uro said proudly. "This island is fertile ground ever since Kaelissa removed the legions."

I tapped a finger on my chin, trying to look like I was large and in charge despite being locked in a cage. "Are you killing those who are with Kaelissa?"

Ontidam waved off the suggestion. "No, nothing so crude, brother. We simply blank their memories and send them on their way."

Bliss locked eyes with me. "As we should do with you."

I bared my teeth. "Why does this Darkling insist on insulting me?" I turned my gaze on the others. "Why do you bear her presence?"

"Because they need me." Bliss jabbed a finger to her left. "Who do you think is the liaison with the Darkling army?"

I grimaced with disgust. "I still cannot believe you would allow a Darkling army on Brightling land."

Uro waved his hands reassuringly. "It will be a united effort. It is time to end the animosity between Darklings and Brightlings so we can unite under the rule of Victus."

I pursed my lips and paced back and forth. Victus's plan was as ingenious as it was insidious. How many minions had he placed here to see his will done? No true Brightling would ever consider allowing a Darkling army to invade Guinesea, but Ontidam, a Brightling who'd fought in the first war and the second one had the clout to make something so unlikely a reality.

I offered a curt nod. "I see the wisdom in this plan."

"It is very wise," Uro said fervently. "We will take over Guinesea from within, and avoid bloodshed. Then we will continue our efforts in other cities until the empire is ours."

I spread my hands and smiled. "Well, brother, I can't very well help you trapped in this cage."

"Of course not." Ontidam channeled a sphere of crackling Brilliance and let it drift menacingly toward the invisible wall separating us. "I must warn you, however, that if you plan deception, it will be short lived. I am not to be trifled with."

I held up my hands like someone surrendering to the cops. "Understood."

Uro looked up at Ontidam. "Shall I free him?"

Ontidam turned to Bliss. "Are you convinced?"

"I would keep him in that cage until we know what he is hiding." She folded her arms across her chest. "We should blank his mind and be done with him."

"I think he will be an asset." Ontidam nodded at Uro.

Uro stepped forward and touched his palm to the invisible wall. The air pressure dropped ever so slightly and the darkness outside lifted, revealing a large chamber. I stepped out and splayed my fingers toward Ontidam. "Well met, good seraph."

Ontidam replied in kind. "Well met, good seraph."

We weren't alone in the room—not even close. Over a hundred robed figures stood at the edges of the chamber, some of them with cowls still hiding their features. There was no way out of this mess except to put on an Oscar-winning performance. "How may I serve?"

"There are less than a thousand civilians on this island. I have seen every one of them and interviewed many in this very room." Ontidam looked around the room. "Does anyone here recognize Justias?"

My nerves went tight as drums. Out of the corner of my eye I saw Elyssa tense as if preparing for an attack.

No one raised a hand.

Ontidam nodded as if he'd expected it. "In other words, Justias, you are new to this island."

"So what if I am?" I countered. "I've made no secret of it."

"You began asking questions about Kaelissa the moment you arrived." He turned to Uro. "Specifically, you asked if she was in Zbura or elsewhere."

I shifted into a wide stance, an attempt to look big and unafraid despite the flutters in my stomach. "Your point?"

Ontidam spread his hands palms up. "It is exactly why I thought you a worthy candidate to interview, Justias." He smiled. "I believe you did not want to know Kaelissa's location to worship her, but to assassinate her and claim the throne yourself."

Chapter 21

Holy crap.

How in the hell had Ontidam surmised all that? It took everything I had to keep my jaw from hitting the floor. I stared blankly at him and thought desperately about my response, but Elyssa came to my rescue.

"Assassination is too crude for my master." She bowed slightly toward me. "Apologies if I speak out of turn, but they should know the truth."

Uro's eyes widened. "Justias, do you mean to challenge Kaelissa to the ancient Challenge of Ascension?"

I didn't know what that was, so I did what every wise man in the movies does and answered a question with a question. "Do *you* think I should issue the challenge?"

Ontidam's forehead furrowed. "There is no guarantee Kaelissa or Arturo would abide by the outcome." He looked me up and down. "Provided Justias is even powerful enough to overcome her challenger."

I puffed out my chest and tried to look as confident as possible. "I am more than capable of overcoming any champion Kaelissa puts in my path."

Once again, Elyssa stole the show. "But that is not his plan."

A susurrus of robes whispered throughout the chamber as all attention shifted toward her.

Uro raised his nose to look down on her, but he was too short to even make a dignified attempt. Condescension dripped from his voice as he spoke. "What is his plan, child?"

Elyssa's jaw tightened, but she covered with a bow. "Master, may I tell them?"

"Of course." I flicked my hand as if I was totally cool with it, all the while thinking, *What in the hell is she talking about?*

"The Mzodi have in their possession a gem—a bloodstone— which can control minds." Elyssa pressed a finger to her forehead. "The bloodstone will allow Justias to control Kaelissa and force her to transfer power peacefully. Seraphina will be a neatly wrapped gift for Victus when he arrives."

Hey, that's a great plan! Even though the Mzodi had destroyed the bloodstones and didn't have another in their possession, these guys didn't know that. I also began to understand why Elyssa was pushing the assassination angle. If it looked like my goals aligned with Ontidam's then they might cut us loose to work on our own instead of trapping us here indefinitely.

I gauged the expressions on the unhidden faces in the chamber and saw confusion and doubt. "Have you ever heard of a bloodstone?"

"I've heard the ancient tale of King Thussor," Uro said, "but I had always thought it a myth."

"I can assure you bloodstones are real," I said. "Using my contacts with the Mzodi, I am very close to procuring a bloodstone and the secrets to using it."

Bliss's eyes flashed. "You wish to find Kaelissa so you can take the throne for yourself! I knew he was hiding something!"

I threw up my hands. "Yes, of course, I hid my intentions to usurp the throne from Kaelissa." I looked around incredulously. "What sane person would openly admit treason?"

"But here it is not treason." Uro grinned stupidly and clasped his hands together like a child who'd just seen the presents under a Christmas tree. "Our plan to undermine a city at a time would take decades, but if this bloodstone exists, we could have the throne in months!"

"Indeed." Ontidam stroked his beard. "It would seem we have a lot to talk about, Justias."

Bliss scowled. "I will not let this seraph steal the throne from our master."

I managed a look of shocked outrage. "You think I would dare steal the throne from someone as powerful as Victus?" I folded my arms across my chest and looked down my nose at her. "I do want the throne, but will gladly hand it over when Victus is ready."

Yeah, right. I wished Victus would show his smug little face because I'd punch him into Earth orbit.

Bliss's forehead scrunched with a mix of anger and disbelief. "Why should we believe him? Let us take the bloodstone for ourselves."

Uro nodded fervently. "Regardless of his intentions, it would be best for us to undertake this mission."

A chorus of agreement echoed in the chamber.

It felt like someone had just slammed a door in my face and locked it. I waited for a quick response from Elyssa, but she looked just as unsettled as me. Instead of talking us out of a corner, we'd just backed ourselves into one. Ontidam was far too perceptive for my good.

I took another shot at getting ourselves out of this mess and hoped it worked. "I am the only one with the Mzodi contact who can get the bloodstone. I am the only one powerful enough to wield it." The murmuring around me ceased and the chamber went silent. "I will gladly take one of you with me to meet my contact, but I will not relinquish the bloodstone."

Bliss grabbed Elyssa's arm and bared her teeth in a fierce grin. "You will do as we say, or your servant will su—" She didn't have a chance to finish before Elyssa flipped her so hard onto the floor, I heard her skull smack it.

Elyssa bent over her. "Don't touch me without permission, bitch."

Uro's eyes went wide as spinner rims on a pimped out pickup truck. "I did not realize Edenites were so strong."

"The girl is more than she seems." Ontidam's lips curled up slightly. "I saw you holding hands with her, Justias. I know there is more to your relationship than servant and master."

I didn't like where this was going. "Are you threatening to use her if I don't cooperate?"

He held up his hands to ward off more accusations. "Let us just say that your plans should include us every step of the way."

It was obvious they wouldn't let us mosey out of here alone, but that was okay. All I needed to do was whittle the crowd down to three or fewer and then we could get free on our own.

Bliss groaned, eyelids fluttering. She sat up, leaving a spot of blood where her head had hit the floor. "What happened?"

Uro giggled like a kid and put his hands over his mouth.

I motioned to the ring of robed people in the room. "So, Ontidam, what's the deal with all the other spooks in here?"

"Converts," he replied. "Perhaps if you prove yourself, you'll earn a robe and a place among the Allied Seraphina Soldiers."

It took everything I had not to clap my hands together and say, "Oh, boy! Really?" in the most sarcastic tone possible. I also wanted to point out that their acronym spelled ASS, but that joke was only funny in English. Instead, I simply nodded. "For now, I will settle for food and wine."

"Agreed." Ontidam raised a fist into the air. "Listen, brethren."

The room once again fell silent.

"Today, we may have found the answer to ending Kaelissa's rule. I will not call a vote on Justias because he has yet to prove himself worthy of the cause." Ontidam turned around the room as if trying to look everyone in the eyes. "We will keep him in the city as our guest and judge him on his actions. Should he decide to help us of his own volition, we will accept him as our own. Should we have to force his hand, then we will do as we must."

A chorus of agreement echoed his sentiment.

Ontidam turned to me. "Justias, you are free to move about the city, but you will not leave. There are many of us, and you will be watched at all times. Should you try to leave without permission, then we will do what we must. Understood?"

"Sounds fair," I replied. *Suckers!* "Now, can we go eat?"

227

Ontidam smiled and flourished a hand toward a doorway. "Be our guest."

I couldn't have been happier if an animated candle and clock started singing to me, but I kept my expression serious and nodded. "We will talk about the bloodstone later. Perhaps we can reach an agreement."

"I am certain of it," he replied.

His tone sent a chill of apprehension down my spine, but I pretended it didn't bother me and marched toward the doorway, shoulders stiff, chest puffed out. Elyssa apparently didn't see the need to continue the subservient servant charade and walked by my side. We emerged back in the outdoor marketplace, now bustling with people.

The sun had set, but shimmering spheres of white light orbited low over the buildings, trailing stardust like miniature comets and illuminating the way. The odor of cooked food tickled my nose and tantalized my tongue. I followed the scent to a patio with chairs set around small round tables. A waiter set a platter of steaming meat and veggies on the table.

I nudged Elyssa. "I guess Brightlings really do eat meat."

Elyssa peered at the meal. "Looks like chicken to me." She glanced back toward Uro's emporium. "I wonder if that's always been the case, or if their visit to Eden changed eating habits."

"I could use some food."

"How are we supposed to pay for it?" Elyssa looked around. "I don't see anyone paying."

"Maybe they deal in gems like Pjurna," I suggested.

"Maybe." Elyssa glanced over her shoulder. "I say we keep acting casual, until we're close enough to the gates to make a run for it."

The gates waited with open arms about fifty yards beyond the end of the market. As we strolled closer, a large group of people stepped onto the roadway and stopped, eyes narrowed with suspicion. I stepped into the nearest restaurant and pulled Elyssa with me.

"Table for two?" a host seraph asked with a smile.

I shrugged off my apprehension. "Yes, please."

The inside looked an awful lot like a restaurant in Eden—booths with padded seats, hardwood floors, and even wait staff bustling from table to table. The host seated us in a booth for two. "What would you like to drink? Beer? Wine?"

"Um, water?" I said weakly.

"Of course." The moment he stepped away, I leaned over the table and started talking.

"Did you see all those people blocking our path?"

Mouth set in a grim line, Elyssa nodded. "They've got us hemmed in."

I looked out the window and tried to see if our greeting committee was still there, but couldn't get a good angle. "How high do the walls look to you?"

"A hundred feet at least." She shook her head. "We can't climb or jump them if that's what you're thinking."

"Just dandy." I ran a hand down my face and tried to summon a good plan to get us out of this mess. "Someone will come looking for us soon, and I don't want them getting stuck here too."

A waiter approached with our water and set them on the table. He bowed slightly to me. "The alliance is excited to have you, Justias."

I groaned. "Can't I get some food without being hassled?"

"Of course." The seraph didn't so much as glance at Elyssa. "We have many Eden delicacies available."

"On a menu?" I held out my hand suggestively.

"We have not copied their menu system, but I can recite them to you," he replied. "First up is a meatloaf with a side of moist mashed potatoes. Or perhaps you'd prefer the vivacious saucy taste of a gourmet food called a sloppy Joe."

Elyssa's mouth dropped open a little and her nose wrinkled. "You consider that gourmet?"

The waiter looked a bit irritated by her interruption, but continued listing foods that sounded like the menu from a street vendor instead of a fancy restaurant.

"I'll take the meatloaf." I smiled sheepishly. "Um, how much is it?"

"No charge for you, Justias." The waiter bowed again. "The alliance sends its regards."

"Wonderful."

"What would you like for your servant?" he asked without even looking back at Elyssa.

Elyssa bristled, eyes flaring with anger, fists clenching. For a moment, I thought she'd whack him in the neck and knock him out. Instead, she forced a smile and said, "Tell our *server* I would like the sloppy Joe."

The server looked at me expectantly until I nodded. "Yeah, get her the sloppy Joe."

"As you wish." He whisked away.

"I'd like to pound him into a sloppy Joe," Elyssa growled. "These Brightlings think they're too cool for school."

"I just hope the meatloaf doesn't give me diarrhea." I frowned. "Do you think it's really made from beef?"

Elyssa grimaced. "I have no idea what mystery meat is going into this food. I'm sure they'll use only the best ingredients for a nobody like Justias's servant."

I was in the middle of a chuckle when an idea hit me. It wasn't a great idea, but it wasn't horrible either. The biggest problem was that Elyssa would hate it.

"Oh god." Elyssa sighed. "You just got an idea, didn't you?"

"How did you"—I waved away the question—"never mind. Yes, I did, and I think it'll work great."

Elyssa pursed her lips. "Does it involve stripping naked and setting yourself on fire as a distraction?"

I blinked a few times. "No, but that could work, I suppose."

She snorted. "Seriously, what's the idea?"

"I want you to walk out of town and go back to the ship."

Elyssa's brow pinched. "Yeah right. You heard what Ontidam said. We can't leave town."

"*I* can't leave town." I raised an eyebrow. "You can. Like you said, they barely acknowledge your existence and probably wouldn't care if you left."

"Let's assume that's true." Elyssa leaned forward on her elbows. "Do you really expect me to abandon you?"

I shook my head. "Nope. I expect you to come back on a flying carpet and whisk me away."

Elyssa looked stunned. "Wow, babe. That's actually a half-decent idea."

"Geez, you make it sound like I never come up with good ideas."

She reached across the table and patted my hand. "You're better at coming up with escape plans than naming living creatures, I'll give you that."

I stuck out my tongue just as the waiter returned with our food. He looked a bit confused by my expression, but set down the plates and wished us bon appetite, or at least the Cyrinthian version of it.

The meatloaf had a saucy tang to it and burned my tongue with spices. It wasn't what I'd expected, but it tasted delicious. Elyssa took a bite of her sloppy Joe and moaned. "Wow, this is really good."

We finished our meals quickly and left. The group that had blocked the street earlier was gone, but I spotted some familiar faces loitering near the market exit.

Elyssa took a deep breath. "Well, here goes."

"Smooches, babe." Kissing her the way I wanted to wasn't a good idea. Ontidam had eyes everywhere and I didn't want to confirm his suspicions that Elyssa and I were romantically linked.

Elyssa prowled forward, casual as a panther daring anyone to come near her, and walked straight toward the market exit. Several pairs of eyes watched her, but nobody made a move to stop her. I held my breath until she exited the gate and sighed with relief.

Something sharp prodded me in the back, and a familiar voice whispered in my ear. "It appears our dear Justias no longer has his protector with him. Now, tell me how to get the bloodstone, or I will gut you in the streets."

Chapter 22

Bliss, you stupid bitch!

She must have been waiting for an opportune moment to strike. After Elyssa put her down like a sack of potatoes, Bliss must have assumed Elyssa was my bodyguard.

"Is that right?" I tried to turn around, but the pointy object pushed harder into my flesh. "Do you plan to kill me in front of other alliance members?"

"I plan to let you live if you tell me how to get the bloodstone."

Bliss didn't trust me, nor should she. But why this lone wolf act instead of just keeping an eye on me? "Are you trying to be a hero, or do you just want the stone for yourself?"

"I simply do not have the same faith in you that Ontidam does." Bliss pulled me into an alley, spun me around, and shoved me against the wall.

I could have resisted, but she was awfully quick with the razor-sharp crystal dagger in her hand, pressing it against my throat before I had a chance to do anything. I might be fast, and I might have super healing, but a slashed throat would put me down like a butchered hog.

Fierce green eyes glared at me, inches away. Lips peeled back, jaw set in determination, Bliss looked like someone who'd just been ordered to clean the dumpster behind a fast-food restaurant without gloves. I noticed something else lurking in her gaze—desperation.

She must be staking everything on this. If she fails, Ontidam will probably kill her.

Or was it something more?

Ontidam was completely beholden to Victus. In fact, the real Ontidam might have been replaced by Victus during the war against Daelissa. Bliss, on the other hand, was a more recent construct. What if there was an insurrection inside an insurrection inside an insurrection going on here?

Kohval's insurrection against Pjurna. Ontidam's insurrection against the Brightling Empire. Bliss was here as an envoy from the Darkling rebels, but she seemed to have an agenda of her own.

"Respond," Bliss said. She leaned her other elbow against my chest. "Tell me where it is."

"I don't have it," I hissed. "I have to reach my Mzodi contact."

She scowled. "Where are they?"

I wondered if she could sneak me out of here. "Outside of town."

"Lies." She went silent, probably going through the options.

A light bulb flickered on in my head, crackled and went out, then came back on again as I tried to latch onto Bliss's true purpose. It seemed unlikely she would strike out on her own. Instead, it was more likely that Kohval, a wholly owned subsidiary of Aerianas, had sent her here to connect with another of Victus's agents. But Aerianas didn't want to neatly wrap Seraphina for Victus. She wanted this realm for herself.

"That's it!" I almost snapped my fingers, but Bliss probably would have slashed my throat.

Bliss dug a fist into my stomach hard enough to drive the wind from me. "What are you talking about?"

I gasped and caught my breath, giving myself a moment to think. I finally came up with a way to delay Bliss from murdering me and to give Elyssa a better way home in on my position. "I have to signal the Mzodi ship from a high vantage point, but they won't be in the area for another hour."

"Once you signal them, then what?"

"I wait for their return signal and they send someone into town to meet with me." Somehow, I had to get this knife off my throat. While I could channel a shield from the pores of my skin, I didn't think I could do it fast enough to keep her from killing me first.

Bliss looked up and around, but the alley blocked her view. "Where did you plan to signal them from?"

"I hadn't decided yet." I offered a tight smile. "I'm new here as Ontidam pointed out."

"Tell me the signal."

"Even if I give you the signal, you won't get the bloodstone." My mind worked furiously to come up with a way to keep me useful to this backstabbing bitch. I had a distinct feeling she'd kill me if she thought she had everything she needed. On the other hand, I didn't want to kill her because she might have information about Kohval's plans.

It was a conundrum, but I'd been in worse situations before. Then again, even a stupid situation could get me killed. I might slip on a banana peel and impale my head on a spike, or light a fart and explode my intestines.

In other words, Bliss could kill me and really ruin my day. Thankfully, I came up with a wonderful reason for her to keep me alive.

She asked the next logical question. "Why won't they give me the bloodstone?"

"Because you don't have the proper payment." I resisted the urge to nod in the direction Elyssa had gone, because again, didn't want my throat slit, and settled for telling her without any gestures. "My servant went to retrieve payment and bring it back. Either you can take me outside of the city to meet her, or we can both wait at the vantage point where she'll meet me."

The realization that she couldn't just kill me and be done with it finally penetrated Bliss's thick skull. The more I stared at this low-budget copy of Nightliss, the more disgusted and angry I became. It was like watching my favorite TV show only to find out they'd replaced all the actors with look-alikes who didn't know how their characters were supposed to act.

Issana had been a total jackass when we met her. She'd tied us to a tree and threatened our lives. Though she'd mellowed after we told her about Nightliss, I couldn't say the same for her other siblings. I wondered what made her different from the blindly loyal dolems.

Bliss remained quiet for a long moment, then finally nodded. "We'll go to a vantage point. You will signal the Mzodi, and your servant will pay for the bloodstone, which she will hand to me."

"Do you even know how to use a bloodstone?" I said. "There's no on-off switch."

The analogy made her face scrunch with confusion, but she got the point. "You will tell me what to do while we wait."

"Fine." I looked up and to the right with just my eyes. "Shall we go look for a vantage point?"

Bliss backed up a step and jerked me off the wall. Her dagger poked me in the back. "I think I know where to go."

I sighed. "Okay, well you'd better give me directions if I'm supposed to lead."

"Go to the end of the alley and take a right," she said.

I followed those instructions and the ones after it until we reached a tower near the northwestern edge of town. The buildings here were dark, the streets mostly deserted. She charged a gem on the side, and a doorway appeared.

"This is where they housed many military families," Bliss said. "There is no one to see us and no one to save you if you try to escape." She looked back over her shoulder as she'd done many times during the walk here, presumably to make sure no alliance members were tailing us.

"You're a cocky little brat, you know that?" I stopped walking. "I'm not going another step until you apologize."

"Move!" She jammed the dagger against my back. It would have been enough to draw blood, but instead, it clinked against the shield I channeled against my skin moments before.

I blurred forward a few steps and spun to face her. "Do you really think you can best me, you little rat?"

She lunged with the dagger. I channeled a shield of Murk and slammed it hard against the weapon. Crystal shattered. Bliss shouted and fell backwards. I channeled a blade of sizzling white Brilliance with my right hand and slashed it toward her neck.

Bliss gasped and tried to back away, but she had nowhere to go.

I held the humming blade inches from her throat. "You're a pathetic shadow of the real Nightliss. A mean, inferior copy of a great sera."

Bliss's eyes went wide. "H-how did you know?"

"I know you're not here to help Victus." I leaned over her. "You're here to help Aerianas take control of the other golems here, aren't you?"

"How—"

"Answer the question!" I roared. "Answer it now before I end your miserable existence!"

"Yes!" she cried. "Aerianas is my creator. I am here to ensure her rule."

I heard a grinding noise and realized it was my teeth. I was so furious, I wanted to destroy this *thing* where it sat. I knelt in front of her, my light blade at the ready. "I knew Nightliss. She was one of my dearest friends. Your very existence offends me."

"Then kill me and be done with it," Bliss said, defiance rising in her voice. "If I am nothing to you, then it should be easy."

I shook my head. "No, not yet. You have a purpose to serve."

Slow, rhythmic clapping echoed in the empty streets.

Bliss's looked around like a frightened rabbit. I leapt to my feet and searched for the source, but saw no one.

Another pair of hands joined that one, and soon it sounded like I was in the middle of a stadium full of invisible spectators clapping to the same maddening metronome beat—clap, pause, clap, pause. And then those spectators emerged from behind nearby buildings—more and more of them until they surrounded me and Bliss on all sides.

I released the channel on the shield and sword. Neither would do me much good now.

Ontidam stepped from within the crowd, a smug grin on his face. "Thank you, Justias. You have confirmed my suspicions. Bliss is a traitor to the cause—she has betrayed Victus as has her mistress, Aerianas."

I suddenly knew why Ontidam had let me go. He knew Bliss wouldn't be able to resist the siren lure of my shortcut to the Brightling throne. He knew she'd try to take possession of the bloodstone. And now I'd just unmasked her in front of the alliance. The problem was, he also knew that I knew about Aerianas and the dolems. He knew that there was more to me than met the eye.

I had likely unmasked myself.

Play innocent until you know for sure. "What's this about?"

"Ensuring the rule of the true master, of course." When Ontidam looked at me, he seemed to see through me. "Is it time to signal the ship, Justias?"

That son of a bitch heard everything I told Bliss! "You never intended to keep me around, did you?" I tapped into the aether, pouring energy into my body. There was no way in hell I could overpower all these people. I might be able to punch a hole in the circle, but I wasn't fast enough to escape.

I could run inside the tower Bliss had opened. With just a narrow doorway, I could probably hold off Ontidam and his people.

240

"I would not rid myself of a valuable asset," Ontidam said. "I saw you channel both Murk and Brilliance at the same time—a feat only the most powerful Seraphim can perform. If you proclaim your loyalty and give me the bloodstone, I swear no harm will come to you and we will fight together."

It might have been the truth, but I wasn't counting on it, especially since I didn't really have a bloodstone to bargain with. As with Bliss, I needed to buy some time. I hoped Elyssa had plenty of time to get the flying carpet and return.

"Fine, I'll signal the ship." I jabbed a finger toward the tower. "But I need to do it from up there."

"You can do it just fine from right there," Ontidam said. "I have already witnessed your power."

Oh, you ain't seen nothing yet. "Sure, but I can send it higher from the building."

The Brightling shook his head. "Do it from right there."

Yeah, he wasn't going to give me a chance to get away. "Fine." I summoned a crackling sphere of Brilliance around my fist.

Dozens of other Brightlings channeled their own much weaker, smaller spheres and aimed fists at me—an insurance policy in case I opened fire on them. They might be shades weaker, but it would take only one to slice me up.

I held my fist high and fired three pulses into the air. The miniature stars exploded into English letters, SOS, briefly lighting up the sky. The Brightlings wouldn't know what they meant, but Elyssa would.

I looked around, hoping and praying for a sign from above.

Bliss backed up against me, teeth bared like a cornered dog. "Do not trust them," she hissed. "Use your power to fight back. It is better to die than live as prisoners."

"As a wise man once said, you've got to know when to hold them. Know when to fold them. Know when to walk away, and know when to run." I looked at the circle of Brightlings. "This is the time to fold and run."

"Fold what?" Bliss barked a sarcastic laugh. "Run to where?"

I didn't answer. I didn't want this *thing* to betray my flimsy plan of escape. Elyssa would scout the ground. She'd see the mess I was in and figure out something. Would she swoop in and snatch me? Create a diversion and pluck me during the confusion? What if I was supposed to do something?

As the minutes ticked past, I began to wonder if she'd even seen my signal.

None of the others had their eyes on the sky, and I remembered why. I'd told Bliss the contact would come into town on foot. That meant they were expecting someone to waltz in here any minute with a bloodstone in hand. They certainly didn't expect my girlfriend on a flying carpet.

"My sentinels report no one new has entered the city," Ontidam said. "How long will this take?"

"They may not have seen the signal," I said. I raised my fist and fired three more pulses. Once again, SOS lit the sky briefly before fading. I used the opportunity to scan the sky. A shadow flitted past. Was it a bird? A flying carpet? My super woman?

An explosion rocked the buildings fifty yards south. Another explosion lit up the city to the east. Ontidam and his people cried out with surprise and began firing wildly.

Even I was surprised by what happened next.

Chapter 23

The *Falcheen* rose over the wall, levitation foils burning bright, and opened fire on the alliance. Shouts and screams of fear echoed in the streets. The powerful beams smashed through buildings and threw up crystal shards all around the fleeing alliance members, intentionally missing them while driving them away.

I pumped a fist in the air. "The cavalry to the rescue!"

Bliss grabbed my arm. "Please take me with you. Don't leave me here to die."

I jerked my arm free. "Why should I save you? You planned to take the bloodstone and kill me."

"*Please!*" Her wide green eyes filled with tears. "I do not want to die."

I knew it was all a ploy, an innocent façade intended to buy her a little more time to do what she was ordered to do. But she looked like a real person. She sounded like a real person. I couldn't just leave her to the mercy of Ontidam and his goons.

"Fine," I growled. I jabbed a finger toward the ship where the Mzodi crew lowered shimmering nets over the side. I saw Elyssa waving to us frantically over the railing. "Run!"

244

"Justias!" Ontidam cried over the roar and din of his fleeing comrades. "How is it the Mzodi fight on your side?"

One of the nets hanging off the *Falcheen* came into range. I clambered up it a few feet, then turned and gave Ontidam a jaunty salute. "I'm just so damned sexy they can't resist," I shouted back.

Bliss climbed up beside me and held on for dear life as the *Falcheen* spun and sped away. "I thought the Mzodi stood alone and apart from the other Seraphim." Her face pinched with confusion. "And yet they rescue you—a reborn Brightling who fought for Daelissa."

Wind buffeted the nets, banging us against the hull as we traveled away from the city and out over farmland. I looked away from Bliss without answering. She'd been ready to kill me thirty minutes ago. *Don't trust her no matter what.*

"Babe, are you okay?" Elyssa called down.

I gave her a thumbs up as the ship slowed to a halt so we could climb up. I grabbed Bliss's arm tight enough to draw a wince from her. "You owe me." I showed her my teeth in an attempt to look fierce, but it probably just looked like indigestion. "I want to know everything you know, got it?"

Her eyes hardened with anger, but she nodded.

I was surrounded by family and friends the moment I reached the deck. Bliss received a more guarded welcome since nobody knew who she was, but recognized her for a dolem.

"I take it the mission went exactly as planned," David said dryly. "That's my son, everyone. He makes even the toughest mission look effortless."

245

Adam barked a laugh. "You were supposed to go in and ask a few questions, not rouse the entire city against us."

Alysea stared coldly at Bliss. "Who is this?"

"Someone with information." I gripped the railing as the *Falcheen* accelerated for open waters. Illaena caught my eye and shook her head disapprovingly as if even she couldn't believe what she'd just had to do to rescue me.

Shelton held down his wide-brimmed hat as wind gusted across the deck. "Man, I can't wait to hear this story."

I turned to Elyssa. "I guess you didn't have time to explain everything?"

"Since when do I ever?" She shook her head in disbelief. "Justin and I spent a while walking around casually inquiring about Kaelissa, but on the way back out, an insurgent group caught us and tried to recruit Justin."

"Justin?" Bliss seemed confused. "I thought your name was Justias."

"Uh, yeah." I realized Bliss didn't know who I really was. "I'm Justin Slade. I'm not a reborn Brightling who fought for Daelissa."

"Then who are you?" Bliss asked.

Shelton barked a laugh. "Man, are you kidding me?" He slapped me on the back. "This here is the guy who killed Daelissa and sent her army packing back to Seraphina."

Bliss gasped. "No, this cannot be!"

"Oh, it is, all right." Shelton blew out a breath. "So what's this about an insurgency? Is there a rebellion against Kaelissa?"

246

"Not a natural one." I jabbed my thumb at Bliss who seemed to be recovering from the shock of my true identity. "Bliss here pinky-promised to tell us everything she knows, but it's complicated."

"Complicated how?" David said. "Plots within plots within plots?"

I blew out a breath. "Let's just say it's more complicated than a Russian nesting doll with mommy issues."

"I fail to see how an inanimate object could have relationship problems," Cinder said. He stood at the back of the crowd, Issana by his side.

Issana stared at her dolem sibling, a blank expression on her face, as if she still didn't know what to think about everything. I could imagine how traumatic it might be to discover you were one of many demonic constructs with no past, no family, and no idea how long your body might last.

Cinder's confusion got a round of chuckles, but I couldn't help worrying that now we had two dolems on board, both of whom might be programmed to act against us. Just as Ontidam worshipped Victus, did that mean Bliss would do absolutely anything for Aerianas? Had Issana been programmed to follow Cephus's every whim?

Victus might have colluded with Cephus and Aerianas, but everything I'd witnessed indicated that all three of them had their own agendas. Cephus had used Issana to spy on Kohval and the Brightling beachhead—now abandoned—north of Kohvalla. Kohval had been replaced and was under the control of Aerianas, while Ontidam had been cloned by Victus.

It was enough to make my head swim.

"Son, you okay?" David clapped me on the shoulder.

"Yeah." I leaned back against the railing and tried to clear my head. "I don't know which way is up with all these conspiracies." I told the group everything that had happened in Guinesea, and tried to convey why I was so confused. "There are three sides vying for power, not including us. Issana for Cephus, Bliss for Aerianas, and Ontidam for Victus, and those are just the agents we know about."

"Cephus is dead," Issana proclaimed. "I owe him no loyalty and will not betray you."

"You say that," I countered, "but can you be sure you're not programmed to respond in specific ways to certain situations?"

"I have free will!" Issana's mouth widened with horror. "I choose to lift a hand, and the hand responds. I choose to be loyal to you, and I am."

"There is nothing to indicate she is brainwashed." Cinder put a protective arm on Issana's shoulder. "She is in many ways more real and human than I am."

Issana nestled like a frightened bird in Cinder's arm, though I knew she was anything but. She looked a lot like Nightliss, but she was rude, aggressive, and demanding. Was this an act, or was she really so frightened?

"I'm more concerned about Bliss." Elyssa folded her arms and delivered a stern gaze to our newest dolem in the group. "What are your intentions?"

Bliss turned her narrow-eyed gaze from Issana to Elyssa. "Aerianas is my creator. My mission is to ensure the Brightling throne goes to her and no one else. She originally worked for Victus, but he is no longer in Seraphina and cannot return since the Alabaster Arches no longer work. I was sent to undermine Ontidam since his blind loyalty to Victus will work against my mistress's goals."

248

"Simple enough." Thomas had remained quiet at the back of the group, but his calm words drew everyone's attention. "You were sent to Guinesea to undermine or take control of Ontidam's efforts because Aerianas knew about him from her time working for Victus."

"I was sent to prevent Victus's agents from claiming the throne," Bliss replied. "That duty has not changed."

Thomas walked between the others until he stood only a few feet from her. "How many more of Aerianas's agents are there?"

"I cannot say."

"Cannot or will not?"

Bliss's eyes darted back and forth as if gauging the expressions of the others in the group. "Will not."

"Then why are you so forthcoming with your own mission?" Thomas asked.

"Because it is no longer a secret." She folded her arms and clammed up like a pouting child. "I will not tell you everything about her plan."

"Would torture loosen your tongue?" Thomas asked.

Bliss's eyes flared. "No!"

"The threat of death?"

"Just try it!" she shouted. "I will not give in."

Thomas fired off another question. "How long were you in Guinesea?"

"Less than a month."

And another. "Are you important to Aerianas?"

Bliss's fists clenched. "Very important."

"I don't think so. Why were you chosen above the others?"

Bliss stomped a foot on the ground. "I am the best."

"The best at what?"

"At the mission!"

Thomas rapid-fired several more questions on a wild variety of topics, all of which seemed to impugn Bliss's ability to do her job.

As Bliss grew more agitated, I began to see a pattern. It was something I'd noticed in all the other Nightliss dolems, whether it was Issana, Bliss, or any of the numerous Daskar.

Bliss responded like an angry child who'd just been scolded by a parent. Her vocabulary might be more advanced than a child's, and her physique might be that of an adult, but maturity hadn't caught up with the rest of her.

All of the Nightliss series of dolems were, by default, under a year old since it had only been months since Cephus captured Nightliss and stolen some of her soul essence. They came out of the oven looking like adults, but their attitudes were like spoiled kids.

Thomas broke off questioning and looked at Elyssa. "I don't think Aerianas entrusted her with troop numbers, much less anything else. She's just a tool."

"There are nearly a hundred of us and more all the time!" Bliss shouted. "Aerianas is powerful beyond your comprehension."

"How did Victus expect to return to claim his prize if the arches are closed?" Thomas said.

"I don't know." Bliss didn't even seem to realize she'd just served up the whole enchilada on a silver platter to Thomas already.

"Where is Aerianas now? What are her plans for conquest? How did she expect to overcome Kaelissa? Where will she retreat if she fails? Has she summoned other demons to her aid?" Thomas peppered Bliss with more questions until at last, she broke.

"Just stop it!" Bliss covered her ears. "I have no more information."

"Yes, I know," Thomas said. "Your knowledge of Aerianas's plans is rudimentary, probably gleaned from observation and not directly conveyed by superiors."

David pinched the bridge of his nose. "Man, remind me to never let you interrogate me."

Thomas folded an arm across his chest and rested the other elbow on it. "I don't see any signs of direct cognitive interference. If anything, I would say she was force-fed propaganda during her brief training."

"She has free will?" Alysea asked.

Thomas looked between Issana and Bliss. "Yes, I think so."

"I concur," Cinder said. "Though a golem spark can be programmed quite specifically, the dolems also possess soul fragments."

Shelton scratched the back of his neck. "You're saying soul fragments automatically give them free will?"

"To a certain degree, yes," Cinder replied. "Free will can be overridden, but it would take many months of intense mental programming. I do not think Aerianas wishes to invest so much time into what she looks at as a disposable soldier."

"I'm not something you can just throw away," Bliss said. "I'm a living being with my own thoughts." She pressed a hand to her chest. "I am real."

Shelton grimaced. "Sounds just like a damned teenager."

Bliss glared at him. "I don't know what that is, but I know you're insulting me."

I wanted to hate her. I wanted to objectify her as a thing so it would make it easier if I had to get rid of her or use her like a tool. But seeing the pain and anger in her eyes, whether real or simulated, jabbed my guts with guilt. I held up my hands. "Look, let's take it easy on the name calling. I think we've established that Bliss has her own agenda that we can't sway her from. We'll just have to deal with her when the time comes."

Cinder nodded. "Simply put, we cannot trust her, but that does not excuse rude behavior."

"Amen to that," Alysea said. "We were all created through no choice of our own, whether by birth or at the hands of another." She made eye contact with Cinder. "Someone once said, it's not what we were born or created as that defines us, but what we choose to do with our lives."

David snapped his fingers. "Yeah, that little green dude in the space movie said that, right?"

"Wasn't it Jesus?" Adam said.

Shelton shook his head. "Nah, definitely a Star Trek reference."

Alysea huffed and looked at me. "I'm sure someone else said it before, but I remember a time when people weren't so accepting of my son for what he is."

I felt my face start to burn and the guilt in my guts start to rise. Back when I'd first come onto the scene, nobody wanted to join forces with a demon spawn. Daemos had earned a bad reputation, but I'd proven that I could be more than the negative stereotype. Hell, even my dad had proven he could rise above his jackassery and do some good.

I'd forced myself to think of the dolems as unnatural things that should be wiped out. As blights on Nightliss's good name. They reminded me so much of her that it hurt knowing bits and pieces of her were being used by bad people. But that wasn't Bliss's fault or Issana's. All the dolems had been brought into this world and fed a crock of lies by evil assholes.

But what if the truth set them free? What if they could eventually rise to be as good as Nightliss? My dear friend might be dead, but maybe the world would be a better place with hundreds of versions of her in it, each one growing parts of her soul back into something hopefully resembling the original.

To accomplish that, I had to make the choice right now to treat Bliss and Issana like I treated anyone else—with respect. I had to at least give them a chance to mature into something good, before condemning them.

Thomas took my mother's words in stride despite his adversarial history with me. "I think we've all learned that irrational hatred breeds more hatred." He turned to Bliss. "Because you possess a piece of her soul, you are a daughter of Nightliss whether you want to be or not." Thomas put a hand on her shoulder even as she flinched at his touch. "Nightliss was the Templar Clarion, a revered figure, a powerful Seraphim, and above all, a friend to all of us."

253

I felt my eyes burning with tears. Even Shelton's eyes were red despite doing his best to look unaffected by the memories Thomas evoked.

"You did not know your mother," Thomas continued, "but we did. It is my hope that you, Issana, and your sisters can be more than just a familiar face to us—you can be family."

"Wow," Elyssa said in a hushed voice. She leaned into my ear. "Did my dad just give an inspirational speech about family?"

I wiped my eyes. "Yeah, he sure did."

Cinder clapped. Alysea and David joined him, and soon the others joined while Issana and Bliss looked utterly confused.

Illaena walked over from the bridge and put her hands on her hips. "What is the meaning of this?"

"We're having a moment," Shelton said. "Is that okay, captain?"

Illaena pursed her lips. "I suppose so." She turned to me. "We are safely out from Guinesea, but we have not rescued the Mzodi prisoners. Did you locate them?"

I sighed. "I'm sorry, Illaena, but they were transferred to Cabala. I think Kaelissa wanted them to build her ships."

"Impossible!" she scoffed. "No Mzodi would betray our secrets to the Brightlings."

"I hope you're right." I looked out at the dark sea. "In any case, we need to cross the ocean and go to Cabala."

It was time to visit the Brightling Empire.

Chapter 24

Azoris, the Seraphina equivalent of North America was a long flight from the bottom of the world, but it seemed the next best place to look for Kaelissa. The capitol city, Zbura, sat on a chain of mountain islands where the state of Florida existed in Eden.

In this realm, the landmass of California and Baja lay under the ocean. The western coast of Azoris consisted of the Algan Mountains and treacherous aether vortexes. Cabala was on the other side of those natural barriers, and our next stop in the search for Kaelissa.

Kaelissa had been severely injured during the Battle of Atlantis. Arturo had saved her and they'd escaped on a hijacked Mzodi ship. Since Voltis was almost directly in the middle of the route leading from Pjurna to western Azoris, it seemed likely Arturo had taken his empress to Cabala. That meant the Brightling legions were also still there, for whatever unknown reasons Kaelissa had for concentrating them in one place.

Even if she'd already left Cabala and returned to Zbura, it would save time to stop there.

Thomas called a meeting once we were underway to discuss our options. Illaena left Tahlee in command so she could attend. We held the gathering in one of the large empty holds, and even then, it was standing room only. Thomas, Michael, Leia, and Phoebe stood next to

255

my parents. I chose to stand on the other side of the circle because I liked to keep an eye on Thomas's expressions for clues about how well the meeting was going.

Thomas started things off in his usual blunt manner. "A few days from now we'll enter the Brightling Empire. I don't know what to expect, or what dangers we'll face, but enemies will surround us on all sides."

"Are we stopping in Atlantis?" Shelton said. "We might need more food for such a long trip."

Illaena frowned. "Our food stores are well stocked. There is no need to stop."

Shelton grimaced. "Yeah, we have plenty of glurk, but I don't consider that real food."

"It'll take us nearly a day to get in and out of Atlantis," I said. "If Aerianas has agents near Kaelissa already, we don't have any time to waste. We need to get there first."

Thomas turned to Bliss. "Do you have any information to offer about Aerianas's plans?"

Bliss had been hesitant to say anything after Thomas's interrogation and inspirational speech. Even now, she looked down and shook her head. "I—I don't."

"Is it really a good idea to have her in here?" Shelton said. "What if she escapes and blabs on us?"

"Aerianas must first take control of Guinesea if she plans to follow us to Azoris," Thomas said. "Even from there, the skyways only travel east to Sazoris and west to Ijolica, right into Brightling territories."

"It isn't Aerianas and her army we have to worry about," Adam said, "it's her dolem agents already ahead of us that could screw over our mission."

"Yeah, so what if Bliss knows about those agents?" Shelton threw up his hands. "She ain't talking, so there's no reason for her to be here."

Alysea nodded. "I agree, Thomas. Unless she offers us information, we should exclude her from this meeting."

"Very well." Thomas turned to Bliss. "I'll have you escorted back to the top deck."

Bliss pulled her eyes off the floor and met his gaze. "I will give you something if you allow me to stay."

Shelton grunted. "Better be good."

Thomas tapped a finger on his chin. Nodded. "What do you have to offer?"

Bliss chewed on her lower lip, hesitated a few seconds before answering. "Aerianas will invade Guinesea this very night."

A ripple of murmurs passed through the room.

"How do you know this?" Cinder asked.

Bliss shifted from foot to foot, like a nervous child. "Aerianas gave me very little time to subvert or kill Victus's agent Ontidam. She knew he gathered an army that could come south at any moment to take over Kohvalla while Kohval's legions went south to secure Tarissa. Though Ontidam could not muster a great army, it would be enough to slow her march north."

A puzzle piece fell into place, but I let Bliss explain it.

"Agents were left behind to seal the pass and keep Ontidam and his army out while Kohval and Meera's legions secured Tarissa and conscripted more civilians to join them." Bliss swallowed hard, as if speaking these words was physically difficult. "She has the means to quickly clear the pass so it will not delay her plans to move on Guinesea."

I held up a hand to stop her. "I thought Ontidam wanted to ally with the Darkling army. Why would Aerianas worry about him invading?"

"Victus created Ontidam and other agents in secret. Aerianas only recently discovered some of these moles." Bliss squeezed her eyes shut and took a deep breath, as if overcoming an internal struggle. "It is very difficult for me to tell you this without feeling like a traitor."

Elyssa took out her arcphone and projected a holographic whiteboard. At the top, she put an image of Victus and next to that, one of Aerianas.

Aerianas's thin, pale face brought back memories of Kassallandra's disastrous attempt to wed my father and ally House Assad with House Slade. Despite my nearly being killed by Aerianas and her demonic cohorts, I couldn't complain about the results. It had certainly prevented Kassallandra from becoming my evil stepmother.

Elyssa drew a vertical line beneath Victus and put the name Ontidam at the end. Beneath Aerianas, she put Bliss's name. "This should help sort the convoluted relationships."

"What about Cephus?" Shelton asked. "He might be dead, but he still has agents running around."

"If he does, I do not know of them," Issana said. "As I said, I owe no loyalty to the dead."

"Let's keep it limited to these two," Thomas said. He stepped forward and drew a horizontal line connecting Aerianas and Victus. "If it makes it easier, Bliss, we'll connect the dots, and you tell us if we're wrong."

Bliss stared at the diagram for a moment, then stepped forward and drew another line under Victus. At the end, she put the name Siricle and beneath it, location unknown. "Aerianas discovered the existence of Ontidam and Siricle and sent agents to discover their whereabouts and missions. Ontidam was to be Victus's failsafe for securing Pjurna in case Cephus failed."

"And Siricle?" Thomas asked.

"We know only that Siricle passed through Guinesea and took the skyway to Sazoris sometime after Cephus was killed." Bliss looked at me. "After you and your army killed Cephus." She still seemed disturbed by my true identity.

Shelton whistled. "In other words, Siricle could already be in Zbura with a plan to take over the Brightling government."

A frightening idea hit me. "What if Kaelissa was part of that plan? After all, she took power right after Cephus died."

"Doubtful," Thomas said. "In fact, I think Kaelissa was not part of Siricle's plan, but a monkey wrench."

"Agreed," David said. "Before Kaelissa took over, Siricle might have had an easier time plotting a coup against a weakened Brightling government. Instead, Daelissa's mother took the throne with the backing of Arturo and the military and promptly tried to take over the world."

"The Battle of Atlantis probably weakened Kaelissa, made her vulnerable." Elyssa put an image of Kaelissa on the board and moved

Aerianas and Victus beneath her. "It means we might not have much time before Siricle comes up with a way to complete his mission."

Thomas pursed his lips. "Agreed." He turned to Bliss. "Does Aerianas have agents in Zbura?"

"Yes." Bliss winced. "She sent one to Zbura, and another to Cabala. We have received no word from either."

"Are they Nightliss clones?" I asked.

She shook her head. "All I know is that Aerianas said they were quite special."

"In other words, we have agents ahead of us, and Aerianas's army behind us," Shelton said. "Sounds like a real party!"

Bliss nodded. "Within a week, Aerianas will be able to take the skyway to the city of Olam in Sazoris and then turn north for Zbura."

"What about the Brightling military in Olam?" Shelton said. "They aren't going to just let her waltz in."

"Unless Kaelissa sent her legions back to their posts, there isn't much standing in Aerianas's path." Elyssa highlighted the route from Pjurna to Sazoris on the map. "Kaelissa withdrew all her legions and concentrated them in Cabala. We assume she thought she'd need them to invade Atlantis."

"Though, if she hasn't ordered them back to their posts, she may have had another reason," Thomas said.

Elyssa pulled up a map of Seraphina next to the whiteboard and circled Cabala. "We received intel from an Mzodi ship one week ago indicating the Brightling troops are still concentrated here."

"Did the ship dock in town?" Adam asked.

She shook her head. "They were bypassing Cabala." Elyssa tapped a finger on her bottom lip. "The crew reported several dragon sightings, though they avoided any fights."

David made a thoughtful noise. "Maybe that's why she put all her troops there. Didn't Cephus's experiments with portals open a few holes to Draxadis? For all we know, they might be hip-deep in dragon poop right now."

Alysea rolled her eyes.

"Well, ain't that dandy?" Shelton threw up his hands "Dragons and a Brightling army right in our favorite vacation spot."

I stared at the mark on the map and imagined a badly injured Kaelissa being taken there for recovery. It wouldn't make sense to move her all the way across the continent to Zbura in the southeast, at least not right away. If dragons were a problem, she might have remained to command her forces. I certainly didn't relish the prospect of entering such a dangerous zone.

Cinder raised his hand. "Once we locate Kaelissa, what is the plan?"

"Ideally, we replace her with a dolem," I said.

Bliss and Issana flicked uneasy looks my way.

David raised an eyebrow. "I assume you'll need my expertise with demon summoning to make it happen?"

"Can you do that?" I asked.

David pursed his lips and tapped his chin. "From what you described, I can definitely handle the summoning bit. As for the technical aspects—creating the soul-infused spark and inserting it, someone else will have to handle that."

"The demon summoning pattern in the foundry was for Baal," Shelton said. "The freaking demon king. Do you really think Aerianas got him to show?"

"I don't know exactly what she did." Concern flashed in my father's eyes. "If Baal is truly involved, you can bet there's a price attached."

"Is it true that Baal is powerful enough to resist a summons even with his name?" Bella asked.

David nodded. "His pattern could be attached to a demonicus to lend it extra power even if he doesn't manifest."

"Holy key-rist!" Shelton blew out a breath. "Is his name really that powerful?"

"Most definitely," David said. "Hell, for all we know, he might be pulling the strings."

Shelton made the sign of the cross with his fingers. "Please tell me we don't have to worry about Baal walking in the room and making us his bitches."

"If you'll remember the Demonicus Incident, it's possible for powerful demons to take physical shape, provided enough souls are used in the summoning," Thomas said. "Anything is possible."

Elyssa frowned. "I thought a demon overlord required a daemonculus to take on a permanent physical form."

"In Eden, yes." David motioned toward the hovering whiteboard. "Can I use some space?"

"Be my guest." Elyssa moved aside the evil mastermind flowchart to give him room.

David drew four messy circles with his finger and marked them with cardinal directions, north, south, east, and west. He connected them with a large circle and then drew another circle in the middle of it all. He stepped back and inspected it and nodded in satisfaction as if it was a work of true art.

"Now that's talent," Shelton said. "Need some water colors to make them pop."

David looked hurt. "Hey, I worked hard on this."

Alysea sighed. "David, the point, please?"

"Yes, dear." David touched the northern circle. "Each of these circles is a demonicus." He waved his hand around the entire diagram. "A demonicus usually consists of three concentric circles of demon-summoning patterns, but as with the one at the foundry, it can still operate with only two, especially in Seraphina."

"Aha!" Adam said excitedly. "In Eden, they used ley lines to connect all four demonicus, but Seraphina is overflowing with aether, meaning the patterns don't need ley lines."

"Exactly." David put a hand on the center of the daemonculus. "In other words, it's possible for a Daemas as powerful as Aerianas to create a compact daemonculus, especially if Baal is cooperating."

"Whoa." Shelton took off his hat and ran a hand through his hair. "If that's the case, how do we know Baal isn't already here in physical form?"

"We don't," David said. "If he's here and has an eye on the throne, there's not a whole hell of a lot we can do to stop him."

"We can't kill the physical body?" I asked. "Banish him?"

"Emily Glass could, but she's not here." David shook his head grimly. "We'd just better hope Aerianas needs something else to summon Baal in physical form, or we'll soon be bowing down to my dear old demonic dad."

Chapter 25

The king of Hell might want to be the emperor of Heaven.

Baal was something of an enigma to me. Sure, he was my grandfather, but I'd never spoken to him, nor was I sure I actually wanted to. He'd devoured a lot of souls and spirits to become the most powerful demon in Haedaemos, and in my book, that didn't exactly make him a good guy.

He also despised my father, calling him weak and unfit because David didn't care about acquiring more power. Ironically, it had also made my dad suited to become the first demon spawn, allowing him to merge his spirit with a human soul and fight in the first war against Daelissa.

Baal hadn't wanted the Seraphim to take over Eden, and it seemed that after Daelissa had made a second try at the title, the demon overlord was taking steps to make sure it didn't happen again.

"Baal wants to take over Seraphina so Kaelissa can't continue in Daelissa's footsteps," I said. "Demons hold a lot of power in Eden, thanks to humans. If the Seraphim ever took over, Baal would lose influence."

"Demons feed on human souls," David said. "If that source was taken away, then Haedaemos might wither away."

Thomas nodded. "Baal wants to make sure another invasion doesn't happen by putting an agent on the throne in Seraphina. Let's say we let him do that. What's the downside?"

"Ooh, you don't even want to go there," David said. "If demons have unfettered access to Seraphim souls, they'll slowly but surely kill everything here."

"It's the magical principle of unnatural presence," Adam said. "A powerful demon incarnate in the physical world will kill plants and sicken animals just by being near them. During the Demonicus Incident, there were several recorded instances of it, especially when Karak and the other demon lords manifested."

"It's also why you can be sure Baal ain't walking around Seraphina right now," Shelton added. "If he was here, we would've seen dead grass and plants back in Kohvalla."

Elyssa frowned. "If that's the case, why don't we see similar signs around Issana and Bliss?"

"They aren't demon spirits manifested in physical form," Adam said. "They're demon flesh with Seraphim souls and golem sparks."

I posed another question. "If Baal were here in physical form, would he also sicken the Seraphim he was near?"

"Theoretically, yes," Adam said, "but I can't say for sure."

"Keep in mind we're talking about powerful demons," David said. "Lower level demons don't have a powerful enough demonic aura to affect their surroundings."

Leesha, one of the Mzodi soldiers, appeared in the doorway, an urgent look in her eyes. She came into the room and whispered something in Illaena's ear. The captain frowned and looked at my father. "One of the prisoners we took is asking to speak to David."

"Prisoners?" I said. "When did we take prisoners?"

"The three we took in Kohvalla," Illaena said. "Zero, Two, and Thirteen have been kept apart from the others since they seem to have special roles."

"How do they even know my father?" I asked.

Illaena shrugged. "The one called Zero says he must speak with David."

David raised an eyebrow and shook his head. "Okay, that's strange. Can you bring him in here?"

Illaena nodded and motioned to Leesha. "Bring him under heavy guard."

David turned to me. "Who's Zero?"

"One of the Daskar who was left behind to seal the Northern Pass," I said. "He's a dolem, but he wasn't made in Nightliss's image."

"Interesting." David pursed his lips. "I wonder how he knows my name."

Alysea folded her arms. "That's a very good question."

Moments later, Zero appeared, walking calmly before two Mzodi soldiers. Something about him looked different than the last time I'd seen him. His eyes met mine and lingered, not hint of uncertainty in his gaze. He exuded something more than confidence—something bordering on arrogance.

Zero looked at David and his lips spread into a smug smile. "So, Davashmaklah, you have become comfortable in your mortal bonds."

David staggered back a foot. "How did you know that name?"

Zero shook his head as if disappointed. "Always the slow one. At least you did not disappoint me too much after your incarnation."

"Oh god." Adam's eyes went wide. "We drew his attention by talking about him so much."

"Whose attention?" Shelton looked Zero up and down. "Does he have super-duper hearing?"

"Adam's right." David straightened and stared Zero in the eyes. "Well, what an unpleasant surprise, Father. Hardly a word from you in thousands of years, and now you decide to pay me a visit?"

The realization seemed to hit most of us in the room like a surprise backhand. Shelton made the sign of the cross again. Elyssa bared her teeth and jumped back. Even Thomas took a step back. Zero wasn't Zero right now. He was under the control of the grand overlord of Haedaemos.

David took a step closer to Baal. "What brings you to town? It's not even Christmas yet."

Shelton put two fingers on his neck as if to check his pulse. "Is his presence going to make us sick?"

Baal laughed. "Only a small part of my presence is here, mortal. This puny body could not contain me, in any case." He held out his hands and flexed them. "I am merely using this vessel as a conduit."

"Nothing like a family reunion," David said. "Did you bring your world-famous deviled eggs for the potluck?"

Baal's borrowed eyes narrowed. "Enough of your insubordination, Davashmaklah. I am here to warn you off your course of action, lest you doom all the realms."

268

"Ooh, sounds scary." David quirked his lips and leaned against the table. "All right, Daddy, let's hear your pitch."

Baal's fists clenched and his eyes lit with red flames.

David put his hands up protectively. "Please don't hit me, Daddy!"

Alysea put a hand on David's shoulder. "David, stop provoking him."

Baal relaxed his hands. "Seraphina must be united. My familiars already have things well in hand and your interference would only throw the process into disarray."

"We can't let you control Seraphina," I said. "We would doom this realm to destruction."

"If I do not control Seraphina, then all the realms will be doomed," Baal said. "An even greater threat looms on the horizon." His gaze lingered on me for a moment. "You have served your purpose, Justin, but you have also set in motion the next crisis."

"Leave my son out of this." David turned to me. "Don't listen to him, son. He's twisting the facts to suit his own goals."

"What facts?" I said. "How did I set another crisis in motion?"

"Surely, the boy deserves the truth, Davashmaklah." Baal flashed his teeth at me in a predatory smile. "You released the Apocryphan, Xanomiel, from the Abyss."

A chill of dread worked its way up from my toes, across my spine, and raised the hairs on the back of my neck. I had been told that decision would come back to bite me in the ass. "Let me guess—he plans to destroy the world."

"In a way, yes, but also, no." Baal waved his arm as if to encompass the world beyond the confines of the room. "He plans to remake the world as it was, to unite the realms under his rule and to punish those who banished him to the Abyss."

"Talk about an administrative nightmare," Shelton said. "How is your taking control of Seraphina supposed to stop that?"

"I will unite the realms first," Baal replied. "Together, we will drive the lone Apocryphan back into the Abyss where he belongs."

"Is not your goal the same as the Apocryphan's?" Cinder asked. "Would you relinquish power once the goal is achieved?"

Baal tilted his head slightly and stared at Cinder as if trying to decide whether he was annoyed or not by such a good question. "I can assure you, golem, that my rule is far preferable to that of the Apocryphan."

I cleared my throat. "Um, I'd say that rule by neither of you is far preferable." I held up a finger. "However, we could work with you to accomplish peace and independence."

Baal's eyes narrowed. "Unacceptable. If you continue your reckless course, you will alert Kaelissa, making it impossible to remove her from power quickly. You will spark a war, weaken this realm, and make it ripe for the plucking."

"Not if you help us." I held out my hand toward him. "Join us and we can stop this madness. We'll unite Seraphina and prepare it to fight Xanomiel."

Baal looked at my hand as if I were offering him a moldy doughnut at a weight-loss convention. "Why would I subvert my will to yours? I have the superior force. I have the superior plan. All you must do is get out of the way." He motioned in a general direction. "I'm certain you can find a nice island to relax on."

"The balance of power would tip precariously should we do that." Thomas's icy gaze didn't waver under the heat of Baal's glare. "Our vision is for the realms to govern themselves responsibly. No more wars of conquest. No more interference. We want peace."

"Peace." Baal spit on the floor. "Xanomiel will shatter your peace and kill millions as he remakes the realms. He may be weakened from his time in the Abyss, but his power is greater than you can imagine. Only I possess the strength to oppose him."

That was the second time he'd used a specific word to describe Xanomiel's plans and it caught my attention. "What do you mean by remaking the realms?"

Mirthless laughter boomed from Baal's throat. "Not only did you release him from his prison, but you also found the key to his master plan." Baal swung an accusing finger my way. "Xanomiel now knows of Atlantis, boy."

Elyssa scratched her head. "What does Atlantis have to do with anything?"

"It is a fragment of the original Earth before it was sundered." Baal held his cupped hands apart and pushed them together. "Xanomiel plans to use it as a focus to combine the realms back into one."

"Holy farting fairies," Shelton hissed. "Is that even possible?"

"That would be a horrible idea," Adam said. "A physical recombination of the realms would devastate cities and landscapes. Countless lives would be lost."

"That is correct." Baal offered another condescending smile. "The mortals would stand to lose the most. Supernatural breeds would prevail."

The thought of compressing the realms back into one dimension was overwhelming. I didn't understand the mechanics of how the world was split into separate realms in the first place, and certainly couldn't fathom reversing the process. All I needed to know was that the casualties in Eden would be staggering.

"There's one important fact you left out," David said, seemingly unperturbed by the diabolical plan. "Haedaemos didn't exist before the Sundering." He jabbed a finger at Baal. "You didn't exist."

"I existed," Baal said. "Just not in my current state. I can assure you that I would continue to exist even after the recombination of the realms."

"Maybe you should just get over yourself," David shot back. "Even if you survived, you'd be Xanomiel's little bitch, wouldn't you? I'll bet life everlasting as a servant would be worse than death as far as you're concerned."

Baal's left eye twitched. "I will give you one last chance to accept my offer. Get out of my way or suffer the consequences."

Adam shook his head. "If you take over this realm, the consequences will be bad enough already. Seraphina will wilt and die."

"It will be transformed," Baal said. "The physical cannot survive. It will become an extension of the spirit realm."

Shelton huffed. "Damned if we do, damned if we don't." He lifted his hat and gave his noggin a good scratch. "The way I see it we can't let either of you yahoos take control or we're all screwed."

"I concur," Thomas said. "Seraphina would be a stepping stone to extend your dominion over other realms. Eden would suffer as greatly under your rule as it would if Xanomiel's plan comes to fruition."

"Damn it all to hell." Shelton slapped his hat back on. "And I thought this mission was hard enough already."

David smiled smugly at Baal. "Well, the nays have it, infernal father of mine. I would ask you to reconsider, but I know that nothing penetrates your god complex."

Baal tensed like a tiger ready to pounce. Shelton and Adam flicked out their staffs. Alysea and I held out our hands, channeled energy crackling in our palms. Metal sang and swords appeared in the hands of Elyssa and her family.

"Please wait." Cinder walked around the table and held his hands out, as if to stop the situation from exploding into violence. "Is there no room for compromise?" He looked from Baal to my father. "Surely by working together we can avert destruction."

"Baal doesn't compromise," David said. "It's his way or the highway."

Baal pursed his lips and considered Cinder for a moment. "I am ancient and powerful beyond your comprehension, golem. Only I can stop Xanomiel."

"You have thousands of years of knowledge and wisdom," Cinder said in his simple, logical manner. "Is there not a way to accomplish your goal without conquering the realms yourself?"

"Of course there is." David pounded his hand on the table. "But that's not what he wants. It doesn't matter how ancient or wise the old man is, he's still every bit as weak and covetous as the rest of us. He wants power, plain and simple."

Baal worked his jaw back and forth, eyes burning as he took in the words of his son. For an uncomfortable moment, he said nothing. For a moment, I hoped he was reconsidering his plan. His next words shattered that hope.

"The blind will not see and the deaf will not hear." Baal backed away a step. "So is the price heavy on your heads." He slumped to the floor, like a puppet with cut strings.

The body groaned and eyes fluttered open. "Where am I?" Baal had left the building and Zero was apparently back in control of his body.

And we were officially enemies with the grand overlord of Hell.

Chapter 26

"Well slap me silly and call me Roberta," Shelton said with his usual aplomb. "And just when I thought my day couldn't get any more interesting, now we get to fight an ancient god and the king of Haedaemos."

"Not to mention supplant Kaelissa as the ruler of the Brightling Empire," Adam added helpfully. "This is quite a checklist we've got going."

Thomas stared at Zero. "I need to know how Baal possessed that body and if he can do it to any of the dolems."

"I can answer that question." David turned his gaze on Zero. His eyes went unfocused and I realized he was slipping into demon sight, viewing the dolem's aura.

Auras flickered on around everyone in the room, varying shades of incandescent glows, as I activated my demon sight. Elyssa's sparkling halo beckoned to me with alluring sensuality. Illaena and Alysea's auras glowed brilliant white, a side-effect of their Brightling affinities. Shelton and the other humans burned dimmer by comparison. My father's aura was a strong blue, throwing off sparks of sapphire every now and then. Cinder was the only one with no glow around him since he had no soul.

Zero, on the other hand, looked quite different. His aura was dim, yellow, and flickered fitfully like a candle in a breeze. The edges blurred as if my eyes couldn't quite focus on them, interlaced with a sullen red tinge.

I saw tendrils of my father's essence reaching out and latching onto Zero's halo. David stared long and hard at the dolem for a moment then withdrew his tendrils and blinked his eyes.

I turned off demon sight. "What did you see?"

David grimaced. "Baal personally made Zero and left a piece of himself inside the soul globe. That's how he was able to take control of the body."

"Does that mean Issana and Bliss can't be controlled by him?" Thomas asked.

"So long as he didn't do the same thing to them." David shook his head slowly. "I'll just have to check them out individually."

"Please do." Thomas leaned his hands on the table. "Could he control an entire army of Zeros?"

Shelton whistled. "I sure hope the answer is no."

David shrugged. "I have no idea."

Adam groaned. "Not what we wanted to hear."

"I want you to show me how to scan the others," I told David. "I think it'd be handy having a helper."

David clapped me on the shoulder. "You got it."

Thomas nodded at the Mzodi soldiers. "Please put Zero back in holding."

276

Zero blinked rapidly, clearly in a post-possession stupor, and offered no resistance as the soldiers left with the prisoner.

"Hoo Nellie." Shelton clapped his hands and rubbed them together. "Things just got a hell of a lot more complicated. Does this change our game plan?"

Thomas shook his head. "No, but I think the organizational chart just added another layer." He flicked back to the holographic whiteboard with the names on it and added Baal's at the top before connecting it to Aerianas and Victus.

Elyssa shook her head. "Hang on a second." She mulled over the line between Baal and Victus then erased it. "Ontidam and his followers were blindly loyal to Victus. They never mentioned Baal."

"You think Aerianas made her own deal with Baal?" Adam asked.

"I think Aerianas thought Victus left her here to rot and decided to take things into her own hands," Elyssa said. "Either by accident or intentionally, she contacted Baal and is now doing his bidding."

"You may be onto something," Thomas said. "Very perceptive."

A pleased smile spread across Elyssa's face. She quickly covered it up and pretended to be unaffected by his praise, despite the blush in her cheeks. "Thank you, sir."

Michael released an uncharacteristic snort. "Good work, Ninjette."

Shelton cleared his throat. "Just to be clear—we've got Baal's Darkling army led by Aerianas on our ass, and dolem agents loyal to Victus or Aerianas ahead of us?"

"No problem." Adam snapped his fingers. "Easy, peasy, lemon squeezy."

"More like difficult, difficult, lemon difficult," I muttered.

"We need multiple options for taking the throne," Thomas said. "Right now, we only have the option of replacing Kaelissa with a dolem, and that relies entirely on us securing part of Kaelissa's soul and using it to create a clone of her."

"Can we do that without kidnapping her?" Shelton said.

"Yes, there's a way," Alysea said, "but it requires close proximity and a distraction."

I thought back to what Uro had asked me and decided now was a good time to find out the answer. "What about the Challenge of Ascension?"

Alysea raised both eyebrows. "I have not heard that term bandied about for eons."

David chuckled. "Yeah, I remember things didn't go so well for Gjoernuss when he challenged Daelissa back in the day."

Shelton grunted. "Who the hell is Gjoernuss?"

Alysea winced. "He challenged Daelissa for the throne during the First Seraphim War." She shook her head as if clearing it of an unpleasant thought. "He invoked the ancient Challenge of Ascension whereby any Seraphim could challenge a leader for their position."

"Hang on." I raised my hand. "What about when the Brightling Empire was run by the Trivectus? Could you challenge them as well?"

"Yes, you could challenge any of the three-member council," Alysea said. "In fact, Daelissa challenged each member and killed them all to reestablish the monarchy." She seemed to withdraw into herself, perhaps remembering something long forgotten, and then blinked back to the present. "By using the Challenge of Ascension rather than a coup, Daelissa was able to claim legitimate rule."

Shelton snorted. "Aw, how sweet. Daelissa played by the rules."

"Not entirely," Alysea said. "Daelissa demanded that each member of the Trivectus personally fight her or she would kill their families."

Bella gasped. "Barbaric!"

"Now that sounds more like Daelissa." I shuddered at the thought of what she'd done to those people. "What are the rules of the challenge?"

"I don't know specifics." Alysea tapped a finger on her lip. "A challenger must present themselves and their entourage before the ruler and issue the challenge. The ruler must then select a hero to fight for them, or they can fight for themselves."

"What if they decline the challenge?" Adam asked.

"Once issued, it cannot be declined by either side," Alysea said.

"In other words, any old peasant could run up to the palace and challenge the leader to a duel?" Shelton snorted. "That's ridiculous."

"There were no Seraphim peasants back in those days." Alysea raised her nose a fraction. "Seraphim society is much different than the old feudal ways of man. Until I led Daelissa to Eden and let her drink the souls of mortals, even she would never have considered overthrowing the Trivectus." She shook her head sadly. "If I had never opened the Alabaster Arch, none of this would have happened."

279

"No use crying over spilt angel tears," Shelton said.

Thomas rapped his knuckles on the table. "Do you remember anything else about the rules?"

Alysea squeezed her eyes shut a moment. "The challenged ruler may set the rules of the match. It could be a challenge of wits, skills, or a fight, the outcome determined by yielding or death."

"A challenge of wits to the death?" I pshawed." How does that work?"

Elyssa nudged me. "I'm sure it involves iocane powder, a Sicilian, and wine."

I laughed. "Guess I'd better build up a tolerance for iocane then."

"Here's the real question," Michael said. "Would Kaelissa abide by the challenge, or just outright kill the challenger?"

All eyes turned to Alysea. She shrugged. "Arturo is fiercely loyal but also places great value on honor. If Justin could make it to Kaelissa and publicly declare the challenge without dying first, then Arturo would probably demand Kaelissa abide by the rules."

"That's a very big 'if'," Thomas said. "I think the dolem option is safer. Besides, even if Justin were to prevail in the challenge, he's not pure Seraphim."

"You don't think they'd accept me as their mighty overlord?" I tilted my nose at an imperious angle.

Elyssa snorted.

"Considering how Darklings have been treated for thousands of years, we can't be sure." Thomas leaned his fists on the table. "Anything else we should consider?"

"What if we nabbed Arturo and cloned him instead?" Adam said. "Once we have him, we could order his dolem to assassinate Kaelissa and take the throne."

"Maybe I should clarify a few things," David said. "First of all, while I've summoned plenty of demons, I've never made a dolem. It could take us weeks or longer just to get the process working."

"True," Adam agreed. "Shelton and I can make the spark, but we don't know how to infuse the soul fragment inside it."

"I believe I can help with that," Cinder said. "I studied the foundry extensively and have formulated several working theories about how to incorporate the soul fragment and the soul globe into the demon flesh."

"The gem sorters can recreate the apparatus used to make the soul globe." Illaena stepped closer to the table. "Under any other circumstances, I would never agree to such an abhorrent plan, but the alternative is even worse. Let me know what you need, and I will do my best to get it for you."

I hesitated before asking the next question. "I assume a bloodstone option is off the table?"

"At this point, I would allow it." Illaena held up her hands helplessly. "But we rid ourselves of all the bloodstones, and they are so rare, we could fish a dozen vortexes and never find another."

"Look, there ain't no pretty way to accomplish what we gotta do," Shelton said. "But you have to admit, using a dolem is a lot better than going back to war."

There were plenty of nods and murmurs of assent around the table.

"Here's the next hard question," David said. "I need to practice making these things. That means I need soul essence. That means I have to copy someone and create a living being."

Elyssa grimaced. "Does that mean we're gonna have a bunch of clones running around?"

"I guess it wouldn't be ethical to make a test subject and kill it," Adam said.

"Absolutely not." Illaena bared her teeth. "That would be monstrous."

Adam held up his hands in surrender. "Point taken."

"Look, let's get the basics working first," Shelton said. "We'll start by encasing a simple golem spark in demon flesh."

"It won't maintain corporeal form long without a soul," Adam said, "but it also won't be alive in any sense of the word."

"It will not be self-conscious," Cinder said. "It will not know it is alive."

"Yeah, um, exactly." Shelton grinned sheepishly. "No offense, man."

Cinder flashed a plastic smile. "None taken."

"Then let's get started," Thomas said. "While you work on creating the dolem, the rest of us will work on a plan for replacing Kaelissa."

"I was the best bounty hunter in the Overworld." Shelton tilted his hat back at a forty-five-degree angle. "If we can find out where Kaelissa is, I can come up with a plan to nab and replace her."

Bella gripped his arm. "This isn't the same as bounty hunting. Kaelissa will be surrounded by guards everywhere she goes."

"That don't change nothing," Shelton said. "Believe you me, everyone has a schedule they follow, and every schedule has a weakness." He nodded toward me. "Remember when we hijacked your mom right out from under the noses of Maulin Kassus and his bunch?"

I grinned. "It was epic."

"As I recall, everything went to hell in a handbasket," Elyssa said. "We ended up snatching the trailer off that semi-truck in rush hour traffic. The Custodians were pissed about all the cleanup they had to do."

Shelton held up his hands. "There wasn't anything wrong with the plan. It was the execution we botched."

"Well, a plan is only as good as its execution," Elyssa said.

Shelton chuckled. "That's what we got Templars for." He lifted his hat and ran a hand through his hair. "I may not have what it takes to blow Seraphim out of the sky, but I can come up with a plan to kidnap one for sure."

"We'll consider any plan you have to offer," Thomas said. "For now, we continue onward to Cabala and find out Kaelissa's current whereabouts."

Shelton and Adam huddled with Cinder, discussing how to create a test lab for dolem creation while Elyssa joined her father and brother to discuss strategies for capturing Kaelissa. David tapped my arm and led me into the hallway. "Want to help me scan the other dolems for Baal?"

"Sure." I headed down the organic curves of the corridor toward the ramps leading below. "What exactly am I looking for?"

"It's not too difficult." David tapped his temple. "If I'm right, the auras of dolems without Baal's influence won't have a red tinge around them."

"I noticed you linked with Zero's aura. What was that about?"

"Let's just say that if a dolem carries a soul shard from Baal, you'll know right away." David turned down the rampway. "It's like touching a live wire and getting shocked."

We reached the prisoner quarters and went inside. Diamond fiber hobbled the prisoners' hands and legs together, making it nearly impossible for them to move around, and they were blindfolded as an extra measure.

"Who's there?" Zero called out. "What did you do to me?"

"Just a routine checkup," David said. "I'm here to make sure your prostate is nice and healthy. Do you have any latex allergies?"

"My what?" Zero struggled on the floor helplessly.

David snickered. "Maybe I should've given him a prostate exam while Baal was still in control. I'll be the old man would've loved that."

"Bend over, Baal." I chuckled. "He would've been pissed."

"Believe it or not, he's not always so serious." David stepped closer to Zero's struggling form. "He used to combat boredom by messing with the mortals—possessing pigs and making them talk. Stuff like that."

"That could be fun." I flicked into incubus vision and got down to business. "So, what do I do?"

David motioned at Zero and then at the other Nightliss-based dolems. "Notice the tinges around the other halos are blue?"

I looked at the rim of red around Zero's aura and compared it to the others. Sure enough, their halos glowed dim yellow with sparks of blue at the edges. "So if it's red, that means Baal is in the house?"

"Or it could mean a ruby demon spirit formed the flesh." David extended a wisp of his aura toward Zero. "Tap in and let me know what you feel."

I followed his lead and latched a tendril onto Zero. A surge of electricity jolted down my spine and everything went black. The sound of my beating heart echoed in a void. Dim red light glowed, revealing a chamber. A man stood across a small room from me. He turned slowly and smiled. Eyes glowed a sullen red in a face that rippled like a reflection in water.

"Who are you?" I gasped.

"Haven't you guessed?" His smooth, deep voice seemed to coil around me like a silken serpent. "Soon, you will know me, grandson."

The world rushed away from me, leaving me in pitch black. I gasped and blinked back into the real world. "What in the hell was that?"

"Quite a shock, right?" David said.

"No, I mean was that Baal I saw in that room?"

His jaw dropped open. "You saw something?"

285

"Yeah." I blinked my eyes and shook my head. "I was in another place. It was black, then it turned into a room with a man." I gave him the details.

"Yep, classic Baal." David sighed. "Sounds like he's got plans for you, son."

I gulped. "I don't think I want to be involved with him."

He slapped me on the back. "Wise man."

I left the prisoner quarters and the guards sealed the doorway behind us. The afterimage of Baal was seared in my memory. I had a feeling it wouldn't be the last visit from dear old Grandad.

Chapter 27

The Voltis Maelstrom came into view the next day. Black clouds rose from steaming waters. Whirling waterspouts danced the perimeter of the dark singularity deep in the Castigean Ocean. We'd ventured into the heart of the massive aether storm and found the last remnant of old Earth before the Sundering—Atlantis.

Could it possibly be used to recombine the realms? If so, it was probably the only safe place to be while the rest of the dimensions suffered massive upheaval and casualties. It seemed uniting Seraphina was more important now than ever if we were to combat the Apocryphan I'd unleashed on the realms.

Shelton and Bella stood at the bow, arms wrapped around each other in an uncharacteristic show of public affection—at least from Shelton. Elyssa and her family were busy belowdecks, still coming up with their master plan for handling Kaelissa.

Electricity arced from the fringes of the maelstrom, striking the water and igniting clouds of nearby aether. Though Voltis looked like one giant hurricane, it was actually an interdimensional disturbance caused by the borders of old Earth against the broken realms. Adam and Shelton suspected it was one big portal that led to all the realms, but the only one we could single out was the passage to and from Seraphina.

A sonic boom like a cannon shot thundered in the distance. The air shimmered and tore apart. An orange sun hung in a pink sky above red waters. Hundreds of birds danced above the alien ocean, a massive flock in perfect coordination.

"What the hell?" Shelton said.

The interdimensional rift sealed and once again, Voltis was the only thing in sight.

I joined Shelton at the bow. "Holy crap, that was huge. Another Draxadis rift?"

"It sure as hell wasn't Kansas," he said.

"Yes, it must have been dragon realm." Illaena stood a few feet away, teeth bared in a grimace. "I have never seen such a large tear."

I'd hoped that destroying Cephus's crimson arch and ending his experiments had stopped more rifts from forming. Obviously, the tears in the dimensional fabric were just growing larger.

"Why do the rips always open to Draxadis?" Shelton shouted over the howl of wind as the ship flew past a waterspout on the starboard bow.

"It is thought that Seraphina is closest to Draxadis in the dimensional plane," Illaena said. She turned to Tahlee and shouted something. The first mate roared a command to the aviators and the ship changed course to give wide berth to a trio of waterspouts forming dead ahead.

In between course changes, Illaena told us what little she knew of the Brightling economy and how to blend in. "They use gems as currency to trade with us, but I have heard there are other ways to pay for things."

"Like what?" I asked. "Paper money?"

She frowned. "Paper money?" Illaena shook her head. "Mzodi do not usually venture into cities, especially those with a Darkling affinity. I will give you the sort of gems the Brightlings find valuable and you should be fine."

"Great, I get an allowance," I muttered on my way belowdecks to speak with Alysea. I hoped she had a few helpful tips for me.

My father was teaching a group of gem sorters how to play poker in the main hold. He'd already collected a sizeable pile of gems on the table in front of him, but the Mzodi seemed entranced with the game. Alysea sat in a chair behind him, reading a ragged romance novel she'd brought with her from Eden.

"Hustling the locals?" I shook my head disapprovingly. "Must not be much of a challenge."

"All for fun," David said, folding his cards and standing up to clap me on the back. "Are we there yet?"

"More than halfway to Cabala."

Alysea closed her book. "Was Illaena able to give you more tips for blending in?"

I waggled a hand in a so-so manner. "Sort of. I hoped you might have more insight."

"Cabala was nothing more than a settlement when I was growing up in Zbura." Alysea ran a finger down the spine of her book. "The entire Brightling culture has probably changed drastically since then."

"What do angels do for work?" I asked. "How do you pay for things?"

She offered a wistful smile. "In my youth, Brightlings spent their time exploring and discovering. There was no need for currency or jobs in the mortal sense. Judging from what you told us about Guinesea, it sounds as if all that has changed."

"In other words, you're going in blind." David slapped me on the back and grinned. "Good luck."

I groaned. "Heaven help us all."

For lack of anything better to do, I joined David for a few hands of poker. Alysea pulled up a chair to make it a family affair and proved to be a better bluffer than I thought. She beat David twice while the rest of us nearly lost our shirts. It wasn't until I convinced them to switch to Go Fish that I actually won a game.

The *Falcheen* wove its way between aether storms, geysers of superheated water, and other natural phenomenon for the latter part of the day until the western coast of Azoris came into view. Illaena used a dense bank of fog to keep the ship hidden until we landed in a small cove.

Elyssa and Thomas joined me on deck a few moments later along with Adam and Cinder.

"What's the plan?" I asked.

"Cabala is a few miles south of us," Elyssa said. "We need to get to town and find out if Kaelissa is around."

Shelton grunted. "Try to be a little more discreet this time."

Adam held out his hand. "Justin, let me see your arcphone."

I handed him Nookli. "What's up?"

He bumped his phone against mine. "I'm transferring the gem hacking program Shelton and I wrote just in case you need to get inside any locked doors."

"How long does it take to hack locks?" Elyssa asked.

"Ten minutes, minimum." Adam shrugged apologetically. "We optimized it the best we could, but gem enchantments are complex pieces of work."

Bella gave us each a hug. "Be careful."

I flashed a grin. "You know I will. Elyssa, on the other hand…"

Shelton snorted. "Yeah, she's never careful."

Elyssa rolled her eyes. "I'll try to restrain myself this time."

Elyssa and I threw back on the same clothes we'd worn in Guinesea and hiked up a path to the top of the cliffs around the cove. We found a skyway access node a few hundred yards to the east. I charged the gem on the white pylon with Brilliance and a cloudlet carried us up to the cloudy roadway high in the sky.

Cabala glittered like a pile of diamonds in the distance. Crystal domes and minarets towered above the scrubby hills and cliffs. The city looked at least four times larger than Novus, perched on the edge of a cliff overlooking the Castigean Ocean with a sea wall protecting it from the aether storms Illaena told me frequented the area.

A crystal bridge spanned a wide river where it rushed over the cliffs and into spectacular waterfalls that crashed into the ocean far below.

"It's beautiful," Elyssa said. Her hand tightened around mine. "It looks like something out of a fairy tale."

I grunted. "Too bad it's ruled by an evil queen."

Elyssa jabbed a finger forward. "Look there!"

A sleek black vessel perched on a platform near the waterfall, its prow curving down like the sharp beak of a raven, narrow wings jutting from the sides. It was the *Ptarn*, the Mzodi ship Arturo and Kaelissa had escaped on after the battle in Atlantis. Beyond it appeared to be an unfinished copy of the sky ship.

"Looks like the Mzodi crews are being forced to work." I held a hand over my eyes and tried to zoom my vision, but there were too many people in the shipyard to discern Mzodi from Brightling.

"If the *Ptarn* is still here, that probably means Kaelissa is in town." Elyssa looked down at the landscape blurring past below. "She could have taken a skyway, but why would you do that if you have a flying ship that can get you across the country twice as fast?"

As we drew closer, details I'd missed earlier came into focus. Most of the buildings facing the sea were pockmarked and blackened. Parts of the cliff and seawall had crumbled into the ocean, carrying buildings with it. Flights of archangels flew sentry around the edges of the city, and hundreds of Seraphim crawled along the damaged buildings repairing them.

A horn sounded in the distance. Blazing wings streaked skyward as more Seraphim took flight and glided out over the ocean. A breath caught in my throat when I caught sight of the reason for the alarm. About half a mile out to sea a glowing rift tore open the sky, and a dark armada of winged creatures burst through it and came toward the city.

The two forces crashed together only a few hundred yards off the coast. Brilliance met scales and flame. Bodies fell from the sky, spiraling a trail of smoke until they splashed into the waters. The dragons looked small, but there were hundreds of them.

292

One group of archangels in chromatic blue armor dove from above, slicing through a swath of the scaled creatures on their way down. I knew from the color of the armor that their leader was none other than Primarion Arturo himself. After a vicious bout of reptilian carnage, the battle ended and the archangels retreated into the city.

"Looks like the dragon incursions are even worse here than near Voltis," Elyssa said. "This confirms our suspicions that the troop concentration wasn't simply to invade Atlantis."

"That rift was huge," I said. "The ones we saw during our trip to Voltis were tiny—maybe big enough for one or two dragons at most."

"That really makes me wonder something." Elyssa bit her lower lip. "What if the portals to Draxadis were intentional?"

"Whoa, you think Cephus might have reached out to the dragons as allies?" I said.

Elyssa stared at the battle-blackened sea wall. "At this point, it's hard to say who's done what. Fact: Cephus built a crimson portal that he claimed could open a portal to any dimension. Fact: We have no idea how he did it or who helped him. For all we know, Baal or Victus had a hand in it."

"I wouldn't put it past Baal," I said. "I think he's powerful enough to reach any realm from Haedaemos, with a little help. For all we know, he started working with Cephus even before the Alabaster Arch was operational again. Maybe he coordinated with Victus." I threw up my hands in surrender. "There are too many *ifs* and not enough answers. The only question I can think of is why?"

"If Baal controls Aerianas, Kohval, and the Darkling legions, then the *why* is pretty obvious." Elyssa waved a hand toward the city. "What better way to draw Brightling troops to one location in order to leave the rest of the nation lightly defended?"

293

I smacked my forehead. "You're right! Aerianas would never be able to march her legions up here if the Brightlings still manned their posts. Hell, she'd have a time just getting past Guinesea, even with two legions versus the one."

"Maybe, just maybe," Elyssa said, "Kaelissa went to Atlantis with bloodstones so she could recruit the Sirens to help her against the dragons. Once she secured the dragons, she could have marched on Pjurna with impunity."

"You may be right." I looked east. "For all we know, Aerianas is on her way to take Zbura right now. Once she's entrenched there, it'll be impossible to root her out without major casualties."

"We've got to clone Kaelissa pronto," Elyssa said. "I hoped we'd have a few weeks for a mission of this magnitude, but we have even less time than I thought."

My stomach twisted at the thought of a prolonged war for Zbura. With the dragons occupying the Brightling legions in Cabala, Aerianas could have her way with the other Brightling cities.

The skyway reached the city and a cloudlet detached, drifting down into a wide plaza where dozens of Seraphim rushed around as if they all had somewhere to be five minutes ago. Inquiring minds wanted to know a lot, but our encounters in Novus had taught me a valuable lesson. If we started asking questions, people would quickly realize that we weren't from here and ask questions of their own.

On the upside, nobody gave a second glance at the two newcomers wandering through town.

I scanned the heavens and spotted the archangels in the chromatic blue of Arturo's personal squad. Their helmets obscured their faces, making it impossible to determine if Arturo was among them, but I figured they were heading back to base and that was probably where Kaelissa was right this minute.

I took Elyssa's hand and pulled her along. "This way."

We rushed down the streets, keeping the archangels in sight until they dipped down toward tall walls surrounding an imposing tower with several domed buildings around it. Crystalline obelisks guarded the four corners of the compound and the air rippled as the archangels glided over the wall.

Must be a shield.

Soldiers in crystal armor patrolled the streets circling the walls, and pedestrians gave the perimeter a wide berth. A seraph guiding a platform loaded with food was questioned and searched when he approached the gates to the compound. The gate flickered away and two Seraphim in gray livery took the platform inside.

I stopped a safe distance away and stayed in the shadow of a mini-mansion shaped like a lighthouse. "I'd be willing to bet my eyetooth that Kaelissa is in there."

"So much for letting her guard down." Elyssa sighed and quirked her lips but her eyes never stopped scanning the environs. "Looks like this is going to boil down to good old-fashioned detective work."

I raised an eyebrow. "How so?"

"We'll need to case the place. Find out if she ever leaves." Elyssa looked at the odd assortment of mini-mansions rising along the circular street. "I wonder if we can rent some space to set up shop."

The crystal road encircled the walled compound, providing a wide border that couldn't easily be monitored from just one side. Some of the nearby buildings rose high enough to give a view over the walls, but none were so tall as to give a bird's eye view. Even if one of them suited our needs, there was another problem.

"I don't think they post roommate wanted ads in these parts." I stepped in front of the lighthouse-shaped mansion. "We need someone familiar with the lay of the land."

A group of soldiers hurried our way. Their crystal armor triggered chilling memories of our encounter with the first army Daelissa brought into Eden with her. We'd suffered terrible losses to them before finally discovering how to overload their magic-absorbing armor. In the end, they'd simply been the city guard from Zbura, not even the proper army.

A pair of soldiers broke formation and approached us. "No civilians are allowed near the citadel, by order of the empress," one said. "Leave immediately or be arrested."

"Apologies," Elyssa said. "We did not realize this was part of the forbidden zone."

"It extends to this road and the domiciles around it," the soldier said. "The buildings will remain off limits until the empress leaves for Zbura."

"I hope Her Highness is well," Elyssa said. "When will she depart?"

The soldier's eyes narrowed. "Leave now."

I took Elyssa's hand and backed away, bowing. "Of course, good soldier. We'll be on our way." We walked down the narrow street between the lighthouse and a house shaped like an origami swan and emerged in a plaza filled with the thrum and bustle of Brightlings going about their daily business. A crowd gathered around a chorus of singing Seraphim in one corner. Others sat around a bubbling fountain sipping amber liquid from crystal goblets and conversing like a bunch of yuppie mall rats.

"I should have realized something was wrong when I didn't see anyone else near the citadel," Elyssa said. She stopped and looked at the forbidden residences. "On a positive note, I think that means we don't have to worry about inhabitants. The lighthouse looks like the tallest one. Maybe we can squat there."

I glanced at the house in question. "I wonder if the doors are locked." I led her to a table near the fountain and sat down so we could look around without appearing conspicuous.

A seraph bearing a decanter of amber liquid approached two females at a table behind us. "More nectar?"

"Yes, please." One of the seras splayed her hands and the seraph spread his fingers in return. Ghostly white essence drifted from her fingers and into his. A white gem on a gold band around his wrist glowed softly. The sera lowered her hand and the waiter filled the goblets.

Elyssa's eyes tightened as she scanned the other people around us. "Is that a method of payment?" she asked in a hushed voice.

"Most of the patrons have the gold band," I noted. "Very few don't."

"Was that soul essence?" Elyssa asked.

I watched the waiter return into a nearby shop where he pressed his hand against a large glowing globe behind the counter. The light in the gem on his band winked out as the energy shifted into the larger vessel. "If it is, it's the creepiest monetary system ever."

"Agreed." Elyssa shuddered. "It looks like something demons, not angels, would do."

"I don't see anyone using gems." I observed the crowd, watching how others paid waiters, but most did it the same way the females had

297

paid for their nectar. A sera in a blue fur coat was the only exception to the rule, leading me to wonder if gems were for the wealthy.

The same waiter from earlier approached our table. "Would you like a drink?"

I managed a smile. "Not right now, thanks."

He frowned. "This area is for patrons only. You'll have to leave if you don't order food or drink."

I thought about getting up and leaving, but at the same time, this was a brand new experience for us. *Paying for two drinks won't hurt.* "Fine. We'll have two glasses."

"How would you like to pay?"

Rather than whip out the gems right away, I decided now was a good opportunity to find out a little more about Brightling economics. "What methods do you take?"

"The usual, good seraph—essence, gems, or services." He raised an eyebrow. "Which do you prefer?"

I reached into the pouch on my waist and took out a couple of the aetherite gems Illaena had given me. "Um, how much?"

The waiter's eyes widened and his mouth dropped open a fraction. "Sir, that would be more than enough for all the nectar you wish to drink."

"How about food as well?" I said.

The waiter looked at my wrist. "You have no band stone? We can only return the excess amount with essence."

I didn't have a clue what made these aetherite gems so valuable and really didn't want to make a big deal out of it. Already, the seras at the table next to us were watching curiously. I shrugged and played it off. "I don't care. Just get us food and nectar and keep the excess payment."

"Ah, you must be with the empress's retinue." The waiter's surprise vanished and he bowed deeply. "It is an honor to have you dining with us today." He filled our glasses and set the decanter on the table. "I will return with the best meal in all of Cabala." With that pronouncement, he spun on his heel and headed into the restaurant.

The Brightlings at neighboring tables began murmuring with excitement, some casting uneasy glances our way.

I groaned. "So much for keeping it on the down-low."

"We're apparently not very good at keeping a low profile." Elyssa took a sip of her drink. Pleasure flashed through her eyes. "Oh my. This is the best wine I've ever tasted."

I let the golden liquid roll onto my tongue. Tart and sweet, it seemed to melt into my taste buds, sending a warm flush through my skin. I swallowed and felt the warmth travel down to my belly. "Wow. I think I like angel wine."

"They didn't have anything like this in the Darkling lands," Elyssa said. "It's more like normal wine down there."

I nodded toward a group of richly attired Brightlings chowing down on some kind of roast. "That, and there are definitely more carnivores up here."

"Vegetarians versus carnivores." Elyssa grunted. "It's no wonder the Darklings and Brightlings don't get along."

"I wonder if they've always been that way, or if all Seraphim were vegan back in the day." I looked around and noticed plenty of meals using glurk, quintos, and other vegetables I'd grown to hate during my time here, but most of them were served as sides with meat.

A trio of angels with harps began playing and singing for a couple at a table near the fountain. Their voices harmonized perfectly as they sang a tale about an ancient Seraphim king.

"Sure beats a mariachi band," Elyssa murmured in my ear. "I know we're supposed to be all business out here, but this is kind of romantic."

I pecked a kiss on her nose. "Yeah, it is."

Over the next hour, we enjoyed a meal of tender white meat served over a bed of greens and finished off the decanter of nectar. My senses buzzed with pleasure by the time the sun went down and the soft white glow of cottony wisps illuminated the square.

"How was your meal?" the waiter asked me.

"Excellent!" I patted my belly. "What kind of meat was that?"

He smiled proudly. "Tender loin of dragon, sir."

My mouth dropped open. "Damn, I didn't know dragons were so tasty."

"Indeed, the green ones are the tastiest." The waiter bowed and left.

Elyssa scooted her chair closer to mine and leaned her head on my shoulder. "I could learn to like this."

I sighed contentedly. "What's to learn? I already like it."

Loud chimes echoed in the distance. Patrons hurried away or looked up in fear. Massive spheres of light streaked into the sky, casting dancing shadows on the plaza until the city lit like the noonday sun.

The angels with harps switched to a lively melody and the choir of angels across the plaza chanted a warlike song about a mighty empress who defended the light of Seraphina against the darkness of evil.

Scores of archangels lifted off from the citadel, blazing wings cutting a path toward whatever threatened the city. I didn't have to guess what came our way.

It was surely dragons.

Chapter 28

Scores of Brightling soldiers in crystal armor marched through the plaza and headed toward the sea wall. Elyssa took my arm. "This is the perfect time to check out those buildings."

I hesitated and looked to the west, but the buildings blocked my view of the horizon. "It feels strange to run away from battle."

"This isn't our battle to fight." Elyssa stood up, sweeping her gaze across the area. Of the few remaining people left, none paid attention to the residences.

"It will be if our plan works."

Elyssa gripped my hands. "One battle at a time, Justin. Even if we wanted to help, do you really think Kaelissa would let us?"

I shook my head. "Probably not. Besides, we're just a drop in the bucket compared to her legions."

Elyssa's gaze grew distant, as if an idea had occurred to her. She shook it off and headed between two of the restaurants at the edge of the plaza. We walked down the narrow alley and came out behind the lighthouse. A knee-high wall was the only thing guarding the back entrance.

I switched to demon vision and surveyed the neatly cropped blue lawn. While there was nothing keeping anyone from walking across the grass, dim white beams of energy crisscrossed the entire outside of the building.

"Your eyes just went wide, Justin." Elyssa nudged me with an elbow. "What do you see?"

"The house is protected by a barrier." I described it. "Give me a minute." I followed the weave of magic back to its terminus—the door gem. I took out Nookli and flicked to the hacking spell Adam had given me. "I hope this works."

Elyssa looked back and forth, eyes wary for anyone coming. "Hurry up. I got your back."

I jogged across the lawn and stopped a few feet from the door gem. I wondered what would happen if something touched the barrier around the house. Would an alarm sound? Would it disintegrate the object? There weren't any twigs handy for a quick test, so I kept a safe distance and hoped my arcphone didn't have to touch the gem.

Thankfully, Adam had made it easy enough for an idiot to use his spell. *Touch here to lock onto target gem. Device must be within two feet.* I touched an icon shaped like crosshairs. A beam of soft red light emitted from the LED camera flash, sweeping back and forth until it locked onto the door gem. The light narrowed and increased in intensity.

A Jolly Roger flag icon complete with skull and crossbones faded into view on my screen. Just below it said: *Gem locked. Touch to start hack.*

I did as instructed. Code flashed across the screen and two skeletal pirates began sword fighting in the background. *He really adds some flair to his hacks.* I turned back to Elyssa. "It's running."

"Any time estimate?" she asked over her shoulder.

"No." I tried to remain perfectly still, but even if my hand wavered, the laser remained locked onto the gem. As long as the phone stayed within two feet, it would do its job. That meant I couldn't move—or did it? I channeled a weave of Murk, crafting it into a makeshift tripod with a flat shelf on top. It was a bit crooked and ugly, but it worked. I set my phone on top and tied off the weave, giving it enough power to last for a few minutes.

Elyssa cast a critical eye at my lopsided work. "I don't think you have a future in sculpting, babe."

The western sky lit up with fireworks. Explosions boomed. Overhead, a flight of archangels mowed through a cloud of flying reptiles. Smoking bodies spiraled down onto rooftops and smacked wetly in the plaza. One of them thudded in the yard just a few feet away.

Green eyes with vertical slits stared blindly up at us. The reptilian body was no longer than my arm, studded with brilliant red scales. It had a long lean muzzle with black whiskers and a forked tongue lolling on the grass. Its body was lithe as that of a snake, but with four small legs and a pair of leathery wings.

A series of loud pops behind me sent me scrambling forward. I spun around and saw another small dragon body bouncing off the barrier of the house next door, each impact scorching the scales with a burst of white electricity.

Elyssa knelt next to the dragon and gently touched its scales. "They're like glass." She pressed one between thumb and fingers. "But hard as diamonds."

I heard shouts in the plaza. Elyssa ran to the corner of one of the shops and looked around it. She spun back to me. "They're cleaning up the bodies! We've got to hide!"

I ran over to the phone and looked at the screen. It gave an estimate of five minutes. "We can't just leave this here or they'll see it."

Elyssa ran around the yard, tossing dragon bodies out onto the road. "Don't you know a cloaking spell?"

"Yeah, but I'm not very good with it." My mom had shown me a way to bend light around a bubble of Brilliance, but I'd never mastered it. I probably had an Arcane cloaking spell on my arcphone, but it was busy hacking the door gem. In other words, I didn't have a prayer of cloaking me, Elyssa, and the phone.

Elyssa seemed to know what I was thinking just from the expression on my face. "We're screwed, aren't we?"

"Yeah—unless..." I snapped my fingers and turned to the phone and my makeshift platform. I channeled Murk into the tripod to supply it with enough energy to maintain cohesion, then shifted to Brilliance. Instead of forming a bubble around all of us, I made a tiny one around the phone and platform.

Alysea's instructions echoed in my head. *Will the light to go around it. Imagine it is not there at all.*

I'd tried using this weave during the Seraphim War and things hadn't gone well. Then again, the bigger the bubble, the harder it was to conceal. I folded a small warped bubble around the phone and tripod.

"I can still see it," Elyssa said from her position near the shop corner. "They're almost here."

Light, go around it. Bend, stupid light! Nothing happened. *Just be invisible, dammit!* The bubble shimmered, but instead of vanishing, it turned into a mirror surface, reflecting the blue grass and the walkway. It wasn't invisible, but as long as no one stepped right up to it, it gave the illusion that nothing was there.

Elyssa hurried over to a dragon body and hefted it on her shoulder. "Grab one. Hurry!"

I snatched up a body just as a group of Brightlings in crystal armor came around the corner with a hovering platform piled with deceased dragons. Elyssa and I nonchalantly tossed our loads onto the platform.

"Thank you, good citizens," said one of the soldiers.

"We saw more fall on the houses." Elyssa pointed toward the other McMansions. "Do you require our help?"

"If only you could," the seraph replied. "Unfortunately, only soldiers are allowed in the restricted zone." He pointed to the plaza beyond. "There is plenty of work to be done out there, if you would."

Elyssa nodded. "Of course."

I swallowed nervously and hoped the soldiers didn't inspect the yard behind us too closely. "We are happy to help, good soldier."

"And that is why we will win," the seraph replied. He motioned his comrades onward. They briefly glanced at the yard with my concealed arcphone, but continued past it since Elyssa had cleared it of corpses.

We walked back toward the plaza where other crews worked, but stayed out of sight at the corner of the building. Within a few minutes, the soldiers were gone, but it wouldn't be long until others came this way. Already, the sounds of battle had died and life would soon return to business as usual during the peaceful interim.

I released the bubble weave around the phone and watched the countdown. The completion bar hovered around ninety-nine percent for a seeming eternity until finally the screen lit up with green text: *Hack Successful.* Switching back to demon sight, I watched the energy barrier fade away. Once it was gone, I zapped the door gem and the wall blinked away.

We were in.

Elyssa and I whisked inside and closed the door behind us.

We reconnoitered the residence from top to bottom. Like most houses in Seraphina, it didn't have normal windows. Instead, you could zap a gem in the room and will a window to appear in one of several configurations. I opted for privacy mode, which meant those inside the house could see out, but those on the outside couldn't see in. The top story offered a nice view over Kaelissa's citadel wall.

Scores of soldiers in crystal armor protected the courtyards beyond the wall, and my demon vision revealed magic lasers defending the buildings. I described the situation to Elyssa. "This is hopeless."

"So much for catching Kaelissa off guard." Elyssa bit her lower lip. "We need to survey from a building on the opposite side." She pointed to a tower with a mushroom dome balanced on top. "Let's see if we can get in over there." She took out an ASE—all-seeing eye— and put it in record mode.

"All right." I pushed to my feet. "But unless she comes out of her turtle shell, we don't have a chance of getting to her."

We walked along the outskirts of the forbidden zone, sticking to a road that took us into another residential area where it ended in a cul-de-sac. A simple gravel path led beneath a crystal arch. Vines wrapped around the arch, red tendrils bearing yellow flowers and sweet scents. We stepped beneath it and into a garden.

The path wandered over bubbling brooks, past tall trees covered in blue flowers, and into shelters woven from red and green vines. This place reminded me of the fairy gardens near Arcane University, like something out of a wonderland. Glowing mushrooms offered places to sit, though they were vacant at this hour.

As the glow balls over the city faded away, the mushrooms and bright flowers lit the path.

"Beautiful," Elyssa breathed.

I couldn't break out of my dour mood and simply grunted. The gardens wrapped around the large estates near Kaelissa's compound, a gravel path leading into the back yards of each. This offered us the unexpected bonus of not having to worry about soldiers marching past every few minutes. Apparently, they figured the barriers around the domiciles would be enough to keep citizens out.

I set up the phone hack at the giant mushroom house and waited impatiently for it to complete. Elyssa kept a watch, but this time we finished the task uninterrupted. A wide empty space greeted us inside the stalk. A levitator just inside the door whisked us up and into the living quarters in the mushroom head.

The view from the top was better than from the lighthouse, but no more encouraging. Elyssa counted fifty of the city guard patrolling the interior of the compound. When Arturo and his archangels returned, the number swelled to around a hundred, though they vanished inside one of the domed buildings. Archangels apparently were too good for patrol duty.

Elyssa set up another ASE to record and made sure it sent video to her arcphone before turning to leave.

"Should we try to send an ASE into the compound?" I asked.

She shook her head. "These two are our last ones. We can't risk them getting disabled by the shield protecting the citadel."

"Are we really that low on supplies?"

"Thanks to the surprise attack back in Kohvalla, we're practically down to the clothes on our backs." Elyssa tucked her phone away beneath her dress. "Let's get back to the ship."

We took the skyway out of the city and reached the ship just before dawn.

Shelton greeted us at the top of the gangway with a look of relief and both sets of our parents close behind. "Man, I was getting worried." He clapped me on the back. "So, what's the word?"

"Not good." I yawned so hard my jaw cracked. "We need a pow-wow."

"Dude, you look beat." Shelton held up a steaming mug of coffee. "Want some caffeine first?"

I shook my head. "No, I'm hitting the sack the minute I'm done with this report."

"We've seen a lot of strange activity off the coast," Thomas said.

"Strange doesn't begin to cover it." My stomach grumbled for breakfast.

Alysea took me by the arm. "Why don't we discuss everything over food?"

Shelton clapped his hands together. "Now we're talking!"

We headed down the ramps and reached the galley a moment later. In addition to the standard vegetarian fare the Mzodi preferred,

309

Shelton had stocked the preservation chambers with bread, cheese, eggs, and bacon. Alysea heated up a couple of plates with her angel skillz and we sat down to eat.

Cinder and Adam came in a moment later. Adam's face lit with excitement when he saw us. "What's the word?"

Shelton rubbed his hands together. "That's what we're about to find out."

I let Elyssa do the talking because I was too busy stuffing my face to say a word. She told them about the small dragons, the restricted zone, and then showed them live video from the ASEs we'd left in the houses.

"And all this time we thought Kaelissa moved all her troops west so she could invade Atlantis." Shelton studied the holographic pictures Elyssa had taken of the dead dragons. "I think you're right. These dragon attacks were the perfect diversion to draw all the Brightling troops west."

"That's probably part of it," Thomas agreed. "Judging from the size of the dragons, I think these forces are a prelude to a major invasion."

"I don't understand," Alysea said. "You can't just open gateways between realms without the help of an arch."

"That we know of." Adam took out his arcphone and flicked on the screen. "Cinder and I collected data from the previous rift we encountered out at sea, and the one that opened while you two were in town." He projected the image and scrolled through rows of symbols. "The magical signatures for these rifts are identical, which means the same device opened them."

"The same arch?" Shelton said.

"We don't think it's an arch." Adam pointed to a row of symbols. "An arch doesn't project beyond its boundaries, but whatever created these rifts is projecting the portals into the sky."

"Wonderful." Shelton grimaced. "All we need is a bad guy equipped to project portals to Draxadis anywhere he wants."

"But how?" I said. "And can we use this magic to take us home?"

"We are hopeful it might provide a way," Cinder said, "but there are no guarantees."

Adam switched to an overhead map of Voltis. Bright tendrils snaked out from the massive storm, many of them crossing thousands of miles to distant shores. One of them reached all the way to Cabala. "Remnants of Atlantis extend beyond the borders of Voltis, each a tiny fragment of the original Earth. These fractures rub against reality and spawn aether vortexes."

I stopped chewing for a moment. "You mean Atlantis isn't wholly confined to Voltis?"

"Precisely." Cinder traced a line with his finger. "Adam and I believe the device causing the rifts is tapping into these fragments. Since Voltis is like one large malfunctioning portal, each of these fractures are smaller versions."

"Whoa." Shelton snapped a piece of bacon in half. "No wonder you guys were so excited earlier. That means we could probably find this thing and get home."

"That is our hope." Cinder said. "We must stop whoever is behind it before they open a rift that allows through the large dragons, for they would surely doom this realm to a major war."

Chapter 29

Shelton let out a long, low whistle. "Holy farting fairies. This has Baal written all over it."

Elyssa nodded. "That was our conclusion as well."

Adam shrugged. "Baal might be behind it, but that means he has a physical agent on the ground somewhere in this town."

Cinder tilted his head, eyes curious. "I believe I have had a revelation."

Shelton snorted. "You know who Luke's father is?"

The golem turned his deadpan eyes on the Arcane. "I was not aware we had a travelling companion named Luke."

Elyssa sighed. "Cinder, just ignore Shelton and tell us what you're thinking."

Cinder blinked and turned to Adam. "I require a better map of Seraphina."

Thomas took out his arctablet and projected his strategic map, complete with skyway routes, stronghold cities, and estimated troop numbers. "How's that?"

"That will suffice." Cinder studied the map a moment then traced his finger from Tarissa to Guinesea, made a circle, then traced a line east toward Cuital, a major Brightling city in Sazoris.

Shelton rapped his fingers on the table impatiently. "Well, are you going to tell us or just draw lines on the map all day?"

Cinder ignored him and traced his finger up the northern skyway from Cuital to the capitol city of Zbura.

"Yes, that makes complete sense," Thomas said.

Cinder backed up from the map and pointed to Guinesea. "The two Darkling legions led by Aerianas will easily crush any resistance in the city of Novus and the troops loyal to Victus will likely join with the superior force in order to avoid annihilation."

"And Aerianas gains a few hundred more troops," Elyssa said.

Cinder continued to follow the line. "I suspect that by now they have already reached Cuital via the Imperial Skyway."

"It's only a three-day ride," Thomas said.

"In which case, they have already absorbed the skeleton troops left behind, along with any citizenry they conscripted to join their army." Cinder moved his finger north. "I suspect they are well on their way to finish their mission in Zbura."

Shelton frowned. "I think we already established that she's headed there sooner or later."

Cinder tilted his head. "True. She will likely control the capitol city within days. That is all the time we have before a major dragon invasion occurs and all is lost."

A moment of silence filled the room as reality punched us in the face.

"I knew we didn't have much time, but this is ridiculous." I turned to Thomas. "We can't let Aerianas take Zbura that fast. We need more time to clone Kaelissa."

"We have nearly created our prototype dolem," Cinder said. "Once we have Kaelissa's soul fragment, there is no guarantee we can clone her on the first try."

"Here's the next question," Shelton said. "Who is Baal's agent in charge of the rift device?"

"All evidence points to one person," Cinder replied. "Cephus."

Shelton nearly spit out his coffee. "Cephus? He's dead!"

"More accurately, a Cephus dolem." Cinder turned to Adam. "Do you concur?"

Adam pressed his lips tight. Nodded. "Baal would want an agent familiar with the crimson arch construction. Making a Cephus dolem would be easiest."

Shelton pounded the table with a fist. "He's worse than a cockroach."

"There are other possibilities," Adam said. "It's possible Cephus had assistants with the knowledge to build the crimson arch."

"But Cephus wanted to open a portal to the friggin Void." Shelton chewed his bacon suspiciously. "If he planned to let the Beast destroy Seraphina, why would Baal keep him around?"

David grunted. "I think that's a case of Cephus having no idea what he was doing."

314

"Baal may be powerful, but he's not omniscient," Alysea said. "Perhaps Cephus wished to end everything, or perhaps he thought the Beast could be an ally. The reality was certainly something none of us expected."

"The Beast is and has been an enigma." David's gaze lost focus. "I wonder if it was created by the Sundering, or if it already existed."

"Just knowing that the consumer of realms is only a dimension a way gives me the chills." Shelton stared at his bacon as if he'd just lost his appetite. "If Xanomiel combines the realms, what's to stop the Beast from coming back with everything else?"

"Nothing," Thomas said. "What we choose to do on this day could put the realms on the path to salvation or doom."

"When it rains, it pours." David chuckled. "So, in addition to cloning Kaelissa, we have to deactivate this rift apparatus and then march to Zbura to liberate it from Aerianas if we don't want billions to die at the hands of Baal or Xanomiel."

"Perhaps we can delay the full-scale dragon invasion." Thomas tapped out some figures on his arctablet. "If the *Falcheen* leaves today, we could reach one of the skyway nodes on the island of Cuba, several hundred miles south of Zbura. If we disable it, we can trap Aerianas's forces in the middle of nowhere. That might push back Baal's time table for unleashing the dragons."

David pursed his lips. "That's a tight schedule." He nodded his head in the general direction of Cabala. "What about Kaelissa?"

"We'll have to leave a crew here to take care of Operation Dolem." Thomas turned to Adam. "How long would it take to unload everything you need from the ship?"

"An hour." He looked at Cinder. "Sound right?"

"I believe so," the golem replied. "We will need to find a suitable place to create our foundry."

Thomas got up from the table. "Justin, choose your personnel and make preparations. We don't have time to waste."

"Wait a cotton-picking minute," Shelton said. "How are we supposed to make this happen without a base of operations? What if we need to get the hell out of Dodge?"

The commander shook his head. "Fighting an entrenched enemy in Zbura will waste countless lives. If we can cut them off, we'll have a much easier time, provided we're successful here."

"Rushing off and leaving us here might set us up for failure." Shelton got up and slapped his hat back on his head. "You ever think about that?"

Thomas gave the Arcane an icy stare. "Improvisation is a part of war, Shelton. If there was any other way to do this, I would, but the *Falcheen* is the fastest way for us to reach Cuba." He looked at me. "Do you agree, Justin?"

His question caught me off guard. Once Thomas Borathen made a decision, it was nigh impossible to make him change his mind. Thankfully, I wouldn't have to do that. I gripped Shelton by the arm. "Look, this won't be easy, but we've got the brains and the brawn to do it even without the *Falcheen* here to babysit us."

Shelton groaned. "Fine, but I'm taking all the bacon with us."

David chuckled. "I like a man who's got his priorities straight." He slapped my back. "Well, son, looks like you get to give us the nickel tour of Cabala."

I frowned. "I don't know if taking everyone to Cabala is the greatest idea. Wouldn't it be better to set up shop in a hidden location outside of town?"

"Not really." Elyssa narrowed her eyes in concentration. "It would be best if we used one of the residences near Kaelissa's citadel. That means we have to smuggle everyone inside."

"Does this mean I have to wear a kilt?" Shelton said.

Adam grinned. "You'll finally get to showcase your pretty legs."

Shelton looked like he was going to cry.

The next hour was a whirlwind of activity. Adam and Cinder packed up everything they'd need to build a dolem foundry and put it in one of the levitating crystal chests the Mzodi used to transport gems along with several preservation cases filled with food. Since the chests were commonly used for transporting goods, this one wouldn't stand out.

Illaena provided us with clothing and more gems in case we needed to pay for anything in town. When it was all said and done, we had two crates and a small crowd accompanying us. Shelton, Adam, David, and Cinder compromised the core of our dolem crew with Issana accompanying us for reference.

Michael, Elyssa, Alysea, and I would be responsible for gathering a soul sample from Kaelissa and eventually replacing her. Bella came along to assist us, and because she wasn't about to travel across the world and leave Shelton behind.

Eor made our group an even eleven. No one had wanted to bring along the grouchy gem sorter, but we needed him to help us attune the gems needed to make the summoning pattern soul spheres.

Meghan wanted to come with us, but Thomas requested that she come with them in case they needed the Templar healer.

We said quick goodbyes to everyone, then the *Falcheen* lifted off from the cove and hugged the coast heading north. Once they were safely away from Cabala, the ship would turn southeast and make a beeline for Cuba.

"I still can't believe Cuba is called Cuba in Seraphina," Shelton said as he unrolled a flying carpet and stepped onboard.

"Maybe it's spelled differently," Adam said.

Shelton turned around and gave him a look. "How in the hell else would you spell Cuba?"

Adam got on his own carpet. "With a Y."

"You need to go back to spelling school." Shelton activated the hover spell on the crystal chest and guided it upward next to his carpet. "And take some geography lessons while you're at it."

Adam snorted. "God, I love messing with him." He activated the other crystal chest and followed Shelton up the cliff.

Elyssa climbed on a carpet behind me and wrapped her arms around my waist. "Ready to go, flyboy?"

"Ready as I'll ever be." I jabbed a finger upward and the rest of our crew piloted their carpets up to the top of the cliff. We flew as far as the skyway then stowed the carpets in one of the chests since no one used carpets in Seraphina.

The others changed into their Brightling clothing and lined up to get onto the skyway. I heard scuffling and shouting from behind one of the chests as Bella shoved Shelton out into the open.

Adam clapped his hands together. "Oh my god, you look adorable."

Elyssa clamped a hand over her mouth, face red with laughter. I couldn't suppress giggles of my own. Shelton wore a handsome red shirt and a matching kilt. His pale white legs practically glowed in the sun. Even more ridiculously, he still wore his wide-brimmed hat.

Bella jerked it off his head and shoved it in the chest. "Harry, you're worse than a child."

"I look like a friggin idiot!" he shouted, face red with embarrassment. Shelton buried his face in his hands. "Just kill me now."

"Aw, you look fine." Adam glanced down at his own skinny legs. "I mean, I look pretty chic myself."

Shelton grunted. "You look lovely." He sighed and shook his head. "Man, I miss my jeans. I miss my duster."

"You're barely through your twenties and you're more set in your ways than an eighty-year old man," Bella tutted. "Change is good, Harry."

Cinder and Adam guided the crystal chests to the skyway node one at a time. Cloudlets formed beneath them and carried them up to the highway of clouds. The rest of us followed and jogged to catch up since the skyway moved at a healthy pace.

"How suspicious will it look to take two chests through town?" Alysea asked Elyssa. "Provided the two are kept close to each other, I can bend the light around them."

"I saw about a dozen of them around town yesterday," Elyssa said. "I think as long as we look like we know what we're doing, no one will give us a second look."

"The mushroom house is the best location to set up shop," Adam said. "That garden gives us a buffer of privacy we won't have in the lighthouse residence."

"Provided there is enough space in the stalk," Cinder said. "The summoning pattern must be laid in the ground, preferably bedrock, and we dare not do it outside."

"Not a problem," Elyssa said. "The stalk is about fifty feet across at the base and sits on a foundation of rock. There's literally nothing in there except the levitator shaft since all the living quarters are up in the cap."

"Perfect." Adam tapped on his arcphone. "We located a suitable demon to summon. We just need to inscribe the pattern and have Eor set the gems in place."

"What are the gems for?" David said. "Usually the pattern is all you need."

"The gems support the soul sphere so the body can form around it," Cinder said. "They also magnify the magical energy in the summoning pattern which seems to give the demon flesh added cohesion."

"Gems make everything function better," Eor said in his usual humble way. "Without me, your plan would fall to pieces."

"Glad to know it," I said. "What about the soul capturing process? Do we have soulstones?"

"Even better," Eor said. "Thomas explained precisely what your soulstones do, and it turns out we already have gems which serve a similar purpose."

My thoughts flashed back to the restaurant. "When we were at that restaurant, some of the patrons paid for their drinks with soul essence." I described how the waiter had transferred it to a large globe.

"Yes," Eor said. "That would be soul essence, but to get what we need, we require an actual fragment of the soul, not just the essence."

Alysea's mouth dropped open. "Are you telling me that Brightlings are paying for common goods with their soul essence?"

Elyssa and I had forgotten to mention that detail since it didn't seem important at the time. I nodded. "That's what it looked like."

"Is it valuable?" Elyssa asked.

"While it does not amplify powers like human essence, it could certainly increase the powers of anyone who consumes it." Alysea shuddered. "I cannot believe civilization has sunk so low."

"Before you know it, they'll have discount warehouses where you can buy glurk in bulk," Shelton quipped.

"Eww!" Elyssa shivered. "I'd rather eat Cheezy Poofs all day."

I got back to the subject at hand. "I take it there's a difference between soul essence and a fragment?"

Eor nodded. "I have modified a gem, which will cut a bit deeper, past the essence and into the soul itself."

"Will the person feel it?" I asked.

"There is no way to lose a piece of your soul, no matter how small, and not feel something." Eor shrugged. "Unfortunately, you will need the subject to willfully open their soul essence to you for this to work."

"Willingly?" Shelton snapped. "How in the hell are we supposed to get Kaelissa to give anyone her soul essence? She's the freaking empress, for god's sake. Royalty doesn't pay for anything."

"If your willpower is strong, you can, of course, force her to raise her hand," Eor said. "But I doubt any of you have what it takes to force Kaelissa to open up."

Daelissa had been strong enough to force others to allow her to feed on them, but her mother was something else altogether. "Willpower isn't the same as being magically or physically strong. It's a test of inner strength that usually comes with experience and time." I looked at Alysea. "I hate to say it, but you're the only Seraphim old enough to stand a chance."

"Kaelissa is centuries older than me." Alysea shook her head. "I was affected by the Desecration and lost a lifetime of memories and experiences. I don't know if my willpower is strong enough."

In other words, the most important part of our plan seemed impossible.

Chapter 30

David took Alysea's hand. "What if Kaelissa is under full demonic assault at the same time you try to coerce her?" He winked. "I can mess with her mind in ways that will make her lose all willpower."

"Not alone," Alysea said. "Seraphim are able to resist the lure of the Daemos better than most."

"Yeah, but if you and I hit her at the same time, I'll bet we could get the job done." He pecked her on the cheek. "Teamwork, babe."

Alysea's cheeks blushed. "I remember the first time I willingly opened my mind to you. It was exciting."

My stomach squirmed. "Hell to the no, Mom!" I held my fingers in the sign of the cross. "Not another word about that."

David and most of the others burst into laughter.

Cinder tilted his head. "Justin, coitus is a natural and, in fact, necessary component of procreation. Had your parent foregone intercourse, you would likely—"

I clamped a hand over his mouth. "Cinder, I know how I got here, but that doesn't mean I want to ever think of it in my entire lifetime. Got it?"

The golem blinked at me then nodded, and I removed my hand.

"I am sorry, Justin." Cinder simulated a frown. "I will not speak of your parents' sexual relations again."

I took a deep breath to ward off my rising gorge, much to David's amusement, then managed to speak again. "Will we need to capture Kaelissa for you two to work on her?"

David shook his head. "Look, if there's one thing I've learned, it's that the more guards someone surrounds themselves with, the safer they feel. That means they let their guard down—pun intended." He winked. "Deception is the key here."

"Why am I not surprised to hear a Daemos say that?" Shelton muttered.

David flashed his trademark grin. "Because it's what we're good at." He tapped a finger on his chin. "Now, if I remember correctly, Kaelissa is on a quest to repopulate the world with healthy, immortal Brightlings."

"I know she was when we first met her," Elyssa said. "Most of the children in Ooskai were hers."

I gagged again. "Yeah, she forced the men to mate with her in the hopes one of her offspring would be like the Seraphim of old instead of weaker in power and limited to a few centuries of life."

"She required Joss to mate with her in exchange for her help," Elyssa said. "For all we know, she's pregnant right now."

"She porked Joss months ago," I said, "but she didn't look pregnant when I fought her in Atlantis."

"Porked." Shelton chuckled. "I love that word."

Alysea gave him a sideways look. "Yes, she would have been showing when you fought in Atlantis. I also suspect if she was pregnant, she wouldn't have been leading a battle."

"She could have mated with someone else in the meantime," Adam said.

"What if we offered her a Brightling with a sterling pedigree?" David said. "A seraph who wasn't affected by the Desecration in Eden, or the Schism, as they call it here in Seraphina. A seraph who is immortal and powerful, with the purest semen in all the land?"

Shelton barked a laugh. "No woman can resist gold standard sperm!"

Bella sighed. "Did I really marry this man?"

Alysea folded her arms and looked at David. "Sometimes I wonder the same thing about David."

"Umm, who's this seraph we're talking about?" I asked.

David jabbed a finger at his chest. "Me."

Cinder stated the obvious first. "But you are Daemos, not Seraphim."

"She won't know that until it's too late." David raised an eyebrow in challenge. "I think it's the perfect way to get close to her."

I looked around at the others, but no one offered a better solution. "Well, work out the details and let me know how you're going to pull it off."

"Already on it," David said, eyes glinting mischievously.

Worry flashed across Alysea's face. "David, you do remember what happened when you tried something similar with Daelissa, right? It completely blew up in your face."

He stroked Alysea's hair, twirling a long golden lock in one finger, adoration twinkling in his eyes. "Lessons learned, darling."

She raised an eyebrow. "Those lessons being?"

David's lips quirked. "This time, I'll listen to your suggestions."

"Wise man," Bella said.

Shelton narrowed his eyes in disbelief, but wisely kept his mouth shut.

The crystal cliffs and buildings of Cabala came into view. Milky white clouds concealed the ocean far below and the late morning sun cast velvety red strokes on the cottony surface.

David whistled. "I'll give the Brightlings one thing—they know how to build a beautiful city."

I nearly argued that the Darklings were just as skilled, but their prevalence of drab ultraviolet and black added dark overtones to their structures that looked dull in comparison to the diamond-like walls ahead.

No one looked twice at us as cloudlets delivered us and our cargo inside the gates of the city. It was instantly evident why. Dozens of other groups pushed around levitating chests in a mad dash to repair the city after the latest dragon attacks.

I thought we were in the clear until a soldier approached us. "What's your cargo?"

"Food, clothing and other supplies, good soldier," Alysea replied.

"High Cyrinthian?" The guard's eyes flared and he offered a hasty bow. "Apologies, my sera. I did not realize you were a noble."

Alysea seemed a bit taken aback, but flattened her face into an imperious mask. "We must all do our duty to help the empire, soldier." She shooed him with a hand. "Go about your business."

"At once." He backed away, bowing every so often until he reached the safety of the crowd.

David put a hand to his chin. "Hmm, that was interesting."

"It's your accent," Elyssa said. "You must speak as they did back in the old days."

I hadn't given it much thought, but now that I'd heard her accent compared to the guard's, it was obvious High Cyrinthian was a dialect all to itself.

"We did not differentiate Brightlings on accent when I was child." Alysea's forehead creased with sadness. "The masses have grown, but their culture has declined. Oh, Daelissa, what have you wrought on our people?"

"Your mom is starting to sound like Shakespeare," Shelton said.

Shakespeare was alive and well in Atlantis, thanks to a group of angels called the Fallen. His poetic mode of voice had made me want to punch him in the throat. I cleared my throat. "Let's move out before another soldier decides to get nosy."

I led our party toward the plaza from the night before then detoured down the street that ended at the garden. Of the few Seraphim we passed, none seemed the least bit curious about us. There was a bit of an issue fitting the levitating chests through the vine-covered arch, but we managed to squeeze them through.

Alysea looked sadly at the vines and plucked a leaf. She squeezed David's hand. "It's ivy." A tear trickled down her cheek.

David wrapped an arm around her. "I know she's okay," he said in a hushed tone. "She's probably running the Overworld by now."

"I hope so, David." Alysea wiped tears from her cheeks. "I don't think I could forgive myself if something happens to her."

"It's not your fault, Mom." I took her hand and rubbed it. Despite her immense power, it felt small and frail in my hand. "Besides, Daelissa trained her, and if anyone could teach her to survive, it was her."

Alysea rubbed her eyes and nodded before continuing silently down the gravel path. David put a hand on my shoulder and watched her go. "Can't wait to break Victus's neck with my bare hands."

I smiled grimly. "You and me both."

We continued to the mushroom house without incident. Some took the levitator up into the cap. I remained with David, Adam, Shelton, and Cinder in the stalk. David staked out the best area for the summoning pattern and then got straight to work tracing it with the aid of a holographic outline from Adam's arcphone.

Shelton stood next to me, shifting uneasily from foot to foot. "Man, I hate how my daddy bags hang loose in this friggin skirt."

"They need to air out on occasion." I tried to keep a straight face. "Keeping them locked up in jeans all the time is how you get jock itch."

He scowled. "That's why you slap on some baby powder, especially before a big fight."

I grimaced. "That's an awful visual you just planted in my head."

"Good." Shelton chuckled. "I guess it doesn't matter where my sack hangs if we get into a firefight with Brightlings."

"Still obsessing?"

"Damned right I am." He spit on the rocky floor. "I dug deep in my battle mage arsenal. Came up with squat."

I sighed. "You're too focused on brute force."

"What else is there?"

"You've seen how Kanaan fights, right?" I flicked imaginary wands in a poor effort to mimic the Magitsu master's moves. "He fights with guile and some wicked sick flips."

"If I tried to do flips, I'd die of a pulled groin before a Seraphim burned me to a crisp." Shelton shook his head and looked down. "There's got to be some way I can be useful in a fight."

"You *are* useful in a fight, dammit." I punched him in the shoulder. "Use your head. Outthink someone more powerful than you."

Shelton raised an eyebrow. "That's not how *you* operate. You run in with all cannons firing."

"I've pulled off a few sneaky moves before." I tapped a finger on my chin and tried to think of an example. "Like the time I turned my shield into a mirror and reflected the death rays coming at me."

"I can't make shields as strong as yours." Shelton sighed. "Wish I could get a few tips from Underborn. Now, that's a sneaky son of a bitch."

"That's because he manipulates the entire game and not just one fight." I thought about how the assassin had put a death mark on my father just to test me.

"Mhm." Shelton gave me a sideways glance. "Aren't we rigging the game by replacing Kaelissa with a dolem?"

"I guess we are." I gave myself a moment of introspection to see if I felt guilty about such underhanded dealings, but nope—I felt just fine. "Then again, we're not the only ones trying to cheat."

"You got that right." Shelton blew out a breath. "Can we get out of here for a while? Maybe a walk will help me clear my head."

"Yeah, sure." I walked over to the others. "Shelton and I are going to take a short walk. We'll be back in a few."

"We'll be done with the pattern tracing in an hour," Adam said. "After that, we'll need help burning it into the bedrock."

David looked up from his work and wiped a bead of sweat from his forehead. "Be careful."

I gave him a thumbs-up then turned and left. Shelton and I sneaked out of the back and into the garden, staying alert for any other Seraphim out for an afternoon stroll. I cracked a yawn and remembered I hadn't slept last night. A nice, long nap was in order when we got back.

We continued down the garden path, waltzed through a neighborhood south of the mushroom house, and followed the curving road until it led us back to the south side of the plaza Elyssa and I had been in last night.

"How are the drinks here?" Shelton asked.

I grabbed a chair at an empty table next to a group of gossiping seras. "Why don't you be the judge?" Using a smaller gem, I paid for a decanter of nectar and poured each of us a glass.

Shelton's eyes widened when he took a sip. "Damn, that's good." He took another sip. "It's like liqueur, but not as sweet."

I clinked my glass against his. "Here's to new adventures."

Shelton snorted. "How about an adventure where we don't have to fight all the damned time?"

The angel choir across the plaza burst into glorious song, drawing the attention of other patrons. Shelton and I drank in silence, enjoying the moment of peace before we forcefully threw a load of crap at a fan and hoped for the best.

Shelton poured his third cup and paused in the act of putting down the decanter. His eyes narrowed. "Am I imagining things, or does that dude look awfully familiar?"

I followed his gaze and froze in my seat. The seraph in question locked gazes with me. Recognition flared in his eyes. He spun and stalked away.

I grabbed Shelton's arm. "Come on. We've got to catch him."

"It's him?"

"Yes," I growled. "It's Cephus."

Chapter 31

Shelton jumped out of his chair like a shot and we hurried after our quarry.

Did the real Cephus die or is this him?

Shelton echoed my doubts. "Is that a dolem?"

I switched to demon vision. The aura of our quarry flickered fitfully, a weak candle flame fringed with blue. This wasn't the real Cephus. "He's a clone."

Shelton grunted. "I'll bet he's the one responsible for the rifts to Draxadis."

"Seems likely." I squeezed through a group of chatting Seraphim. "I wonder how he recognized me."

"Maybe he has some of Cephus's memories," Shelton suggested.

The dolem looked over his shoulder and quickened his pace when he saw us following. Unless we broke into a sprint, we weren't going to catch him.

"Even if we catch him, do you think he'll give up any info?" Shelton dodged a running child. "What if he has friends?"

I gave him a look of disbelief. "Are you saying we should let him go?"

Shelton took out his wand. "Nah. I'm just taking your advice and getting sneaky." He whisked his wand through a pattern and flicked it toward the dolem. A tiny dot of light streaked from the tip of the wand and hit the dolem in the back of the neck. Fake Cephus still faced forward and didn't even notice.

"Uh, what was that?" I said. "Pixie dust?"

"Tracking spell." Shelton grinned. "He took out his phone and switched to the map. The phone had already drawn in the parts of the city we'd visited while unexplored parts remained black. A white dot moved from the mapped parts of the garden path and into a black area.

I stopped and stared at the phone. "What's the range?"

"A hundred miles, give or take." Shelton tucked the arcphone back in his pocket. "Even if he walks out of range, we'll have a trail to follow until we pick up his signal again."

I elbowed him in the ribs. "I like it when you're sneaky."

"Later tonight, when he thinks he's lost us and is all snuggled up in his lair, we can spring a surprise." A smug smile stretched his lips. "If we're lucky, we'll snag him and any co-conspirators."

"And maybe figure out what he's up to." I clapped my hands together. "Brilliant!"

"Darned tootin'!" Shelton held up his hand for a high-five. I didn't leave him hanging.

When we got back to our own lair, we told the others what had happened and our idea about capturing the dolem that night.

Once everyone got over the shock of hearing our story, Elyssa shot down our plans. "Tonight won't work."

"Why is that?" I asked.

Alysea stepped forward. "Because tonight, your father and I are going to get Kaelissa's soul essence."

A cube of ice crackled around my heart. "Tonight? Isn't it a little soon? How are you going to get in?"

Alysea clasped her hands below her waist and gave me a pleased smile. "While you were out, I took a walk of my own and spoke with some of the guards in the restricted zone."

"You did what?" I said.

"I told him I was Felysea of Cbora, here with my mate, Ijoruss, and that we wished to pay respects to the empress this evening." She saw the puzzled look on my face and clarified. "Kaelissa will recognize our aliases as those of ancient Seraphim only two generations removed from the first of Seraphina. Cbora is far to the north and out of range of any Alabaster Arches, which means the Schism would not have affected us."

"I thought the idea was to dangle David as a potential mate," I said. "Why not introduce him as a brother or something?"

"The ancient Seraphim did not hold to such traditions as marriage," she said. "It was not uncommon to switch mates to politically bind two households."

I wrinkled my nose. "Are you saying the ancient Seraphim were a bunch of swingers?"

Alysea looked scandalized. "Of course not! It was done out of necessity."

Shelton smirked. "I'm sure they all say that."

"Suffice it to say, we have been granted a private audience tonight." Alysea held up a white gem. "With this modified soulstone, I should be able to capture a soul fragment tonight. If David and I perform flawlessly, Kaelissa will not even know."

Thoughts about what that meant snaked through my guts, leaving a trail of nausea. "You're not—uh"—just the thought of it made me want to throw up—"going to have—" I stopped myself right there before I puked.

David barked a laugh. "Son, it's absolutely normal to have a threesome to save the world."

"Gah!" Elyssa plugged her ears. "That is definitely not part of the plan."

Shelton burst into laughter. "Whatever it takes, right?"

Bella elbowed him in the ribs. "Harry Shelton, don't encourage him."

David doubled over with laughter. "Oh, Justin. You've seen war, death, and a lot of nastiness, but you get queasy thinking about parental sex? That's adorable."

"David, stop torturing your son." Alysea walked over and patted my shoulder. "We should be able to complete the mission without coitus, but we're prepared to make any sacrifices necessary to get the job done."

I took a deep breath to drive away the terrible thoughts clouding my mind. "Whatever you do, don't give me the details later, okay?"

David snorted. "Don't worry, son. We'll preserve your delicate sensibilities."

"It's my sanity I'm worried about." I shuddered like a wet dog. "When do you leave?"

"In two hours." Alysea gave me a wistful smile. "Everything will be okay."

I didn't know if I could believe that.

The time came and my parents left. I worked on a plan with the others to capture Fakor, as I nicknamed the Cephus dolem. "We have enough people to pull this off," I argued. "Why don't we get it done while my parents are gone?"

Michael stroked his chin. "What if Fakor has a dozen allies? What if he has traps set near his lair?"

"Then we adjust our plans."

"We need a full team just in case." Michael looked at his sister. "Thoughts?"

"I'd feel better with Alysea and David backing us up." Elyssa touched my arm. "Justin, we can't take chances in a city full of enemies."

"Can we at least recon the place?" I said. The tracking dot on Shelton's arcphone had stopped about a mile east of us. "If we know what we're up against, it'll make capture a lot easier."

Elyssa nodded. "As long as that's *all* we do." She gave me a pointed look.

I held up my hands in surrender. "Recon. That's it."

Michael nodded. "Sounds good."

Shelton held up his arcphone. "Let me transfer the tracking spell."

I bumped Nookli against his phone and downloaded the tracker.

As we turned to leave, Adam and Cinder burst into the room. Cinder wore a manic look on his face, like someone who'd taken too much ecstasy at his first rave.

A person I didn't recognize walked unsteadily behind them, a blank expression on his face, and his tender bits swaying freely for all to see.

"What in the hell?" Shelton said. "I thought you were going to wait for me."

"Eureka!" Adam shouted. "We've got our first dolem."

Elyssa blinked. "How very naked he is."

Shelton snorted. "Man, is he related to a horse?"

Bella looked at the dolem with a critical eye. "He is certainly well-endowed."

"I have no idea why he came out like that," Adam said. "Anyway, this form won't hold cohesion for more than an hour because there's no soul essence binding it together."

"This is proof of concept," Cinder said. "Once David returns with soul essence, we should be able to use it as a template to copy Kaelissa."

"Excellent work," I said. "Will it be easy to control the Kaelissa dolem?"

"That all depends on the programming we put into the spark," Adam said. "The dolem should do whatever we say." He turned to the newly minted creature. "Do jumping jacks."

The dolem complied without a word, his inordinately large junk putting on quite a show.

I grimaced. "I think I've seen enough."

"Just a few more," Bella said.

"Hey now!" Shelton said. "Stop looking at it like it's a hunk of meat."

I took Elyssa's hand and led her around the exercising dolem. "We're going to spy on Fakor." I tapped the communication pendant on my shirt. "Let me know if there are any problems."

Michael nodded. "Whatever you do, don't try to capture him on your own."

"We won't," Elyssa assured him. She gave me a sharp look. "Right, Justin?"

"I already said I won't." I raked my gaze across the room. "Let's just hope today isn't the day he plans to unleash the dragon apocalypse on the city."

I left them with that grim thought and headed down the levitator with Elyssa. We made good time through the gardens, heading in the general direction of the tracking spell while letting the map fill in the blank spots along the way. The crystal road climbed a steep hill and meandered to a section of town with cramped residences crammed into compact neighborhoods.

This section of Cabala illustrated clear differences in Brightlings social classes that I hadn't seen in the Darkling nation. The buildings showed little variety, the Brightling equivalent of townhomes—two story crystal cubes with permanent windows built in instead of the magical sort back in the fancy section of town. There were no door gems on the outside either. The doors slid open and closed.

"Why don't they use door gems?" Elyssa said.

"Gems are currency," I suggested. "Maybe they're expensive to install."

She shook her head slowly. "At least the Darklings didn't discriminate like that."

Upon nearing the target building, we slowed our pace and became more vigilant of our surroundings in case Fakor had sentries watching the streets. There were few Seraphim out and about— probably because they were busy with repair duties after the dragon attacks of the previous day. That made it easier for us to spot anyone suspicious, but it also meant enemies didn't have to pick us out of a crowd.

The domicile in question resembled all the other two-story domiciles. Curtains shielded the large windows, preventing us from seeing inside. Elyssa turned into an alley and scouted the back of the residence. There were no fences, just a long swath of red grass dotted with large mushrooms and shrubberies. Curtains also blocked the rear windows of Fakor's joint.

Elyssa didn't seem deterred. "He's got to come out of there sometime. Let's find a place to watch."

We settled on a narrow alley just down the road that allowed us to look around the corner and observe the abode without revealing ourselves to anyone leaving it. Nearly two hours later, Elyssa raised a hand to interrupt a serious discussion about the possible plot of a Princess Bride sequel to say, "He's coming out."

I joined her at the corner. Fakor emerged from the residence and looked back inside, apparently conversing with someone inside. Seconds later, a figure in a dress and cowl stepped outside, back to us.

A random seraph and sera walked past our hiding spot. The female stopped, eyes narrowed. "Who are you and what are you doing next to our house?"

Oh, crap. I fumbled with an explanation. "We're looking for a place to live. Heard this was a nice neighborhood."

"Does it look like a nice neighborhood?" the sera said in a sarcastic voice. "If you have no gems, then yes, this is the perfect place to live."

"Come now, darling, no need to take out our woes on strangers." The seraph put an arm on her shoulder. "These are desperate times for all of us, and with the dragon attacks, things will only get worse."

Tears formed in the female's eyes. "How could it possibly be worse? We have already lost so much!"

This was definitely a desperate time for me. Out of the corner of my eye, I saw Fakor and his companion headed our way. The moment they passed the alley, we'd be in plain view.

I offered a curt bow to the sera. "I'm sorry for intruding. Live long and prosper." I backed further into the alley since stepping onto the street would reveal us. The seraph looked confused, but the sera buried her face on his chest and distracted him.

The moment we reached the back end of the alley, we headed down a few houses and peered around the corner. Fakor and his female companion gestured at each other, apparently engaged in lively conversation. The sera shook her head and glared straight ahead, finally giving us a clear view of her profile.

"Oh no," Elyssa said in a horrified voice. "It can't be."

My heart dropped like a lead brick on steroids. "You've got to be kidding me."

If Fakor and this sera were in league, it meant my parents were in terrible danger.

Chapter 32

The gray-haired sera was one of the first people we'd met in Ooskai, and the person who'd first taken me to meet her mother. I switched to demon view just to make sure the sera before me wasn't a dolem. Though her aura glowed with far less vigor than Brightlings untainted by the Schism, she was the real deal.

My guts twisted with apprehension at what this meant: Djola, daughter of Kaelissa, was in cahoots with Cephus's dolem.

"Why is Djola talking to Fakor?" Elyssa said.

It certainly boggled my mind. "I never in a million years thought she'd betray Kaelissa."

Elyssa's forehead pinched. "I don't think she has."

"No?" I swung my head her way. "Why would Djola hang out with the dude working to undermine Kaelissa's rule?"

"Djola reveres Kaelissa." Elyssa tapped her chin with a finger. "This is something else, but we have to get closer to overhear their conversation."

"Yeah, that and we have to capture them." We crossed behind more houses to keep pace with our targets. "What if Fakor told her that I'm in town? What if Kaelissa puts two and two together and realizes she's meeting with my parents?"

"Has she ever met your mother?" Elyssa poked her head around the corner and waited before crossing the next alley.

I shook my head. "No, Kaelissa was banished to Pjurna with all the other Darklings before my mother met Daelissa. But if Fakor recognized me, then he probably knows what my parents look like."

"The question is, does Fakor know everything Cephus did?" Elyssa bit her lower lip. "I think the safe assumption is yes." She tapped the pendant on her dress. "Michael, we have intelligence suggesting the Fakor dolem is working with Kaelissa. We need to capture him immediately for interrogation."

"You're certain?" her brother replied.

"He's with Djola, one of Kaelissa's most loyal servants and children."

"Follow him," Michael said. "We'll coordinate."

Daggers of ice sliced at my heart. *What if Kaelissa already knows who my parents are? What if her meeting with them is a trap?* I couldn't think about that right now. We had to make a clean capture of our targets without alerting other citizens.

Elyssa and I skipped ahead and took cover near the street so we could overhear the conversation between our prey.

"Their blooms will be lovely this year," Fakor said.

"Indeed," Djola replied, spreading her hands apart as if she had just nailed an opponent in a debate contest. "The land will flourish."

Their botanical discussion faded in the distance as they left the neighborhood and entered an open stretch of road heading back to the gardens.

I stopped to let them get out of sight over the rise before continuing after them. "Why in the blazes are they talking about flowers?"

Elyssa bit her lower lip. "Something isn't right, Justin." She headed up the rise and stopped to watch Fakor and Djola enter the gardens ahead. "This doesn't make sense." She tapped her comm pendant and updated Michael on our location.

I put on my thinking cap and tried to make sense of it. "Let's assume Fakor's plan is to create a dolem version of Kaelissa. If that's true, making best buds with Djola is a good way to gain access to her."

"But he can't harvest a soul fragment by himself," Elyssa said. "And Djola certainly wouldn't help him do it."

"Maybe he hopes to trick her into doing it." I shook my head. "Nah. Too hard."

"He must have another team helping him," Elyssa said. "That's the only answer."

"Too many questions," I said. "Let's hope he talks when we catch him."

Fakor and Djola vanished around a bend in the garden. If they continued this route, they'd end up at the exit near Kaelissa's citadel.

Shelton's voice emanated from my pendant. "Turkeys spotted. Ready when you are."

"Ready," Michael said.

"No civilians present," Phoebe said. "Capture is a go."

It was over in an instant. Michael and Phoebe blurred in from opposite sides and grabbed Fakor and Djola while Shelton and Adam shackled them with diamond fiber. Shelton wore his hat and duster instead of the local garb. "Why are you outside without your disguise?"

"Didn't have time to change," Shelton said. He turned toward our prisoner. "We'll have him nice and tucked away before anyone sees me."

Fakor didn't look the least bit perturbed. "Hello, Justin Slade."

His voice sent ice spiders skittering down my back. "In case you hadn't noticed, you're our prisoner now." I stepped closer to him. "Maybe you should be a bit more concerned about your future."

Djola stared impassively at me. "Once again, the Destroyer seeks to shatter order with untamed chaos."

"Order?" I scoffed. "All I've seen is a warmongering empress who wants to pick up where her daughter left off."

"Mother provides," Djola said. "She will show you the error of your ways."

"It is as I said," Fakor told Djola. "I have seen the recorded history of the Eden War. I instantly recognized the face of Daelissa's murderer when I saw him."

"Mother will be pleased," Djola said. "She may even grant you a blessing."

"Are you two insane?" I threw up my hands. "You're our prisoners, not the other way around!"

Michael frowned, head cocked to the side as if listening for something. I heard a faint susurrus in the skies above. Alarm bells rang in my head.

Metal sang as Elyssa drew her sword from a sheath hidden in the folds of her dress. "Something's not right."

Shelton whipped out his staff. Bella and Adam followed his lead.

Armored figures crashed through the trees above. Branches crackled and the ground shuddered with the impact of dozens of armored feet landing all around us. Primarion Arturo's blazing wings flickered away as he regarded me down the length of his nose.

Murk and Brilliance burst into spheres around my fists. "You!"

Fakor smiled smugly. "Consider yourselves baited."

That son of a bitch had led us straight into a trap.

I flung a hand toward him, but archangel lightning spears angled toward my jugular. Arturo held up a hand. "There is no need to die this instant, young Slade." He offered a faint smile. "You will, of course, be publicly executed."

"No!" Elyssa shouted. "We'd all rather die first."

"I know," Arturo said. "Since the execution of the Destroyer would be far more symbolic than simply killing you all here, I propose a deal."

This is hopeless. Even on my best day I couldn't take on more than a couple of archangels at once. Elyssa and Michael could probably take out a few, but without Nightingale armor to protect them from the lightning spears, even our resident ninjas wouldn't last long.

I lowered my fists and snuffed the burning power. "What's the deal, Arturo?"

"I will spare your friends if you come peacefully." He raised an eyebrow. "Your death is the one that matters."

"You give your word?" I said.

"On my honor." Arturo pressed a hand to his heart.

I swallowed the hard lump in my throat. "Then I accept."

"No, Justin!" Elyssa gripped my arm. "I won't let you!"

Shelton gave me a haunted look. "Justin, you can't just—"

"I can, and I will." I turned back to Arturo. "What now?"

Arturo looked at Michael and the others. "Lower your weapons."

I nodded at the others. "Put them down."

Elyssa stepped in front of me, her sword at the ready. "I won't let them take you, Justin. I won't let you die without a fight."

I gripped her wrist. "Babe, we can't fight them all." I gently took the sword from her hand. "If we fight here, we die now," I whispered. "Let's buy some time. Maybe there's a way out of this mess."

She shuddered, nodded. "I won't let you die alone."

"Believe me, it's not at the top of my list either." I held the sword out to a nearby archangel. "We're ready."

Archangels released Djola and Fakor from their bonds then snapped crystalline bands around each of our wrists. At a word from Arturo, the bands hummed and glowed. A magnetic force jerked my wrists and the wrists of my friends together with a snap. Then our new wards herded us toward Kaelissa's citadel.

My nerves tightened with every step. "Can I talk to you, Arturo?"

The primarion nodded and stepped closer to me. "Speak."

"Do you know the name Cephus?" I said.

He shook his head. "No. Why should I?"

"Djola's friend." I tried to spot him in the throng of archangels, but couldn't.

Arturo's expression gave nothing away. "What of him?"

"He's part of a plot to overthrow Kaelissa."

Arturo raised an eyebrow, but said nothing.

"Look, the Darkling legions are controlled by a Daemas named Aerianas." I tried not to let the desperation creep into my voice. "Using demon magic, she's already cloned the leaders of the Darkling legions and controls them now. Djola's friend is part of that plot."

Arturo gave me a sideways look. "I find your story hard to believe."

"Not only that, but he's the one opening the rifts to Draxadis." I motioned my bound hands toward the sky. "It was a ploy to draw all the Brightling forces here and leave Zbura and your other cities undefended."

Arturo pursed his lips. "The rifts are caused by instabilities in aether storms. Our theorists assure us they will eventually cease."

I'm not getting through to him. "I know it sounds crazy, but that seraph with Djola isn't even a real person. He's one of the demon clones Aerianas made."

"Let's assume you speak the truth," Arturo said. "How can I tell this Cephus person is a clone?"

Since Seraphim didn't have demon vision, I couldn't tell him to check it out that way. Dolems bled and died like anyone, so that wasn't proof either. "There's only one way." I knew he wouldn't go for it. "If you cut him open, there's a soul sphere inside his chest."

"Enough of this." Arturo's face hardened. "As a warrior, I know you fear death by execution, Justin Slade. I would rather kill you in open battle than lead you to slaughter. It is beneath your dignity to seek escape by pretending to care for Kaelissa's welfare." He gave me a pointed look. "You nearly killed her in your last encounter."

"That was kind of the point," I muttered. "She tried to use a bloodstone on me, Primarion. She wanted to use Sirens so she could slaughter helpless people. Where's the honor in that?"

"No, she merely wanted the Sirens to help hold the dragons at bay," he said. "It would spare lives on both sides until the rifts stop manifesting."

"Kaelissa is not honorable," I repeated. "And neither is that seraph with Djola." I hissed a frustrated breath between my teeth. "Look, I want what's best for Seraphina. A unified Seraphina is stronger and better."

"That is eventually our goal," Arturo said as our formation came to a halt outside the citadel gates. "Die well, Justin Slade." He left my side and signaled for the gates to open.

The soldiers led us inside and stopped in front of a low square building behind the citadel. One of the guards zapped a gem. The air shimmered and a door appeared in the wall. The archangels herded through the door and into a wide room.

My parents looked up in surprise and dismay.

"Son of a bitch," David said. "I really hate being outsmarted."

"Pardon the sparse accommodations," Arturo said. "The citadel does not have a dungeon."

"What kind of a hellhole is this?" David muttered. "Doesn't even have cable television."

Arturo ignored the jibes. He and his soldiers backed out of the room and the doorway materialized into a wall. I heard a faint hum as the shield activated. My wrists sprang apart as the bangles deactivated.

I tried to channel a beam of Brilliance to see if I could burn them off, but my magic fizzled in a show of fitful sparks.

"Magic blockers," Alysea said grimly.

I pounded the crystal floor with the bottom of my fist. A miniscule crack rewarded my efforts. "Doesn't affect my strength."

"I can still aetherate," Adam said. He held up thumb and forefinger and displayed an arc of magical energy. "The bracelets affect channeling, not casting."

"As if it matters," Shelton said darkly. "Even at full strength I couldn't take down an archangel with his hands tied behind his back."

Adam blew out a breath. "You're so friggin negative. Of course you're not going to overpower them." He reached into his pocket and groaned. "I feel naked without my arcphone."

Elyssa paced restlessly back and forth. "We've got to figure out how to get out of here. I won't let Kaelissa execute Justin."

"We need to lose these bracelets." David held up his wrists and clanked the offending bangles together. "I can't summon a damned thing with them on." He winked. "Pun intended."

I rolled my eyes. "Kaelissa's going to execute me, and you're making jokes?"

His irreverent façade dropped into a scowl and he pounded a fist on the ground. "What else can I do? I'm powerless."

I held up a hand to calm him down. "What happened with Kaelissa?"

"We met with her, worked our spiel, and snagged a bit of her soul essence." David tugged on a bracelet to no effect. "Then we ran into your old buddy Fakor and twenty city guards."

"Somehow, he knew who we were and why we were there." Alysea shook her head in disbelief. "He took the stone with Kaelissa's soul fragment in it and locked us in here."

I dreaded the next question nearly as much as my impending execution. "Did you have to do anything nasty with Kaelissa?"

"Just a bit of talk and touching." David shrugged. "She fell for our ruse hook, line, and sinker."

"That's it?" I dared feel hopeful.

"Yep." He frowned. "Then Fakor came along and ruined everything."

My mother's forehead creased. "How could he have possibly known about our plans?"

"He used Djola to get on the inside," Elyssa said. "He probably knows most of what Cephus knew, and we just did the work of getting Kaelissa's soul fragment for him."

"Man, I thought we'd outfoxed Fakor." Shelton reached up as if to take off his hat, but the guards had confiscated it and his duster. "Looks like we played right into his hands."

I closed my eyes and rewound to earlier today, replaying the encounter with Fakor. He stood maybe fifty yards away from where Shelton and I sat. All I had to do was turn around to see him. When he and I locked gazes, something important was missing from his expression. "Fakor wasn't surprised to see me," I said. "He knew I was there. In fact, I think he intentionally showed himself to me, knowing we'd track him."

"How could he possibly—" Shelton clamped his mouth shut and growled. "We have a traitor—probably Bliss or one of the other dolems."

"We left Bliss on the ship," Adam said. "She had no way to communicate with him, and I know she didn't sneak off the ship."

"We kept close tabs on her at all times," Elyssa said. "I don't see how she could have spoken with Fakor."

Shelton steepled his fingers. "I'd bet dollars to donuts she has a way to communicate with him."

Michael nodded. "It makes sense. For all we know her soul sphere has built-in communications magic."

"Gah!" I smacked my forehead. "Why didn't I think of that?" I smacked a fist into my palm. "If that's true, Fakor knew we were here all along. He knew the *Falcheen* went to Zbura and left us on our own!"

Adam ran a hand down his face. "I feel like a complete moron for not checking her more closely."

"Too late," David said. "We'll be dead before long, and Fakor has everything he needs to make a dolem of our beloved empress."

Chapter 33

"Well, ain't this a pickle?" Shelton ran a hand through his hair. "By the time Aerianas arrives, we'll be dead and she'll have all the ingredients to make herself a nice Kaelissa clone."

"If Bliss found a way to communicate with Fakor, it's likely Aerianas knows our plans." Elyssa bit the inside of her cheek and her gaze went distant. "What if Aerianas sent her army to Zbura while she and a small contingent came to Cabala to clone Kaelissa?"

Adam grimaced. "The Imperial Skyway branches west and northwest before it leaves Sazoris which means she could totally bypass Cuba."

"And the nodes Commander Borathen sabotaged," Michael finished.

"That's all fine and dandy," Shelton said, "but how does knowing that help us? We're trapped like rats in here."

"Simple," Adam said. "Let's tell Kaelissa what Fakor is up to."

"She may think it's a desperate attempt to save our hides," David said.

Shelton snorted. "That's because it is."

I shook my head. "I tried to tell Arturo, but he wouldn't listen."

"We have to assume that Fakor concocted a story we'll be hard-pressed to prove false." Bella held up her hands helplessly. "We have the disadvantage of being prisoners while Fakor has connections within the imperial court."

"Agreed." Elyssa's eyes grew worried. "Kaelissa won't listen. All she cares about is executing Justin."

Alysea's eyes flared. "Unless we come up with a plan, we'll all be in line for death."

I cleared my throat. "Not exactly." I swallowed the knot forming in my throat. "I made Arturo promise not to execute anyone else."

"Did he include your parents in that plan?" Shelton said.

A chill worked down my spine. "I-I don't know."

"Doubtful," Shelton said. "Especially since you specifically mentioned us and not them when you made the deal."

"It's moot anyway," David said. "Kaelissa doesn't have to abide by Arturo's promises."

"She has no honor," Michael said.

"Let's say we convince Kaelissa." Shelton swept his gaze over the groups. "All that means is that Fakor ends up on the chopping block next to us."

Elyssa pursed her lips. "I just don't think we could earn her trust no matter what."

David chuckled wryly. "Justin nearly killed her in Atlantis. I'm certain Fakor convinced her that Alysea and I were there to poison her or something. There's no way to overcome that trust deficit."

Elyssa fiddled with the bracelet cuffs. "If only we could get out of these!"

"Maybe if I had my arcphone," Adam said.

Bella wrapped her arms around Shelton's waist. "I just want you all to know that no matter how terribly this turns out, I love you all and am proud to call you friends."

Shelton leaned down and pecked a kiss on her forehead. "Hey, I got to marry the woman of my dreams."

I slipped an arm around Elyssa. "I can't complain either."

"Plus, we've saved the world at least five times," Adam said. "I mean, that's not too bad."

"Stop it!" Elyssa slipped out of my arm and shoved me in the chest. "What about Eden? What about Ivy?" Tears streamed down her face. "What about me?" Gone was the cool composure of my ninja girl, replaced by raw emotion, and it broke my heart.

"Elyssa, I swear if there was any other way—"

She bared her teeth. "If you let them execute you, I will make them execute me alongside you."

"Ninjette." Michael shook his head. "That's not the answer."

"I don't care if I have to fight barehanded," Elyssa said. "I would rather die fighting than let them lead you like a sheep to the slaughter."

The doorway flickered open and our wrist cuffs snapped together. Instead of Arturo and his archangels, soldiers in the crystal armor of the city guard entered.

The leader, a seraph with gold insignias engraved in his breastplate sneered at us. "Line up, you traitorous filth."

"I only count thirteen," Michael murmured. "Wait for my signal once we're outside."

Shelton's eyes widened, but he nodded along with everyone else before lining up. Michael's signal never came. The moment we stepped outside, the number of city guard swelled to nearly a hundred, forming a neat box around us and snuffing any hopes of fighting our way out of this. I looked to the skies and prayed for a timely rescue from the *Falcheen*. Hell, even a major dragon attack would be nice at this point. But Fakor probably controlled those rifts, meaning there was zero chance of a last-minute rescue or diversion.

Cinder was the only one of us at large, but he wasn't going to mount a rescue all by himself. I hoped he'd figured out what happened and gotten himself out of town.

We marched through the square and into the citadel tower. Golden tiles led down the center of a great hall. Brightlings thronged inside, most dressed in finery I hadn't seen among the common folks.

"A noble audience," Alysea said from behind me. "Kaelissa wants to parade our heads before a crowd."

I heard my name in whispers as we passed by.

"Is that the one who slew Daelissa?"

"Is that Slade?"

"…the Destroyer who leveled Tarissa?

"I've heard he's half-demon, half-Seraphim!"

I forced a grin and addressed the crowd as we walked past. "I'll sign autographs after the executions."

One sera reached out and tried to touch me, but soldiers blocked her hands. Another female next to her looked scandalized at the attempt. I expected for anger in their faces, but instead found mostly confusion and awe.

Apparently, I'm something of a legend. Like all legends, I was about to come to an end.

When we reached the empty throne at the end, the captain of the guard shouted, "On your knees, filth."

"I'll have you know I take showers regularly," I shot back, trying to keep a bit of levity before I lost my head.

Rough hands gripped my shoulders and tried to force me down along with all the others. Strong as they were, one guard wasn't enough to overcome my strength. I bared my teeth at him. "Do you even lift, bro?"

David chuckled, and made his guard work to push him down as well. Murmurs rose from the crowd, though I couldn't make out if they thought we were cool for resisting, or just stupid for pissing off the guards.

The captain whacked me in the back of my knees with the flat of his sword and my tiny rebellion came to an end. My knees hit the hard tiles, sending a shock up my bones. Once we were all down, a chubby seraph produced a brass horn and trumpeted a few notes. A choir of angels emerged from behind curtains on the sides of the throne, playing a lively tune on their harps.

Primarion Arturo appeared in his brilliant chromatic armor. Brilliant white wings blazed into fire on his back and spread wide. "All hail the rightful ruler, the Mother of Daelissa, the Conqueror of Realms, and soon to be the Mother of Dragons—Kaelissa, the second of her line."

The angels burst into loud song and the crowd burst into chants of, "All hail the empress, may she live forever!"

The curtains behind the throne billowed and Kaelissa burst through. She wore a pure white gown with a billowing cape of clouds. I had to admit she looked splendid, but the cold gaze in her eyes turned my heart to stone.

This is not a good day to die. But soon, I would be dead. My friends would likely live out their lives as prisoners. Seraphina would never be united. I would never see my sister or my home realm again. Every grim realization made my heart wither with sorrow.

Since Fakor had Kaelissa's soul essence, that meant Aerianas would soon rule as a puppet of Baal. I didn't know what that meant for the realms, but it couldn't be good, especially if the Apocryphan I'd freed from the Abyss decided to merge them back together.

I closed my eyes and tried to send a desperate message to the netherworld—to Haedaemos in the hopes of reaching Baal. Unfortunately, the cuffs I wore blocked the window in my soul just as surely as they blocked my magic.

We'd run out of options long ago and the reality crushed my hopes like a tin can in a steamroller factory.

Kaelissa raised her hands and the chamber grew silent. "My daughter sought to bring order where mortals spread chaos. She offered peace and hope to Eden, but the cowards kneeling before you today denied her goodwill."

David snorted as if he could barely restrain laughter. The guard behind him slammed the hilt of his sword into the back of his neck, but that didn't wipe the amused smile from my father's face.

"I have picked up the cause of my daughter," Kaelissa continued. "First, I will bring order to all of Seraphina. No longer will the Darklings sulk in their corner of the world. No longer will the Mzodi ignore the laws and customs of my empire."

The crowd roared with applause, and grew silent just as abruptly. I wondered if someone was holding up cue cards for them or if they feared Kaelissa's wrath for cheering too long.

"Once again, these cowards have tried to block my efforts at every turn." Kaelissa's eyes gleamed with delight. "No longer, children. Today, they will meet the fate they so richly deserve."

I gave a sharp look to Arturo, who frowned and looked at Kaelissa.

"Guards, prepare to deliver justice." Kaelissa motioned at the soldiers behind us.

I heard a hum and felt the heat of Brilliance coalescing around their blades. Michael gritted his teeth and tensed. We would die, but not without a fight.

"Arturo promised clemency for my comrades!" I shouted. "I alone am here to pay the price."

Kaelissa laughed. "Yes, Arturo told me of his promise, but he is not the empress."

"So, you will sully his honor?" I let my voice boom so it would reach the ears of as many people as possible.

"Empress." Arturo bowed deeply and spoke in tones only those nearby could hear. "I gave them my word to avoid needless bloodshed. Surely executing Slade is enough."

"No, my dear archangel, it is not." Kaelissa scowled at me. "These people killed my sweet Daelissa. They dream only of killing my entire family line. I will not have it!"

"By tarnishing the honor of your top commander, you tarnish your own," Alysea said.

"Even the darkest tarnish can be polished back to a clear shine," Kaelissa said. "My daughter calls for your blood." Her voice sank to a hiss. "She calls for revenge." The empress stood, eyes blazing white. "Guards, ready your weapons."

Energy hummed as the crystal blades rose above our necks. A ripple of tension ran down the backs of my friends. Before those swords came down, I knew some of us would explode into action, fighting with bound hands until swords plunged into our bodies from all sides. One of us would be the last to die in a lake of our loved ones' blood.

Will it be me?

I felt so helpless. So lost. I knew of only one possible way out.

I took a deep breath and spoke from my diaphragm so all would hear. "Kaelissa, I issue the Challenge of Ascension!"

Chapter 34

Kaelissa's face clouded with momentary confusion. I saw hesitation in the eyes of the soldiers even as they held their swords aloft. From the galley came a loud murmuring and a scattering of shouts.

"You cannot challenge me for the throne, half-damned creature." Kaelissa spat in my face. "You have no standing to issue such a challenge."

"Is that true?" I directed the question to Arturo. "Or is this another of her lies?"

"It is true," Arturo said in a voice too calm for such a tense moment. "Only a pure Brightling of noble birth can issue the challenge."

"Then I issue the Challenge of Ascension," Alysea said, her voice ringing like a crystal chime in the great hall. "I am Alysea, descendant of Seaa, the Golden Ruler herself. If any have a claim on the throne, it is me."

"Ridiculous!" Kaelissa shouted, spittle foaming on her lips. "Guards—"

Arturo held up a hand and the soldiers looked with confusion between their military leader and the empress. "Alysea has a rightful claim, Empress. Her challenge must be heard."

"This is absurd," Kaelissa shouted. "Guards, execute them."

"Apologies, Empress, but you cannot ignore a rightful challenge." Arturo proved he still held sway over his own people, because none of the guards moved to chop off our heads.

Kaelissa's face grew red with anger, but instead of demanding our heads again, she turned to a short seraph standing near the curtain to the side of the throne. "Bring me the Pearly Tome."

He nodded and darted away.

The murmurs in the crowd rose to a dull roar. I glanced over my shoulder. While the crowd still cast hostile glances our way, they certainly looked entertained. The short seraph returned moments later with a tall, thick book that looked as if it had been carved from pearl and stitched with gold. Kaelissa unwrapped a silky white ribbon from around the cover and opened it in her servant's arms. She turned stiff pages of which there seemed only a few dozen and then stopped.

Arturo stood by her side and looked at the page.

Kaelissa turned to us a moment later, a malevolent gleam in her eyes, and a smirk that made me wonder if she'd found some way to get out of this. "The challenge is accepted," she cried out. "As the challenged, I choose a battle of magics to the death, and Primarion Arturo as my protector."

Alysea didn't seem surprised at all by her choices.

"Mom," I hissed. "Choose me." I knew if I didn't say something, she'd probably fight herself.

David nodded. "He's the strongest of us."

Fear lit in Alysea's eyes, but she knew I was the one with the best chance to beat Arturo. "I choose my son, Justin Slade, as my protector."

At this, Kaelissa laughed with malicious glee. "My dear Alysea, do you not know the rules of the challenge?" She took the servant by the shoulders. "Please show her the tome."

The servant dutifully walked over and held the book low so those of us on our knees could read the Cyrinthian text inside. I couldn't quite see it from this angle, but Alysea's face blanched and her lips parted with shock.

"Yes, you poor fool." Kaelissa grabbed the book from the servant and held it aloft, opened to the page in question. "So that no family line will be wiped out, the challenger may not choose a blood relative." She closed the book, held it out, and dropped it like a mic.

"That's not even remotely fair," I protested. "Choose me if you want a fair fight, Kaelissa."

Arturo held up a fist. "I will gladly fight Justin Slade, champion of Eden."

"Yes, you will fight a champion of Eden," Kaelissa said, her gaze wandering my comrades. "But he must be chosen from among those who wield magic."

Bella stood. "Then I will fight for Alysea."

"No!" Shelton pushed to his feet. "Choose me. I volunteer to fight for Alysea."

My mother looked helplessly between the two. "This is unfair, Kaelissa. Arcanes are outmatched by—"

364

"I do not care!" Kaelissa pounded out each word like a hammer blow. "Choose your hero."

Shelton dropped onto his knees in front of Alysea. "Choose me. Please. I'm much stronger with magic than she is."

"Harry, no!" Tears streamed down Bella's eyes. "I will fight for her."

He shook his head. "No, baby. I can't let you."

Tears pooled in my mother's eyes, but she nodded. "I choose Harry Shelton as my champion."

"The lines are drawn, the heroes chosen." Kaelissa looked at Arturo as if challenging him to counter her word. "Let our champions prepare."

His jaw tightened and his smoldering eyes met mine. Finally, he bowed. "If the empress wishes to protect her honor with such a farce, then I will do it."

Kaelissa leaned down and sneered in Alysea's face. "When your hero fails, and he will certainly die quickly, the heads of your loved ones will litter the floor, foolish Alysea. You were Daelissa's friend, and you betrayed her. You, of all people, should feel such loss as I have felt. That is why I will spare you and give you centuries to ponder your mistakes."

Tears trickled down Alysea's cheeks, but her expression turned to stone. "The biggest mistake I ever made was showing your evil daughter how to reach Eden."

A loud pop rang out as Kaelissa's palm slapped my mother's cheek. She stood and turned to her servant. "Fetch the wizard's tools and arm him however he sees fit."

The short servant bowed and dashed away.

Kaelissa turned to Arturo. "Relocate the prisoners to a suitable arena. Citadel Square will suit our purposes. Let the commoners see this challenge. Let them witness the executions."

Arturo nodded. "Yes, Empress."

Within an hour, Kaelissa stood on a raised dais on the edge of the plaza where Shelton and I had shared drinks only a day ago. A huge crowd surrounded the square, nobles arranged around the empress and the rest of us prisoners on a raised platform corralled by a sea of glittering crystal armor.

Shelton stood in the open space just on the other side of a line of guards. He wore his hat and leather duster. His wand and compacted staff hung on opposite hips, his arcphone strapped inside his duster sleeve. His face had regained some color, but his eyes looked resigned.

"He has no faith in himself," Adam said. "Just look at him."

"How is he supposed to fight Arturo?" Bella said, tears in her eyes. "The archangel can fly overhead and pummel him with magic."

"Not to mention Seraphim magic will blow right through his shields." Adam winced. "I wish I could help him."

"Poor son of a bitch." David glared at Kaelissa. "I guess it's better than getting your head cut off."

Alysea looked on with red eyes. "I swear, I had no idea I couldn't choose you, Justin. It just doesn't seem right."

It didn't seem right, but there wasn't anything I could do about it.

Arturo stood at Kaelissa's side, his chromatic blue armor glinting in the sun. He carried no sword or lightning lance. Since this was a contest of magics, he would have to channel a sword if he wanted one.

"May I have a word with my friend?" I shouted at the archangel.

Kaelissa raised an eyebrow and looked to Arturo. The Primarion nodded his head and the guards helped me down off the platform and parted way. I walked over to Shelton, wishing I could give him a hug, but the wrist cuffs prevented it.

Shelton grinned when he saw me coming. "Jealous that I get to be the hero this time?"

I tried to chuckle, but it only brought tears to my eyes. "God damn it, Shelton, I'm sorry."

"Hey, look, we had a good run." He slapped me on the back. "I mean, at least I get to die for the woman I love and my best friend."

I didn't remind him that we were all doomed to die anyway. "Look, don't try to overpower him, okay? Dodge his attacks and wear him down so he can't fly, then get sneaky."

"Sneaky how?" Shelton glanced over my shoulder. "How am I supposed to beat that magnificent son of a bitch? How am I supposed to wear him out?" He chuckled. "I ain't that light on my feet and I don't have supernatural endurance."

He was right. Arturo had every edge over him and there was virtually no chance.

"Shelton, you're a pain in the ass, but I love you, man." I swallowed the lump in my throat. "I'll see you on the other side, okay?"

He wrapped his arms around me and slapped me on the back. "Hey, at least we can raise hell in the afterlife."

A guard took my arm and escorted me back to the platform with the others. Shelton looked at Arturo, took a deep breath and prepared to meet his fate.

Arturo, at least, showed some class and bowed toward his opponent as he took his place in the arena. Though he'd supported that heartless bitch, Daelissa and now fought to champion her mother, it was clear that he did it from a sense of duty. If Arturo had nothing else, he had his honor. Unfortunately, it meant he was duty-bound to kill my best friend.

"I can't watch." Bella buried her face in Michael's chest.

Elyssa gripped my manacled hand with hers, tears trickling down her cheeks. "I love you, Justin."

"I love you," I said, "and there's not a damned thing I can do to save you or anyone else."

"Sometimes, all you can do is go down fighting," Michael said grimly.

Kaelissa raised her hands and the crowd grew silent. "Alysea of the lineage of Seaa challenged my rightful rule. Now her hero faces mine in a test of magic. Let there be no doubt that the hero of the rightful ruler will prevail."

"Because she's a cheater," I muttered.

"At least I don't think Arturo is all amped up on human essence," Adam said. "That might give Shelton five minutes of dodging bullets."

Bella glared at him with tearstained eyes. "Adam, kindly shut your mouth."

Adam seemed too intent on peering at Shelton to hear her. "C'mon, Harry. Pull off a miracle."

"Let the fight begin!" Kaelissa cried, and fired a burst of Brilliance into the air.

Arturo wasted no time. He leveled his right fist at Shelton and focused a thin beam of Brilliance toward him. Shelton dodged sideways and rolled as Arturo raked the ground after him. He jumped up a little awkwardly in the leather duster and ran in a wide arc, avoiding death beams from the archangel while looking somewhat ridiculous.

Brilliance splashed against an invisible shield around the arena, preventing any casualties, but it also hemmed Shelton into a smaller space than the entire plaza. He quickly found the edges of the zone, bumping against the barrier before dodging another attack.

"'Tis hopeless," Arturo called out. "Come meet your death bravely."

"Shove it!" Shelton shouted, now panting as he ran around in his cowboy boots.

"Those stupid clothes are going to get him killed!" Bella said.

As if in answer to her accusation, Shelton took off his duster and gave it a mournful look. He leapt aside another attack, then whirled the duster above his head and flung it at Arturo. Any normal article of clothing should have fallen a few feet from where he threw it. Arturo seemed to think the same thing because he paid it no mind as he turned to follow Shelton's erratic path.

369

The duster whirled through the air and came down right on the archangel's head, wrapping around it tight. Arturo shouted in confusion and tried to pry off the coat. Shelton pumped a fist and jogged over to his opponent. Sweat poured down his face, and he panted like a long-distance runner on his last leg.

Shelton drew his staff and snapped it out to full length, whirled it, and planted it right in Arturo's gut. Kinetic energy exploded and the archangel flew back fifty feet and landed in a heap.

"Go, Shelton, go!" Adam shouted.

"Kick the *puta* while he's down!" Bella screamed.

Shelton raised his staff and roared out a command. A massive ball of fire coalesced and streaked toward the downed angel. Though he couldn't see, Arturo anticipated another attack and rolled to the side. Burning wings sliced through the duster. Brilliance crackled from the archangel's hand and shredded the coat. Arturo ripped the leather from his face with a roar and threw it aside.

The exuberant expression on Shelton's face died and with it, any hope he might pull this off.

Arturo took to the air, fists pulsing with deadly energy and rained it down on his foe. Shelton growled and touched an icon on his arcphone. A honeycombed barrier sprang up around him, rotating each time it took a hit so another panel could take the brunt of the next.

"That's the geodesic shield spell," Adam said. "I hope it's working!"

Each hexagonal section of the shield flickered out when one of Arturo's blasts hit it, but another was always available to take the next hit. Unlike the last time, it didn't fizzle out and die.

"I don't understand how he got around the power issue," Adam said. "It draws too much aether to sustain."

The shield grew brighter and brighter. Arturo's anger faded to cold calculation as he realized he couldn't penetrate Shelton's defense. He dropped to the ground and channeled a blade of white fire.

"You can't hide behind that shield all day," Arturo said, dragging the tip of his energy sword across the barrier, causing several sections to flicker out.

"Wasn't planning on it," Shelton said.

"Kill him!" Kaelissa said. "I grow weary of this, Primarion."

Shelton spun his staff, and the glowing energy from the shield gathered around it, leaving him open to attack. Arturo wasted no time, swinging his sword at the Arcane's neck. Shelton brought his glowing staff up to block.

Arturo feinted with the light sword. His leg swept Shelton's feet out from underneath him and the Arcane slammed on his back. Shelton rolled away an instant before the sword plunged into the ground where his chest had been. With his other hand, Shelton produced his wand and flicked it at Arturo's feet.

Yellow energy crackled into the archangel's boot. Arturo cried out and jerked off his boot, scratching furiously at the skin.

"That sneaky bastard." Adam grinned wide. "He used an itch spell."

Arturo lashed out with a burst of Brilliance. It rammed into Shelton's shoulder, leaving a black mark on his shirt and flipping him sideways. Shelton smacked into the ground. He tried to push himself up, but his arms gave out.

"No!" Bella cried. "Harry, watch out!"

Arturo blurred toward the downed man, light sword raised high. Shelton rolled over onto his rump and touched his arcphone. Black mist sprayed into the air inches above the ground. The archangel slashed his sword down at Shelton just as his feet touched the mist and lost all traction.

"What a jackass!" Adam said with pride. "He used that joke spell on me a week ago! Nearly dislocated my shoulder."

Arturo flailed his arms. Shelton rolled out of the way at the last instant and the archangel crashed headfirst into the invisible arena shield.

Shelton climbed to his knees. Blood trickled from both nostrils. His arms shook with fatigue. Just one hit from a supernaturally strong being was enough to break bones and end mortal lives. Shelton was an Arcane, but he wasn't supernaturally strong.

"Get up, *papi*." Bella's eyes widened with fear. "Harry, move your *culo*!"

Shelton blinked rapidly and wobbled. Arturo had already gained his feet. He walked carefully, his one bare foot and boot still slick from the oil slick spell. Shelton groaned and gained his feet, tottering in place as the archangel came up behind him, sword raised for the killing blow.

Chapter 35

Gasps sounded all around me. Kaelissa bared her teeth in delighted ferocity. Bella screamed for Shelton to turn around. Everything seemed to happen in slow motion.

Shelton gripped his still-glowing staff for support and tapped his wand to his forehead. He flinched, as if an electrical current had snapped into his brain. His eyes flicked open wide, alert, and focused. He threw up his staff at the last instant and caught the death blow. His staff pulsated brighter and brighter as Arturo pressed down, slowly driving the Arcane to his knees.

"Why is his staff glowing?" I said.

"The shield spell is on his staff." Adam snapped his fingers. "I know how he solved the energy problem."

Arturo forced Shelton to one knee, but somehow, the Arcane held his ground. Arturo's light sword turned from bright white to a sickly yellow. My supernatural sight honed in on something very telling: a trickle of sweat forming on Arturo's brow.

"How is he doing it?" Bella asked in awe.

Shelton shouted something vaguely familiar. Something I'd heard Kanaan, the Magitsu master, use during exercises. He rolled to the side and Arturo's sword sizzled into the ground. Shelton rose to his feet, staff whirling, eyes sharp and devoid of emotion even as blood poured down his face from multiple wounds.

Arturo raised his sword. "How are you still alive, Arcane?"

Shelton flashed him a grisly smile. "Because I'm a survivor, you son of a bitch." He slammed the staff into the ground. The geodesic shield around the staff exploded toward the archangel with brilliant ferocity. The crowd cried out. Kaelissa shrieked.

It was like the world's brightest flash bulb. I squeezed my eyelids shut and felt a wave of heat pass over me. Heard the arena shield humming like an insect zapper as it tried to absorb everything at once.

When I opened my eyes, Shelton stood on unsteady feet above a bloody and blackened Arturo. He held the crackling tip of his staff to the archangel's throat and bared crimson stained teeth. "Yield or die."

"Kill him!" Bella shouted. "You must kill him!"

"No, he doesn't have to," Alysea said. "The rules allow claiming victory if the opponent yields, though he has the right to kill him if he wishes."

"This is a foolish risk," Bella said. "What if Arturo recovers?"

"It's a smart move," Michael said. "Arturo is the only one honorable enough to accept the results."

Arturo held up a badly burnt hand. "I yield, Arcane. You are the victor."

"No!" Kaelissa shrieked and leapt from her dais, fists blazing with energy. "I will not accept this!" She leveled her fists at Shelton and fired.

The arena shield absorbed her attack. While the other soldiers and archangels looked around in confusion, Arturo pushed to his knees and held out a finger. "Restrain the former empress and release our new ruler."

The archangels moved on Kaelissa, but a contingent of city guards surrounded her protectively.

"Do you really think the people will betray me?" Kaelissa said. "No one can take my rightful power. If you dare come after me, I will plunge this realm into civil war!"

An archangel freed my mother. She rubbed her wrists and nodded at the rest of us. "Free my comrades."

"Yes, my liege," he said.

Alysea leapt high over the crowd and landed in front of the guards surrounding Kaelissa. She flung out her hands, weaving Murk and Brilliance into a stream of Stasis. The cloud rolled over the guards and cut off Kaelissa's shouts in mid-shriek as it froze them and her in place. Alysea waved a hand and the cloud dissipated, leaving behind gray statues.

Murmurs and shouts of awe rose around us.

"She controls all the elements!" A sera said. "Only the first were able to do that."

"The ancient Seaa herself has come back to rule," a seraph shouted. "The golden age will return!"

Alysea pointed at Kaelissa's frozen form. "Restrain her and arrest these guards."

The archangels moved at once to follow her orders. Many of the city guard who'd looked uncertain before snapped to order in her presence. Most of them had probably never seen a Seraphim dual channel Murk and Brilliance, much less weave Stasis.

"That's my momma," I said proudly.

The arena shield flickered off and we pushed our way through the crowd, never stopping until we reached the hero of the day.

Harry Shelton wobbled on his feet and collapsed into Bella's arms. Archangels rushed in to aid Arturo. The singed archangel looked in even worse shape than my friend.

Arturo managed a scowl at Shelton. "I underestimated you, Arcane."

Shelton groaned. "Yup."

Alysea grabbed the short seraph who'd been in the throne room earlier. "What is your name?"

He dropped to his knees and bowed. "Absidiah, my liege."

"I need a healer this instant." Alysea's eyes narrowed. "You are a Darkling."

"Yes, my liege." He bowed deeper. "I live to serve. I will bring the healers at once." Absidiah got up and ran toward the compound.

"Man, you look rough," Adam said to Shelton.

"Who me?" Shelton tried to smile, but the blood loss seemed to be affecting him. "I'm prime, man."

"I saw what you did there," Adam said. "How did you modify the geodesic shield to absorb energy?"

"That black aetherite you put in the phone and my staff," Shelton said. "It can soak up some serious energy. Arturo's attacks gave me what I needed."

"Why didn't you use it sooner?" I asked.

Shelton blinked and took a moment to answer. "Wasn't entirely sure it would work." He broke into a coughing fit and spat up blood. "I think my ribs punctured a lung."

"Harry, why didn't you say so?" Bella made him lie down flat. "You foolish man." Tears dripped down her nose and onto Shelton's cheeks. "My brave husband."

"I love you, woman." And Shelton passed out.

The healers raced into the square moments later. One attended Arturo, while the other patched up Shelton.

I spotted Alysea talking to a soldier in the armor of a city guard captain and with the archangels in Arturo's own squad. Guards led Kaelissa and Djola away while another squad raced away on another errand.

Alysea channeled blazing wings and did something she rarely did, levitating above the crowd, her blond hair billowing in the wind. The dull roar went silent as the new Brightling empress addressed her subjects.

"The ancient Seraphim knew that weak leaders would weaken the nation. In their wisdom, they allowed others to challenge leaders and assert legitimate rule through the Challenge of Ascension." Alysea paused to let that sink in, then hammered her point in one more time. "I am Empress Alysea, your ruler and protector. Do you hear me?"

A great roar rose from the crowd.

"All hail the ancient Seaa!" some cried.

A chant rose from the back. "Golden Ruler! Golden Ruler!"

"Damn, she's magnificent," David said with awe. "I'm a lucky guy."

Elyssa gripped my arm. "She really is golden."

I could hardly believe what was happening. "I'm in a royal family. I'm right up there with the Queen of England. The York of Shire. Prince Humperdinck!"

Elyssa groaned.

Shortly after Alysea's speech, dozens of Kaelissa's closest advisors and guards were arrested. However, there was one person missing that gave me great concern—Fakor.

Elyssa tried to reach the *Falcheen*, but communications were spotty using her pendant and we had no way to contact the *Uorion* to relay messages.

"They must be out of range," she said.

"It's a moot point right now," I said. "We have to find Fakor, especially if he's connected to the dragon incursions."

"The guards are questioning Djola, but she isn't talking." Elyssa bit her lower lip. "Let's assume Fakor is using an arch to open the rifts. It would have to be on the coast near the Voltis fractures, right?"

"I don't think it's an arch," I said. "It takes something a lot bigger to make those rifts."

"Regardless, we need to start looking." Elyssa looked west. "For all we know, he's opening a portal right now."

I headed toward the citadel and found Adam outside talking to Cinder.

"Justin, it is good to see you were not executed," Cinder said. "Once I discovered you were captured, I began to work on a rescue plan."

"I'm glad you didn't have to use it." I patted him on the back. "I don't think you stood much of a chance against so many soldiers."

"I must admit, the situation looked hopeless." He shrugged robotically. "As Shelton would say, you pulled a magic trick out of your ass."

I snorted. "Exactly, except it was Shelton who did it this time." Steering the conversation back to more serious matters, I brought up Fakor. "Any idea how Fakor is connected to the dragon incursions?"

"We were just discussing it," Adam said. "We suspect he's using a portal gem similar to the one we used to get in and out of Atlantis."

"If he is indeed using Voltis fractures to power such a gem, then there are few places he could be." Cinder projected the map of the glowing lines radiating out from Voltis. He zoomed in to a small group of islands. "I suspect Fakor's device is somewhere around here."

Gongs sounded to the east. Soldiers raced through the citadel courtyard and lined up in formation. I stopped one of them. "What's going on?"

"An army approaches from the eastern skyway," he said. "The Darkling legions are here!"

My mouth dropped open. "What the hell? Aerianas doesn't stand a chance against—"

Gongs rang in the west. I climbed up a guard tower for a clear view of the horizon. Far out to sea, a thin scar formed against the sky as a new rift began to form. Cabala was about to get squeezed between the Darkling legions and an army of dragons.

Chapter 36

We had a numbers advantage, but the carnage from a clash with dragons and the Darklings would drown Cabala in blood.

I scrambled down from the guard tower. "We need a flying carpet, stat!"

"I am already prepared." Cinder unfolded two high-speed carpets from the satchel on his side. "I was going to use them in my rescue plan."

Adam bumped his arcphone against mine. "I updated your maps with the islands Cinder showed you. If Fakor is using a portal gem, it'll need some time to power up before it can open the rift all the way."

"We'll start north," I said. "You start south."

"Got it." Adam climbed on a carpet behind Cinder. "If my estimates are correct, we have less than twenty minutes before the rift opens."

"That's not much time to stop it," I said. "Speaking of which, how would we stop it?"

Adam shrugged. "I won't know until I see it."

I nodded grimly. "Let's get to it then."

381

We zipped over the city, over hundreds of soldiers rushing toward the sea wall. Archangels soared out of the citadel, splitting off in two directions to face the dual threat. Elyssa directed the carpet northwest while I used Cinder's map and called out directions. It took us five minutes to reach the first island, a small hunk of rock coated in red algae, but nothing resembling a portal gem.

Elyssa veered further out to sea toward a larger island, but a quick survey of the sandy shores revealed nothing.

"This is taking too long." Elyssa stared at the silver split crossing the sky. "If only we could trace it somehow."

I smacked my forehead. "Of course!" I switched to demon view and scanned the horizon. Mist and bright clouds of aether made it difficult to see it at first, but I spotted a wide beam of energy feeding the forming rift.

"There!" I pointed west. "That's got to be it."

"I don't see an island," Elyssa said.

I checked the map and saw she was right. "Maybe there's a floating platform."

She jetted toward it without another word and tapped her pendant. "Adam, head due west. We've spotted something."

"On it," Adam replied.

Time ticked past mercilessly as the rift grew wider and wider. Small dragons filtered through the crack, their hisses and screeches audible even over the crash of ocean waves. I spotted a small island of brilliant pink crystal rising into the air, a massive gem floating on a vortex of aether. The gem spun faster and faster, churning the aether into the widening rift.

A tiny figure stood on a narrow column of rock rising from the ocean. He stood before a black obelisk linked to the rift gem by a stream of aether.

"Fakor," I growled.

Elyssa drew her light bow and aimed for the shelf of rock where our target stood. The susurrus of wings drew our attention above. Dozens of tiny dragons dove at us. These were even smaller than the ones from the other attack, but hundreds of razor sharp teeth and jets of flame still hurt.

I flung a wall of Murk at them and the small reptiles bounced with meaty *thunk*s off the barrier. Elyssa weaved through a cloud of multicolored dragons while I mowed another flock down with Brilliance. We reached the rock column and leapt off the carpet. Fakor spun at the sound of our arrival and backed away.

He tried to run. I snared his foot with a lasso of Murk and reeled him in. Fakor rolled onto his back and shot a feeble spark of Murk at me, but he looked too exhausted to fight back, probably from controlling his rift apparatus.

"How do you turn it off?" I gripped him by his robe and jerked him off the ground. "Tell me now!"

"I'll tell you!" Fakor cried. "Just don't kill me" He opened his mouth to speak. His eyes fluttered and his head lolled to the side. Fakor stiffened, gasped, and went limp as a wet noodle. He blinked, looked up at me. A slow grin spread across his face. "We meet again, grandson."

"Baal, you son of a bitch!" I nearly flung Fakor over the cliff, but held out hope the demon overlord might have a heart and tell me how to turn off this infernal apparatus. "Why are you doing this?"

"It's simple, really." He looked at my hands where they gripped his robes and raised a disdainful eyebrow.

I released him. "Tell me how to disable the rift generator."

"That would be unnecessarily cruel, child." Baal brushed off his shirt as if I'd dirtied it. "You see, the dragons are running out of room in their realm." He waved an arm at the widening rift overhead. "They must expand or die. Seraphina has plenty of room for them to stretch their wings."

"So, you formed an alliance with them."

"Precisely." Baal watched a flock of small dragons flitting overhead. "In exchange for access to Seraphina, the dragons will submit themselves to my rule."

"I'm sure that's exactly what will happen." I wondered why the dragons weren't attacking us and realized something was holding them at bay. "What's to stop them from turning on you? They're just dumb animals."

"The bulk of dragons are indeed nothing but animals, acting on instinct." Baal looked toward the rift where a huge dark form hovered on the other side. "The ancient dragons are something else altogether."

"What's to stop the dragons from overpopulating Seraphina?" I said. "Is your deal with the ancient dragons really strong enough to keep them from warring with the Seraphim?"

"Absolutely." Baal waved a hand toward the ocean. "There are barely enough Seraphim to populate even a corner of Azoris. Plenty of room for dragons."

"Plenty of room to gather an army," Elyssa said. "An army to conquer all realms."

"And save them," Baal said. "Once Xanomiel makes his move, I will command legions that can stop him and put him back in the Abyss."

In other words, Baal would never willingly shut down the rift apparatus. Guttural roars echoed from the other side of the rift. Massive forms waited patiently on the other side, even as their smaller brethren slipped through the widening crack. If they made it in, they'd crush our forces.

I switched to demon vision and observed the beam of energy running from the obelisk to the gem. My mind pieced together how the object operated. Channeling into the obelisk controlled the rift gem. Once the gem began to spin, it pulled magical energy from the Voltis fracture on the ocean floor, drawing up the aether and focusing it into the rift. The obelisk acted like a control console. Unfortunately, I didn't know any of the commands. I didn't know how to stop it.

Ignoring Baal's smug soliloquy, I walked up to the obelisk and channeled into it. *Turn off. Cease and desist.* I went through a mental thesaurus of deactivation commands, but the obelisk ignored me.

"You can't stop it," Baal said. "It's charmed with a passcode only Fakor and I know."

Frustration clenched my hands into fists, but physical violence would solve nothing. How in the hell could I unplug this thing? Blasting it with Brilliance might only fuel it. Encasing it in Murk wouldn't turn it off. There had to be—*that's it!*

"Fascinating," I said as Baal smugly regarded my efforts. I channeled a sphere of Brilliance, silently praying this did the trick.

"Oh, grandson, how little you know." Baal tutted. "Violence is not—"

I summoned Murk and wove it into a beam of Stasis.

"No!" Baal lunged for me.

Elyssa batted him onto his ass, then bound him with the magic repression cuffs.

I threaded the Stasis around the obelisk, suffocating it in a blanket of energy-snuffing fog. The aether dancing on its surface died. The rift gem flickered and fell. It crashed into the ocean with a tremendous splash. The rift snapped shut.

The flock of tiny dragons chirped and warbled in distress, flying in circles where the rift had been. I almost felt sorry for them.

"You got it!" Adam and Cinder glided in for a landing. "Awesome!"

Baal looked coldly up at me. "You have only delayed the inevitable, Justin. By thwarting me, you have given Xanomiel the advantage." With that, he darted from Elyssa's side and leapt over the edge of the cliff before either of us knew what had happened.

I wondered if Baal left the body before it hit. I wondered if Fakor even knew he was about to die. The body bounced off the side of the rock and splashed into the ocean far below.

"Christ Almighty," Adam said. "What an asshole."

"We've got to get back to the city," I said. "There's still Aerianas to worry about."

Elyssa's comm pendant crackled. "This is Commander Borathen. Please reply."

"I'm here," Elyssa said.

"…was a misdirection. Aerianas…coming for Cabala."

"We know." She hopped back on the carpet. "What's your ETA?"

"A day," Thomas said, the connection hissing with static. "…careful."

"You too." Elyssa glanced over her shoulder at us. "Let's go."

We flew at top speed back to the city. Whoever was in charge of troop deployments was damned good at their job, because the soldiers manning the sea wall had already boarded cloudlets and embarked across the city to the eastern front. I spotted more cloudlets laden with soldiers far to the north and south, apparently circling around the enemy forces in a classic pincer move.

Baal had bet everything on getting his big bad dragons through the rift. Now there was nowhere for Aerianas and her army to go. That brought up another problem. Did Alysea control the Brightling soldiers or someone else? Would they order the slaughter of the Darkling legions?

The battle started before we got there. Daskar met archangels. Destructive magic lanced across the sky. Armored figures spiraled to their doom on the ground far below. What the Daskar lacked in numbers, they made up for in firepower and maneuverability. It wasn't enough. Archangels hemmed them in from all sides and whittled down their numbers until the ground was littered with bodies from both sides.

I spotted the bulk of the Darkling legions on the ground below. The forward ranks milled in confusion. The rear turned and ran. Up on the skyway, I spotted a small group of people that could be no one else but Aerianas and her inner circle. The carpet was fast, but the Imperial Skyway whisked them away too quickly to catch.

Her capture was important, but I had other considerations to make. Preventing a Darkling slaughter ranked the top of my list.

Brightling infantry cut off retreat on all sides, their numbers at least four times that of the Darklings. I held my breath, waiting for the charge that would spill blood. Instead, I saw a cloudlet with my mother drift behind a flight of archangels. I saw her mouth moving, but hearing her words over the shout and din of the battle was impossible.

Elyssa steered clear of the few remaining Daskar and circled around to my mother. By the time we reached her, many Darklings were already throwing down their weapons. Some few tried to fight their way free and were killed or subdued. Dozens lay dead, but hundreds more surrendered and preserved their lives. There would be no slaughter today.

The final Daskar fell from the sky and a sense of relief washed over me. Were they truly living beings? Probably. But as long as any survived, I couldn't help but think that Aerianas had spies among us.

It hadn't been much of a battle, but the aftermath would shake Seraphim politics to the core.

The *Falcheen* arrived early the next morning with unexpected passengers. They'd encountered Aerianas and her cohorts heading back east on the skyway and engaged them. The dolems impersonating Kohval and Meera were killed in the battle. Aerianas had given herself up.

Alysea had the Daemas thrown into holding with Kaelissa.

Thankfully, we had good news for Illaena as well. We found the Mzodi crew Kaelissa had captured in holding cells near the shipyard. Kaelissa had forced them to build her a fleet. Unwilling to give her their ancient Mzodi secrets they'd barely constructed half a ship hull.

We told Thomas and the others what had happened in their absence. Thomas had Bliss and the other dolems searched for communications devices but found none. It was Cinder who surmised how Fakor knew our plans.

"Baal could possess Zero or Fakor at any time," Cinder said. "When he possessed Zero and we allowed him in the room where we had discussed our plans, he likely informed Fakor of his observations. It is also likely he overheard other useful information."

"Son of a bitch." Shelton smacked a palm to his forehead. "We didn't even think of that."

"Baal certainly weaves a mighty fine web of deceit," David said. "Even I haven't untangled half of it."

"Are demons able to enter any realm?" Cinder asked.

David tilted his head back and forth. "Lesser demons can certainly possess beings in other realms, but mortals are far easier to possess than other supernaturals."

"Unless you're Baal," Shelton said.

"Exactly." Dad shrugged. "There's no telling how many realms he's reached or how many others he's influenced. The dragons are probably just the tip of the iceberg."

"Then it is imperative we try to secure our own allies," Cinder said. "The Seraphim may not be enough."

I blew out a sigh and nodded. "We need to find a way to hop realms. With Baal and Xanomiel intent on wrecking the universe, we're going to need everyone on our side."

"Can the rift gem be used for that?" Elyssa asked.

"Only if we can access the obelisk," Adam said. "All the enchantments controlling the gem are encrypted. It might be better to return to Atlantis. If we can find the Fallen, they might have the answers to interdimensional travel."

"And a way home," Shelton said, hope rising in his voice.

Elyssa sighed and rubbed her arms as if she was cold. "Well, we'd better get to the plaza. Alysea is supposed to make her speech soon."

I shivered with excitement. *Mom is a friggin empress!* Unfortunately, her new duties kept her incredibly busy. Kaelissa had ignored the little things while she was busy trying to take over the world and the empire was falling apart at the seams.

We met Shelton and Bella outside. Adam, Meghan, and Cinder waved as they made their way toward us. Shelton had a few fading bruises and was missing a small piece of his ear where one of Arturo's attacks had nicked him. He didn't care about all that. His biggest complaint was the loss of his beloved duster.

"Leather in Seraphina just ain't the same as cowhide," he moaned as we walked toward Citadel Square. "Eor offered to make me something with a gem, but there's no way I'm wearing a silky duster."

"I think purple silk would suit you just fine," Adam said with a snicker. "It brings out the color in your cheeks and eyes."

Shelton stopped in his tracks. "Hey, you're right. Plus, I'll bet it's a lot more comfy. I can charm it to wrap around your face and choke you to death too. How's that?"

We burst into laughter.

"Gotta admit, I wasn't expecting a choke charm on your duster," Adam said. "That was really sneaky."

"When they gave me my stuff back before the fight, I went straight to my practical jokes files." Shelton chuckled. "I figured if I could knock Arturo off stride, maybe fluster him, I had a chance."

"It worked," I said. "Plus, it made him pour more energy into your geodesic shield spell."

"How did you know your spell would not explode on you?" Cinder said.

Shelton scratched his chin uncomfortably. "I didn't. It was a calculated risk that my spell would hold cohesion until I released it."

Bella tightened her grip on Shelton's arm. "Maybe now we'll have a chance to slow down and enjoy life for a change."

Everyone looked at each other before shaking their heads and saying, "Nah!"

"Two days at best," Shelton said. "Then Justin will decide it's time for another adventure."

I threw my arms up in surrender. "Hey, don't look at me!"

"Oh, it's all you," Elyssa said with a grin.

I looked into her glowing violet eyes and felt love swelling in my heart. Despite all the battles we'd survived, the executioner's sword had fallen uncomfortably close to our necks this time. The thought of everyone lying headless in pools of blood made me shudder.

We reached Citadel Square just as Alysea began her speech. Dozens of Mzodi ships hovered beyond the sea wall. Mzodi crew stood apart in the crowd. Darklings mingled with Brightlings and the tension was palpable. I saw a Brightling soldier spit on the ground when a Darkling passed. A Darkling soldier cast venomous stares at the city guard.

This is not going to be easy. For centuries, the two factions of Seraphim had lived apart both geographically and socially. I just hoped it didn't take centuries to mend the rift.

Alysea stood on a cloudlet floating above and in front of the crowd. Behind her stood Arturo, Xalara, Flava, and other representatives from the Darkling and Brightling nations. She tapped a gem at her throat and began to speak, her voice amplified throughout the city.

"The first of our people did not know such terms as Brightling or Darkling. They knew only one term for our people: Seraphim. Each of the first channeled creation and destruction. Each wove the primal forces into many other forms." Alysea held aloft white and ultraviolet spheres, sending a ripple of murmurs through the crowd. "What caused the separation in our powers, I do not know. I know it is possible for each of you to tap into both forces. I know that your affinity for Murk or Brilliance does not define you as a person, or lessen your value as a Seraphim."

Several nearby Brightlings scowled while Darklings looked hopefully at one another.

"Only the weak seek differences in others to make themselves feel better. Only the weak claim moral superiority because of their primal affinity." Alysea's voice rose in volume with every sentence. "We are not weak. We are Seraphim. And from this day forward, I decree that every Seraphim has inalienable equal rights and value."

A great roar went up from the Darkling throngs. The Brightlings seemed less sure, though pockets of them raised their voices in cheers.

"Furthermore," Alysea continued, "Pjurna and the Mzodi nation shall be joined with the Brightling Empire. This new nation will be known as the Seraphim Empire. One name, one people, one purpose. An ancient evil threatens all the realms. It is now our purpose to heal the old divides of our people and to move forward. Together, nothing can stand in our way!"

A great roar went up from the crowd.

"Can you believe it?" Shelton said. "A unified Seraphina."

"Not quite," Bella said. "But at least the Seraphim are all on the same path now."

A gruff voice spoke behind me. "Your mom is quite a speaker."

I turned and saw Thomas and the rest of Elyssa's family.

"Honestly, I didn't know she had it in her." I shook my head in wonder. "It's still hard to believe she's an empress. And that my dad is her consort."

"I'll bet he loves that!" Shelton snorted. "What do you plan to do with Kaelissa and her merry gang?"

"She's too dangerous to cut loose," Michael said. "But we also can't keep her locked up in Zbura in case sympathizers try to free her."

"Which is why we worked out a deal with the Mzodi," Thomas said. "Kaelissa will spend some time in their flying cities, first as a prisoner, and perhaps later as a citizen."

"What will you do with the remaining dolems?" Cinder asked.

"Zero is a link to Baal," Thomas said. "We'll have to keep him locked up along with most of the others."

Cinder tilted his head slightly. "What of Bliss and Issana?"

Shelton patted him on the back. "Aww, does Cinder want his girlfriends?"

393

"They have not expressed interest an intimacy," Cinder said, "though with your help, Harry, I am certain to succeed."

Adam snorted. "Asking for Shelton's help with women is like asking a dragon to help you put out a fire."

Shelton scowled. "Hey, I got Bella, didn't I?"

"Against all odds, Harry." Bella smiled sweetly and punched him in the shoulder.

We burst into laughter.

I wished the moment would freeze-frame like the end of a corny sitcom so we could make this happy moment last a bit longer. Unfortunately, we were still stuck in Seraphina with Grand Overlord Baal of Haedaemos and Xanomiel of the Apocryphan scheming to wreck the universe. I'd hoped uniting Seraphina would be my last good deed for a while, but apparently, this was just the first step of many.

Our next moves were clear—find a way into the other realms and gain more allies. If anyone could do it, we could.

Baal, I'm going to kick your demonic ass.

###

About the Author

John Corwin is the bestselling author of the Overworld Chronicles. He enjoys long walks on the beach and is a firm believer in puppies and kittens.

After years of getting into trouble thanks to his overactive imagination, John abandoned his male modeling career to write books.

He resides in Atlanta.

Connect with John Corwin online:
Facebook: http://www.facebook.com/johnhcorwinauthor
Website: http://www.johncorwin.net
Twitter: http://twitter.com/#!/John_Corwin